THE CAPTAIN'S QUEST

THE LEEWARD ISLAND SERIES - BOOK 4

LORRI DUDLEY

Leya,
Always know
you are loved.
Thank you for
all your support
of my books.
much love,
Lorri
1 John 4:19

WILD HEART
BOOKS

Cover design by: Carpe Librum Book Design

ISBN-13: 978-1-942265-34-4

"If a man has a hundred sheep and one of them wanders away, what will he do? Won't he leave the ninety-nine others on the hills and go out to search for the one that is lost?

And if he finds it, I tell you the truth, he will rejoice over it more than over the ninety-nine that didn't wander away!

In the same way, it is not my heavenly Father's will that even one of these little ones should perish."

– Matthew 18:12-14 (NLT)

AUTHOR'S NOTE

Thank you for journeying through the Leeward Island series!

If you have read book three, *The Sugar Baron's Ring*, I ask your forgiveness for jumping around in the timeline. Whereas the Sugar Baron's Ring took place in 1829, *The Captain's Quest* starts back in the year 1814, six months after Lottie Winthrop, from *The Merchant's Yield* (book two), sailed to the island of St. Kitts. Pricilla Middleton, Lottie's closest friend, begged for her story to be written. I couldn't set Priscilla from my mind, for as you'll see, she's a very persistent character.

If this is your first journey into the Leeward Island series, don't fret, for the book can stand alone without having read the prior novels. However, if you enjoy your voyage into the story, please return to the islands with a copy of *The Duke's Refuge, The Merchant's Yield,* and *The Sugar Baron's Ring.*

Wishing you warm and happy reading travels.

CHAPTER 1

Uncover the French infiltrators and compromise their mission.
~ *Letter to Admiral Middleton from his superiors*

*W*hy *did I agree to this?* Priscilla Leah Middleton pressed her loo mask tighter against her face. Other dancer's skirts swirled around her like colorful pinwheels. The music roused the boisterous energy of men and women emboldened by the anonymity gained from their striking costumes. Greek gods, bright bird plumage, historical heroes, and her own Little Bo-Peep costume did nothing to diminish the unease pricking her conscience.

Was she that desperate for a close friendship? Enough to relent to Nellie's whimsical woes of heartache? They'd become acquainted a few months ago, but recently, Nellie seemed determined to entangle them in a scandal.

The violinist concerto finished its movement, and dancers

changed direction. Distracted, Priscilla would have continued straight, but her dance partner's robust frame saved her from embarrassing herself. She flashed her gratitude.

Her stately partner returned her smile, but even behind his mask, she could tell it didn't reach his eyes.

The rapping on her conscience intensified, bottling pressure. "It is quite a party, is it not?" she blurted, though conversing while dancing would be difficult.

"Quite." His gaze floated above her, scanning the room.

A floodgate of nervous prattle opened. "Does Lady Lemoore always entertain such interesting groups of people? I recognize politicians mixing with opera singers, military officers speaking to notorious rakes and gamblers. This is quite—"

"Indeed." A coldness shone in his gaze.

Her breath hitched. Had he taken offense? Perhaps he fits into the latter category. "I love a good party, dancing, meeting interesting people, matchmaking among friends. It's thrilling. Don't you agree?"

As though unaware she'd spoken, his attention drifted to the far corner.

At least she'd learned something about this man Nellie had insisted Priscilla partner with for a dance—he wasn't a conversationist. Priscilla willed the orchestra to conclude.

She scanned the dancers for Lord Fortin, still hearing Nellie's pleading in her head, "Please, you must attend the masquerade with me. Lord Fortin must hear what's on my heart from my own lips. I must look into his eyes and see for myself if he returns my sentiment."

Priscilla should have inquired further before agreeing to attend the ball. Had her need to replace the friendship she'd lost when Lottie moved to the Leeward Islands blinded her to Nellie's selfish immaturity?

Nellie had begged her. "Please do not cut off our chance at

love. The masquerade shall be a splendid time. Everyone of notice shall be in attendance."

Nellie had neglected to mention that by *everyone* she meant those affiliated with the Tory party.

The coattails of the outspoken political party leader dancing next to her brushed the back of her skirt as he swept past. His sloped gait and high-pitched voice made him easily identifiable despite his raven costume.

Would he recognize her? Why had she been so foolish? She could hear her brother's scoff in the back of her mind. *You're either daft or half-crazed, and I think I know the answer.*

After this dance, she should have the coach brought around before anyone recognized her underneath the mask. Otherwise, *The Morning Star's* headlines might read: *Daughters of Two Prominent Whig Party Affiliates Seen Dancing Among Tories.*

A loud cheer erupted from the card room, and Priscilla jumped. A gentleman threw down his hand of cards as Lord Barret, who'd always voted opposite Priscilla's father, scooped up his earnings. Lady Lemoore whispered in his ear and leaned in a way that offered a provocative view of her low bodice.

Priscilla turned her head to hide her face. *Silly, you're wearing a mask.* Lord Barret would hardly recognize her without a costume, certainly not while she wore one. However, she couldn't be so sure about other familiar faces. If she identified them, then surely, they could do the same for her. "It's time for me to leave."

"Leave?" Her dance partner reared back.

Oh, dear. Had she said that out loud?

"Relax, the night is still young." A lazy half-grin spread the lips of her dance partner, revealing white, even teeth.

Now at least she had his attention. *Blast*, what was his name? Guy, Gould? No, *Goulart.* How could she relax when their host, Lady Lemoore, an esteemed woman of the Quality, chose tonight to become politically outspoken.

Mr. Goulart swept her across the floor. "How does a lovely woman like yourself sneak away unchaperoned?"

She stiffened. "How did you know we're unchaperoned?"

"Miss Archard mentioned it to Lord Fortin."

Drat. Why would Nellie reveal such a thing unless she wished to encourage a clandestine interlude? Priscilla caught sight of Nellie, basking in the adoration of the well-dressed Lord Fortin, who was guiding her across the crowded dance floor. By Nellie's dreamy expression, he had once again wooed her with his fanciful flummery.

Could Nellie not see the man was a rogue? They needed to flee from this looming disaster sooner rather than later. Would this dance never end? "Our chaperone was merely delayed." It wasn't a lie. Her duenna had fallen ill with a severe headache, and Nellie's chaperone had nodded off during the carriage ride over. Nellie convinced Priscilla to let her sleep. How convenient for Nellie. She lifted her chin. "She shall be arriving shortly."

An intoxicated couple nearly collided with Priscilla. Mr. Goulart adeptly reworked steps to avoid disaster. She had to give her partner credit. He danced superbly.

"How did you and Miss Archard become acquainted?" His gaze landed everywhere but upon her.

"We met at a political soiree. Our fathers are closely connected."

"Really?" His attention snapped to her, dousing her with the rich warmness of his russet eyes.

Priscilla blinked at the handsome gentlemen's compelling gaze, generous mouth, and tightly trimmed beard. She tensed as he drew her closer than the proper waltz distance. He, who'd ignored her earlier attempts at conversation, now wanted to discuss her father?

Persistent brown eyes bored into hers, waiting for her to elaborate further.

"I beg your pardon, Mr. Goulart. I lost myself in the steps."

She raised her chin. "My father used to dabble within the War Department, but he has recently retired." She stole another glance Nellie's way.

"Ah. The War Department you say. You must be Admiral Middleton's daughter." He raised his hand and ushered her under his arm for a turn. "No one truly retires from the War Department."

"Quite right." She flashed a knowing smile. Papa's visits, callers, and hand-delivered missives certainly hadn't slowed.

Mr. Goulart leaned in and whispered, "I adore a lady with dimples." His breath tickled her skin. "I do hope to see more of them."

Heat spread across her cheeks and chest. It seemed flummery was catching. She'd heard many a compliment before, but not regarding her dimples. Dimples were adorable on children but not on a grown woman. She cleared her throat. "I'd thought, after Napoleon's surrender, activity would have diminished, but my father still spends endless hours in his study, ambassadors and generals filing in and out."

Mr. Goulart's eyes widened. "You don't say?" He removed his hand from her lower back and scratched his nose with his thumb.

The movement subdued the flash of eagerness she'd witnessed in his gaze a second ago. Perhaps vapid females who only discussed the latest fashion trends weren't his type. Maybe she'd misjudged him. Better he knew she had a brain and an opinion.

"Tell me more about my competition for your affection," he said. "I'm certain, after discovering Admiral Middleton has such a lovely daughter, they called upon you as well?"

An inelegant snort erupted from her nose. "You jest."

His expression remained serious.

She bit back her laughter. "Most of the men who call upon my father are well along in years, except perhaps Officer Campbell and Lord Asterly, but I daresay, they see me as an annoying intruder."

His eye twitched. "An intruder, you say?"

The song concluded, and Mr. Goulart bowed while Priscilla curtsied. Laughter erupted on her left, belonging to Lord Eversley, another key leader in the Tory party.

She mentally measured strides to the main exit.

Mr. Goulart offered her his arm and escorted her off the dance floor.

"Care to take a turn about the room?" he asked.

"I just remembered another obligation I promised to attend. I'm afraid Miss Archard and I must be leaving soon."

"I insist you stay. I'd be loath without your company." Mr. Goulart placed his other hand atop hers.

In any other situation, she might have enjoyed the affectionate gesture, but not tonight. His heavy hand snared her in a trap. She had no choice but to stay on Mr. Goulart's arm or make a scene, drawing unwanted attention.

When Priscilla didn't respond, Mr. Goulart guided her to the perimeter, away from the crush of guests.

To her right, Lord Fortin strolled Nellie past the refreshments. Priscilla detested the curved smile Lord Fortin cast Nellie as though she were a feast he intended to savor. Could she not see that the man was a knave?

Mr. Goulart turned left away from Lord Fortin and Nellie. "Officer Campbell is an interesting chap. He and I became acquainted in the West Indies." He stopped next to a large marble pillar in a secluded corner.

The knot in her spine released once she was out of the crowd's direct line of sight. Priscilla angled so her gaze tracked Nellie.

"Have you seen him lately?" he asked.

"Who?" Priscilla had lost track of their conversation.

"Officer Neil Campbell, the man you said sees you as an interloper."

"Last week, perhaps. He paid Papa a brief visit."

Nellie and Lord Fortin headed toward the guest wing.

Priscilla's jaw tightened. Her friend lacked an ounce of sense, and Priscilla was twice the fool for involving herself. More than ever, she missed Lottie, who'd married and moved to the Leeward Islands. Lottie would never have placed Priscilla in such a predicament.

"I thought he was supervising Bonaparte?" Mr. Goulart leaned his shoulder against the pillar. His chocolate eyes melted into hers as if she were the only person in the room, the only person left in England.

Her heart pattered. What she wouldn't give to be the sole focus of a man's admiration. Anyone's regard for that matter. She thought of the time her Papa asked her to go for a stroll. He'd given her his undivided attention until he ran into a passing friend. From then on, she'd trailed behind as the men conversed. When they returned, the gentlemen walked straight into her father's office and closed the door. She'd remained in the foyer utterly forgotten.

Mr. Goulart's eyes glinted with victory as though he sensed her desire to be considered in such a way.

Priscilla steeled herself. Not tonight. She would not let her guard slip.

"Officer Campbell was known in Guadeloupe for having an eye for beautiful women." Mr. Goulart grazed his knuckle down the bare skin below her capped sleeve and above her satin gloves. "Were you party to their conversations? If so, you may have learned of his rogue ways."

The balcony doors opened, and a buxom woman dressed as Rapunzel from the Brothers Grimm story burst in and squealed laughter. A robust gentleman dressed as a huntsman pursued her.

Priscilla used the distraction to step from Mr. Goulart's reach. She scanned the room for Nellie's flowing white Greek goddess costume. *Please let her be in here.* Priscilla shouldn't have taken her gaze off her reckless friend.

"Miss Middleton?" Mr. Goulart's tone held a note of impatience.

"It's surprising you wish to speak politics with a woman."

He stepped closer, blocking her view. "I can tell you are not like most women. There is an intelligence about you." His gaze flicked to where she'd last seen Lord Fortin and Nellie, and he, once again, rubbed the side of his nose with his knuckle. "I appreciate a woman with a mind."

Each time he scratched his nose, a tingling prickled the back of Priscilla's brain, sounding an alarm of unease. Was he distracting her from going to Nellie's aid?

She followed his gaze, spotting Lord Fortin's wavy hair and proud swagger across the ballroom. She released a sigh. "If I were an intelligent woman, I wouldn't be here."

Mr. Goulart blinded her with his full smile, and his deep chuckle reverberated. "And a delightful sense of humor, might I add."

Lord Fortin stepped into the dim hall near the guest's quarters. The wall candles had been snuffed out. His outstretched hand beckoned and Nellie emerged from behind a column.

Curls framing Nellie's face swayed as she peeked both ways before slipping into the shadows with Lord Fortin.

"Blast." Despite the room's stuffy warmth, Priscilla's palms grew clammy. She stepped forward, prepared to chase them. "Pardon me. I must go."

"You never answered my question." Mr. Goulart halted her with a hand on her arm.

"I must return to my friend." She attempted to brush from his grasp, but he didn't release her. "Thank you for the dance, Mr. Goulart." She stared at his warm hand on her arm.

"Let me help you locate her."

"I'm capable of finding her myself."

"In good conscience, I cannot allow a young woman with delicate sensibilities to traipse about unescorted. Lady Lucille Lemoore has been known to allow"—he cleared his throat —"certain indiscretions. I wouldn't want you to happen upon anything shocking."

Priscilla's insides hollowed. "All the more reason for me to locate Nellie immediately." She nodded toward the guest hall. "I last spied her over there."

He ushered her around the wainscoted perimeter. The cool breeze blowing in from the open terrace doors cooled her heated skin. As they approached, she glimpsed the flickering torches and their host Lady Lemoore slapping a man's groping hand away with her mask stick. The woman entered the ballroom, passing Priscilla and Mr. Goulart, leaving in her wake the scent of expensive orange-blossom perfume.

Priscilla's stomach tightened. What sort of debauchery would ensue when the hour grew late? She used Mr. Goulart's body as a shield from view as they passed the refreshment table. She craned her neck for a brief moment only to spy her neighbors', Lord and Lady Griffin's, two elder sons filing through the entrance. Lady Lucille extended her hands in warm greeting.

Priscilla sucked in a breath. Thomas Griffin, the eldest, was easily identified by his bright red mop of hair. How many school holidays had he joined their family because his family had traveled north to their country house? She shrunk back behind Mr. Goulart, caving her shoulders to appear smaller and hopefully pass unnoticed.

Thomas could easily recognize her, and if he did, gossip would spread quickly. Only a couple more paces and she'd reach the dimly lit hallway where she'd last spotted Nellie. Priscilla gripped Mr. Goulart's arm and lengthened her stride. As they rounded the corner, she tripped on the lacy trim of her Little

Bo-Peep hem. Fortunately, Mr. Goulart's grip kept her from falling.

"My neighbors." The tight strings of her corset restricted her heaving chest. "If they saw me..." It could affect her brother's distinguished naval career and her father's status at the War Department. Her mother would not be able to face the co-chairs of the charity boards on which she served. "I need to leave." She pressed against the wall of the vacant guest hallway. Doors lined either side where out-of-town guests slept.

He nodded as if understanding her predicament, but his slow exhale seemed more annoyed than empathetic. He guided her past a small jog in the hallway where they'd be less visible from the ballroom. "No one saw us. Everyone's focus was on the door or Lady Lucille." Mr. Goulart pushed her against the wall, hiding her from view with his body as a busy servant scurried past.

Priscilla lowered her face, grateful for her mask. "Are you certain?" The ornate wainscoting ledge dug into her lower back. Earlier, she believed only her reputation would be at risk, and she'd been willing to endure insubstantial gossip to gain a friend. But heaven above, why hadn't she considered how this would affect her father's political connections? And why hadn't Nellie divulged that the masquerade party would be teaming with Tories? Priscilla's fingers curled, and her nails scraped the wainscoting, though her gloves prevented any damage.

He stepped away and pressed his ear to a closed door before trying the latch and discovering it locked. "Things are about to get complicated. If you know what's best for you, you'll forget me, this night, and everything about it." He moved to the next door.

How could things become more complicated? The casual way he spoke such ominous words scraped her nerves raw. "What do you mean? What are you suggesting?" She gripped his sleeve. "Where is Nellie?"

"Forget your friend. Leave without her and go to another party." He tried the brass knob, but it didn't turn. He strode toward the next door, his boots hardly making a sound against the hardwood.

While he tried the lock, a wicked smile twisted his lips. "You turned out to be a treasure, chérie." He dipped his head. "Thank you for the information."

Priscilla gasped at the brazen term—spoken in French when their country was at war with France. *Merciful heaven.* With whom had she been conversing? What information had she divulged?

She wracked her brain to recall their exact conversation while he stayed in the shadows, sneaking to the next door and once again pressing an ear to it. This latch gave, and he poked his head into the room, whispering Lord Fortin's name. No answer. He repeated this process down the hall, moving like a stealth cat on the hunt.

Her body refused to move as her brain frantically tried to process Mr. Goulart's threat.

He glanced at her and shooed her away with his hand.

She backed up, peeking around the corner toward the ballroom at the hallway entrance where the guests mingled. Her spine straightened. She couldn't leave without Nellie. Laughter sounded nearby, and a door to one of the closed bedrooms opened.

She darted back toward Mr. Goulart only to discover him gone.

She was alone.

Her lungs refused to inhale, and the fine hair on her neck rose. She couldn't have one of her episodes here. Anthony warned her that if anyone knew of her attacks, she'd be locked up in Bedlam. *Calm down. You're not alone.* There were over fifty guests down the hall. Her feet, however, moved of their own accord as she dashed to the end of the hall through a study and back parlor. She flung open a door and collided with Mr. Goulart's back.

He spun and stared at her as if she'd sprouted another head.

"Pardon. I didn't mean to… I was…" She wracked her brain for an excuse, lest he believed her half-crazed for running blindly through rooms. "I was inspecting my manicure." *Manicure? With gloves on? Truly? Think, Priscilla.* "My nail snagged my glove. I fear I wasn't paying attention."

He glanced around the back hall before pressing a finger to her lips and pushing her through an open closet door. "If you know what's good for you, stay quiet and don't move." He shut the door, but the hem of her costume caught in the jam, keeping it from closing. The door cracked back open.

She stood frozen in the dark space. The smell of linens and cedar filled the cramped room. Her heart lodged in her chest, and sweat beaded on her brow. She no longer wished to be around Mr. Goulart, but being alone was even worse—especially in a darkened room. She clenched her fists to keep her hands from shaking as she peeked through the sliver of light, choking on an inner scream.

In the open door of a richly decorated sitting room, Lord Fortin stood before Mr. Goulart, adjusting the frill of his cuff. "I have what I came for."

"We have company." Mr. Goulart indicated over his shoulder, but not at her.

"Out the back, then?"

Mr. Goulart nodded, and they both strode toward the servant's entrance. Mr. Goulart held the door open for Lord Fortin.

After they left, she crept out from her hiding place.

"You there. Stop!" Her father's voice halted Priscilla's steps. She braced for the disappointment in her father's eyes and a stern set-down. However, Papa wasn't in sight. Priscilla tiptoed to the open window. The night air chilled her heated skin. The flickering torchlight of the terrace revealed a man chasing two shadows. The vanilla scent of Papa's favorite cheroot still hung in the air.

Papa wasn't here on her account? He hadn't been listening when she mentioned she was going out for the evening. She certainly hadn't stated where she was headed. Papa would rather clean chamber pots than be seen mingling with Tories. If he hadn't come for her, nor the event, then he must have come on assignment. The shadows skidded around the corner of the main house, her father's silhouette disappearing shortly after. Was the War Department looking for those men?

You turned out to be a treasure, chérie. Thank you for the information.

Mr. Goulart's words hollowed her chest.

Good heavens. Had she danced with a French spy?

CHAPTER 2

Your services are requested for a black bag job to deci-
pher the allegiance of two individuals. I oblige you to
obtain intelligence of the foregoing particulars speedily.
~ *Letter from Admiral Middleton to Agent White*

*P*riscilla spun around, desperate to locate Nellie. She
pressed her palms against the eyeholes of her mask.
What had Lord Fortin done to her? Was Nellie distraught?
Where should she go? Back to the ballroom or the powder room
to freshen up and fix her hair? *Think Priscilla.*

A soft weeping emanated from the adjoining bedchamber.

"Nellie?" She dropped her hands and darted to the nearby
door. "Nellie? Is that you?"

Nellie responded with a wail.

Priscilla pushed the door open only to be met with darkness.

"He-he told me he loved me." Nellie choked on a sob.

Priscilla felt her way across the room toward Nellie's staccato breaths. Nellie sat on the edge of a poster bed, and Priscilla
crouched beside her.

Nellie wept into her hands. "He used me."

Priscilla covered her gasp. Dear Lord, she'd been too late. She'd known the man was a cad. This was her fault. She should have tried harder to talk Nellie out of coming.

"All those pretty words he told me. I felt beautiful, appreciated, wanted. He said he'd never met another woman like me, and he'd traveled the world."

"He's a blackguard."

"He made me feel special. He looked at me as if the rest of the world no longer existed." She burst into wails.

Drunken laughter sounded in the hall.

"Shh." Priscilla draped an arm over Nellie's shoulder. "God will avenge you for his misdeeds." She stared at the doorknob, willing whoever was outside to keep walking past their room.

Lady Lemoore purred in the hall, "That wouldn't debate in the House of Lords, but in the bedchamber..."

Priscilla waited until she heard a door slam and muffled laughter before she pulled Nellie to a stand. "What's done is done, but we shall only exacerbate the problem if anyone within our circle recognizes us. We must slip out the back and quickly before anyone sees us."

Nellie turned and cried into Priscilla's shoulder. "I'm so grateful you are here."

"Of course. You're my friend. I shouldn't have left your side for a minute."

"Why didn't I listen to you?" Nellie pulled back, her face melting into a fresh round of tears. "What a henwit I am."

She grasped Nellie's hand and dragged her to the bedroom door. "We can discuss the merits of sound advice later." She peeked into the hall and looked both ways. All clear. She pushed Nellie, who was quietly sobbing, out the same way Lord Fortin and Mr. Goulart had escaped, through the servant's door.

A maid jumped, dropping the dirtied bedsheets she carried.

"Forgive us," Priscilla told the wide-eyed maid. "Where is the closest exit?"

The maid pointed to a door on the right.

Priscilla yanked Nellie behind her into the unusually tepid November night. They exited near the gardens and quickly slipped along the hedge to the carriages parked along the drive. She spied Nellie's family coach across the lawn, but men and women hovered around the main entrance, so Priscilla arched a wide path to avoid being spotted. She instructed the coachman to take her home. She must pack and convince Miss Dodd, her chaperone, to join her on Anthony's ship. If she pretended to have visited her brother this evening, perhaps she could emerge unscathed.

Nellie climbed in across from her elderly chaperone, who didn't stir when they entered the conveyance. Priscilla sat next to the woman and tried to nudge her awake, but she only snored louder. "By Jove, she is a heavy sleeper. I daresay, if word reaches your father that she neglected her duty, especially while we were in mixed company, she'll be tossed out on her ear without a reference."

Nellie bit her swollen bottom lip. "I might have aided her sleep."

Priscilla jolted. "What?"

She twisted a loose hair tendril between her fingers. "I knew she wouldn't approve of my dancing with Lord Fortin, so I put a bit of laudanum in her tea to make her nod off."

"You drugged her?" Priscilla's lungs deflated. Her predicament worsened by the minute.

"I couldn't have met with Lord Fortin otherwise." She leaned forward, her eyes pleading with Priscilla for understanding. "He told me it was perfectly safe and would have no ill-effects." Nellie's face crumpled once more. "I know I've made a mull of things."

Priscilla rubbed her temples before opening the door and instructing the driver. Her elder brother would know what to do. Anthony would alleviate her fears about Lord Fortin and

Mr. Goulart. He would explain her father's presence, and if everyone believed she'd spent the weekend visiting her beloved brother instead of flitting about at a salacious party, all the better to quash any rumors about her reputation.

"I thought he loved me." Nellie wailed into her gloved fingers. "And to think I would have given myself to him."

Priscilla jumped, bumping her head on the carriage's fabric ceiling. "You didn't... He didn't... You're still..." She stumbled to form a full sentence.

"But don't you see?" Nellie's tear tracks glistened in the lamplight. "I would have."

Priscilla melted into the seat cushion as if her bones had turned to water. *Thank God for miracles.*

~

*P*riscilla pressed her forehead to the Archard carriage's pane. It cooled her heated skin as she scanned the street. She wracked her brain for any pertinent information she might have slipped and given to Mr. Goulart.

My father still spends endless hours in his study, ambassadors and generals filing in and out.

Last week, perhaps. Officer Campbell paid father a brief visit.

Pricilla's stomach soured. *Oh, Lord.* What had she unwittingly done?

Two unfamiliar black conveyances had parked in front of her parent's London townhome. She tapped the roof, and the coachman stopped in front of the neighboring house.

"Wait here while I grab my things. I'll be but a moment." She alighted from the coach into the damp night. Mr. Goulart's threat still rang in her ears—*forget this night, forget me.* The quiet street dispelled her misgivings. He'd merely been trying to scare her away, frighten her so she wouldn't warn her papa.

Priscilla kept a hand on the carriage door and eyed Nellie.

"Don't speak a word to anyone. You hear me?" She waited for her to nod before traipsing the dark alley between the two houses. The all-too-familiar prickle of fear hastened her heartbeat and her steps. She crept in through the servant's entrance, thankful the scullery maid's back was turned while she scrubbed the pots and pans. Priscilla snuck up the back steps.

Anthony would know what to do. She'd tell him what she'd told Mr. Goulart, and then if he deemed it necessary, they could approach Papa later together. She'd face a heap of trouble for attending a Tory party, but that wasn't her primary concern. Her parents already considered her a disappointment. She feared not only having been recognized at the party but having revealed something damaging that would affect her family's reputation and perhaps the war effort.

Not wanting to wake her maid, she packed a few dresses, corsets, and unmentionables into a carpetbag. Moments later, her fingers glided along the chair rail as she crept down the unlit hall toward Miss Dodd's chamber. She stepped over the creaky floorboard near the hall table and paused in front of her chaperone's door. Inhaling a deep breath, she gathered her courage. Her heart clenched at waking the poor woman, who'd taken to bed with a splitting headache.

Priscilla knocked lightly on the door. She had no choice. Boarding her brother's ship without a chaperone pushed the bounds of scandalous behavior further than even she would dare. No reply followed, but Priscilla heard stirring. She cracked the door and peeked inside. "Miss Dodd?" she whispered. The wind blew through the open window, shifting the curtains and spilling moonlight over Miss Dodd's form under the covers.

"Can't it wait until morning?" The covers muffled her reply.

Priscilla stepped into the room and closed the door behind her. "I'm afraid not. I've gotten myself into a hobble, and I need your help."

Miss Dodd pulled the covers off her face. "What kind of a hobble?"

Priscilla started at the beginning of the party. By the end of the retelling, Miss Dodd was resting against her fluffed pillows, and Priscilla sat on the foot of her bed.

Miss Dodd pinched the bridge of her nose with two fingers. "As disturbing as this news is, I concur that visiting your brother is the best course of action." She threw back the covers. "Are you packed?"

Priscilla nodded as Miss Dodd crawled out of bed, still donned in her earlier dress. "Do you always sleep in your clothes?"

Her hands smoothed wrinkles from her sturdy gown. "I was too weary to change."

"I'm terribly sorry." The pang in Priscilla's heart deepened. "I didn't know what else to do."

Miss Dodd stuffed several gowns and writing materials into another bag. "You did the right thing in coming to me."

Male voices murmured from Papa's study a floor below. Priscilla stiffened. Had Papa returned? She clasped her hands at her waist. Should she face him alone without Anthony's support?

Miss Dodd pressed a finger to her lips, and they both listened.

The voices resonating through the grate spoke French.

Priscilla stopped breathing. Had Mr. Goulart and Lord Fortin followed her home? Were they here to harm her or her family?

Miss Dodd grabbed Priscilla's arm and moved to the door. She popped her head out into the hall and looked both ways before facing Priscilla. "Take the back stairs and wait for me in the Archard coach." Even in the dim light, Miss Dodd's face was lined with strain from battling the headache that had plagued her for days. "I will alert the servants and meet you out front."

Priscilla clung to Miss Dodd's arm. "What of my parents?"

"Your family isn't home. I shall send a runner to warn them."

"Could it be prowlers? Should we try to scare them off?"

"And risk your life?" Her tone sliced through Priscilla. "I think not. You don't know their intentions, or if they have weapons."

"Get to the carriage." She pushed Priscilla out into the hall. "Go quickly."

Priscilla snuck down the stairs, out the servants' entrance, and into the night. Thank heaven for Miss Dodd's take-charge nature. Priscilla stayed low, using the hedge as cover. She was certain her heart was thundering loudly enough for others to hear.

The carriage is in sight, and Miss Dodd will be right behind you. Shadows mocked her, and icy cold chills ran down her spine.

You're not alone, she reminded herself. At least she wouldn't be for long. One more clearing, and she'd join Nellie in the carriage. She darted across the yard, praying for her safety and that of Miss Dodd, Priscilla's parents, and the staff. Hopefully God would overlook the fact that she rarely prayed and listen to her earnest plea. She swung the door wide before the footman even noticed her coming, climbed into the carriage, and sat on her hands so they wouldn't shake.

Nellie, beside her, wavered between tears and utter panic. Her fingernails clawed down her cheeks. "What if my father finds out? He'll never allow me to leave the house again. My season will be ruined."

Nellie hadn't a clue of the real trouble she'd perpetuated. Priscilla rounded on her. "Have you stopped to think about how this would affect your father's career? His connections? Nellie, you had us attend a party teeming with Tory supporters. If word gets out that his daughter fancies the opposition, he'll be a laughingstock."

Her hands dropped into her lap, and she stilled. "I hadn't thought of that."

"And how well do you know Lord Fortin? Have you made his acquaintance long enough even to know if he is friend or foe? Will he brag about his conquest with you to his Tory friends?"

"I don't know." Her bottom lip quivered. "I thought I knew him, but now I'm not sure."

Priscilla pressed her palms to her eye sockets. She turned her back on Nellie and rubbed dew off the window. Where was Miss Dodd? It seemed they'd been waiting for an eternity, but the clock on Drummond's Mercantile up the road attested barely five minutes had passed since she'd entered the carriage.

The evening's events replayed in Priscilla's head, piling questions in her mind. *Did anyone recognize her? Who were Lord Fortin and Mr. Goulart? Had she revealed British secrets? Had she accidentally committed treason?*

"If Lord Fortin didn't tup with you, what did happen?"

The carriage door opened, and Miss Dodd scooted along the bench seat next to Priscilla. "To the wharf." She instructed the coachman.

Nellie pressed her lips tight. The discussion was over.

This time of night, it wasn't safe for women to visit the docks—another thing to add to Priscilla's growing list of crimes, putting Miss Dodd in danger. Her chaperone glared at the sleeping woman beside Nellie. "How can she sleep at a time like this?"

Nellie nudged her duenna, but she didn't show any sign of waking.

"What is the matter with her?" Miss Dodd grabbed Miss Reynold's wrist, her fingers pressing to feel a pulse.

"Nellie put laudanum in her tea."

Miss Dodd's eyes widened, and her gaze swung to Priscilla.

"I swear I had no idea of her plan." Priscilla held up her

palms. "Nor would I ever have agreed to it. What she did was unthinkable."

"If you ever consider drugging me, it better be with poison." Miss Dodd speared them with her sharp glare. "For if I remain alive, you'll regret it with every ounce of your being." She rounded on Nellie. "What if you gave her the wrong dose. What if you'd killed her?"

"I don't need to listen to this." Nellie stiffened and raised her chin. "He told me the proper dosage, and as you can see, Miss Reynolds is perfectly fine and will wake well-rested tomorrow."

Miss Dodd grunted and eyed Priscilla. "A friend of fools shall suffer harm."

Priscilla gulped back her guilt. *Good gracious.* If Miss Reynolds had died, would she have been considered an accomplice to murder? How does the possibility of having committed treason and murder in the same night happen without one's knowledge? Both punishable offenses by hanging. The carriage grew warm and stuffy despite the chilly night air. She opened her fan and waved it near her face, hoping it would whisk away her menacing thoughts.

Their family name would be tarnished. Her mother would be banned from her charity boards, her father's distinguished accomplishments sullied. Her brother's promising career would end. To hide their disgrace, they'd send her to the country to stay with her elderly aunt, who slept most of the day. Priscilla would rattle around, isolated, in the old musty house. She swallowed past the lump in her throat. *Alone.* Waves of hot and cold washed over her. She dragged breath into her tight chest.

She only thought about being alone, and her heart raced like a horse around the Ascot track. Her episodes were increasing in number and now for the most subtle cause. Dizziness swept over her. Not here. Not in front of people. She'd be mortified if they witnessed one of her attacks. Once she had told Anthony in confidence about one of her spells. He stared at her as if she'd taken leave of her senses. She couldn't look at him for an entire week without dissolving into tears. Later, she tried to regain his respect through kind gestures. She'd saved three months of her allowance to purchase a sextant as a gift because every good captain needed a sextant. On multiple occasions, she'd bragged about his accomplishments to his friends over tea and scones. However, Anthony's droll upper lip curl signified he knew the real reason she lavished his friends with attention.

Why was this happening now? She wasn't alone, and thus far, her attacks only plagued her when she was by herself. Was it the strain of the evening, or had the fear of being alone brought on this one? Was she getting worse?

Her lungs strained against her corset. She drew aside the window curtain. She needed to get air... to breathe.

Miss Dodd placed her hand over Priscilla's. "Is best to keep the curtain closed, lest someone recognize you under the light of a passing oil lamp. It would ruin our alibi."

Priscilla's cheeks burned. *Inhale. Exhale.* Her heart slowed. She cleared her throat and straightened her back. "How silly of me. I overheated and thought to get a bit of air. Perhaps I merely need something to drink." She loathed how scatter witted she sounded.

Nellie perked up. "I have refreshments." She pulled a container from a side compartment, along with a teacup, and poured her a spot of tea. "It's probably cold now."

Priscilla gripped the cup like a lifeline and drank.

"Hold!" Miss Dodd's command froze her mid-sip. "Is this the same tea from which Miss Reynold's partook?"

"Why, yes." Nellie nodded and then blanched. "Oh, goodness."

Priscilla spit tea back into the cup, but she'd already swallowed some.

"I'm dreadfully sorry." Nellie removed the cup from Priscilla's fingers.

The carriage drew to a halt.

Miss Dodd's lips pinched tight.

The footman opened the door, and Miss Dodd hauled Priscilla out.

"Wait for me." Nellie ventured to join them.

Miss Dodd stopped her with a glare. "You, Miss Archard, are a disaster waiting to happen. Return home immediately, and if I hear even the slightest rumor linking Priscilla to this evening, I will ensure your hand in tonight's events are printed on the front page of every gossip column in England."

Nellie's jaw dropped, her expression comical. The strain must have pushed Priscilla into madness, for ill-suited mirth bubbled inside her. Lunacy appeared catching because she'd never seen Miss Dodd lose her composure and issue such a severe tongue lashing.

Miss Dodd poked the tip of her parasol at Nellie. "And if you even come near Miss Middleton again, I will make certain you are brought before the House of Lords."

Priscilla covered her mouth to smother a giggle. What was the matter with her? Such a display was inappropriate at a time like this. Yet the warm lightness starting in her stomach spread through her until her lips and fingertips tingled.

Miss Dodd's sobering grip hauled her in the direction of the looming ship.

CHAPTER 3

Engage the ships from our Brimstone Hill fortress in St. Christopher to provide support for Lieutenant General Pakenham.

~ Letter from Admiral Sims to Captain Prescott

Captain Tobias Prescott inhaled the aroma of lye soap as it drifted into the wardroom even after the clanging of pots and pans being cleaned had ceased. In a few short hours, this crew area would be bustling once more as men broke their fast and began the morning shift. The swishing of mops swabbing the deck above moved in rhythm as the night crews completed their assignments a tad late for his liking.

He laid his quill beside the ink well and leaned his forearms upon the weathered table across from the shell of a formerly great man. "I'm giving you one last chance to remove yourself from this vessel or suffer the disgrace of your former crewmembers forcibly removing you."

Tobias's patience had set with the sun. The thrill of his hard-earned promotion had long since been shadowed by his first act of duty—to remove the previous captain. Admiral Sim's orders had been clear, to write a full report as to why Captain Anthony Middleton had commandeered British Naval property and then demote Middleton and remove him from the *Trade Wind*. He'd keep his title of captain, but from this day forward, he'd command a smaller vessel.

"It's not right." Middleton grabbed for the rum bottle.

Tobias pulled it just out of his reach. "Enough."

"I suppose you're going to tell me how much I can drink now?" Middleton snatched the bottle. "I thought we were friends." He held it to his lips, downing three big gulps before slamming it on the table.

"So. Did. I." Tobias punctuated each word. His fingers curled as he fought ripping the gold buttons off Middleton's Navy coat. The man didn't deserve them.

"I always figured you for the settling down type," Middleton said with disdain.

"You'd like that, wouldn't you?"

"A good woman would keep you out of my blasted hair, always claiming the prize even though I'm gentry and you're from common stock."

Bitterness hung palatable in the air between them.

Middleton's expression crumpled, and his eyes glassed over. "It's all a misunderstanding."

Tobias wished it were that simple. For the second time, Middleton had proved to be a spineless, unscrupulous man who would swear an oath of allegiance to their king and then make a mockery of the king's Royal Navy. Tobias's jaw ached from reining in his temper. Such sins were unforgivable.

Middleton held his head in his hands. "I'll go to Admiral Sims. He'll return my command."

"You've forgotten it was Admiral Sim's order."

He shook his head with a vacant stare. "Once he knows the truth of what happened—"

"And which truth is that? The one where merchantmen

boarded your ship and sailed off to Barataria on a pleasure trip, probably ruining Britain's chance to align with the smuggling pirate-king against the Americans? Or the one where you misused British Navy property for a clandestine rendezvous with a ladylove?"

Middleton's shoulder's slumped, and he dropped his forehead onto the table. "I had no choice."

"I'd consider it a boon you're not leaving here in shackles." A muscle in Tobias's jaw twitched. "You probably have your father's connections to thank for that."

Tobias glanced at his watch—half past midnight. He had his report. It was time to put an end to this. He'd summon Holland to escort Middleton home since Mr. Holland's leave began the next day. The midshipmen probably wouldn't mind an extra night with his family—what was left of it. Tobias rose. At least he'd had the forethought to send a man to pack Middleton's personal effects. Lord knew how much longer this would be drawn out if Middleton needed to collect his things.

"Wait." Middleton raised his head and spread his fingers upon the table. "One more drink for courage. Please." His eyes begged. "To face my father."

Tobias couldn't fathom the shame Middleton would endure, having to inform his friends and family members of his disgrace. "Make it quick. We're wasting precious sailing time."

"Sims already gave you a mission?" Middleton gaped at him.

Tobias pushed back from the table. "We weigh anchor within the hour."

∼

*B*riny air smelled heavily of seaweed, and waves lapped against the ship's side. Priscilla waved to the midshipman who patrolled the *Trade Wind*.

Priscilla's voice broke the placid night, "Good evening, Mr.

Holland." Her smile felt over-bright, but she couldn't harness it. "Is my brother awake?"

Mr. Holland's lean frame held an unusual stiffness. "Indeed, Miss Middleton, but now may not be the time fer a visit."

"It's of the utmost importance."

"I'm afraid he's in a meetin' with a higher up." He shifted as if uncomfortable and lowered his voice to a whisper, "I wouldn't want to interrupt him unless it's dire."

Miss Dodd's parasol pressed into Priscilla's back, urging her up the gangplank.

Priscilla glanced back at Miss Dodd's tight expression. One hand rubbed her temple. Her headache must have worsened.

Mr. Holland's brow folded like a Roman shade. "There hasn't been a death in the family, has there?"

"Heaven forbid. We are all hale." For the moment, at least, or so she hoped. She shook the negative thoughts away. "We shall await my brother in his cabin. Please let Anthony know of our arrival as soon as his meeting concludes."

"Of course, miss." He bowed. "I'll escort you."

"I know the way." She hooked her hand around Miss Dodd's waist. The woman's pale face glowed in the dim moonlight. When afflicted with these severe headaches, she needed a dark room and complete silence for several days. Other than loud snores vibrating the timbers as they passed the crew room, the ship floated quietly. Priscilla aided Miss Dodd below deck to Anthony's cabin.

She knocked softly on her brother's door, where eyes of a lion carved into the thick oak panel stared back at her. After hearing no response, she lifted the latch.

Miss Dodd winced at the burning oil lamp hanging in the room's center.

Her brother's strong cologne and distinct male odor permeated the cabin, but it lacked any décor or personal effects.

Anthony had spent some time at home. Perhaps he hadn't unpacked yet for his next voyage.

Priscilla dimmed the oil lamp, and Miss Dodd sighed her relief. Lines of strain marred her pale face. Her headache must have been worse than she'd let on.

"Why don't you lie down until my brother returns and provides us with sleeping arrangements." Priscilla pulled the thick coverlet back, resisting the desire to crawl underneath herself. "I'll wait for him in the chair."

Miss Dodd opened her mouth perhaps to protest but instead sat on the bed, closed her eyes, and removed her bonnet. "This is the best course of action." Her voice held a lilt as though convincing herself. "While you listened to Nellie's preposterous chatter in the carriage, I wrote notes to several other companions stating that I've been accompanying you while you visited with your brother aboard his ship and passed them to the footman to deliver. That should explain your disappearance and cast doubt upon anyone's claims that you attended the Lemoore house party."

Priscilla caught a rare glimpse of Miss Dodd's shoulders slumping before she rested her head upon the pillows. She lay on her back as one would stand—her spine stiff, her arms straight by her sides, and toes pointed upward.

"Although I disapprove of your earlier provoking of your parents, it has made the current circumstance viable, especially since the staff overheard your sarcastic remark about visiting your friend in the islands."

Priscilla sank into the wooden chair and fought dizzying fog clouding her head. She'd forgotten about her disgraceful behavior earlier. "I didn't know you'd been listening."

"Even in my sorry state, it is my duty to ensure you're in good hands."

She wanted to be angry at her parents for not listening to her—for not questioning where she went or whose company she'd kept until it was too late. A yawn forced its way out, and she covered her mouth. Her irritation fizzled. She'd witnessed through her friend Lottie how her mother's controlling nature had driven her across the Atlantic. Priscilla should be grateful her parents raised her to be independent, but it left an aching loneliness that she took drastic measures to fill. Ultimately, she knew attending the Lemoore party was a horrid idea, yet she went anyway.

She rubbed her eyes, hoping to erase her earlier behavior, but against her will, her jumbled thoughts decided now to be a good time for introspection.

"I'm going to a masquerade with Nellie. Miss Dodd is in bed with a headache." Priscilla had stood in her shepherdess gown in the same room as her parents. Her mother scratched behind their Persian cat's ears and read the latest gossip column. Her father sat across the room, engrossed in a letter. Neither had responded to her comment.

Priscilla fought the swarm of insecurities stinging her exposed heart. She raised her chin, shooing the feelings of being unloved and unwanted away, and defiantly tested their apt for listening, "I promised Lottie I'd visit her in the Leeward Islands. I'll be sailing with Anthony. Don't worry. I'll endeavor to write you."

"Have a lovely time, dear." Mama flipped the gossip column page. "Make sure you heed Miss Dodd."

Priscilla had stomped from the room in a huff. Little had she known, a couple of hours later, she'd be in a nasty scrape and boarding Anthony's ship.

Miss Dodd opened one eye. "I no longer approve of your association with Miss Nellie Archard."

As if the woman hadn't been clear about her feelings. "Neither do I." Priscilla sighed.

"Good. That's the most sense you've shown all evening." Miss Dodd's clipped tone didn't scare Priscilla. She owed a great deal to the woman. Despite her gruff exterior, she was the only person besides Lottie who'd cared a wit about her.

With Lottie married and in a distant land, Priscilla had entered the London season like a ship without a rudder. Desperate for friendship and insecure about her episodes, her gregarious nature was mistaken as too eager or flirtatious. Miss Dodd had quickly set her to rights. She disciplined Priscilla by forcing her to decline two weeks of invites as punishment for wandering the gardens unchaperoned. She'd only left with Lord Belton because an acquaintance she'd hoped to befriend had dared her. Before any indiscretion could occur, the tip of Miss Dodd's parasol marked Lord Belton in the ribs.

Priscilla covered another yawn. Her eyelids grew too heavy to hold open, and her head bobbed forward. She jolted upright. What was taking Anthony so long?

Miss Dodd's breathing deepened, and Priscilla didn't want to wake her. She leaned upon Anthony's desk and propped her chin upon her folded hands. Nellie's sobbing echoed in her memory. *He used me... And to think, I would have given myself to him.* Priscilla's mind groped for the words Lord Fortin had said. She needed to dispel this unsettled niggling that wouldn't leave her alone. She could see him adjusting the frill of his cuff. If Nellie's innocence remained intact, then why did Lord Fortin claim he had gotten what he came for?

❧

The creak of door hinges pushed through the fog of sleep and stirred Priscilla. Footfalls of heeled boots entering the cabin roused her to consciousness. She squinted in the oil lamp's glow.

"What is the meaning of this?" A brusque male voice—not Anthony's—bit out.

Miss Dodd moaned, and the man lifted the oil lamp and swung in her direction.

"Explain your presence!" A pair of dark eyebrows sliced toward a straight and narrow nose.

Priscilla rubbed her eyes to clear her vision.

Her companion released a feeble cry and pulled blankets over her head. "Dim the light," she whispered with a weak croak. Her head must still be splitting.

The night's events flashed through Priscilla's mind—the Lemoore party, Nellie, those awful men, waiting for her brother. She jumped to a stand. "How dare you enter and disturb us." She shoved the strange man's chest. Her hands hit solid mass as if encountering a brick wall, but surprise must have been on her side, for he stumbled back.

"You better have a good explanation, for I shall be reporting this to the captain." She pushed again with all her strength.

He grabbed her wrist as he toppled backward over the threshold, pulling her into a heap on the passage deck.

Priscilla yelped.

The man grunted as her forearms rammed his chest. He still held the oil lamp up, and it swung, knocking Priscilla in the back of her head.

"Ow." She'd landed nose to nose with the man. His dark eyes blazed, and not only from the flickering lamp.

"God's thunder! What are you doing on my ship?"

"Your ship?" She pushed from his chest, knocking her head, once again, against the oil lamp that prevented her rising. "This vessel is the *Trade Wind*, is it not?"

"Indeed, it is." Other than the bobbing of his Adam's apple, he remained utterly still.

"Then you are mistaken. Anthony Middleton is its captain."

He set the lamp on the floor and attempted to push up to his elbows. "Was."

"What do you mean was?" Priscilla pressed him back down.

She'd heard horror stories of men being caught in the rigging or crushed by cargo.

His mouth opened, but he didn't appear capable of speech.

"What happened? Is he hurt? Ill?" Mishaps happened on ships all the time, even when they weren't at sea. Would Anthony ever again tussle her hair or chide her about her dimples? She imagined her parents' devastation at losing their beloved son and their disappointment to be left with only an impetuous daughter.

"He's fine."

She sagged against his warm chest, which quickly drew her attention to their precarious position. *Merciful heavens.* She was constricting his breathing. No wonder the man couldn't speak. She scrambled to rise.

Dizziness swept over her, and the floor tilted. "We're moving?" She braced against the wall, but the ship shifted in the opposite direction. "Lord, help us, the ship is moving." She tripped over the man's booted leg and staggered back into the cabin.

"Miss Dodd, get up quickly." Her spine stiffened with determination, but inside, her stomach and emotions rolled. Priscilla gripped the door frame. "The ship is sailing. We must get off."

The lantern's glow brightened behind her.

"Sailed." The single word from his deep throaty voice slashed the air with finality.

CHAPTER 4

I believe it is of the utmost importance for you to hear of your son's demotion from my own hand in case other representations indicate entirely opposing statements.
~ *Letter from Admiral Sims to Admiral Middleton*

"What do you mean? It can't be too late."

Tobias winced at the frantic, high-pitched tone of his petite female attacker's voice as she wielded her index finger under his chin like a knife, a crazed look in her wild eyes. "Who are you?"

"Captain Tobias Prescott." The presence of women had an adverse effect on him, drawing out his brusque side, but the last thing he'd expected was an attack from Anthony Middleton's ladylove.

"Then, you *can* turn this ship around."

The day's weight hit him with full force, and he leaned his shoulder against the door frame. First morn's light had been rising on the horizon before he'd sought refuge in his new cabin. Would he have enough time to read his daily devotional before it was time to return above deck and start another day?

He was too tired to spar with a female verbally. The fact that Middleton had brought women aboard for his pleasure added another black mark against the man and another mess Tobias would be cleaning up. *God, give me strength and words.*

He shifted his gaze and exhaled a steadying breath. If he didn't look at her, he could formulate the words. "If we turn around, we could compromise the mission. Time is of the essence. Men's lives are at stake." And he'd already wasted precious time, documenting Middleton's excuses.

She rose on her toes, forcing her way into his line of vision. "Where is the ship sailing? Bristol? Dublin? France?"

"The Leeward Islands in the West Indies."

Her lips parted, but only a winded squeak emerged. "A-across the Atlantic?" Her head shook. "That's not acceptable. I must speak to Anthony."

"He's not here. He's been demoted and given another command."

"What?" Her eyes widened. "You must turn around immediately."

"I'm under orders."

"To abduct us?" Her squeak turned into a shout.

The woman in the bed groaned.

Tobias eyed the bunk and gestured with his chin. "Is she ill?" The last thing he needed was his men succumbing to sickness when all hands were required on deck.

The demanding woman glanced over her shoulder before resuming her glare at him. "Miss Dodd suffers from a severe headache. Might we discuss this elsewhere?"

Her gall raised his hackles and emboldened him, loosening his tongue. Mockery laced his tone. "Of course, where are my manners." If she detected his scorn, she showed no sign. He stepped back, extended a hand toward the wardroom, and guided her down the corridor.

The scent of biscuits and coffee rumbled his stomach, but he had much to do before breaking his fast. Two young sailors, starting their day early, sat at the table. Meals on wooden plates lay before them. Their mouths dropped open when the woman entered. One lad's bite of biscuit fell from his lips.

Tobias cleared his throat, and they jumped to attention. "Pardon me, men. You'll need to finish your meals above deck."

They grabbed their plates and retreated from the room, but Tobias didn't miss their over-the-shoulder glances at the dainty miss. Having females on board was going to create a nest of problems. He pulled out a chair and gestured for her to sit. He then positioned himself in the seat adjacent, exactly where he and Middleton had sat mere hours before.

The crew room light shined brighter than the cabin, offering him a better view. Her complexion was blemish-free and wrinkle-free, except for the creases from sleeping at his desk. She couldn't be much over twenty years with a lovely aquiline nose and large, intelligent eyes. He could see why Middleton would be taken with her. She'd be an unwanted distraction to his crew and another demand upon his time, for he'd need to ensure her safety. Ships and men long at sea were a dangerous combination for a woman. He laced his fingers and stared at his hands. "Why did you board this ship?"

"Anthony wasn't expecting me." She gripped the table so hard her knuckles turned white. "But I need to speak with him. It's urgent."

Anthony. They were on a first-name basis. He could see she'd dressed her best for him. Her gown seemed strange, like a dressy sheepherder, but he didn't have the slightest clue nor interest in women's fashion trends.

Tobias's lips curled. Middleton was a liar. He'd sat in that very seat and claimed to have used the British warship to rescue the woman he loved. All the while, his paramour awaited him in his cabin. "What discussion was so important that you needed to sneak aboard his ship in the middle of the night?"

Her lashes lowered, and when she didn't speak, Tobias followed the storyline to the obvious conclusion. "Are you carrying his babe?"

She gasped and pushed back from the table. "How dare you insinuate... accuse me of-of...?"

He might have chuckled if the situation hadn't been so dire. Usually, he was the one fumbling for words in the presence of a woman, not the other way around.

Her eyelids narrowed. "Anthony is my brother."

He blinked, caught in her frosty glare. "My apologies." Those flashing blue eyes turned something inside him, like rusted gears moving once more. "I was remiss." He lowered his gaze to the table and shook his head. "I beg your pardon. I made an unfortunate assumption."

Miss Middleton crossed her arms under a heaving chest. "An unsettling presumption."

He tugged his sleeve. "Let's return to the situation at hand."

"My abduction."

"Whoa." He raised his palms as heat poured through him anew. "Your boarding my ship without my knowledge is hardly a kidnapping."

"So you'll turn the ship around?"

"No."

"Then you're holding me against my will. How is that not an abduction?"

He locked gazes, no longer seeing her as a woman as much as a foe. Madness must run in Middleton's family. "I do not see another option." He itched to toss her and her companion over-board. Instead, he tilted his head to crack the tension in his neck and concentrated on formulating the right words. "I cannot place a woman's demand above our country's mission. You will have no choice but to travel with us to St. Kitts."

"That's absurd." She leaned over the table toward him, stretching her slender neck until their faces were only a hand's width apart. "People will question my disappearance. My family will be frantic with worry, and I fear for their safety." A shadow dimmed her light eyes, and she paused. "They'll wonder about my whereabouts." Her wide-eyed determination fizzled as she wilted into a slump. "What is so pressing in the Leeward Islands that you cannot help a woman in distress?"

Tobias's resolve slipped. He saw his own mother's eyes pleading with him to accept a commission within the Royal Navy so there would be one less mouth to feed.

"I cannot lose six months of my life. I beg you." She clasped her gloved hands. "We couldn't have sailed far. How long would it take to return—a day—day and a half? The prince regent won't die if he has to wait a few days for sugar in his tea, whereas my life would be ruined if I were to vanish for six months."

His sympathy evaporated. Disloyalty ran in their family. He pounded his fist on the table, and she flinched. "I will not abide slander of our king on my ship."

She drew back. Her chair hinged on its back legs before slapping the floor.

This woman didn't come under his command, but that didn't stifle his compulsion to impart respect for those who'd fought and died for England. Reigning in his temper, Tobias evened his tone. "Men have sacrificed their lives, spilt their blood on this very deck, to bring England honor and to spread its principles to the world. Such talk disgraces our king and those who've defended the crown."

"I beg your pardon." She inhaled a staccato breath. "I'm merely frustrated and trying to understand why my life has been upended over an honest mistake." Her eyes grew overly bright. "And why my family shall suffer needlessly wondering what has happened to their daughter."

She retracted her hands underneath the table, but not before he witnessed their shaking.

Please, Lord, don't let her start crying. He didn't know how to speak to a woman. Other than when he was a small child, he'd had very little interaction with females. He wanted to explain his mission so she'd understand the urgency, but he didn't know her, nor did he trust Anthony Middleton's sister enough to reveal the Admiral's war orders.

Her lower lip quivered, and fear shone in her unblinking eyes.

He softened. He should pity Miss Middleton. She was sailing far from home on a ship full of warriors off to do battle after gathering reinforcements in the Leeward Islands. This was nothing like the London drawing rooms and house parties to which she was accustomed. If she were like the women Henry, his lieutenant, spoke of, it was a wonder she hadn't swooned or fallen prey to a fit of vapors. In a way, she'd earned his respect for facing her problem and demanding a solution—even if she was infuriating.

"I'll tell you what." He leaned back, resting his face against the L-shape of his thumb and index finger. "I will inform our lookouts to watch for any British ships headed into port. If we can hail them, we might be able to set you and Miss Dodd aboard one."

"Truly?" She blinked, and her face illuminated as though an oil lamp had been turned up.

He nodded.

She inhaled a deep breath. "Thank you." A brief smile flitted across her lips, and a set of dimples winked at him.

The sight expanded his chest as if he'd been hailed a hero. He wanted to shout *huzzah*, for he'd spoken to a woman, and his tongue hadn't become leaden. His burst didn't last long before a wave of exhaustion crashed over him. He stifled a yawn. He could bunk in the lieutenant's cabin until the women's situation was rectified. An hour's rest was necessary to restore his energy before introducing himself to the day-shift crew and explaining their new orders.

"What are we to do in the meantime?" Miss Middleton twisted in her chair. Her hand gripped the seatback, and her clouded eyes peered at him with questions.

Questions he was too tired to answer. He rose and moved to the center of the room, waiting to escort her back to the cabin. He pulled her to a stand and stood tall himself, despite the weariness permeating his bones. He'd just gone twelve rounds in the ring with Anthony Middleton. He may have owed it to his country to obtain the truth from the man, but he held no obligation to alleviate the distress of the man's sister. He ushered her down the hall and opened the door to the captain's chamber.

"We'll discuss further concerns tomorrow." He gently pushed her over the threshold. "In the meantime, remain in your cabin and out of the way of my crew."

~

"May I get you anything?" Priscilla tucked the sheets under Miss Dodd's pale face.

"No," she murmured.

Priscilla matched her whisper. "I'm afraid we've boarded a ship sailing for the Leeward Islands. The captain is going to unload us on any passing vessel headed to London if they can hail them." Her voice cracked. "It's the best I could get the exasperating man to promise, but I will work on him." She kneeled at the bunk edge. "I'm truly sorry to bring you into this mess. I will make it up to you."

Miss Dodd made no response. Only the rise and fall of bedcovers indicated she still lived.

Priscilla's list of sins continued to grow. Miss Dodd never spoke of any family, but she was often sending letters. Would her family be worried when they didn't hear from her? "I hope no one will fret over your absence. Anthony will stay holed up in his townhouse pouting and imbibing, so he won't realize I'm gone." Her heart ached as though it had gotten caught on a rib. She inhaled a deep breath. "I can only hope the butler who overheard my sarcastic remark about sailing to the islands took it seriously." It could be weeks before her parents noticed her disappearance. They'd assume she was visiting with Anthony at his lodging or her friends in the country. As long as Miss Dodd was missing also, they'll believe their needy daughter was in good hands and probably be relieved she was gone.

However, to disappear for six months, especially during the season, would draw attention. Would those in her circle merely gossip about her absence, or would they be concerned? Nellie would miss her, but mostly because she'd need help to plan another secret rendezvous, which Priscilla wanted no part in.

"This could be a new start." She inhaled deeply. Perhaps getting away would distance her from some poorer influences on her life, like Miss Nellie Archard and men like Mr. Goulart and Lord Fortin. Mayhap things would clear up during her absence. She'd return to discover she was worried over nothing. Besides, she'd always wanted to see the Leeward Islands. "Lottie resides in St. Kitts. She's the only person, other than you, who gave me pause to rethink my actions."

Still no reply.

"Lottie will know what to do. She'd probably tell me this is God's hand, drawing me back under His protection and encouraging me to do what is right." Lottie's faith had always been strong, but when she and Miss Dodd spoke of ancient Bible stories, Priscilla had considered them more of a history lesson. The Middleton family never put much stock in prayer or church attendance. However, now she wished she'd paid closer attention. "You'd be happy to know that I actually prayed a hasty prayer earlier, for your safety and that of my parents. Do you think God honors those prayers? Even from someone like me?"

Silence.

She listened to Miss Dodd's rhythmic breathing, but it didn't lend her comfort. In the dark confines of the cabin, Priscilla's heart pounded in her chest, and perspiration dampened her palms.

No. Miss Dodd lay near her. She wasn't alone.

Priscilla opened her carpetbag and hung up her gowns to take her mind off the prickly tingling of her spine. The all too familiar feelings rushed back.

Twelve times two is twenty-four. Twelve times three is thirty-six. Twelve times four...

The lurking darkness seeped around her, pressing in. She wiped her clammy hands on her skirt.

Even doing sums in her head wasn't working. Should she wake Miss Dodd?

And tell her what? That her charge's mind was slipping? She'd mistakenly told Anthony, and now he believed his sister to be nicked in the nob.

Her pulse accelerated.

"You're not alone," she whispered into the darkness, but the silence of the cabin mocked her, and her mind wouldn't listen to reason.

Her racing heartbeat pounded in her ears.

The echo of the scraggly man's sinister voice rang in her mind. *Scream all you want. No one will hear you.*

Priscilla sprung to her feet. She was still in control. She wouldn't let this happen. Grabbing her skirts in one hand, she threw open the cabin door and sprinted down the corridor.

Darkness pursued her like an attack animal gnawing at her heels. She needed to stroll above deck, be in light and around people.

A sailor descended the stairs and halted. His eyes bulged, and he rubbed them as if she were an apparition.

Priscilla stopped. Was he surprised to see a woman in general or shocked because he'd witnessed her fleeing like a banshee? What would he think about her odd behavior? She intended to smile a greeting, but her lips faltered. Darkness gripped her mouth and throat.

"Good day, miss. May I assist you? You seem to be in a bit of a hurry."

Darkness retracted its tentacles from around her mouth, and she generated words. "I-I thought I saw a mouse." Her lips mustered a smile. "I was thinking of taking a stroll above deck. Might you accompany me?"

The man's ruddy face illuminated. "I'd be delighted." He bowed. "At your service, miss. Name's Cecil St. Ledger. I'm the new midshipman."

"Pleased to meet you, Mr. St. Ledger. My name is Priscilla Middleton."

"Middleton?" Mr. St. Ledger tugged on his earlobe with his free hand. "Why does that sound familiar?" He paused. "Are you related to the previous captain?"

She nodded. "I'm his sister. There was a bit of a miscommunication. I called upon him because his ship wasn't supposed to leave until Monday, and he wasn't notified of my presence."

"Hound's teeth." He stared at her with a slack jaw. "The ship sailed without yer knowing?"

"I'm afraid so."

"Yer stuck on board."

"Indeed."

"Well, I can't say I'm disappointed." A crooked smile lifted one side of his face. "It's nice to have the company of a lady. It keeps the men in line, cleans up their speech."

"I'm glad someone is pleased. Captain Prescott seemed less so."

"Our captain is a disciplined man." The stairs were too narrow to ascend side by side, so he stepped aside and allowed her to climb first. "I've sailed under his command fer two tours. He runs a tight ship and crew. He's probably worried you'll keep the men from their duties."

"In all the confusion, I never thought to ask him why he'd replaced my brother?"

Mr. St. Ledger glanced around but pressed his lips tight as if to hold the juicy gossip inside.

"He's my brother." She held his gaze. "I have a right to know if there are any grievances against my family."

"Rumor has it"—he leaned closer and lowered his voice—"Captain Middleton absconded with a British ship to meet up with his lady love."

Anthony? The only woman in whom he'd shown any interest was Lottie, but he lost his opportunity when she married the St. Kittitian, Nathan Winthrop.

"The up and ups think he might also have been secretly dealin' with smugglers in Louisiana."

"Barataria?" Where Lottie wrote that Anthony and Nathan had helped rescue her.

"That's the place." He nodded. "Captain Prescott gets real sore about it, cuz the admiral rang a peel over him. Gave Captain Prescott a good set-down. We worried he might lose his command because he was the one who'd referred Middleton. Went and stuck out his neck for him and all, then Middleton went and betrayed Captain Prescott and the Crown. The admiral saw reason, though. He took Middleton's command of the *Trade Wind* and gave it to Captain Prescott."

Priscilla swallowed the disturbing information.

Lottie. She would have the answers. She could clear Anthony's name. If Priscilla couldn't return to England, then she would seek the truth in St. Kitts.

Mr. St. Ledger gestured to the deck. "Ladies first."

She emerged into the sunshine, and the darkness's remnant fingerprints melted away. Fresh, salty air swept aside the musty smell of damp wood. Men like spiders climbed the web of lines and rigging. Orders echoed, followed by "look alive" or "smartly men." Large white sails cupped the wind. Sweaty sailors grunted as they heaved ropes and tied them off. If they noticed a woman on deck, they didn't pause from their tasks.

"Cecil, did you get the auger?" A burly sailor looped a thick rope around a cleat.

"I've found another job. Send Benton for it."

"That lad wouldn't know an auger if it bit him in the—" The burly man halted, and his eyes widened. He checked behind him before strutting over. His bandanna flapped in the breeze, protruding like a rooster's cockscomb.

He stepped around her and swatted the back of Mr. St. Ledger's head.

"Ow." Mr. St. Ledger rubbed the spot.

"What were you thinking sneakin' a woman on board. The captain'll hang you from the riggin' when he finds out."

"It's not like that. Captain Prescott knows. Her bein' onboard was an accident." He stepped aside and extended his hand as if presenting the queen. "Miss Middleton, may I introduce you to our sub-lieutenant, Jacob Raleigh."

Mr. Raleigh tugged off his bandana, put a hand to his waist, jostling the frill of his sleeves, and bowed. "Pleasure to meet you"—he eyed Mr. St. Ledger—"as surprising as it may be."

"Delighted to make your acquaintance, Mr. Raleigh." She curtsied.

Echoed commands ceased, and the ship quieted except for the sound of waves breaking against the bow. All eyes had shifted to her.

Mr. Raleigh glared at the men, and they half-heartedly resumed their duties. When he turned back, his eyes gleamed. "I must hear your tale."

"It was merely a misunderstanding." She sighed. "I needed to speak to my brother."

Men gathered around with curious expressions. A few scowled at her with crossed arms.

Mr. St. Ledger stood tall, as though proud of knowing the information his higher-ranking official didn't. "She's Captain Anthony Middleton's sister."

Murmurs floated among the crowd.

"Is she sailing with us to the islands?" A bran-faced lad wiggled his eyebrows. His freckles covered practically every square inch of his skin.

His query burst open a dam of questions, one shouted on top of the other. Mr. St. Ledger put his fingers to his lips and whistled to quiet them. "Let's remember we are naval men." He took Priscilla's hand and parted the men, offering her a seat on a nearby bench made out of a barrel. "Where are our manners. Why doesn't someone fetch Miss Middleton something to drink?"

The bran-faced lad ran to do their bidding.

"Stand back, men. Give Miss Middleton room." Mr. Raleigh stood over her like a sentinel. "If you would be kind enough to tell us your tale and assuage our curiosity."

She peered at all the eager faces. "I'm afraid it's not much of a story." Under such scrutiny, her retelling spilled out into nervous rambling, and she explained more details than she intended. "Next thing I knew, Captain Prescott held a lamp over my head in an utter rage, demanding to know why I was on his ship."

A handful of men chuckled, but a man with a curled mustache planted his fist into his palm. "And for a good reason. Mark my word, women bring bad luck to a ship."

"Bah." Mr. Raleigh waved his hand. "Don't mind him. He's a superstitious old sea dog."

"I, fer one," said a sailor kneeling to her right, "am mighty pleased to have such a lovely lady to look upon, if you don't mind me sayin', miss."

Many other questions followed. They wanted to know the captain's exact reaction to her presence, if her family knew of her whereabouts, and if she had any suitors who'd be devastated by her disappearance, which led to invitations to dine as their guest.

She laughed, flattered by their compliments and endeared by their concerns. "Thank you, all for your generous hospitality, but I've yet—"

"It's the captain," whispered a sailor.

Men scattered faster than miscreants when the constable arrives.

Priscilla froze like a rabbit without a place to hide.

Captain Prescott's hulking form loomed in front of her. His mouth dipped in a deep scowl. "What's the meaning of this?"

CHAPTER 5

I shall do my best to keep your daughter from further trouble.

~ *Letter left behind by Miss Dodd to Admiral and Mrs. Middleton*

"*B*ack to your stations." Tobias leaned into his shout with curled fists. He prided himself on always running an efficient ship. One man asleep at the helm could spell certain disaster. His reputation preceded him, at least he'd thought, until this moment, when a mere woman turned his crew into bumbling fools.

Cecil stepped in a looped line in his haste to get below deck. Timothy and Griffin collided, and Benton hid behind a barrel.

This was not the first impression he wanted to give his new crew. Tobias wasn't a hot-headed tyrant. He prided himself in being tough but always fair with his men. Yet this woman raised his hackles faster than his most disobedient crewman.

Why couldn't he have a stowaway boy, running from his family? She had to be a woman and a Middleton, no less.

She clutched the bench's side as if forcing herself to stay put. "I'm afraid we have gotten off to a bad start."

Tension knotted his spine, and his voice deepened to a deadly growl. "I thought I told you to stay out of my men's way?" For his sanity and her safety.

"You did, indeed." To her credit, Miss Middleton didn't run or shrink back. Instead, she met his gaze and held it despite the ferocity she must have witnessed in his eyes.

He stepped closer. Her distraction of his crew not only would slow their progress when timing was of the essence, but it could also lead to men getting injured. For their safety, they must be alert, aware, and obey commands without question. *Lack of leadership sinks a ship.* His commanders had engraved the saying into his brain. The sooner she understood his crew wasn't at her disposal, the better. "Why, then, didn't you obey my order?"

Her head tilted back, and wind whipped loose strands of her hair about her delicate face. She released her hold on the bench and met his gaze with guarded blue eyes. "Because it was an unreasonable order."

Her mutinous words slapped him. How dare she show such insubordination in front of his men? Never had he witnessed such disrespect. If she were any other person on his ship, she'd be on chamber-pot-scrubbing duty for the rest of the voyage. But what to do with a disobedient woman—a lady at that?

His fingers clenched, itching to throttle her right here in front of his men. He ground his teeth and grumbled under his breath, "Middletons are a blight upon society."

She leapt to her feet. "What did you say?"

Blast. He hadn't meant to say the words aloud, but this wee thing drove him to madness.

Her lips set into an indignant line, and she stepped forward until their toes touched. "I'll have you know my father was an admiral and works for the War Department."

How many times had her brother thrown that fact in his face? "It seems your father's honorable patriotism didn't pass to the next generation."

She gasped. "My brother has been sailing ships since he was in leading-strings and had always endeared his crew to him." She glanced around at the men now busy at work but with curious ears leaning in their direction.

He'd speak to his men later about minding to their own business.

"Whereas, from what I've seen, you instill fear into your men and work them like dogs." Her arms stiffened at her sides.

Tobias's control ignited into an inferno hot enough to turn those around him to ash, but she met him with an equal blast of rage from her icy glare.

"Whoa, now." Lieutenant Henry Dalton, who should have been at the helm, slid between them. "I daresay tempers have run a bit high." He peeked over her shoulder and scratched the side of his beard. "Our guest, Miss Middleton, is probably not aware of the chain of command on a ship."

"I most certainly am." She poked her head around the first mate.

Henry shifted to keep her behind him. "Captain Prescott, you are needed at the helm."

Tobias inhaled a deep breath and gulped down the acid burning in his chest.

A smile wobbled on Henry's lips, and he turned to escort the captain back to the brig.

Tobias couldn't leave without clear proclamation of who was in authority. He pivoted in front of Miss Middleton and snapped an order. "You are to return to your stateroom at once. Do you understand me?"

"Quite."

"Do I need to escort you?" He peered down his nose at her.

Her face turned to stone. "I can find my way."

"Very well, then."

Her lips twitched. "But we have more to discuss."

"On this ship, delayed obedience is disobedience." He nodded his chin toward the stairs.

She didn't budge.

He dismissed her by inspecting the rigging, but he felt her scowl burning a hole through him. If she didn't obey his direct order in under a minute, he'd pick her up and carry her there himself. His men would not be subjected to her mutinous standoff. He'd place her under house arrest and set a sentinel at her door. It would mean one less hand on deck, but he wouldn't hesitate to issue the command.

She murmured under her breath, "You are being irrational."

"Speck," he called to a sailor, ignoring her comment. "Secure that line before it gets away from you."

With a huff, she strode in the direction of her cabin. Her blond tresses whipped about her face in a fiery dance. She passed him one last glare over her shoulder before disappearing below.

Good girl.

Tobias strode to the bridge.

Henry lifted a questioning brow.

"I will explain later." A deep sigh dispelled any remaining anger. "It's been a long night."

Henry followed him onto the deck. "I thought you couldn't talk to women?"

"I can't." Tobias gripped the helm.

"I guess yelling is the exception then."

Tobias grunted but considered his first mate's comment. *Odd.* His words had flown freely.

A wry smile tipped Henry's lips.

"Middletons show a talent for infuriating me."

Henry chuckled and filled him in on the crew's progression. "Middleton's men are lazy and overindulge on spirits, but I believe we can fix them up right quick. A couple of weeks under your command, and they'll be in tip-top shape."

"Good to hear." Rumors had spread to Tobias's ears that Middleton ran a slipshod ship, drinking and carousing in every port. Perhaps it wasn't as bad as Tobias had feared.

"The wind is steady. We should see smooth sailing."

"That is yet to be determined." Tobias grimaced, still focused on the problem of the high-spirited Miss Middleton. He didn't relish bringing such a shrew to heel, but he couldn't allow her rebellious nature aboard his ship. Her safety and the safety of the whole crew mattered more than an individual's comfort.

Henry hooked his thumbs behind his lapels and rocked back on his heels. "I don't mean to speak out of turn, captain."

He waved his hand. "You know you may speak freely. We've done battle together, and you've had my back."

"Indeed." He rocked backward and forward. "That being said, you've had limited experience with females, so I must warn you. The tropics will freeze over if you continue to treat our guest in such a manner."

"What sort of manner?"

Henry arched an eyebrow. "Like an insolent child."

"She was acting like one." He despised the childish tone of his voice. He cleared his throat and adjusted his hold on the wheel. "Are you saying I should ignore such disrespect?"

Henry held up his palms. "I'm merely saying that women are like delicate flowers. They must be treated with special care, or they will wilt."

Tobias inhaled a deep breath of salty air. The vast ocean spread before him, and above him long stretches of canvas sails harnessed the wind. His hands directed the ship's path. The sea was where he found peace. Like shifting waves and unpredictable weather, women were incomprehensible creatures he could not navigate. They made his palms perspire. They only brought trouble. This particular woman was a Middleton, which magnified the issue.

The image of Miss Middleton's blond tresses blowing in the wind and her expressive eyes narrowed upon him sent his heart beating erratically.

His grip tightened on the wooden handles. He would not let her steal his peace.

She may have the beauty of a rose, but underneath, women had thorns that pricked and made you bleed.

~

*A*rrogant lout.

Three days later, Priscilla and Miss Dodd strolled above deck past the helm to take in the air. According to the list of commands, folded and left in the crease of their cabin door, they were to do so only during designated hours. As she'd read each decree aloud to Miss Dodd, who by the third day appeared much improved in health, Priscilla's opinion of Captain Prescott soured even more. Not only had he outright ignored her, turning his back as if she no longer mattered, now he believed he could govern her every move. She raised her chin a notch. There must be a way to bring an unreasonable man like Captain Prescott around. If not to sail them back to England, then at least to come to a more acceptable arrangement than this list.

Grunts carried on the wind along with wafts of unbathed male. Each moved in rhythm to hoist a sail, tugging and releasing as if taking a simultaneous breath. As much as Priscilla didn't want to allow Captain Prescott any credit, he ran an efficient ship.

The bran-faced sailor slowed swabbing the deck long enough to tip his hat. "Good morning, ladies."

"Good day, cadet..." Priscilla couldn't remember the young man's name, but she remembered his face from the day before.

He leaned on the mop handle. "It's Fredrick Combs, milady, but I'd be honored if you'd call me Speck. Everybody on board does. Not because I'm small, but because I'm speckled." He pointed to his face, and his smile widened. "See me Freckles."

"Enjoy the lovely day, Speck." Priscilla flashed a polite smile and continued their walk. She nudged Miss Dodd. "We mustn't smile overly long. We wouldn't want to distract the men and break one of the captain's rules."

"I daresay you are making too much of this." Wind fluttered Miss Dodd's bonnet, but it was held tight by the knot under her chin. "The captain's loyalty is to his crew, not to unexpected women who board his ship."

Priscilla greeted each sailor they passed as her father used to do with a firm nod and a cheery smile. "I understand a captain's loyalty more than most, thanks to my father and brother. The captain created that list to spite me."

Miss Dodd harrumphed. "Perhaps you should have reconsidered calling his order unreasonable, stayed in the cabin, or possibly remained silent in a respectful manner. If you use your emotions as your compass, you'll end up sailing in circles."

Under the flapping brim, Priscilla spotted Miss Dodd's chastising arched eyebrow. Clearly, she thought Priscilla in the wrong. "He called the Middletons a blight upon society."

"Mayhap that has been his experience?" Miss Dodd kept a perfectly even pace. "Captain Prescott is under the impression that your brother betrayed him. The additional trouble of our being aboard and your less-than-admirable regard of him might lean the captain toward an unfavorable opinion of your family."

Her logic made sense, but Priscilla couldn't relent. "A gentleman would never refer to a lady as a blight, nor a man for that matter unless he wanted to be called out and met on a grassy knoll at dawn."

"Then how fortunate for us there are no grassy knolls at sea."

Lieutenant Dalton approached. "Good morning, ladies. I hope you are faring better with some fresh sea air."

Priscilla introduced her companion to the first mate.

He faced Miss Dodd. "I'm glad to see you're up and about these days." His stiff body, standing at attention, contrasted with his warm expression. Against his deeply tanned skin, white lines formed from squinting in the sun, highlighting the crinkled corners of his eyes. Priscilla guessed him to be of a similar age to her companion.

"We have a surgeon on board," Lieutenant Dalton said. "He's not a physician, but he's fairly knowledgeable in herbs and poultices if, heaven forbid, you find yourself ill once more."

Miss Dodd clasped her hands in front of her. "Thank you for your concern. I'll be sure to visit him. These afflictions are few and far between, but I could use something to help me sleep. All this rocking to and fro churns my stomach and keeps me awake."

"His name is Samuel Evans, but we all call him Doc." He clapped his hands together one time. "I won't keep you from taking in the air, but now that you are up and about, the captain extends a special invitation for you both to join us for supper in our cabin."

Priscilla's gaze flew to the imposing figure standing at the helm. She should decline, ignore his offer as he'd blatantly ignored her, but he had let them remain in Anthony's—er—the captain's cabin. The gold buttons of Captain Prescott's navy coat reflected the early morning sun. His snug uniform hugged his broad shoulders, and his bicorne hat added several more inches to his already impressive height. She could only imagine the commotion he'd have caused among her marriageable friends if he strode into a London ballroom.

The duress of their situation had emotions running high. Perhaps Miss Dodd was right, and she'd misjudged him. Could it be he was extending a peace offering by inviting them to dine as his honored guests?

"How lovely. We would be delighted." Miss Dodd nudged her elbow into Priscilla's side to wake her from her woolgathering.

"Splendid." Lieutenant Dalton bowed and stepped aside for them to pass. "Supper will be served at eight."

They nodded their thanks and continued their stroll. Priscilla soaked in the warm sun. They'd been sailing for less than a week, but already the sun radiated stronger than it had in England. As they drew close to the bow, a strong gale plastered the front of their gowns to their skin and whipped their skirt hems about their ankles.

On past voyages, Priscilla had looked forward to the captain's dinner. Her father or brother's special guests usually discussed interesting topics on politics or their travels. Could dinner with Captain Prescott be enjoyable, or would it be a litany of more regulations she must uphold?

They rounded the bow, and as they drew closer, she caught Captain Prescott's scowl upon her. The intensity in his eyes conveyed a challenge. She shouldn't stare, but she couldn't pull her gaze away. It soon became a battle of wills, and she dared not show weakness. A strange fluttering sensation flowed through her. Heat spread from her stomach to her limbs, and her pulse beat erratically. Her eyes burned, but sheer determination kept her from looking away.

A wispy cloud formed over his shoulder and reflected the sun. Priscilla squinted. It wasn't a cloud. It was a ship.

A way home.

She grabbed Miss Dodd's wrist. "Is that what I think it is?" She pointed at the boat.

Miss Dodd pushed Priscilla's finger away. "It is impolite to point."

"But it's a ship. We're saved." She frowned. "We should be hailing them—changing direction." Priscilla scooted around her companion. "I must inform Captain Prescott." Lifting her skirts, she dashed toward the bridge.

A line snapped, popping like a musket shot.

"Comin' around!" A sailor yelled.

A swinging boom creaked behind her.

CHAPTER 6

There is a hullabaloo growing over the departure of the *Trade Wind*. Prepare for a tongue-lashing from the disadvantaged parties.

~ Letter from Admiral Sims to Lieutenant Sparks

*T*obias's blood chilled.

A couple of crewmen reached for Miss Middleton to prevent impending disaster, but she was too quick. The heavy boom swayed toward the back of her head.

"Halt!" It was the only word Tobias's lips could form.

His entire crew froze, but not Miss Middleton.

He vaulted the helm's rail, extending a hand toward her, but he could only wince as the boom swished above her head, clearing it only by a few inches. His hand dropped to press his heart back into his chest. *Thank heaven.*

Miss Middleton eyed the thick timber without any change in her expression and proceeded to step in a coil of rope.

Lord, help them, the woman had a death wish. "Stop!"

She froze in the center of the coil.

"God's thunder. What in blazes do you think you're doing?"

She crossed her arms under her bosom. Her eyebrows snapped together above a set of flashing blue eyes. "I was coming to speak to you." She pointed behind him. "Do you see the ship on the horizon?"

His heart's rapid beating sent blood rushing through his ears and throbbed a vein in his temple with a dull ache. Her offended look tightened his jaw to the point of nearly cracking a tooth. As much as he wanted to throttle her, the safety of his crews and its guests—invited and uninvited—must remain his top priority. Tobias forced his hand to reach out. *Remember, she's a delicate flower.*

She reared back.

Again, with the defiance.

He dropped his gaze to the rope.

Miss Middleton glanced down and stepped outside the circle.

"You never want to stand in a coiled rope on a ship." She flashed him a small smile, and a pair of dimples winked at him, throwing him off-kilter. "Next thing you know, you'll be swinging from the rigging."

Had she just lectured him on ship safety? The woman must be daft. His jaw clenched. *He* must be daft for not turning the ship around and expunging his vessel of the awaiting hazard that was Priscilla Middleton. "Did you not see the swinging boom or hear the warning?"

"Not at first." Her gaze drifted over his shoulder, most likely to the ship behind him. "But it doesn't matter."

"Doesn't matter?" She wasn't daft. She was completely mad. He closed his eyes and pinched the bridge of his nose between his fingers, fighting to suppress anger burning like acid in his chest. "You might not care a wit for your life, but the last thing I need is a delay for a sea burial"—he opened his eyes—"nor the endless documentation explaining the situation to your family."

Her gaze snapped back to his. "Are you saying, if I die, you'll be inconvenienced by the paperwork?"

Was she even listening? "That's not what I'm saying." He glanced heavenward and beseeched God to help him spit out the right words. "I'm trying to keep you from meeting a bitter end, despite your attempts otherwise."

"I'll have you know." She stepped forward, planting fisted hands on her hips. "I've been around ships all my life, and unless I've grown a full five inches, then there is no chance a boom will come near hitting me."

Tobias flexed his fingers to keep from strangling the impertinent chit. The arrival of her companion kept him from having to respond to Miss Middleton's statement.

Miss Dodd's already pale face appeared whiter than before. "Heavens above, that was a near catastrophe." Even her lips seemed tight. "Praise the Lord for favor."

He eyed Miss Middleton, letting her know Miss Dodd proved his point.

Two angry splotches reddened the younger woman's cheeks. "I'd like to address the ship on the horizon before it disappears." Her gaze darted between him and the ship. "If you'll recall, you mentioned, hailing another vessel to return us to England." She nodded toward the far horizon. "Well, there is a ship."

Tobias turned to glimpse the object of her fixation. His barrelman had notified him of the ship's presence three hours ago. He pushed back his jacket lapel and hooked his thumb over the waistline of his breeches. "As much as I'd like to remove you from my ship, especially after this little stunt, I'm afraid that unless you'd like to sail into Canada to wage battle with the Indians against the Americans, then you're better off staying aboard."

Her lips parted. "But, it's sailing northeast."

One side of his mouth lifted into what he intended to be a

sardonic smile. "Unless the earth has pivoted, it's sailing northwest."

She located the sun's direction, and he could see her mind doing calculations. "I see." She bit her bottom lip. "Very well, then. Please keep a lookout for any ship sailing for England."

He issued her a mock bow. "At your service, milady."

She hesitated. Her foot angled in a way to indicate she wished for a quick escape. "I apologize for any fright I may have caused you. I know our presence has frustrated you, but we do not wish to be any trouble."

Trouble and Middletons were synonymous. Tobias used restraint. Instead of snorting his disbelief, he accepted her apology with a nod.

Miss Dodd curtsied. "We appreciate your hospitality and look forward to dining with you and the lieutenant this evening."

He struggled to keep his expression neutral. He'd completely forgotten about the invitation Henry had convinced him would be considerate to extend. Tonight, he needed to be reviewing maps of Louisiana and planning battle strategies, not playing host for the pampered daughter of an admiral. However, he'd given Henry his word, and so he would suffer through.

"You are welcome."

Miss Dodd issued him a polite smile. Miss Middleton's looked forced. They continued to stand before him.

Did they expect him to bow or say something else? "I look forward to dining with you at eight." He crossed his arms and dipped his chin in a dismissive nod, as he would to one of his men.

A play of emotions danced through Miss Middleton's crystal blue eyes. Miss Dodd hooked her arm through Miss Middleton's and strode in a safe route toward the port leading below deck.

To ensure they safely removed themselves to their cabin,

Tobias trailed them with his gaze. A breeze billowed Miss Middleton's gown. He hated not being able to read her thoughts. Did she find his presence insufferable, or would the honor of being a guest at his table dispel some of her anger? Blast. Why must women be so complicated? He exhaled the remaining heat of his rage into the wind then returned to his post. Men needed direction and new courses drawn with the change of currents. He'd have better luck contemplating a peace agreement between his country and the Americans instead of wasting time considering the confounding inner workings of Miss Middleton's mind.

Lieutenant Dalton, who directed the helmsman in his absence, eyed him after the women had gone below deck. "You never mentioned hailing another ship."

"I'm afraid I might have been rash in trying to appease our uninvited guest."

Lieutenant Dalton stepped aside and let him have the helm.

"We cannot afford to delay our mission." He gripped the wheel, once again the ship's master as he steered it toward the sun, parting the waves. "Men's lives are at stake. As it is, we'll barely have time to replenish supplies in St. Kitts before leading the fleet into the Gulf of Mexico to battle."

The sooner they entered the fight, the sooner he could fulfill his purpose like his father and his father's father before him. He'd win or die fighting for England.

~

"This is a terrible idea." Priscilla tugged the sleeve of her glove as Miss Dodd prodded her through the dim passage toward the captain's quarters. The last thing she wanted was to dine with the ill-tempered captain, especially after making a fool of herself by stepping in a coiled line. She knew better. Her brother would have flown into the boughs giving her a proper set-down. "You saw his face. He didn't mean it. He'd prefer to dine with Napoleon."

"It is an honor to dine with the captain and an opportunity to redeem yourself in his eyes."

Even after a long discussion with her companion, Priscilla didn't believe Captain Prescott should be fully exonerated. Yes, they'd accidentally stowed away on his ship, posed a distraction for his crew, and frightened everyone when the boom swung above her head. But Prescott had accused her of being Anthony's mistress. He'd insulted her family and infuriated her with his haughty demeanor. Dinner with the lout would most certainly be dreadful.

"I shall be on my best behavior, as I promised, but you cannot make me like this man." She lowered her voice as they neared. "I'm merely enduring him until other arrangements can be made."

Something brushed past her kid boots and scampered aloft.

Priscilla jumped and clutched Miss Dodd's arm. "What was that?" She couldn't keep the shrill tone from her voice.

Lieutenant Dalton's head peeked into the passageway. "That's just Sneaky Pete, Cecil's pet weasel." He exited his cabin and awaited their approach. "He's a friendly sort, nothin' to worry yer head over. We like him 'cause he keeps the rat population down."

Priscilla scanned the passageway, half expecting to see beady little eyes shine within the shadows. She shivered.

The lieutenant's tanned skin appeared darker in the poorly lit corridor, making the speckled gray in his beard and the kind glint of his eyes seem to glow white. "Good evening, ladies." He stepped aside with a bow. "Please, come in and be seated."

As Miss Dodd bobbed a curtsy and entered the cabin, she cast a long-glance the lieutenant's way under lowered lashes.

Was her companion developing a fondness for the lieutenant?

Priscilla smiled at the lieutenant with new interest. Miss Dodd had been a socialite until her father passed suddenly, leaving her bereft and lacking funds. Her life choices narrowed to governess or a paid companion. Miss Dodd had chosen the latter.

Priscilla nodded. "Lovely evening, Lieutenant Dalton. Thank you for your gracious hospitality."

The man shifted his weight. "It's—er—the captain's idea and partially mine, but I won't take credit."

She questioned the truth of his statement.

Lieutenant Dalton gestured for her to enter, and she stepped into the double-sized room, much like the one she and Miss Dodd shared. A large mahogany table with four chairs graced the center. A folded hammock hung on a hook for additional sleeping arrangements, and two trunks lay underneath, strapped to the wall. She'd forgotten Lieutenant Dalton shared a cabin with the captain to make room for extra female passengers. A slight pressure squeezed her heart for putting them out.

"May I offer you a glass of claret while we await the captain?" He held up a bottle and an empty glass.

Miss Dodd and Priscilla nodded.

"How long have you been in the Royal Navy, Lieutenant Dalton?" Miss Dodd moved near the cupboard as he poured the red wine.

"Since I was a lad of thirteen."

Miss Dodd's lips pursed. "That's awfully young."

"Ah yes, but the fifth male child of a baron must earn his keep early. My eldest brother inherited a small estate, but for the rest of us, we had to make our own way. Being at sea was my birthright. I started as a cabin boy and ascended to first lieutenant."

Priscilla used the opportunity to stroll about the room. Whereas her brother kept mementos from his travels as inspiration—African masks, Caribbean coconuts, a Peruvian silver flask given to him as a gift—the lieutenant displayed maps, ship renderings, and weapons on the walls.

Miss Dodd's voice rang out. "I'm certain they're proud of your accomplishments."

"Aye, if they were alive, they would be." The deck boards creaked as he moved.

"I'm sorry."

Priscilla glanced over her shoulder and saw him pass a goblet to Miss Dodd. A long look was exchanged. Interesting. Was it to express her condolences or perhaps something more?

Priscilla didn't want to be an interloper, so she stepped over to a long cot tucked in a small alcove. Above it hung alternating rifles and cavalry swords all upside-down. Curious. Why would one display their weapons with the sharp blades facing the ceiling? She leaned closer to admire the sword's intricate metalwork on the gold hilt and highly polished edges.

Lieutenant Dalton approached her side, holding out her drink.

Priscilla accepted the glass, gripping it in both hands. "Impressive weaponry."

He nodded. "I had these hung today. Captain Prescott likes to have his men at the ready. Our weapons are to be on our person or close by at all times—even while we sleep."

"Are they positioned upside down because you worry one might become dislodged and... well, impale you?"

The lieutenant's head drew back, and he laughed.

"What is so amusing?" Captain Prescott's voice sounded from the doorway, startling Priscilla.

His stern gaze fell upon her and held before moving to the lieutenant. The captain's presence filled the room even before he shifted sideways a bit to fit through the narrow cabin door. Gold-fringed caps on his jacket shoulders made him appear even more formidable. As usual, he'd dressed impeccably. He clutched his hat to his chest, covering some of the gold buttons lining his jacket. His milk-white breeches hugged his legs and led to his black boots polished with such a sheen she could practically see her reflection in them.

Every inch of him spoke of a captain who was very much in command. Enough to give her pause but at the same time quicken her pulse.

Lieutenant Dalton straightened to attention, but Captain Prescott waved him at ease. He pointed to the weapons. "Miss Middleton wondered if we kept our weapons positioned blade side toward the overhead because we feared they'd fall off and stab us while we slept."

Hearing her question repeated made it sound foolish, and Priscilla hoped he couldn't see her squirm under her gown's layered fabric.

Captain Prescott's gaze swept past her to the weapons. "It's an astute observation..."

She inhaled a breath and held it. Had the captain just praised her? Was complimenting her so repulsive, he had to force the words past his lips?

"...but the theory is wrong."

She exhaled. Of course.

The captain leaned an arm upon the beamed bulkhead of the alcove and examined the blade. "I invented a U-bracket clip that unlatches only when great pressure is applied. All officers are trained to wield their weapons at a moment's notice because sometimes that is all we have." He peered over at her with a boyish glint. "We often run drills. Would you care to watch?"

His gaze searched hers with a nervous eagerness she couldn't refuse. This was a side of the captain she had yet to witness, and it tugged a smile from her mouth. "Indeed. I would be delighted."

"Very well, then." He gestured to the bed. "Lieutenant, if you would participate as one of our officers and lie in your bunk, and I will play the part of a French marauder."

Lieutenant Dalton assumed his sleeping position.

Captain Prescott touched her elbow, and a current of energy spread up her arm and down into her stomach.

"Please, step back a bit." He guided her over to Miss Dodd's side at the far corner. "I'd lose my crew's respect if I didn't take precautions to keep our passengers safe."

Was he explaining his reasoning behind his rules? Or why he became so enraged when he believed her to be in danger above deck? She searched his gray eyes for any indication, but he glanced away.

"Be ready to observe." He cleared his throat and, with stealth movements, crept around the table, reaching for the hilt of sword belted at his hip. He removed his weapon with a zip of sliding metal only to be met with a loud clang as Lieutenant Dalton, in a single sitting-up-motion, whipped a cavalry sword off the wall and thwarted his attacker. The lieutenant continued his combat, but Captain Prescott countered with the fluid grace of an orchestra conductor.

Miss Dodd gasped and fanned her face with her gloved hand.

Priscilla couldn't resist clapping at the magnificent display of skill.

The captain saluted with his sword to both the lieutenant and the ladies before sheathing his weapon.

Lieutenant Dalton returned his weapon to the U-brackets on the wall.

Two cabin boys entered and swiftly set the table with plates, silverware, and glasses.

Priscilla grinned at the captain and the lieutenant. "Quite impressive."

Lieutenant Dalton moved to Miss Dodd's side. "Captain Prescott not only runs these drills with the officers but with every crewman on board."

"Truly?" Priscilla raised both eyebrows. "Even the cabin

boys?" Anthony barely acknowledged anyone ranked below midshipmen. She couldn't imagine him taking time to train the boys who swabbed the deck.

"He believes every able hand must be ready to defend their ship. The captain has just begun training the new men, but quite a few came with us from *The Bergamot*." The lieutenant's voice rang with pride.

Captain Prescott placed a hand on the shoulder of one of the cabin boys. "This is Oliver."

The lad stood stiff with his arms at his sides.

"He's been under my command for a full year." Captain Prescott nodded in a silent command.

"Aye, aye, captain." Oliver scampered to the bed and pretended to sleep.

The captain once again reached for his sword.

Oliver popped from the bed, snatched the sword, and wielded it in an arch to slam into the captain's extended blade. "Take that, you filthy pirate."

"I appreciate your enthusiasm, Oliver." Captain Prescott corrected the boy's grip. "Very well executed. Next time, tighten your wrist a bit more, and you'll be knocking the sword clear out of the marauder's hand."

Oliver glowed at the captain's praise.

"Now, back to your duties."

"Aye, aye, Captain." Oliver returned to his work. The cabin boys' eagerness to please showed in their frequent glances at Captain Prescott and their care in the table presentation.

"Well done, Benton"— Captain Prescott nodded—"Oliver."

Both boys saluted, their lips fighting to suppress grins, before exiting the cabin.

Priscilla's heart stirred. How deeply had she longed for such approval from her papa? She glanced at Captain Prescott. Had she misjudged him? Could a man be so terrible who cared to recognize even the lowest ranking persons under his command?

"Please." Captain Prescott held out a chair for her, and Lieutenant Dalton held out a chair for Miss Dodd.

The boys returned carrying serving platters and tureens of soup, roasted duck, and root vegetables.

Priscilla unfolded the silk napkin and spread it across her lap. "I must commend you on an efficiently run ship." She sipped from her glass. "I've never seen the like."

"Indeed." One corner of Captain Prescott's mouth tightened in…a sneer?

He'd insulted how her brother managed his ship, and now this man was apparently so high in the instep he couldn't graciously accept a compliment. And to think, she'd begun to see him in a favorable light. He might run a tight ship, but he could use a lesson in manners.

He parted his lips as if to speak but swallowed the comment with a frown. Instead, after a long pause, he merely said, "Thank you."

She focused her attention on the food set before her and drew conversation from Lieutenant Dalton. Within the span of the first and second course, she learned the names, livelihoods, and towns of residence for all his siblings and Lieutenant Dalton's interests, including model ships, fishing, and a good game of slide groat, which consisted of sliding a coin across a table to a specific spot. Captain Prescott confirmed Lieutenant Dalton's competitiveness and how they practiced every evening on this very table.

"Captain Prescott." Lieutenant Dalton nudged the captain with his elbow. "Is the only man who, on occasion, can best me in the game. While I practice the craft religiously, he'll simply pick up a coin, slide it across the table, and knock mine out of play." He shook his head. "Makes me cross as crabs."

"I have other priorities that demand my time." The captain speared a potato.

Lieutenant Dalton whacked him on the shoulder. "All work and no play makes life dull."

Captain Prescott swallowed his bite. "But keeps my crew alive."

"Aye, it does, and we're grateful for our captain's thoroughness." He eyed Priscilla. "But one day, I'd like to see him meet a nice girl, settle down, and raise a brood of little tykes."

Priscilla flashed back to their first encounter—Captain Prescott's hard flesh under her palm as she shoved him out of what she thought was Anthony's cabin. Her cheeks heated.

"You know I'm not..." A muscle in Captain Prescott's jaw twitched.

"Couldn't you picture him gracing a ballroom?" Lieutenant Dalton winked at Miss Dodd. "If one look at our dashing captain doesn't send ladies into a swoon, then he can sweep them off their feet by pretending the waltz is a gunner drill." He guided his arms through the air in a combination of a dance hold and lighting a cannon. "Lift—two three, load—two three, light—two three."

Priscilla coughed into her hand to hide her laugh at the lieutenant's outrageous suggestion.

Even the captain couldn't contain his smile. One side of his mouth lifted in a crooked grin, revealing even white teeth.

Priscilla implored Lieutenant Dalton to tell more about himself and the crew, and he focused on his first days of service under the young captain, growing more animated with each telling. The socially relaxed atmosphere got everyone, including the grave captain, laughing. Without the dark furrow of his brow, Captain Prescott appeared quite handsome and even approachable in a boyish way. His shoulders shook when he laughed with an unguarded heartiness.

The evening had somehow taken an unexpected but delightful turn.

Priscilla enjoyed Lieutenant Dalton's charm and enthusiasm.

He even drew subtle smiles out of her stoic companion. Each time he did, the lieutenant's chest expanded, like a king who'd won a hard-earned battle. Only when Priscilla inquired about their voyage and plans did he peer at Captain Prescott. The captain issued the barest shake of his head, and Lieutenant Dalton changed the subject.

The simmering heat of her ire rolled below the surface. Apparently, Captain Prescott believed two women to be a threat to his mission. As if they were spies. What rubbish. She sipped her drink, swallowing the memory of her interaction with Mr. Goulart and her anger.

Miss Dodd leaned forward. "And, how long have you been in the Royal Navy, Captain Prescott?"

"Since I was ten."

"Also, very young." Her fork stilled. "Why is that?"

"I wanted to serve my country. The navy offered posts at a younger age than the infantry."

The twinkle returned to the lieutenant's eyes. "Unlike myself, Captain Prescott was commissioned."

Priscilla reared back. "Someone paid for your commission at such a young age?"

"His father was Captain Lawrence Prescott from the Battle of Cape St. Vincent."

Miss Dodd dabbed at her lips with her napkin. "The captain who died saving Commodore Nelson Horatio?"

"The very same." Reverence quieted the lieutenant's voice.

Priscilla blinked. "*The* Lord Nelson?" The same man whose renowned maritime tactics Papa raved about? "The hero from the Battle of Trafalgar?"

Lieutenant Dalton nodded. "The man earned every bit of his legend."

Her gaze shifted to Captain Prescott. "Which makes your father's sacrifice all the more heroic."

Captain Prescott merely scratched the corner of his jaw with his thumb, but his eyes darkened. A heaviness seemed to fall upon him, deep mourning, and it radiated through the air, compressing the walls of her heart.

Lieutenant Dalton raised his glass. "His father was a true hero."

They followed, raising their glasses in reverence before sipping from the rim.

Silence fell over the cabin, broken only by the creaking of the ship.

Captain Prescott straightened. Priscilla didn't see the movement as much as she felt it. The Battle of Cape St. Vincent had occurred when she was an infant, but many still referenced the epic event where the outnumbered British ships captured the Spanish fleet.

She glanced at the captain. Not a single gray hair tinged his thick, dark hair. He couldn't be a day over thirty, which meant he'd lost his father at a young age. Her heart twisted. She placed a hand in the open space on the table between them. "I'm so sorry for your loss. It must have been hard being so young."

He dismissed her acknowledgment with a slight wave of his fingers. "It was a long time ago." The shadows on his face deepened.

He remained quiet for the remainder of dinner.

CHAPTER 7

Lieutenant General Sir Edward Pakenham shall lead the
battle of New Orleans from the helm. No doubt to
victory as he did during the Peninsular Wars.
~ *Correspondence from Admiral Sims to the Prince Regent*

*P*riscilla lay in bed, replaying the evening's dinner in
her mind. Miss Dodd's light rhythmic snores
sounded next to her. She'd fallen asleep reading the Bible out
loud to Priscilla. She lifted it, careful not to wake her companion, and set it on the bedside table next to the empty glass once
filled with an elixir the surgeon instructed Miss Dodd to drink
to help her sleep.

Priscilla drew the covers back up and stared at the dark
overhead.

What was it about Captain Prescott that rattled her so? Lieutenant Dalton treated him as a dear friend, his crew respected
and admired him, and the young cabin boys adored him. Even
Miss Dodd defended him instead of siding with her. It seemed
the captain treated everyone fairly except her. He'd disliked her
the moment he'd awakened her in a fit of rage. Either he

ignored her or issued her one set-down after another. Was accidentally boarding his ship that unforgivable?

A lump formed in her throat, and she swallowed around it. If he discovered she'd unintentionally spilled British secrets to a potential French spy, he'd tighten a noose around her neck himself. Before the masquerade, she'd have found such devout loyalty an attractive quality, but now the trait set her on edge.

Why did it matter? Captain Prescott meant nothing to her. The sooner they happened upon a returning British ship, the sooner she could be separated from him. A sinking feeling hollowed her stomach. The further they sailed, the less likely they were to meet a ship sailing to England. She needn't be reminded of the vast expanse of the Atlantic. Many an evening, she'd hide in the bookshelf cabinet while her father worked at his desk. Her nanny believed her asleep in her bed, but she'd sneak down the servants' stairs, escaping the darkness that sought to snatch her from her bed, and through the library's open door. Light from her papa's candle would shine through the old grate between the rooms. She'd lay, memorizing maps of the oceans, continents, and countries until she drifted off to sleep. Somehow come morning, she'd awaken back in her bed, a servant likely having carried her there.

The ship creaked as it climbed a wave, and the walls groaned their displeasure. A gnawing sounded in the far corner, and Priscilla's breath caught. Was it Sneaky Pete? A tiny mouse? A large rat?

It stopped.

She clutched the bed covers to her chin. Her eyes widened in the darkness as if attempting to absorb more light. Her thudding heart pounded in her ears.

An itchy feeling of needing to get out of her skin twitched her muscles.

The gnawing sounded again.

She rolled over and shook Miss Dodd.

The woman groaned. "What is it?"

"I heard something."

Miss Dodd rolled over, pulling the covers with her. "We're on a ship. There are always going to be noises. Go back to sleep."

Priscilla squeezed her eyes shut. *It's merely your imagination. Calm yourself.* Perhaps if she counted sheep. *One.* A fluffy white body leapt over a fence. *Two... Three...*

Miss Dodd's snores resumed.

Sweat broke across Priscilla's forehead, and a silent scream lodged in her chest.

In her mind, she shooed another cuddly white sheep over the fence. *Four...* A cloud passed over the green pasture, shadowing the sheep until their white wool turned black. The scraggly man, wielding a butcher's knife, emerged from the red barn. The sheep wandered away to greener pasture, but one lonely little lamb with shaking legs huddled against the fence. It was too small to jump over, and its bleating cry was left unanswered.

No one will hear your screams.

Priscilla's eyes sprung open. The darkness reached up from under their bunk and squeezed a hand tight around her throat. She struggled to breathe. *It's not real.* She sucked in a deep breath, but her lungs still screamed for air.

The grip on her throat squeezed, turning her blood to ice.

The crew's laughter sounded from the wardroom.

She bounded from her bed, grabbed her robe, and fumbled with the latch. Her fingers refused to work right. It finally gave. She exited into the passageway and scrambled down the hall, evading creatures lurking in the corners. The oil lamp's glow through the port eased her steps. She stuffed her arms into her robe and tied the sash tight about her waist.

Years of etiquette training rang in her head. Entering a room full of men dressed in her nightclothes would be indecent. They'd believe her a wanton woman. She swallowed and turned back down the dark passageway, and cold dread clawed anew.

The door behind her opened.

"Miss Middleton, is something amiss?" Mr. Raleigh's voice held a note of surprise.

She spun to face the stout man at eye-level. "I was..." Her mind whirled for an explanation. "I was merely thirsty, is all."

He backed into the room, holding the door for her. "Please come join us. I'll have one of the men fetch you some fresh milk." He shook a finger above his head at one of the six men seated at the table.

Speck set down his cards and rose to do Mr. Raleigh's bidding.

"Thank you, Mr. Combs," She nodded. "Mr. Raleigh."

Mr. St. Ledger chuckled. "We're not formal. If you use our surnames, we're not gonna know to who yer referrin'." He placed a hand on his chest. "Please call me Cecil." He gestured to Mr. Raleigh. "He's plain Raleigh. This is Lefty. You've met Speck, and we've got Nash and Jacob, but Jacob's not his real name. He got it 'cause he has his little heart set on a lass named Rebecca."

"Pleasure to meet you again." She nodded. "And I hope you'll treat me as one of the crew."

"You look like you've seen a ghost. Perhaps you should sit." Raleigh touched her elbow and guided her over to the men.

Cecil stood and pulled a chair off the wall hook for her to sit.

She slowly lowered into it, uncertain about the wisdom of her actions.

"Did you see headless Ben?" asked Nash, a man with an unruly mass of curly hair atop his head. "I've never seen him myself, but Chauncy said he's seen him stumbling around above deck in the wee morning hours searchin' for his head."

Raleigh slapped the back of the curly-haired man's head.

"Where're your wits, Nash? You shouldn't be telling such Canterbury tales in the presence of a lady."

Nash colored such a dark red it was perceivable even in the dim light. "I beg yer pardon, milady."

Priscilla mustered a weak smile. "Do not change on my account." She waved a hand at the cards on the table. "Please, continue as if I weren't here."

Six pairs of eyes peered at each other, uncertain.

"We couldn't in front of a lady." Raleigh sat next to her. "Captain Prescott isn't too keen on us playin' as it is. It involves wagers, not fer money, captain wouldn't allow it"—he held up a wooden circle—"but fer these."

She studied the plain wooden disk. "What are those worth?"

Like a pair of curtains being drawn, his lips pulled back into a bright smile. "Respect."

"Then, I have no qualms at all about it." She sighed. "I've witnessed my brother wager with his crew right here at this very table." She eyed two of the men whose faces she recognized from under her brother's command. "Isn't that right, Mr. Smith —I mean Lefty?"

Lefty scratched his head under his bandanna. "If I recall, you bested your brother that night, Miss Middleton."

"Indeed. And a little fun is good for morale. This is your free time, is it not?"

The men nodded.

"Then the captain shouldn't complain as long as it doesn't interfere with your duties."

"Shall I deal ya in?" Raleigh arched the cards with a hum and a final snap.

She shook her head. "Not tonight. I'm content to watch."

"Mayhap you'll bring us luck." Cecil reached for his cards.

The rest took the queue as permission. They snatched up their hands and began placing *respect* bets.

Speck returned and placed a cup of warm milk in front of

her. "It's fresh goat's milk. Ships not big enough for a cow, but Cook brings a few goats fer milk and cheese. It doesn't taste quite the same, but you become accustomed to it right quick."

She thanked him and sipped. The earthy, sour taste filled her mouth, but she swallowed it down. "Mmm."

Speck resumed his seat. "Did you deal me in?"

Raleigh slid the cards on his right in front of Speck, and he scooped them up. He studied his hand under a furrowed brow and scrunched his lips to one side. "I'll see you two."

"I'll take that and raise you three." Nash slid his wooden chip stack into the center.

Priscilla relaxed back in her chair and sipped warm milk. As the men laughed and teased each other, the darkness became a distant memory.

Several hands had gone by when Cecil narrowed his eyelids above the rim of his cards at Nash. "Yer bluffin'. You can't take that many tricks."

Nash tapped his index finger on the back of his cards. "Try me."

"What do you think, Miss Middleton?" Cecil lifted his eyebrows. "Do you think he's shamming me?"

She glanced at Nash's index finger before returning her gaze to Cecil. "I think not."

Cecil folded, and sure enough, Nash held the best flush, taking all five tricks. As he scooped his winnings, his eyes shone brightly at Priscilla. "How did you know?"

She merely shrugged. It was easier than explaining that she noticed things others didn't—little nuances, subtle gestures. It drove her brother to distraction. After a while, he stopped allowing her to play.

They dealt a few more hands, and it became a game for them to check with her when they suspected someone of cutting a sham. So far, she'd been accurate.

Priscilla saw Jacob wipe his palm on his breeches. "He's bamboozling you."

"Blast." Jacob flung his cards on the table, and the men guffawed. "How are you doing that?" He screwed his face into a perplexed frown. "Are you a mind reader?"

"Nothing of the sort." Priscilla sipped the last of her milk. "I'm merely observant." Her ability to notice and interpret gestures wasn't a perfect science. Certain people were easy to read, but others, like her father and even Captain Prescott, for that matter, were impossible.

Raleigh stiffened and checked his pocket watch. He pressed a finger to his lips, hushing them. "The captain's coming. Those are his footfalls."

The men grabbed their chips. Nash held out his shirt and scooped the cards into the makeshift sack. They pushed back their chairs and dashed to the door. Raleigh grabbed her elbow and gently pulled her to a stand. "This way, Miss Middleton."

She blinked at the confusion. Were the men afraid of Captain Prescott? Were they truly not allowed to play cards? Have a little fun?

He nudged her toward the door, but she held her ground. "My room is the other way."

"I can show you another route."

And have someone see her sneaking around the crewmen's quarters? *No, sir.* She'd already risked her reputation by being in a room full of men without Miss Dodd. She shook her head. "I will stall for you."

~

*P*riscilla Middleton's dimpled smile remained fresh in his mind. The memory of its radiance distracted Tobias from the tasks at hand long after dinner had finished, and he'd returned above deck to instruct the night crew. Helmsmen Taylor had to repeat his question because, while locating the North Star, Tobias found himself comparing stars twinkling to the glints in Miss Middleton's eyes as she laughed at one of Henry's tales. Cadet Benton had to tap him on the shoulder to get his attention because Tobias noticed how the moonlit-filled sails brightened like the glow of Miss Middleton's enthusiasm. He'd witnessed another side of her tonight, one that caused him to question his original judgment. Initially, the woman chafed him like wet wool, but he'd found himself enthralled by her ease with people and positive outlook during dinner.

"Taylor?"

The helmsman straightened to attention. "Aye, captain."

"You have a wife and daughters?"

"Aye, captain."

"How do you...?" He scratched the side of his face. "How do you—er—get along with them?"

Taylor frowned. "I treat them as I would one of the crew. I'm honest, and I set the rules. As long as they stay within those limits, then we get along right well."

"What if they—er—cross those boundaries?"

He shrugged. "Then there are consequences, I guess. Unfortunately, I'm away at sea for months on end, so my wife does most of the dealings with our wee ones, but she manages well."

"I see."

A smile broke across Taylor's face. "Are ya asking because of Miss Middleton?"

"Aye."

"She's a bonny lass, that one."

"Quite." A warning stirred in his gut, a reminder that Middletons were as dangerous as fire aboard ship. Contained, they could be beneficial, but out of control, they'll sink you.

"She can charm the spots off a leopard, and the old crew says she's a sharp at dealing..." Taylor shifted his head to stare forward out over the bow. "I mean, her dealings are masterful—a quick-witted woman."

Masterful? Tobias ran a hand over his face. Nothing made sense. He needed sleep. He'd been driving his crew hard to make good time, and his mind demanded rest before delirium set in.

He left the helm in Taylor's command and removed himself below deck. He ducked his head under a low hanging beam and turned down the passage to the crew room on his nightly round before turning in. A figure stepped into the hall—not just a figure—the one who had plagued his thoughts for the last few hours.

"Miss Middleton?"

"Good evening, Captain Prescott."

His jaw tightened as he neared. "I thought my instructions were clear." Her feminine scent, like that of wild strawberries, overtook the usual smell of damp wood. He stopped, blocking her path. "You shouldn't be roaming after dusk. It's dangerous."

Her delicate chin lifted, and even in the shadows, he could see the sweep of her long lashes. She held a wooden cup between her graceful fingers. "I was merely thirsty."

Set boundaries. "Next time, bring Miss Dodd along with you."

"I didn't want to wake her at this late hour."

Be honest. He rubbed his forehead and released a deep sigh. "I can't be the only person watching out for your hide. I run a tight ship, but not all these men have been under my command for long. I cannot, yet, vouch for their character." The last thing he needed was for her to be compromised and have to hold a court-martial assembly to see a sailor flogged. Did she not know how alluring the soft curves of a woman could be to a man who'd been away at sea?

"Those were men under my brother's command. I'm—"

"Exactly." He'd seen the leeway Middleton allowed his men. He gripped her elbow to return her to her cabin.

She yanked her arm from his grasp. "What happened to the

gentleman I sat beside at dinner? Who was that man? For I daresay, he wouldn't drag a woman in his wake or insult her and her family."

He wasn't dragging her. He shook his head and forced his jaw to relax. "Listen."

The reflection of the flame in a nearby oil lamp blazed a warning in her eyes.

"I'm not trying to be unkind, but the minute you stepped aboard my ship, you made yourself my responsibility, and I take my obligations seriously. Since you seem to be unaware of the dangers, let me list them for you." He held up his thumb. "You could accidentally fall overboard." He lifted more fingers as he enumerated the risks. "You could knock yourself unconscious on the low ceilings. You could step in a line and be hoisted like a sail. You could lose your footing as the ship crests a swell and fall through an open hatch to the deck below." A memory he'd long wished he'd forgotten flashed through his mind. A bunk still made—a search of the decks. A shout of *man overboard* and a body fished up on deck—Annie or Adam as she was known. She'd joined the ranks, pretending to be a lad, to avoid an abusive father. Only to wind up dead. He uncurled his last finger, and his voice lowered to a deadly whisper. "You could encounter lustful men with an eye for a pretty face who'd lure you to where your screams wouldn't be heard."

Her eyes widened.

For an uncanny moment, the creaking ship silenced, and the stillness of the air bellowed a grave warning.

Something fell from her pocket and rolled down the seam in the deck. A small wooden disk?

They both bent, bumping heads.

"Pardon." She held her head but snatched the piece.

"My apologies." He spoke through gritted teeth and curled his fingers around her upper arm, escorting her the remaining steps to her cabin. "If you cannot obey my list of instructions, then I will have no choice but to confine you to your room and put a guard at your door."

Miss Middleton's face paled in the dim light. She wrapped her free arm around her midsection, and the strong-willed woman from moments ago withered.

"No." Her voice trembled. "Please." Her knees folded.

"What's the matter?" His grip firmed, holding her steady. Maybe their small collision injured her. "Are you hurt?"

She shook her head.

"Are you ill?" He stepped closer for a better look. Her face tightened, and a wild look filled her gaze, but it might have been his imagination or merely an effect of the light from the oil lamp. He leaned her against the wall and searched her features for clues. "Has something happened?"

She recovered, standing on her own. "I'm fine," she said, but her eyes remained shadowed. She unlatched the door to her cabin and quickly stepped inside. "I shall do better to heed your instructions in the future."

She moved to close the door, but he stopped it with his palm.

She gasped. Even though they stood inches apart, her shiver vibrated the air.

He'd frightened her with his blunt speech. *A delicate flower.* He was a cad. A complete cad. He had to say something to smooth over the rough way he'd treated her. "Miss Middleton."

Only the creaking of the deck answered.

"I enjoyed our dinner tonight." He must say something charming to redeem himself.

She nodded.

"I..." He swallowed, forcing his lips to work. "I am that gentleman." He shifted his weight. "I apologize if I frightened you. It was not my intent."

"Very well, Captain. Good night." She closed the door.

"Sleep well, Miss Middleton," he said to the stained wooden planks. The lion's face carved into the thick oak door appeared to laugh at him. He rubbed the back of his stiff neck before trudging back down the passage to his shared cabin.

Lud. That didn't go well.

Something was amiss. He'd been able to smell her fear. He entered the cabin to the sound of Henry's deep exhale of sleep. Tobias's fingers undid the gold buttons of his dress coat and removed his jacket.

Miss Middleton remained his responsibility, and he would get to the bottom of what had upset her so.

CHAPTER 8

We shall drive back those dirty shirts and show their beloved General "Hickory" Jackson the full brunt of Britain's naval power. They shall wilt before our formations.

~ *Letter from Lieutenant General Sir Edward Pakenham to Admiral Sims*

*P*riscilla unbuttoned the top button on her pelisse and faced Miss Dodd. "I'm still holding onto hope."

The ship swayed, and Miss Dodd gripped the back of a chair for balance.

"However." Priscilla lifted her chin. "It's time to face facts. We've been at sea for almost two weeks. At this point, it's not likely we are going to pass any inbound British ships. The weather above deck grows warmer to the point that we no longer need a jacket, muff, or even a pelisse for when we stroll above deck." She'd even donned her thinnest petticoats. "We must accept we'll be voyaging with Captain Prescott to the Leeward Islands."

As she shrugged out of the light jacket, she struggled to speak the words she knew to be true. Surely, her parents had noticed her disappearance by now. Would they be worried? Would they realize she'd accidentally sailed with the *Trade Wind*, or would they think she'd run off—eloped with some fop in Edinburg? Or that she had visited with friends at a house party, or met a bitter end?

The minute Captain Prescott had mentioned the possibility, she'd clung to the idea of boarding a returning ship, but she'd grown up studying maps in her father's office. Navy and merchant ships maintained an easterly route closer to the Americas on the way to the islands, and a westerly direction using the trade winds up the European coastline on the return voyage. The paths didn't often intersect. She wanted to retain hope, but she feared the captain had only mollified an unhinged woman who threatened the speed of his mission.

She draped the jacket over the back of the chair. "It's time to accept our fate and make the best of it."

Miss Dodd hung Priscilla's pelisse in the wardrobe.

Priscilla inhaled a deep breath. "Why do you think the captain hates me so much?"

"Pshaw." She closed and latched the cabinet door. "Captain Prescott doesn't hate you. You're making much out of nothing. Captain Prescott merely keeps an orderly ship, and you, my dear, even with the best intentions, are an imposition. If circumstances were different, if the two of you had met in a London ballroom, you would get along famously."

Priscilla imagined him requesting a dance but dismissed the preposterous notion. "Could he be punishing me for what he thinks Anthony did? He mentioned Anthony used a British ship for personal gain, but I believe Anthony sailed to save my friend from pirates." Priscilla rested a hand on her hip. "If that's the case, then it's one big misunderstanding. I might be able to explain the situation, mayhap even have my brother reinstated."

"Lottie?" Miss Dodd's brows drew together. "Oh, yes, Lady Etheridge's daughter, the one discovered with an island merchant."

"Don't hold that ridiculous incident against her. It was completely innocent. One big mistake that fortunately ended well. Lottie is an exemplary model of respectability." She exhaled a deep sigh. "Oh, how I miss her. I've longed to see if island life is as grand as she states in her letters. Even though I might not have chosen this voyage, I'm going to count it as a blessing." Priscilla checked the watch pinned to her walking dress—fifteen minutes before their allotted time to stroll above deck. "Lottie has always been the voice of reason, talking me out of doing something rash." Until Lottie caught her dress on fire, and the merchant was seen extinguishing the fire with his hands. Gossip mongers had a frenzy. The one-time Lottie did something foolish, she did a bang-up job of it.

"Harrumph. I could use another voice of reason to keep you in check."

Priscilla paused in tying the strings of her bonnet. If only someone understood her reasoning. She usually didn't mean to land in precarious predicaments. Sometimes, it was of her own doing—a desperate ploy to gain her parent's attention, like the time she'd tried spirits and cast up her accounts on mama's Axminster carpet. Mama was late for her charity meeting because she was busy boxing Priscilla's ears. Even worse was that Priscilla almost enjoyed having her mother's undivided attention. What kind of person was she?

Most times, her messes were born of desperation not to be alone. The night of the masquerade, she could have stayed home, but with Miss Dodd laid-up and her parents preoccupied, it would have been her and the servants, and her mother disapproved of her being friendly with the help. If only she could explain how her heart raced, throat tightened, and body shook when she found herself alone.

However, that would only confirm her madness. It was best if she remained quiet. She wanted neither Miss Dodd or Captain Prescott suspicious of her whereabouts. They certainly could never discover that she regularly snuck out at night to play a round of cards in the wardroom. She laughed at the crew's frequent schemes to sham her and see if she'd call them on it. Cecil once refused to move a muscle in an effort not to give himself away, but that very act showed his intentions. She adored the way the men acknowledged her. And, as the pile of wooden chips growing under her pillow declared—respected. Something she craved. If the surgeon's elixir didn't cause Miss Dodd to sleep so heavily, Priscilla wouldn't need to go to the wardroom. Or if Captain Prescott didn't always adhere to a strict regimen, which concluded with one last inspection below deck at precisely half-past eleven before he retired, she wouldn't be able to pull off the nightly game.

Priscilla could set her watch by the man. Last night she'd put it to the test because she held an excellent hand and didn't want to fold. She played out her cards but risked encountering him in the hall. Fortunately, she'd finished with two minutes to spare and dashed back to her cabin unnoticed.

Being around the men's chatter helped her relax and temporarily relinquished the darkness, at least until she could fall asleep. Once asleep, she'd slumber until Miss Dodd woke her in the morn.

Miss Dodd bent and picked up a piece of paper that had wedged itself under their trunk. She unfolded it and read its contents. "We've been invited to join the captain and lieutenant again for tomorrow's evening meal." She placed the note on the desk.

She might have been pleased if she knew they'd be dining in the presence of the gentleman captain and not the brute, over-bearing captain, but his moods changed faster than the weather. "Are you ready to take in the air?" Priscilla unlatched the door.

"Is it time yet?"

Priscilla fanned her face with her hand. The cabin had grown stuffy. She couldn't imagine the heat that must permeate the gun room where men slept in hammocks and folding beds. "I'm sure it's fine." Priscilla entered the narrow passageway and waited for Miss Dodd to follow.

She hesitated but complied with a frown.

Once aloft, Priscilla paused to drink in fresh sea air and tilted her head up to feel the sun's energy radiate into her depleted bones.

"Brace and lift aft." His crew echoed Captain Prescott's deep baritone voice, and the clacking of pulleys followed in a rhythmic pattern. His fisted hands rested on his narrow hips as he peered at the tall masts.

As the men heaved the lines, Raleigh bellowed out a sea shanty a little off-key, "Farewell and adieu to you, Spanish ladies. Farewell and adieu to you, ladies of Spain."

The crew sang the next line as they moved in one motion, hoisting sails. Some of the young lads looked barely out of the schoolroom—no muscle on their lean frames.

Raleigh spied her, and his dark eyes twinkled. She'd aided him in besting Cecil last night in a round of loo. Without releasing the line, he wiped sweat from his forehead with his arm and nodded to his mate.

Cecil glanced up and caught her eye as she and Miss Dodd strolled in their direction. He raised his chin in a silent promise to pay her back this evening, but the effect ceased when his mouth cracked a smile.

"Lovely day, isn't it, Mr. Raleigh?" she teased.

Cecil didn't miss a beat. "Tomorrow, I suspect it will be even better. The best day of the week, I've heard."

Priscilla fought hard to suppress her smile.

"Miss Middleton." The captain's booming voice caught her by surprise, and she tripped over a length of uncoiled rope.

Both Cecil and Raleigh released their hold to steady her. The line whizzed through the pully. Benton's high-pitched cry sounded as the lad thrust forward, hitting the rail with enough force to send his legs flipping up and over.

CHAPTER 9

There has been no word of your daughter. I understand your fears, but I can assure you Captain Prescott is an honorable man.

~ *Missive from Admiral Sims to Admiral Middleton*

*P*riscilla screamed.

Captain Prescott lunged, grabbing the boy's ankles to keep him from going over while Nash swiped air in an attempt to grip Benton's britches. Cecil and Raleigh scrambled to retrieve the line and resume their hold. The captain eased Benton's feet back onto solid ground before rounding on his men and ringing a peel over them for being lax in their duties.

Priscilla shifted uneasily, feeling guilty for her part in the crew's distraction.

His nostrils flared, and he blasted her with a frosty glare. He marched in her direction until he loomed over her like a dark storm. She had no choice but to tilt her head back. The crew and Miss Dodd inched away.

"A man would receive twenty-four lashes for the stunt you just pulled. You think you can parade about the deck, doing as you please"—his lips twisted into an angry snarl—"but this is no longer your brother's ship. Would you have people die because of your foolishness? Do you want Benton's death on your conscience?" The cords of his neck tightened like lines hoisting full sails. "From now on, you'll abide by my rules, or you'll suffer the same fate as anyone else under my command."

She bit hard on her lower lip as hot tears flooded the back of her eyelids. How dare he embarrass her in front of the crew.

He glared back over his shoulder at the frozen crewmen. "If my men don't understand the importance of holding fast, then we'll run trainings through our break times until it's fresh in our head."

The men's shoulders slumped.

His gaze sliced through her, and he jabbed a finger in Benton's direction. "If one man slacks off even for a second, it could mean certain death." He turned his back to address the crew, and she quickly blinked away any sign of tears. "When on deck, every duty must be carried out to ensure one another's safety. That even goes for your own." He spun on his heel back to face her.

Priscilla inwardly drew back but physically held her ground. "It was an accident. I tripped. They tried to help me."

His nostrils flared. "I saw what happened." He closed his eyes and pinched the bridge of his nose, inhaling a deep breath. "How would you feel having to be the one to write cadet Benton's family to inform them of his demise, knowing it was due to careless behavior?" He opened his eyes, awaiting an answer.

In his gaze, she witnessed the raw pain of losing a loved one. She swallowed, straining to form words.

"Well?" His lips thinned into a white line.

"Horrid," she choked out in a hoarse whisper.

"When you disobey my orders and come above deck before the allotted times, you put the crew's lives at stake. I don't know how to get that through your thick skull other than with a good thrashing."

Heat rushed into her cheeks at the image of him paddling her over his knee. By the set of his jaw, she didn't doubt he'd do it.

His expression darkened. "Go below. Your above deck privileges are revoked. For your own safety and that of my men, you'll be confined to your room for the rest of the day and tomorrow."

Ice froze her veins. She'd be alone—trapped—prey for the darkness that would feast upon her lifeless bones. Lightheadedness filled her.

Miss Dodd hooked her arm.

Dear Miss Dodd. Could she see her plight? Priscilla forced her muscles to tighten. She would rather die than faint in front of this man.

"I shall ensure Miss Middleton complies from now on." She gently guided Priscilla in the direction of the ladder leading below, but Miss Dodd paused and eyed Captain Prescott. "Could you spare the exact time? I fear her watch runs a bit fast."

Dear, sweet Miss Dodd.

Captain Prescott's expression fell slack, and he stared at them for the briefest of seconds before reaching into his pocket and removing his watch. "Seven minutes past the hour." He clamped the watch shut and turned on his heel to return to his duties.

His moment of visible self-doubt held enough of a victory—albeit small—for Priscilla to summon the inner strength to remove herself below—to dreaded isolation. Even if her companion remained in their cabin with her, Priscilla's mind no longer cared to see reason.

∽

*T*obias rubbed the back of his head and returned to the helm. He lived by order. Routines, duties, and trainings kept his life and ship gliding on smooth waters. He'd been to battle and under siege. Foes were often predictable with attack measures and countermeasures. He'd thwarted many a French ship because they'd been at the ready. Through hard work, routine drills, and perpetual study of battle tactics, he and his crew had become known for their preparedness, yet this one woman continued to ambush him. And she wasn't supposed to be his foe.

Men's grunts and the pulley's clacking ceased.

"Give a little counter rutter."

Henry turned the wheel accordingly and glanced at Tobias.

Tobias shaded his eyes from the sun. The British flag showed the wind blew at forty-five degrees. "Brace up aft," he commanded his men, and they looped the lines around the cleats.

Benton stared blankly for a second before working to tie the knots. The poor lad remained shaken.

"Brace around forward," Tobias yelled.

"Brace around forward," echoed his men. They shifted to the forward and mizzen. The grunts and clacking began anew.

Still, he felt Henry's gaze upon him.

Tobias rounded on him. "What is it?"

Henry scratched under his chin. "Don't ya think ya might have been a bit unfair to Miss Middleton?"

His head pulled back. "Benton nearly landed in the drink. He could have lost his life." Tobias paced. "The ship would have had to come around. Think of the time lost. Men will die if we don't get reinforcements to Louisiana before Christmas."

He pivoted to face his longtime friend. "I cannot allow my ship to fall into a state of chaos. I don't care if she's a pretty sight for the eyes. The men must not be distracted."

The wind filled the sails, and the bow angled to the precise course.

"Set the mainsail and haul out the spanker," Tobias bellowed over the wind.

His men repeated his command.

Henry shrugged. "I'm merely saying, the incident seemed innocent enough, and Miss Middleton wasn't the only one to blame. I'm thinkin' you might need to have a word with Raleigh and Cecil."

Tobias crossed his arms and studied the distant horizon. Henry was right. Raleigh and Cecil dropped the line, not Miss Middleton. And if Miss Dodd reported truthfully and her pocket watch had merely been fast? Was an apology in order? He rubbed his eyebrows. "Give Benton the next two days off, and I'll speak to Cecil and Raleigh and let them know they will be doing double duty."

"Aye, captain." Henry nodded.

Tobias sighed and clasped his hands behind his back, seeking peace.

A moment passed, and a wide gleaming smile spread across the lieutenant's face. "So you think she's a pretty sight fer the eyes, ay?"

CHAPTER 10

Per your request, Bonaparte has complete freedom upon the island, but he never travels far from my sights.
~ *Letter from Colonel Neil Campbell to Lord Castlereagh, Britain's Foreign Secretary*

*P*riscilla had spent the last day and a half keeping Miss Dodd occupied so she wouldn't nap. She'd begged the guard posted at her door to find them a deck of cards and taught her companion every game she knew. Priscilla borrowed needles and thread and worked on embroidery. She prattled on about what must be happening in London, as they worked on the latest stitches. However Miss Dodd tended to dose off, so Priscilla woke her for a rousing game of charades.

Daylight no longer streamed in through the large glass portal, and Miss Dodd drew the curtains. An invisible hand walked its fingers up Priscilla's spine and settled a threatening grip on her throat.

After changing into their nightclothes, they both crawled under the covers. Miss Dodd sat against the pillows and cracked open her Bible, as was her routine.

"Could you...?" Priscilla cleared her throat and dragged air into her constricted lungs. "Would you read to me?" She hated the wistfulness in her voice.

"I'm in the book of Matthew, chapter eighteen." Miss Dodd placed a finger on the page as a guide and began to read. "If a man have a hundred sheep, and one of them be gone astray, doth he not leave the ninety and nine, and goeth into the mountains, and seeketh that which is gone astray? And if it be so that he find it, verily I say unto you, he rejoiceth more of that sheep, than of the ninety and nine which went not astray. Even so, it is not the will of your Father which is in heaven, that none of these little ones should perish."

A shadow grew in the corner. In her mind's eye, she saw Benton flipping over the rail, his small, frail body sinking into the deep, the waves drowning his cries for help. The other men's heads slowly turned her direction, condemnation in their eyes. A shiver ran through Priscilla's bones. What if Captain Prescott hadn't gotten to the lad in time? What if she had caused Benton's death?

Priscilla turned to face the wall and allowed silent tears to flow. She would try harder to follow the rules. Would God truly go after His lost sheep? Miss Dodd had told her once that God was all-knowing. Did that mean He understood her plight? Could He find it in His heart to forgive her? *God, I didn't mean to cause any harm.*

Miss Dodd's voice eventually drifted off. Priscilla wiped her tears and slowly turned to find her companion asleep with the Bible lying on her chest. Priscilla lifted the book and closed it. Reaching over her snoring friend, she laid the book on the side table next to the empty glass of elixir and turned down the lamp.

Darkness filled the room.

She turned the lamp back up, only to consider the amount of oil allotted for the voyage. If she let it burn all night, would they have enough for the week? Would they have to stay in darkness? With a weak cry of protest, she forced her fingers to turn off the flame.

Priscilla buried herself deep under the covers, her knees drawn to her chest. and pretended she was, once again, huddled in the corner of her father's study, memorizing his map. She listed off the islands they would surely be passing within the next few days, and it worked to keep her mind focused. But Miss Dodd's soft snores pulled her back into the present and reminded her of the darkness hovering, its weight pressing upon her. She squeezed her eyes shut, wishing she were in the crew room with the men dealing out a hand of cards.

Her body began to shake. A weight pressed on her chest. She couldn't breathe. She'd once overheard her brother tell his friends a ghost story about a man who died of fright. His heart had stopped. Would that, too, be her fate? Would her parents wonder what had caused her death at sea? Would her body be cast into the ocean?

Would they mourn her? Had they even noticed her missing?

Priscilla closed her eyes, but the childhood memory flooded back.

Her parents had brought her to the park to witness a balloon's launch and marveled at how high it soared. Priscilla moved to get a better look because a cluster of tall men in dark top hats blocked her view. A silken skirt bushed her body. She reached up and slid her hand into her mother's but kept her eyes on the distant balloon.

"I beg your pardon," said a strange feminine voice.

An unfamiliar face with a pointy chin peered down at her. She snatched away her hand and backed up. She searched the crowd, but no one looked familiar. She parted a blockade of cream and yellow skirts to peer through the wall of ladies and called for her mother once more.

"Where is your nanny?" A dour face frowned at her, and boney arms reached for her.

Priscilla ran as fast as her little legs could pump. She darted around onlookers and followed the hot air balloon to Hyde park's edge.

She was lost.

She bit her lower lip to keep from crying because Anthony had said, "Only babies cry," and she was no longer in leading strings. The crowd dispersed until only a few spectators remained, and not one resembled her parents. A tall, scraggly man came up behind her. His hat blocked the sun's low rays. "Where are your parents, little girl?" Spittle formed in the corners of his lips as he spoke. His gnarled fingers snatched her upper arm, and his other hand muffled her mouth. Terror smelled like worn leather gloves. He hauled her down a dark alley. She screamed when he uncovered her mouth to pry open a cellar door. He tossed her into the darkness like the grocer heaves a sack of potatoes and closed the cellar tight, leaving her there—shaking and alone.

Priscilla awoke from her nightmare sleep drenched in sweat. She scrambled from the bed and lunged for the door. Her fingers jiggled the latch, but it was locked. She clawed at the crack, trying to pry it open with her bare hands, but it didn't budge. She propped a leg up on the wall and pulled with all her might. Still, it held fast.

Sapped of all strength, she sank to the floor. She panted hurried breaths, unable to fill her tight lungs. She crawled to the center of the floor, uncertain how it became wooden when it had been a dirt cellar. She lay down and curled on her side. Darkness had her by the throat. Even if she could scream, no one would hear her anyway. No one knew where she was. Tears slid helplessly from her eyes.

Oh, God, help me.

She couldn't drag in enough breath. Like a pillow pressed

over her face, darkness suffocated her, and there was nothing she could do to fight it.

~

*T*he following morning, Tobias raised a hand to knock on the cabin door but hesitated. He'd planned to come yesterday to apologize, but signs of a storm had materialized. Thin, wispy, cirrus clouds streaked the blue sky, and the barometer gauge dropped like a ship down the backside of a wave. Maps were unrolled, and new routes were plotted. Fortunately, the early omens allowed time to prepare, but amid the additional tasks, he'd forgotten about Miss Middleton.

He rapped on the hardwood panel and stepped back to await an answer.

The door cracked open, and Miss Dodd's austere face peeked through the crack. "Captain Prescott, welcome."

She swung the door wide.

Priscilla whirled around. She'd been staring out the portal, her face strained. He'd grown accustomed to seeing her azure eyes flash with a challenge, but today they appeared disheartened, hollowed by sadness, and... was that fear? She composed her expression with a polite smile and a tilt of her chin, but the haunted look in her eyes persisted.

A knot twisted in his gut.

Lord, forgive me for losing my temper whenever Priscilla Middleton is concerned. Help me to find the right words to offer her grace and mercy.

A good captain dealt with conflict within his crew immediately instead of letting it fester. Yet, here he was two days later with an apology lodged in his throat. He prided himself on keeping a steady ship, but by Jove, when Priscilla was above deck, chaos erupted. She'd capsized his crew. His men stumbled over themselves because they were endeared to her. He may have earned their respect, but somehow, she'd acquired their devotion. Ever since she tumbled him into the corridor that first night, her presence had been maddening, but she, too, was a victim. When she boarded, Priscilla'd had no idea her brother had lost his command. She couldn't help being Anthony's sister. And, she hadn't meant to put his men in harm's way.

He blinked. Since when had he started thinking of her as Priscilla and not Miss Middleton?

"Captain Prescott." She curtsied. Her blond hair tied with a simple ribbon glowed white in the sunlight streaming in through the window.

Miss Dodd gestured him inside. "Please join us."

He entered with his hat in his hands and met with a flowery aroma of feminine toilet water perfume, so different from the raw unbathed male smell he'd grown accustomed to onboard. Other than his mother, he'd had little experience with women. He saw no point in courting a woman since captains notoriously made for poor husbands. He'd seen firsthand on his mother the result of his father's prolonged absence. Back when he and Middleton had trained together, Anthony needled him for staying behind while other sailors caroused with tavern ladies. When he'd finally let Anthony convince him to go, the rowdy environment and forward women had only made him uncomfortable. By evening's end, he sipped his ale alone, unable to hold polite conversation with a woman and convinced that other things were more trustworthy. Like the weather.

The same awkwardness wedged itself in his throat anew.

Miss Dodd seated herself in the corner and picked up her needlework. So much for her aiding conversation.

Silence filled the air between them, but Priscilla broke it first. "I'm afraid I don't know how to feel about your visit. It's an honor for you to pay us a call, but part of me braces as if I'm about to undergo another surprise attack." She sighed and held her palms face out. "If you're looking for a fight, I'm afraid I shall disappoint. I don't have it in me today."

He admired her openness. Being free of speech wasn't a luxury a captain could hold. He had to weigh every word and keep his head in all situations, which he did, except when it came to her.

She glanced at the window.

Were those dark smudges under her eyes? The knot in his stomach tightened.

"Are you concerned about the pending storm?" She turned back to face him.

He leapt at the familiar topic. "You can tell a storm's brewing?"

One side of her inviting mouth lifted, and a dimple appeared on that cheek. "Can't everyone?"

He shook his head and stepped closer. Reaching past her, he pulled the white cotton curtain aside to see the view. "Hardened deepwater sailors and fishermen raised on herring bones will know the signs, but you'd be surprised at how unobservant men can be." He stepped aside but still held back the drape. "What do you see?"

She pivoted, and her skirt hem brushed over his boot. The scent of wild strawberries swept under his nose.

"See how the clouds resemble white peacock feathers?"

He nodded.

"And the waves have swelled." She pointed at a white cap dancing upon a large crest. "You can feel the increase in the rise and fall of the ship."

"That explains my queasiness," Miss Dodd commented without looking up from her stitches.

A crease formed in Priscilla's forehead, and Tobias resisted the urge to erase the line with his thumb. By George, two days ago he'd wanted to throttle her, but now he desired to soothe her concerns?

"Another sign, I fear, is Miss Dodd rubbing her forehead."

He glanced at Priscilla's companion, who quickly lowered her hand back to her sewing. He arched an eyebrow. "Due to the drop in barometric pressure?"

"I'm afraid so." Priscilla waved her hand. "A sudden drop can pain joints and sometimes cause headaches."

Miss Dodd stabbed her needle into the cloth. "Most unfortunate."

"Lieutenant Dalton's hip pains him where some shrapnel hit back when he was a midshipman." He released the curtain.

Miss Dodd's gaze slid his way before snapping back to her embroidery.

"On his left side?" Priscilla leaned against the bedpost but anticipated its position wrong. She let out a gasp and toppled.

Tobias caught her with his arm and righted her. His hand tingled from the softness of her smooth skin just under her capped sleeves. "I believe so." Was she trembling?

She shrugged off his touch and lowered her lashes. "It's merely that sometimes he favors his left leg."

"You're very perceptive."

She peered up at him, and for a long moment, their gazes held. Her lips pinched together, and two dimples winked at him from each cheek.

His stomach crested as though he rode a wave. When had he become so fascinated with dimples?

Her eyes brightened, growing round and liquid as if he were the only man for a thousand leagues, and she found wonderment in having his attention.

"I didn't come here to discuss the weather." He shifted his feet and fingered the brim of his hat. "I came to..." He cleared his throat. The earlier blockage of words disappeared. "...apologize." His squared shoulders relaxed, and a warmth spread through his chest. A half-smile raised the side of his mouth.

Who smiles during an apology? "For my hasty reaction the other day."

"I've had two nights to think things over." She faced him as if he were about to be disciplined. "Although your manner of yelling is disagreeable, I realize it was out of fear for my safety and the safety of your crewmen."

He swallowed. She understood.

"I was too flippant regarding your orders. Ships can be dangerous." She placed a hand on his arm. "I would never intentionally do anything to hurt anyone." Her brow puckered, and she shook her head. "If anything had happened to Benton, I could not have lived with myself."

"All is well." At her gentle touch, his residual anger melted. "Praise God. Benton is hale, and I spoke to Raleigh and Cecil and obtained a better understanding of what transpired." He swallowed around his thick tongue. "You were not to blame."

Her hand dropped back to her side. "Mr. Raleigh and Mr. St. Ledger weren't punished, were they?" Her clear-blue eyes widened.

He could still feel the warm imprint of her hand as if it was forever branded into his skin. "They're doing double duty this week—Benton's tasks and their own." He tucked his hat under his arm. "A little extra work won't hurt them over much."

"I still feel at fault." Guilt clouded her eyes. "I may have come above deck a trifle early."

He knew it. However, it took a brave woman to admit it. "If you can forgive me, then I shall do the same." He offered a courteous smile and turned to leave but paused as he remembered his other reason for coming. "Will you and Miss Dodd be joining the Lieutenant and I for supper?"

"Does that mean I'm no longer confined to my cabin?" Her eyebrows lifted, and her face lit like the sun breaking through clouds.

His constrained smile broke free, parting his lips.

"Did you hear that, Miss Dodd?" She inhaled, and her entire body lifted. "We're free."

A light chuckle rumbled in his chest at her enthusiastic candor. "Just stick to the schedule for when to come aloft. It's for your safety and that of my men." He pivoted to leave. "Lord, help us all if we'd been having a firing drill."

CHAPTER 11

Agent White has fallen silent.
~ Letter from Admiral Middleton to Britain's Foreign Office

*A*s Priscilla dined with Captain Prescott, Lieutenant Dalton, and Miss Dodd, she found herself smiling often. Their engaging conversations across the table ranged from favored cities in which to come into port to strange foods they'd been forced to eat. Priscilla asked questions longing to understand cultures different than her own. She added stories her father and brother shared from their voyages.

Of course, the lightheartedness fluttering in her stomach stemmed from relief of no longer being trapped in her cabin and not due to Captain Prescott regarding her with curious interest. His once contemptuous, menacing gaze now held an inquiring intelligence, as if she were a puzzle he savored piecing together.

Lieutenant Dalton leaned over his plate and pointed his upside-down fork at Captain Prescott. "He bleeds seawater." He eyed the captain. "It would be good for you to relax and, for once, not think about our next mission."

Miss Dodd dabbed at her mouth with her napkin. "Has no woman met your fancy, Captain?"

Priscilla held a breath wanting to hear the answer but, at the same time, wanting to throttle Miss Dodd for broaching the topic.

"One has my undying loyalty."

She paused in chewing a bite of salmon. Of course, a man as handsome as Tobias Prescott would have a love interest. She pictured him returning home from a long voyage at sea, unlatching his front gate with a broad smile as a lovely woman with rosy lips sprinted down the front steps to greet him.

"She has the beauty of a single red rose."

Priscilla clenched her teeth. She knew it.

His eyes grew distant, and a small smile lifted the corners of his lips. "She is a queen among her people and patriotically dons a gown of red and blue."

Priscilla wracked her brain for whom she knew among the Quality who wore such bold colors. "Is she from England?"

"Indeed." His smile widened. "But her land expands past its borders."

Her gaze lowered. Was she the daughter of a nabob who gained his fortune from importing spices from India or sugar from the islands?

"What is her name?" Miss Dodd tapped a finger on her lips as her eyes narrowed on him.

"Britannia."

Why did the name sound familiar?

"She proudly carries her trident—"

"England." Priscilla slammed her palms on the table so hard the silverware ricocheted.

"—and commands the greatest navy in all the world." He peered at her with a conspiring twinkle in his eyes.

Her mouth fell open. "You've been describing our country."

He raised his glass in salute. "To England. The love of my life."

Lieutenant Dalton released a hearty laugh and lifted his drink. "To England."

Priscilla shook her head and elevated her glass along with Miss Dodd, even though they'd both been a little slow to catch the jest.

"Gets 'em every time with that one." Lieutenant Dalton swigged a large gulp. "I must say, Miss Middleton has been the quickest to figure out your riddle."

Tobias eyed her above the rim of his cup. "I, for one, wouldn't underestimate Miss Middleton's intelligence." His cool gaze studied her face in an approving, unhurried manner. "Nor her other attributes."

His words trickled over her, absorbing into her mind like rain to a parched plant.

Dessert was served—bread pudding with rum raisins—and Priscilla felt his regard as he observed her slightest move. When she dared to meet his gaze, his eyes darkened to a stormy gray, and the intensity of the look crackled the air. He didn't say a word, which only increased her nervousness. She began to babble on, asking questions about the islands and how often they were stationed there. Henry answered most of them, offering to give them a tour upon their arrival if there was time.

Something brushed against Priscilla's slipper. She peered at the captain and caught him glancing her way. Moving her foot, she focused on her dessert and downed a large bite.

The nudge happened again, more insistent this time.

Her gaze snapped to Tobias.

He arched an eyebrow.

She caught her breath. Was he flirting with her?

He made contact with her foot once again.

The ship dipped on a wave, taking her nervous stomach with

it. She must distract him from such bold intensions. "The storm seems to be picking up. I hope we're not keeping you from your men."

"I've already given the crew instructions." He leaned back, extending his legs further under the table. "They have coordinated and are trained for storms such as this. Many have been through much worse."

"Reminds me of that time we were sailing in the Gulf." Henry leaned back in his chair and rested his hands on his full stomach. "We battled waves larger than the ship itself."

Priscilla pretended to listen with rapt interest and ignored the prodding of Tobias's foot as it slid under hers, lifting it in the air. She ground her teeth, unable to tolerate his taking such liberties. She pivoted in her chair to face him. "I beg your pardon. What do you think you're doing?"

He blinked, and his eyes narrowed on her with a wary glare. "We have two choices—ride it out at sea or flank speed and anchor in the safety of one of the Lesser Antilles Island's coves." He crossed his arms. "If we ride it out, we'll be blown off course and could lose several days to a week of travel. We cannot afford that time with our mission."

His foot withdrew, and Priscilla relaxed a bit, hoping her message was received. "You've decided to anchor in one of the coves?"

"Anegada is the closest."

She studied images of her papa's maps in her memory. "Yes, but the reefs make it dangerous."

"Storm surge will aid us."

"Or toss us onto a reef." She turned her spoon over between her fingers. "Why not sail on until Tortola and shelter in Wickham's Cay?"

Lieutenant Dalton rubbed his bearded chin. "She poses a good suggestion."

Crossing his ankle over his knee, Captain Prescott stared at the ceiling. "I've considered Tortola. If we can make it, it's a better option."

His foot returned even more persistent, rubbing against her ankle.

"Captain Prescott!" She pushed her seat back from the table. "I shall not stand for such rude..."

Her gaze riveted to the heel of his booted foot crossed over his knee and his other firmly planted on the ground. Her blood pooled in her feet. If it wasn't Tobias, then...?"

She shot up with a scream.

The men leapt to their feet, hands on the hilts of their swords.

Priscilla stared at a fuzzy face and pink nose, sniffing the air under the table. "Sneaky Pete, you little weasel!"

Lieutenant Dalton bent under the table and scooped the critter into his hands. He carried him to the door. "Back to the bilge you go." He opened the door and pitched it into the passageway. "If that dratted creature weren't so good at catchin' rats, I'd have told Cecil to get rid of him long ago." He dusted off his hands and rejoined them at the table. "Well now, what were you about to say to the captain, Miss Middleton?"

Priscilla's lips parted. "I-I was... I thought..." Heat rushed into her face, and she fanned it with her hand. "It nudged my foot most persistently, and I believed..." She glanced at Tobias.

He raised both eyebrows as dawning swept over his features. His lips quirked, and he pretended to cough, but his laughter wouldn't be constrained.

Miss Dodd straightened. "I wouldn't have stood for it." She crossed her arms. "Not under my watch."

Lieutenant Dalton threw back his head and released a hearty roar of laughter.

Priscilla's ears burned like red-hot pokers.

"You thought." The lieutenant clutched his stomach and

fought to get the words out. "You thought the captain was playing footsies with you?" Tears streamed from the corners of his eyes, and he didn't bother to wipe them.

Tobias, no longer able to hide his laughter with a cough, turned his head and covered the lower half of his face with the crook of his arm. However, the shaking of his shoulders gave him away.

At the sight of the men struggling to contain their laughter, a bubbling fit of mirth rose within Priscilla. The entire situation was rather ridiculous, embarrassing as it may be. A little snort escaped through her nose, which sent the lieutenant and captain into another round.

Priscilla succumbed to the helplessness of her predicament and enjoyed the moment of merriness.

Only Miss Dodd observed them with a stern expression of disapproval.

Which, of course, threw them all into another fit.

~

The following day, signs of an approaching storm grew stronger, but there was no sign yet of rain. Perhaps they'd been fortunate enough to skirt around it. Priscilla spent as much time above deck as allowed, making sure she stayed within designated safe zones. She and Miss Dodd stood in the shade of the mizzen mast as men several years younger than herself climbed ratlines, undaunted by the stiff wind.

"Try the upper tops and see how she behaves," Tobias yelled over the wind to Henry.

Henry bellowed out the command, "Let down the royals!"

"Let down the royals," echoed from above as men unfurled uppermost sails.

White canvas billowed, harnessing wind for the captain's

LORRI DUDLEY

governance. The ship's speed increased. Wind batted the hair about her face as the bow cut through the waves.

With one hand on the rail, Tobias stood tall, peering up at the raw power under his command. The bold red and blue of the British flag hailed high above him. His jacket was unbuttoned, flapping behind him in the wind. His fitted waistcoat outlined his chiseled form hardened from years at sea, and his breeches clung to his muscular legs braced in a wide stance.

Her heart pressed against her sternum to the point of aching. She rubbed the pang with her fingers. Captain Prescott made an impressive figure. Nellie would have swooned on the spot.

Tobias pivoted, and their gazes locked. His mouth corners lifted into a smile, probably remembering her ridiculous assumption last night. She glanced down at her skirts, but not before a rip-tide current pulled at her heart.

She knew better than to fall for a man like Tobias—er—Captain Prescott. She straightened, giving herself a mental shake. For one, they were always at odds, and he'd be months at sea. She couldn't live alone all that time. She'd go mad.

Lieutenant Dalton said something, stealing the captain's attention.

Priscilla rubbed her temples. How had her thoughts even drifted in that direction—as if she'd consider marrying Captain Prescott—as though it were even an option?

Thank heaven she was to visit Lottie. She needed her practical friend to shake some good sense back into her skull. Priscilla rose and said to Miss Dodd, "I believe I shall retire below deck for a bit."

Miss Dodd eyed her with a puzzled expression.

Since when did she offer to go below deck?

The man was making her daft.

As the day progressed, she and Miss Dodd vacillated between above and below deck. With Tobias's permission, they were allowed to watch from a distance as the men practiced storm drills with impressive efficiency. All pulleys, sails, and lines were double and triple checked, and hatches battened down. She and Miss Dodd stood on the ship's stern as the sun lowered in the sky. Dark clouds loomed on the horizon, painting the heavens a vibrant red.

Tobias approached behind her. His presence stirred her long before he placed a hand on the rail next to her. She peeked at his profile as he gazed out at sea. He stood tall and confident, his sword resting at his side, an impressive figure. He didn't speak, merely soaked in the salty air and sea spray misting his skin.

She allowed her gaze to linger on his square jaw and the aristocratic slope of his nose. If only she held such a disposition—firm, braced, and ready to handle whatever storm came her way. His maleness frazzled her nerves, and her lips twitched to fill the silence. She licked them, tasting their saltiness. Why did she need to ramble? Why couldn't she be content with silence like the captain? "I don't like the look of that sunset."

"Neither do I." He stared into the eastern sky. His tanned skin glowed bronze in the diminishing sunlight. "Storm's coming quick. I expect it to bear down on us tomorrow."

"Will we make it to Tortola in time?"

"We've picked up the pace but still have a day at sea before we reach land."

He rested his forearms on the rail, laced his fingers, and issued her a sideways glance. "Worried?"

She inhaled a deep breath. "I should be. I've heard all the horrid tales from my brother and Papa, ships that have sunk or gone missing, men washed overboard." She turned so her back leaned against the rail, and her loose hair tendrils flared out behind her.

The crew worked in unity to maintain speed, reminding her of the time her papa removed the hall clock's back to repair the chime. She'd been fascinated with its mechanism—gears, springs, shafts, and small hammers seamlessly working together as a whole.

Tobias silently watched her.

She met his stalwart gaze with one of her own. "But I'm not afraid. I've never seen a ship so well run, and I was born into a naval family." Men often complained about their demanding captain during the late-night card games, but they did so with a loyal, reverent tone. They admired Captain Prescott and felt safe under his command, and to be honest, so did she. "Your men are well equipped because you are an excellent captain, and you have their loyalty because they understand you have their well-being at heart."

"I..." He broke off as if carefully formulating his words. "I would readily give my life for God, country, and my men." He paused, studying her face. "That means being a good steward of what is under my command. I can't put self-interest or the interests of any one person above the crew."

Would Anthony have said the same? She loved her brother, but he became a captain more for prestige because it was what his father wanted.

"I must get back to the helm." He stood and tapped the railing. "Eat a hearty meal and get a good night's sleep because we may have to hold tight for a day or two."

⌇

*N*either the swinging lanterns above their heads nor the stiff wind blowing sea spray into his face could hide Tobias's grin. The words of praise Priscilla offered him at the stern billowed his chest like a sail. She no longer seemed like a hindrance to his mission, nor the undermining sister of a man who'd betrayed him. Priscilla wasn't like her brother. She'd displayed a gentle kindness and unflappable aplomb even when he lost his temper. But also, her perceptiveness and intelligence continued to impress him. He'd grown accustomed to her presence and found himself speaking more freely than he ever had around a female. Most men and probably women, too, would have taken offense at their amusement last evening, especially when it was at their expense, but not Priscilla. Red-faced and rosy-cheeked, she'd laughed at herself.

Henry glanced his direction and chuckled. Pinching his side, he yelled over the wind. "My stomach still aches from last evenin.'" A massive wave smacked the ship's hull, raining ocean droplets upon them. He wiped saltwater from his face. "That Miss Dodd, though, is a tough personality to get to know. Despite us being hunched over in hilarity, she didn't crack a smile."

Tobias strained to keep the wheel steady. "You seem to have taken an interest in Miss Middleton's companion."

"Even though I may be stricken with years, it doesn't mean my heart isn't as soft as a greenhorn's. I'm certain Miss Dodd was a prime article back in her day, just came across a bit of bad luck. But as they say, one person's misfortune is another man's luck, and I still haven't given up on the dream of one day havin' a wife to warm my bed."

"I can't picture you with a stern woman."

"I have enough merriment in me for both of us." Henry gripped his shoulder and grinned. "How about you? I know you think yer destined to give yer life for yer country like yer father before you, but have you considered the good Lord may have something else in mind? I've seen the way you look at Miss Middleton. Bickerin' and wantin' to pull caps is a sure sign that you've become sweet on her. Don't deny it." He removed his hand.

"She's Anthony Middleton's sister." He snorted. "If that doesn't dissuade your way of thinking, then imagine a family gathering. I highly doubt it would be God's will, and besides, I will not put individual needs over that of my country or crew. If

I've indulged in any so-called looks, it'll not come to anything. You can be assured of that."

"You may be able to fool yerself with those words, but I can guarantee Miss Middleton will see right through it. She can tell when someone's pitching the gammon just by lookin' at them. She's perceptive, that one."

"Indeed, very observant, except for when it comes to herself. She's toppled me in the passage, almost took a spanker boom to the head, tripped over a coiled line, and played footsies with a weasel. If guardian angels exist, and I believe they do, hers must be exhausted from keeping her out of one scrape or another."

Henry chuckled, then groaned and gripped his side. He shook his head. "The crew's noticed too."

Tobias frowned. His crew should be seeing to their duties, not eyeing Miss Middleton.

"I overheard Nash and Cecil arguing over whether Cecil rubs his ear when nervous, as Miss Middleton says, and then Raleigh held his hands behind his back as he told poor Oliver a Canterbury tale. Cecil called him on it, saying he was hiding his hands like Miss Middleton noted because he didn't want them to know he was fibbing. They're all acting like they're calling each other's bluff over a hand of cards."

A memory flashed of standing in the dim passage with Miss Middleton and the sound of a wooden disk hitting planks and rolling. She'd been playing cards. A fresh surge of sea spray pelted him but immediately turned to steam. Hadn't he told her to stay away from his men?

"Blast." Tobias flipped open his pocket watch but had to wipe the beads of water to see the time. "How long has the night crew been on duty?"

Henry shrugged. "A couple of hours. Why? You turning in early?"

"The little vixen," Tobias muttered and snapped his watch shut. "I have to remove a card sharp before my men wind up without a sixpence to scratch with." He grabbed the rail to go below deck.

"Tobias."

Tobias peered over his shoulder at Henry's beaming grin.

"Go easy on her."

CHAPTER 12

I suggest a two-part frontal assault.
~ Letter from Admiral Sims to the British Naval Fleet

*P*riscilla relaxed against the wooden back of her chair, happy to escape the dark confines of her cabin and join the loud ruckus of men playing cards. Ladies didn't gamble, but the men convinced her that there was no impropriety since no actual money was being transferred, merely wooden dowels. She neglected to mention, her sitting as a lone female in a room full of men would start enough gossip to set all of London on fire. If Miss Dodd had a stronger stomach and didn't have to drink the concoction the surgeon gave her each night to sleep, Priscilla could have stayed in her cabin, but not even a thunder boom could stir the woman.

Priscilla held her poor hand of cards. Too late, she realized she couldn't take as many tricks as she'd claimed. She was going to have to bluff her way out of this and hope they didn't notice.

She struggled not to squirm. All gazes rested upon her, carefully observing every movement, twitch, and gesture. It was absurd. She fingered the corner of a card and glanced up.

Sailors' eyebrows rose in unison.

She burst out laughing at the ridiculous scene.

Gold buttons flashed from the doorway, and drips of water raining from a navy overcoat puddled on the floor.

"Captain." Priscilla gasped and tucked her hand of cards under the table.

The men leapt to their feet and saluted, sending flittering cards raining like leaves to the table.

Captain Prescott tucked his hat under his arm and ducked under the low portal to enter the crew room. Water dripped from his hair and trickled down his forehead. He swiped it with his sleeve, never taking his gaze off her. "Men, it would be best for you to turn in early due to the impending storm and trying day we shall endure on the morrow."

"Aye-aye, captain." Men made quick work of returning their chairs to the wall hooks and clearing the cards.

Priscilla rose to do the same.

He stilled her with a sharp look. "You may remain seated."

Blood siphoned from her face, but she swallowed hard and lifted her head. She resumed her seat with a straight back. Why must he assume everything to be her fault?

Jacob and Nash slowed their cleaning, and Cecil and Raleigh hovered near the crewman's door.

Cecil stuffed his hands in his pockets. "Captain, I... uh... I just want to say that Miss Middleton, she was merely obligin' us. We begged her to stay because she—" A nervous chuckle rumbled in his throat. "She can always tell if one of us is shammin' another. It's uncanny. God's truth."

Raleigh stepped forward, cupping a handful of wooden disks to his stomach. "She notices everything, even the slightest movement." A crooked grin wobbled on his lips. "Turns out, I hold my wrist when I'm tryin' to humbug somebody." His eyes widened, and he shifted his hand away from the other.

Nash nodded. "I tap the top of my cards." He slashed air with his index finger.

"She's a downy one." Cecil peered at her with what resembled pride. "There's quite a mind behind that pretty face."

"I do not doubt her intelligence." Tobias turned a chair around and straddled it across from her. "It's her common sense that is in question." He eyed his men. "You're dismissed."

Sailors flashed her sympathetic glances before slipping out the door.

Tobias waited a moment longer before rebuking her. "The loyalty of my crew is shifting." His tone leaked cynicism, and one side of his lips twitched in a brief smirk. He folded his arms, leaning on the chair's backrest. "What do you think you're doing?"

"I was enjoying a hand of cards in the delightful company of your men."

"After you were supposed to have turned in for the night."

"I'm not above deck." She counted her reasons out on her fingers as he'd once done to her. "I'm not distracting them from their drills nor putting any of your men in danger."

"Only yourself."

She remained silent.

"A lone woman playing cards with a roomful of men at night—do you not care about your safety?"

"I had no other choice. Miss Dodd sleeps like the dead since she's been drinking the elixir the surgeon offered her, and I dare not wake her while she is suffering from one of her headache spells."

He closed his eyes as if to subdue his ire. "Your choice was to stay in your bed."

"I couldn't."

His gaze opened upward in a silent plea before returning to her. "Why not?"

"You wouldn't understand."

"Try me."

She bit her bottom lip. Anthony told her not to speak of her episodes, thinking she'd be sent straight to Bedlam for her madness. What if she made light of it? "I had a nightmare." Normal people had those.

His eyebrows drew together. "What kind of nightmare?"

"It's merely a feeling. Like something's there with me in the dark." His hard eyes peered into hers. Her stomach twisted, and she babbled. "It grips me and I..." Heat filled her cheeks under such intense scrutiny. She waved a hand. "It's silly."

His lips thinned, and he turned his head to the side to stare at the bulkhead. A muscle in his jaw twitched, and a long moment passed before he faced her. "You're right." His voice sounded strained. "I don't understand. I'm used to dealing with men who've seen their mates speared by a bayonet or peering at a cannonball hole through their gut." He leaned forward. "Those men have nightmares. You, my dear, merely have bad dreams."

Priscilla swallowed. "I've never witnessed the horrors of battle. The worst I've encountered was a scraped knee or elbow." She must sound ridiculous—petty even. "But the icy fingers choke out my breath. I can't cry..." Questions and doubts swirled in the captain's hardened gaze. He believed her to be disturbed. She folded her shaking hands. Perhaps she was.

"My apologizes." He blew air past his lips. "Such talk was uncalled for."

She studied her fingers, and weariness swept through her.

"Priscilla, look at me."

The use of her given name and the soft change of his voice startled her into looking up.

His gray eyes had softened into liquid metal. "I cannot protect you if you continue to do irrational things." He sighed. "Anthony spoke of your rash behavior. I know your parents allowed you free reign, but at sea—"

Priscilla jumped to her feet. Anthony had said that about

her? Is that how everyone saw her? "Do not pretend to understand me." Her hurt drew unwanted tears to her eyes, and she looked away. What did he know? And, what did Anthony, for that matter? Her brother had been mostly at sea for the past ten years. Neither of them understood her fears or the lengths she underwent to hide them.

"You're right." Warm fingers touched her arm, gently reeling her back into her seat.

She summoned the courage to face him.

He clasped her hand in his warm palm. "I have little experience or understanding of the gentler sex." He released a resigned sigh. "I'm merely trying to keep you safe. Help me find a way to do so."

His touch fluttered her pulse, setting her even more ill-at-ease. She withdrew her hand, and a shadow passed over his gaze, returning the liquid metal to the usual steely gray.

"I shall escort you back to your room." He rose.

She did the same.

"Tomorrow." He narrowed his eyes. "You're to stay inside your cabin and remain there until I come and get you after the storm passes." His hard glare penetrated to her toes, icing her inside out. "Do you understand me?"

Inwardly she screamed in terror, but her lips whispered, "Yes, Captain."

A gentle hand pressed against her lower back, guiding her toward her stateroom. As they stepped into the passage, she swore she heard him mumble, "Or, Lord help me, I'll bolt your door."

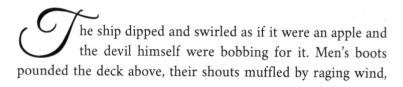

The ship dipped and swirled as if it were an apple and the devil himself were bobbing for it. Men's boots pounded the deck above, their shouts muffled by raging wind, rain, and waves. The spanker banged as the ship tipped leeward, followed by more bellows.

Miss Dodd's Bible slid across the desk. Priscilla reached for it but only brushed the edge before it thumped on the floor and proceeded to the far corner. She lunged after it, scooping it up as Miss Dodd emptied the contents of her stomach into the chamber pot.

The boat shifted again, and Priscilla released a tiny scream as she fell back into her chair. She clutched the Bible to her chest. "Would you like me to read to you some more?"

"Not when my pounding head threatens to split it in two." Miss Dodd rested on the bed with the chamber pot wrapped in her arms. After five hours of casting up her accounts, how could anything remain in the woman's stomach? Miss Dodd released a low groan and sipped on another dose of the doctor's elixir. "I'm going to rest awhile to let the medicine take effect, hopefully, it will stay down this time."

Priscilla ran a hand over the leather cover. Over the past few weeks, as Miss Dodd read from these pages, Priscilla found a sense of comfort in knowing there was an all-powerful God who created her and loved her. She put the Bible away and set the chamber pot in a stand on the floor to keep it from tipping. She glanced at the watch pinned to her gown. It was only half-past ten in the morning. Dark clouds blotted out the sun, and the oil lamp remained lit, swinging back and forth with the rocking boat.

The storm had blown in quickly. If the captain's projections had been correct, they should be near the Lesser Antilles Islands. She hoped they could shelter in the safety of an island cove, but that in itself posed risks. Would the storm surge be high enough to protect them from being cast against the dangerous coral reefs?

The ship rose on a wave and dropped out. She gripped her chair's arms as acid lurched into her throat. Down the corridor, dishes bounced in the galley's pantry. If it had been her mother's china cabinet, not a single cup or saucer would have remained intact, but the ship's metal plates would survive. The constant shifting of balance muddled Priscilla's mind. She wanted to hold her head and scream for this to end.

The ocean, however, continued to rise and fall as quickly as Tobias's moods. One minute he fooled her into thinking he cared, but the next moment he flew to the boughs, raging at her for whatever he disapproved of at that time. There'd been moments at dinner when she'd caught him staring at her with a curious intensity as though he were a fisherman who'd reeled in a mermaid. Thinking of his stormy gaze sent her pulse pattering like raindrops on a sail.

A cold splatter of water landed on the crown of her coiffure and seeped through the roots of her hair. She peered at the ceiling. Beads of water formed on damp boards above her head, ready to drip. She moved to the opposite side and sat on her trunk. Hull planks creaked as the ship rolled onto its side and back upright. Priscilla's fingers dug into the soft pine wood to keep herself from tumbling.

Miss Dodd moaned in her sleep.

The ship answered with a groan.

Priscilla's stomach dipped.

The ship grew oddly still. Silence roared in her head, lodging another scream in her throat.

Wind whipped up again, creaking the deck boards.

Hair on her arms rose. The darkness huddled in the far corner whispered to her.

You are alone. Scream all you like. No one will help you.

Lies. Miss Dodd was near. She certainly would wake. Wouldn't she? Priscilla dared not look at the darkness for fear of it taking hold of her.

Above deck, Tobias's baritone voice reverberated a muffled command. Even below, she could hear the authority in his tone.

She tilted her ear to discern the words but couldn't. She needed something to take her mind off the storm—off her fears.

As if sensing her isolation, the darkness inched closer. *You are a nuisance. No one wants you on board. If you were drowning, no one would save you.*

Priscilla shivered. There was nothing to fear. She was safe below deck.

Two more drops of water splashed onto the chair—*plip plop.*

Miss Dodd released a deep exhale, the kind a person makes before leaving this world for the next. Priscilla scooted to the edge of the trunk closest to the bed and gently nudged Miss Dodd with her finger to make certain she was still alive. Miss Dodd mumbled and swatted at Priscilla's hands while she rolled over. *Praise God.* She only slept. Priscilla had half a mind to replace the surgeon's elixir with watered ale, but she would never do that to dear Miss Dodd, nor would she dare after the masquerade debacle.

The ship tilted, and Priscilla grabbed the wooden hull to keep from falling. The damp boards sent an icy chill through her bones, and she ripped her hand away. Her pulse accelerated, throbbing in her ears, and tightness formed in her chest, quickening her breath.

Priscilla squeezed her eyes shut. *No, no, no.* Perspiration beaded on her forehead as she fought to keep from shattering like a mirror. Her fingers gripped the trunk harder.

You're mine.

Her throat constricted like a fist tightening its grip. She pressed her palm to her chest. Her heart pounded as though determined to break free of its confines.

She squeezed her eyes shut. "This will not happen again. I won't allow it. I'm not crazed."

Only a madwoman would say such things.

Somewhere, a cabin door banged shut. She jumped, for it sounded like the slam of a cellar door.

The boat rolled starboard. The oil lamp swung on its chain, almost hitting the bulkhead. Priscilla fell off the trunk onto the deck with a thump, landing sprawled out on her hip and side, just like the scraggly man had tossed her all those years ago.

"Help." Her cry squeaked past the tightness in her chest. She scrambled backward on her hands until she bumped something in the dim light. Her mouth opened to scream, but there was no air in her lungs. Only a pathetic whimper emerged. *Mama, Papa, where are you? Please find me. I'm scared.*

No one can hear you.

Priscilla trembled, unable to move.

The pounding of her heart slowed to an occasional tick, and darkness crept into her periphery, closing in.

Was she dying?

No one cares.

She closed her eyes, resigned to her fate.

Cast your cares on me because I care for you.

This gentle whisper spoke directly to her heart.

The darkness flinched.

She regained control over her limbs and sucked in a deep breath. Jumping at the opportunity to escape the terror, she dashed for the door. Whatever dangers the rest of the ship might pose would be nothing compared to the torture of remaining isolated in her cabin. She lifted the latch and barreled into the passage. Darkness lunged after her.

The boat rocked again, slamming her into the wall and banging the door closed behind her. She scrambled toward the galley.

She had to find somebody.

Ricocheting back and forth like a lawn tennis ball, Priscilla stumbled down the corridor. She gripped the wardroom portal and pulled herself inside. Not a soul. Surely, Chef would be in the galley. The ship dipped, and a chair unhooked from the wall, clattering onto the wooden deck. She staggered to the galley door. The narrow room usually teemed with men, vegetables, and pots, but today there wasn't a one. The stove coals remained unlit, the knives and food prep materials tucked away.

"Is anyone here?" she yelled in the direction of the sleeping quarters.

No response.

Once again, darkness closed in on her periphery, narrowing her line of vision. A sob escaped. The need to locate someone consumed her, but her fragile control slipped. She ran back through the wardroom and into the passage, but instead of her footsteps creaking deck boards, her kid boots pounded against cobblestone. She glanced back over her shoulder and saw the back alleys of London's streets. The murky fog slowed her pace. Her dress caught on a peg. He had her.

The boat tilted, and she slipped, hitting hard against the damp wood. She clawed her way to the hatch. She turned the latch and met resistance.

"Help!" She banged her fists on the cellar door. When that didn't work, she slammed her shoulder into it. Pain shot down her arm, but she barely felt it through the numbing, dark haze. She rammed it again and again until something gave. The wind caught the hatch and flung it open.

Sheets of rain pelted her face, drenching her in seconds, but Priscilla burst into the whipping winds of the perilous storm.

⸏

"Get that spanker secured!" Tobias bellowed over the wind. He and Henry both strained at the helm to hold her steady. The storm smothered the sun even at high noon, leaving them with only the faint glow of their lanterns. Lightning streaked the sky, illuminating the mast and furled sails bright as day. The rigging snapped aloft. They rode up a massive wave and down its backside, but another hit from the side, washing over the deck. He yelled to his men, "Hold fast—one hand for you, one hand for the ship. Secure yourself before you help your mate."

A bang sounded to his right. The hatch had blown open. By George, hadn't he watched crewmen triple-check the tarpaulins? He twisted to see his men struggling with ropes to tighten the spanker. The hatch would have to wait. Hopefully, below deck wouldn't take on much water. He returned his focus to the helm, but motion caught his eye.

A woman scrambled above. Her billowing gown whipped in the wind, and rain soaked her in seconds. Priscilla wiped water from her pale face, etched with panic.

Tobias's blood stilled. Something was wrong. "Nash, take the helm."

As soon as Nash put a hand to the wheel, Tobias vaulted the rail onto the main deck. His boots slipped on the wet surface, but he remained upright.

The ship tipped starboard, toppling Priscilla like a ragdoll into the outer railing.

"Hold tight. I'm coming."

The ship righted more to port, and she struggled to stagger back to the hatch, but her legs weren't used to maneuvering in a storm. She slid past the opening, luckily in his direction.

"Got you." He grabbed her shoulders and turned her to face him. "Get below." He placed a hand on the back of her head, forcing her to crouch low. He guided her against the wind to the hatch. Tobias braced his stance and leaned forward to aid her down the stairs.

Her nails dug into his arm, and she balked.

Blast. "It's too dangerous. Stay in your cabin."

Wide, terrified eyes blinked away rainwater.

"Did something happen?"

He was met with a vacant stare.

A growl rose in his throat, and he clenched his jaw to keep it locked within. She was mad. Completely mad. Why else would she come above ship during a severe blow? "Stay in your cabin." He shook her. "Do you hear me."

Thunder rattled above them, as if in emphasis.

The ship heeled sharply to starboard. A large wave darkened the dim lamplight.

Priscilla yelped and wrapped her arms around his midsection. Her cheek pressed against his chest. Through his wet clothes, he could feel her trembling.

He grabbed the hatch, but the sea ripped Priscilla away, slamming her into the rail. *Lord, have mercy.* Tobias released his grip and slid after her. A second wave washed over them like a giant hand, scooping them off the deck and pitching them into the sea.

CHAPTER 13

What do you know about this Captain Prescott fellow? I grow more concerned with each passing day since your sister's disappearance.

~ *Letter from Admiral Middleton to his son Anthony*

eightlessness swept over Priscilla. The ocean roared in her ears and ripped Tobias from her fingers as she tumbled through oblivion. She plummeted below the ocean's surface, and her scream muffled into large bubbles. The shock of the water stiffened her body, not deadly cold but chilly nonetheless. The howling wind and pelting rain ceased. Only the sound of distant crashing of waves and water swishing above remained.

She was alone and most certainly going to drown.

What had she done with her life? Would anyone mourn her death, or had she merely been a body, another dance partner at a ball?

She wanted a second chance—to do better—to be better. She wanted to live.

Lord, help me.

Priscilla kicked toward the rising bubbles with all her might. Muffled thunder boomed above. Her clothing impeded her legs. Thankfully she'd donned a cotton gown and a thin petticoat due to the warmer weather. The layers were only slightly heavier than the chemise she usually swam in with her brother. Heavy wool would have weighed her down like a millstone. She kicked her legs and stretched her arms in long strokes. If she lived, she would buy her brother a bottle of his favorite port for teaching her how to swim. Finally breaking the surface, she gulped in a deep breath only seconds before a wave hit her face. Her lungs coughed out saltwater in time for another to strike. She blinked away seawater and rain. A wave lifted her, and she looked for Tobias. His head emerged within a few yards, and Priscilla choked back a thankful sob.

"Priscilla!" Tobias's voice traveled on the wind.

Streaks of jagged lightning sliced the night sky. She twisted around to find a swell lifting him as he swam against the current to her.

"Tobias!"

He disappeared under a wave.

"Tobias?" Her breathing quickened.

He resurfaced a few seconds later.

She gripped his arm as she would a life raft. "Where did you go?"

"I had to remove my boots and my saber. They weighed me down."

Her chin dipped below the surface.

"You can't swim in these skirts either." He bunched up her skirt and petticoats into a knot at her side, leaving only her thin chemise to contend with.

She floated easier without the weighty fetters.

"Man overboard!" echoed in the distance. Waves carried them away from the ship.

Tobias placed a hand on her arm, and she gripped his shoulders. His hair plastered his face, and water dripped from his nose and chin. "You can swim?"

She nodded. "Anthony taught me."

He wiped a hand over his face. "Praise God."

A swell lifted them. Priscilla glimpsed the ship over the waves. It floated further away and showed no sign of turning. "Won't she come about?"

Lightning flashed as a wave curled above their heads, illuminating Tobias's face an aqua glow. He grabbed her arm, helping her dive through it. She kicked to the surface and gasped for breath, clinging to his warmth.

Dark sky and black waves shadowed Tobias's face while she awaited his answer. "No."

Her jaw dropped, which she regretted when seawater sloshed in her mouth. She spit it out. "What do you mean, no?"

"They can't turn her around in this storm. If they lower sails in this wind, they'll tear or go missing in minutes."

Priscilla choked on her panic. "They can't leave us." Her grip tightened on his arm. "We'll die."

He held her chin between his thumb and index finger, forcing her to look at him. "We're not going to die. Do you hear me?"

She nodded, but her energy was sapping. How long could she stay afloat?

"Good." His gaze bore into hers as if transferring a bit of his strength.

It worked, for she calmed, trusting her captain.

"They lowered the dinghy." He inclined his chin behind her.

She would have turned to look, but he still gripped her face.

"We have to swim for it." He spit out water. "If we get separated, do whatever you need to do to stay afloat, and I will find you. I promise."

Separated?

He nodded and stretched out with long strokes.

Priscilla dove after him, swimming with all her might to keep up.

Saltwater dripped from her nose and fingertips with each stroke. She sucked in deep breaths, her muscles burned, and her arms and legs shook. Was she making any ground? A glimpse of Tobias rising on a nearby wave caused tears to fill her eyes. She wasn't going to make it. A wave crashed over her, and she stayed suspended underwater. Her hair swished in the colliding currents waving above her as if in a final farewell. She closed her eyes.

It is not the will of your Father which is in heaven that one of these little ones should perish. The Bible passage Miss Dodd had read rang clear in her mind.

Her eyes sprung open, and she kicked with a renewed strength that couldn't have been her own. It was not God's will for her to die. Her lungs compressed and her throat convulsed, needing to draw breath. She clawed her way to the surface, breaking through the rough surf. She gasped in big gulps of air. Her lung expanded, filling with life.

"Priscilla!" Tobias's voice rolled over a wave.

"Here." She tried to yell, but it came out more of a squeak. Fatigue washed over her with the most recent wave. "I'm here," she repeated, her energy sapped once more. "Please, help."

Her arms refused to obey what her mind commanded. A large wave plowed water toward her. She no longer held the strength to swim up it.

"Hold fast!"

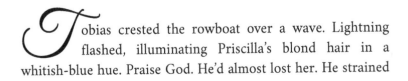

*T*obias crested the rowboat over a wave. Lightning flashed, illuminating Priscilla's blond hair in a whitish-blue hue. Praise God. He'd almost lost her. He strained against the oars to get to her while positioning the dinghy so the rough waves wouldn't tip it.

"Over here." The volume of her voice increased, but her head barely topped the surface.

He rowed beside her and stretched out a hand, keeping his weight distributed evenly. "Give me your hand."

Her head sank underwater.

Tobias lunged, grasping the back of her gown and hooking a hand under her arm. The boat tipped, taking on water. He thrust his weight back, dragging her inside.

Priscilla collapsed into the boat and coughed out ocean water.

Tobias grabbed the oars, thankfully still hooked into the oarlock. Rain pelted his face, blurring his sight. He blinked to clear his vision, and his gaze darted to Priscilla every chance he could to reassure himself she would survive. It pained him not to tend to her, but he couldn't let a wave flip the dinghy. "Are you all right?"

She expelled a deep breath and nodded with a weak smile. "I am now."

A wave crashed on port side. He maneuvered the craft to avoid flipping, but it was a daunting task. He rowed vertically up a rising swell.

Ignoring his screaming muscles, he concentrated on the waves' direction. He had to keep the bow pointed head-on toward each wave. Occasionally a whipping wind caught him by surprise, and a wave curled over the dinghy, threatening to sink them.

Priscilla sat across from him on the bench seat and clutched the edges with white knuckles. She shivered.

"Are you cold?" he yelled above the wind.

"N-no." She shook her head, but her teeth rattled, barely able to get the word out.

The water was unseasonably warm, and a tropical wind

blew. He wasn't sweating from exertion, but he wasn't cold. She must be in shock.

By Jove, he'd also be in shock if he didn't need to row. They'd fallen overboard in the worst squall he'd seen all year, nearly drowned, but that wasn't the last of it. They still needed to survive by finding land or hailing a ship before thirst or starvation killed them.

Another tremor ran through her. Her face and lips had paled, white as a sail. She stared wide-eyed at the towering waves around their small craft. Her matted hair hung limply down her back and about her shoulders, and her bare feet sat in pooled water. She must have lost her slippers in the ocean.

A triangle-shaped wave lifted the boat, spun it around, and set it back down on the other side.

Priscilla held on tight and watched his face.

Her haunted gaze clung to him. He'd been well trained as a captain to school his expressions. Fear spreads, but calm could also be contagious. He preferred the latter.

"Priscilla." He rowed over a harrowing swell before continuing, "God's going to pull us through the storm."

She stared at the mix of rain and seawater sloshing in their boat, at least a hand deep. "Are we sinking?"

"Nothing to worry about." *Not right this moment.* Instead of bombarding them with large breakers from what seemed every angle, the waves let up a bit. The current traveled more in a general direction, and bigger waves attacked only every few.

Each minute spanned out like an eternity. It was difficult to determine through the clouds what direction they were headed, nearer the Lesser Antilles Islands or away. The wind had been blowing in a northwesterly direction, pushing the ship closer to the Bahamas, but it could easily have changed as the storm passed. He dared not close his eyes or bow his head, but he prayed nonetheless. *Lord, save us. Don't let us die out here, not without fulfilling our purpose.*

Wind raged around them as if it might never let up. Tobias's fingers and arms cramped. His hands bled where his callouses had torn. He could barely lift the oars. A square wave approached, a white cap dancing along its top edge as though giddy to take them under. He couldn't turn the bow to meet it. The wave crashed into the side, pushing the dinghy sideways and flooding the interior.

The impact knocked Priscilla onto the floor, where water rose to her elbows. Instead of panicking, the splash seemed to wake her from her shock. She righted herself. "You need a rest. Let me take the helm for a while."

"I'm fine." He struggled to ready the boat for the next wave with one oar. A bolt of lightning struck in the distance. A few seconds ticked by before the roar of thunder followed. "Did you hear that? The storm is moving north. We're through the worst of it."

"How can you tell?"

"Before, thunder immediately followed the lightning. Now you can count the seconds between the lightning and thunder. The squall's pushing further out."

Another massive wave rolled in, but Tobias's hands refused to cooperate. He dropped the oar.

Priscilla grabbed the paddle before it slid from the rowlock into the ocean.

His arm shook as he reached to take it from her.

Her moon-pale face softened with sympathy. "You should rest. Let me row for a bit."

"I'm fine."

Her gaze was insistent. "A normal man would have given up after twenty minutes, but you are staunch, steadfast, and most of all, stubborn."

"You do not understand ocean mechanics."

The rowboat rose backward over a wave and dropped down the other side.

Her clammy hand rested on top of his. Rainwater splashed off her shoulders and the crown of her head, and her eyes softened, pleading with him. "You can teach me."

He blew a breath from his lips, and it sprayed water. "We'll take turns." He shifted out of the position he'd sat in for what must have been hours. A grunt escaped his throat as he moved to the other bench. Every muscle and joint in his body protested.

Priscilla slipped into position and gripped the oars. She battled to keep the boat steady, straining against the waves. "Our country home resides on a large lake. Anthony taught me to swim in it, and I used to row a boat across to visit with Lottie, for the Etheridges resided on the other side."

She may know how to row, but her gentle hands weren't calloused like his own. They had probably never seen a hard day's work. He figured she'd last two waves, and then he'd be back rowing.

"Position her so that the bow faces the wave. The pointy ones will pick her up, spin her around, and set her back down on the other side. It's the square rimmed waves you must be wary and watch. Those can easily capsize us. Point her straight at them." He indicated with his chin because his hand refused to move. "Here comes a big one. Row harder with your left."

She adjusted and released little grunts with each stroke as they climbed a wave.

There's one.

At a brief lull in between waves, she rubbed her hands, massaging the skin. Another wave followed. This one frothed at the top, threatening to curl into the boat. "Keep her steady. A bit more on portside."

She pulled harder on the starboard side.

"Portside. Your left." He lunged to place his hands over hers, resuming command.

"I can manage." She corrected the direction.

He sat back, leery. "When I give the order, row with all your might up the wave."

The wave lifted the stern.

"Row. Now!"

She leaned forward and arched back into the stroke, cutting through the wave top, its white foam crashing down once they passed.

There's two.

A wave barreled in from another angle. It was smaller but would hit them square in the side.

"Swing her around thirty degrees port."

Priscilla obeyed his commands as if she were one of his men.

"Hold her steady."

The wave passed.

"Back thirty degrees starboard."

She situated the boat, and they rode over another wave.

The whipping wind and rain had eased into more of a steady constant. Tobias wiped water from his face with one hand and fought to re-open his heavy lids. When he lifted them, Priscilla had already positioned the rowboat to the proper angle to meet the wave. Impressive.

"How are you faring?"

"Fine." She grunted with an oar stroke.

She looked like a wilted daisy in a waterlogged flower bed. Granted, he probably looked worse. The rain had lessened, but water still ran in streams down his neck and back. "Are you certain you don't want me to take back the oars?"

She paddled up an incoming wave. "Go ahead and rest. I will let you know when I'm tired."

Tobias struggled to keep his eyes open. Every part of his body ached with exhaustion. He should have taken the advice he'd given the men, eaten a good meal, and gotten a good night's sleep, but he hadn't. There'd been so many things to tend to, check, and double-check. Had it only been last night that the storm hit? It felt like days since they'd tumbled into the ocean.

Priscilla pulled the oars back, lithe muscles in her slender arms straining. She was stronger than she appeared and, for once, surprisingly biddable. As soon as he thought he had her figured, she did something unexpected, like offer to row.

His chin hit his chest, and he jerked his lolled head up. He mustn't fall asleep. Steep waves continued, but at least the wind died and the soaking rain softened into a drizzle. By Tobias's calculations, based on catching a glimpse of a gray orb through the dark clouds a while back, he figured it must be near dusk. His guess was correct because what seemed like minutes later, the sky turned purple. Not a pinkish purple seen often in sunsets but a deep royal purple. The waves, too, reflected the color as though they'd entered a strange realm where sky and sea mirrored an unlikely hue. In this strange, surreal realm where he sat bobbing in a purple sea with a beautiful woman at the helm, anything seemed possible—perhaps even their survival.

～

"Tobias."

A female voice pulled him from a deep sleep. His mother? She was the only female who meant anything to him. Wait, Annie. Was Annie trying to stir him from his bunk to let him know the lieutenant would be coming around shortly for bed check? The familiar pang of sadness slapped his face as guilt punched him in the gut. Why did she have to lie to him? Why did she have to die?

"Tobias! Wake up." Priscilla's shriek jolted him into consciousness.

His head jerked, and he absorbed his surroundings. He was ankle-deep in water in a rowboat with Priscilla at the helm. He had no idea how long since he'd drifted off, but the sky had turned dark indigo, almost black. The rain had stopped, but there were no stars to guide them. The occasional large wave continued to toss the dinghy around like a toy boat in a swollen stream after a deluge.

"I can barely see." Her voice shook as if she might burst into tears. "I don't know what to do."

"You've done splendidly." He slid in between the oars and sat next to her to take over rowing. The heat of her skin soaked through his shirt, and his body delighted in the warmth, craving more. But he was a gentleman. "I'll take the oars."

She scooted to the other bench. "Do you have any idea where we are?"

"There's no way to know for certain without a sextant and the stars, but once the clouds clear, I can figure out a general location." His muscles ached as he rowed, but he rested in between waves. There was no point in rowing a specific direction until he knew which direction to navigate.

Priscilla wiped the wet hair from her eyes. "Now that the worst of the storm has passed, will the *Trade Wind* come back to find us?"

He didn't want to steal her hope, but it would be better for her to understand the truth. "She won't come back for us. The mission is more important."

She stilled. "What mission is more important than rescuing their captain?"

"The one the prince regent issued." He strained his eyes to locate any approaching waves.

"No one is coming for us?"

He hated the fear in her voice, especially since he'd been the one who caused it. "Once my crew arrives on St. Kitts, they will send another ship to search for us. Lieutenant Dalton trained under me, so the *Trade Wind* will continue on its mission, because that's what I would have done."

"Oh."

He heard a thousand questions in her reply. How long would that take? Would they survive until then? What would they eat and drink? Questions that weighed heavily on his mind too. "Once the sky clears, we need to get our bearings and row in the direction of Tortola or Anegada. If we locate an island, we can find help or at least find food and shelter until a ship reaches us."

He could barely discern the outline of her shoulders, but they seemed to relax. Her breath returned to a steady rhythm. He concentrated on the sound, so soft, so feminine. A wave behind him rose. *Blast*. He'd been distracted, and darkness made it hard to determine direction.

"Priscilla, hold tight."

The boat rode up the wave sideways, but the fizzle died out before they reached the top. Tobias exhaled a loud sigh. "That was clos—"

A second wave hit them without warning. It crashed into the side, knocking her and Tobias portside. For several seconds, the wave used the rowboat as a plow through the ocean before flipping it over.

Priscilla screamed.

He barely had enough time to suck in a deep breath before plunging into the dark depths.

CHAPTER 14

Bonaparte appears content to hold a lilliputian court on Elba Island. However, I daresay, he grows giddy whenever men speak of events in mainland Europe. There is a suspicious glitter in those dark eyes.

~ Letter from Colonel Neil Campbell to Lord Castlereagh

*P*riscilla sputtered to the surface. She dragged in a deep breath, inflating her lungs. Saltwater dripped into her mouth, and she spit it out. Once again, she was in the ocean.

"Priscilla?" Tobias's voice sounded muffled.

The air seemed darker, and the waves sounded stifled. A swell lifted, and her head bumped wood. Lord, help her. She was underneath the boat.

"Priscilla!" His voice pitched higher, frantic.

"Under here." She banged on the boat. "I'm coming." She inhaled and dove under, re-emerging on the other side a few feet from where Tobias bobbed in the water.

He grabbed her arm and pulled her next to him. "You gave me a fright."

She couldn't determine his expression in the evening light, but his voice fluctuated between relief and anger. Why was he always angry in her presence? She wanted to yell back, *I wasn't the one who flipped the rowboat.* That would only lead to him reminding her that it was her fault they fell overboard, which she couldn't deny.

He placed her hand on the overturned boat. "Grab hold." He patted the dinghy's side. "Try to pull yourself up."

She felt for anything to grip on the rounded surface. Her nails dug into wood, but they wouldn't support her entire body weight. "There's nothing to hold."

He gripped the edge of the boat and raised his knee. "Step on my leg for a boost. Try to grab the keel."

Her sensibilities recoiled at placing her bare foot on a man's leg, but everything since she'd stepped aboard the *Trade Wind*, had been beyond sensible. She put her hands on his shoulder to balance her weight.

"Ready, one, two, three... lift."

She pushed off his leg, submerging Tobias. She stretched to reach the keel, and one hand gripped the edge, but the other missed. A high-pitch growl erupted from deep in her chest, and she gritted her teeth, pulling with what little finger strength she had. She grabbed hold of the keel with both hands. The overturned dinghy sank lower in the water as she hung like a wet towel over the side. Tobias's head bobbed below.

"I got it." An almost giddy bubble gurgled in her throat. "Now, what."

He wiped water from his face. "Pull yourself up further until you can straddle the keel."

She obeyed, but it wasn't a ladylike position with her calves bared. Survival, however, trumped propriety.

"I need you to reel me on top. Keep your weight back. Don't lean out too far."

She extended her hand.

He pushed off the boat rim with one hand and reached up with the other. Twice she couldn't hold his grip, and he splashed back into the water. On the third attempt, Priscilla gritted her teeth and used her elbows as a pivot point for leverage. *Please God, give me strength.*

Tobias pulled a leg up and caught the boat edge. The side dipped low, but he hefted himself onto the ridge. Water ran off his drenched body, cascading over the side. Instead of sitting up, they both collapsed on top of the overturned hull, breathing heavy.

"We did it." She panted.

He turned his head and laid it upon the wood. "It's a small victory."

"But a crucial one." How long could he have continued to tread water in these rough seas? The man was inhuman.

"Indeed."

Moonlight flittered through fast-moving clouds. The rain had stopped, and the waves settled a bit, but they still had to grip the keel with one hand so as not to fall off. How long did they have before the dinghy sank? A few hours? A few minutes?

She stared at Tobias's outline, exhausted, spent, but alive. A knot rose into her throat, and tears stung her eyes. She, too, was tired, her emotions raw, but her heart twisted as realization sank in. This man had sacrificed everything for her, his ship, his crew, and his sword. Papa always said a saber marked an officer. Even in the dim lighting of the storm, she could see Tobias's solemn expression. Sacrificing his weapon must have pained him, especially when he prided himself on always being prepared.

An undeniable fact sliced her heart wide open. Tobias had almost given his life to rescue her.

"Thank you." She choked out the words in a soft tone.

He remained silent.

Had he fallen asleep before she could express her gratitude? "For saving me."

A long pause followed. "It's my duty to protect my crew."

"I'm not one of your crew." She hadn't meant to correct him, but a part of her wanted him to admit she was more than a duty. "I was an accidental stowaway. You said so yourself."

"You became my responsibility the minute you boarded my ship."

Ridiculous tears threatened to spill over. She slowed her breathing so that he wouldn't notice. The silence between them raged louder in her ears than the earlier wind. When she could bear it no longer, she tried again, "I'm sorry for getting us into this hobble."

"Hobble?"

"Well, this terrible mess." She wiped a stray tear. He didn't need to rub it in, even if it was true. Couldn't he see she was trying to make the best of this? "Whatever label you want to place on it, I'm sorry."

"The thanks go to God." He rubbed his head, shaking the water from his hair, before adding in a weak whisper, "Who hath gathered the wind in His fists? Who hath bound the waters in His garment? Who hath established all the ends of the earth?'"

"That's in the Bible. I think Miss Dodd read that to me once."

"It's from the book of Proverbs." He sat up and shrugged out of his jacket. "It's wet and will feel cold at first, but it will retain your body heat." He draped it over her like a blanket and lay back.

"What about you?"

"I'll be fine."

She curled her fingers around the fabric, inhaling his masculine scent mingled with wet wool, and settled as best she could beside the keel on her back. Tobias lay on his stomach. Tropical wind whipped dried strands of hair about her face as she stared up at the clouds zooming past the moon. The dinghy rested low in the water. Would it remain afloat or eventually sink? She needed reassurance they would be all right, but Tobias didn't appear in the mood. He wasn't a man of many words. Would they be able to find land, or would they die on this little dinghy of dehydration? How long did they have? A week? A few days? *God, I know I haven't given You much thought until recently, but please help us. I realize now You were trying to get through to me in the cabin. I'm sorry I didn't listen. I'm sorry to drag Tobias into this mess. I don't want either of us to die.*

A gust of warm wind blew, but only deafening silence followed. Images of the maps she used to memorize for comfort now tormented her. In the vast ocean, islands had been tiny green dots. How much smaller was she compared to those islands? No one would ever find her. No one may ever look. Not for her. Tobias—perhaps.

Lord, please answer me. Let me know you're there.

"What happened before we went over?" Tobias lifted his head and propped his chin on his fist. "You looked like you'd seen headless Ben."

Her blood surged, and she half sat up. Had God heard her? Was Tobias's speaking a sign? She shifted onto her side to face him. "The phantom Chauncy swears he's seen? You know it's all flummery. You don't believe in such things, do you?"

"You're evading the topic. What had you so frightened? The storm?"

"I can't explain it." Nor did she want to. The last time she'd tried, it had angered him.

"Try me."

The waves turned from jostling to a rhythmic rocking. "It happens when I'm alone."

"Wasn't Miss Dodd in the room with you?"

"She was. My fear"—she turned her face away—"it's not rational. My past and present merge. I can't control what happens nor what I do." She choked on a hollow laugh. "Believe me, I've tried." She moved her arm under her head and wiped away her tears. "Perhaps I'm becoming mad, like King George."

He released a heavy sigh. "First of all, you are not mad. Second, please refrain from speaking ill of our king."

"Isn't his madness common knowledge?"

"He's still our king, and I'll not tolerate slander."

Once again, she'd offended him. Why had she thought he'd understand?

Other than the constant breeze flapping her damp skirt and the waves lapping the sides of the boat, a stillness fell upon the night. Priscilla had begun to succumb to her exhaustion and drift off when he spoke again.

"I didn't take it seriously when you first told me about your nightmares. I shouldn't have dismissed it so lightly."

A grateful smile twitched the corners of her lips. "We're a sorry pair."

"Indeed." He said the word with such despondency it hung on the air like a discordant note.

The somber mood nagged at her like a constant dripping of water. She couldn't stand it. "We're still alive."

"Which is a miracle." He turned his head away from her and murmured. "We need to find land, or we may not be alive for long."

Priscilla gulped as she rolled back to her stomach and rested her head on her arm. It was not the reassurance for which she'd been hoping.

Tobias's warm fingers settled on top of hers.

It wasn't a guarantee they'd see tomorrow, but at least she didn't have to face whatever happened alone.

∾

a deep-throated bird's cry woke Priscilla. Her eyelids sprung open. Tobias's head rested on his arm beside her. His mouth hung slightly open, and his hair ruffled in the breeze. She was alive, and Tobias was still with her. Thank God. Light colored the horizon as the sun rose above the waves. Thankfully, most clouds had dissipated, and their dinghy had remained afloat, even if the stern dipped under the water.

Her back ached from her stiff position. She moved, but every muscle protested, so she relaxed against the wood, only turning her head. The ocean shimmered a brilliant shade of turquoise blue, and it shone so clear that she could watch fish swimming below. If she could avoid being wet for the rest of her life, she might do it. Even now, her skin was damp from either dew or sea spray. The cool breeze sent a chill over her skin, and she tucked her arms back under his jacket, closer to her body for warmth.

A seagull cried, and a pair floated past her. Their white-and-gray wings glided on the wind. Something tapped her memories, persistent in getting attention. She stared at the gulls. Something was remarkable about them. They're alive. They're flying. They reminded her of the docks at home.

Priscilla lurched into a seated position. *That's it.* Seagulls fly near land. Sure enough, jutting out of the sea of blue rose a small crop of verdant islands. She shook Tobias. "Wake up. I see land."

His eyes snapped open. He blinked and sat up straight.

"Over there." She pointed.

A smile lifted the corners of his mouth.

"We're going to live, aren't we?" A giddiness swept through her body. "We're saved, right? Someone on the island can help us."

Tobias's smile widened, and he turned to face her. "Quite right."

She wrapped her arms around him. "We're saved."

His warm hands slid up her back.

She melted into his embrace, overjoyed at a chance at life. Her lips murmured into this shoulder. "I prayed, and God listened. I didn't think He heard, because He didn't answer. There was only silence, but then you spoke—"

Tobias pulled away, and his arms dropped back to his sides.

Her body protested the loss. She'd been rambling.

He frowned and stared at the water.

She must look a fright. Her hand touched her hair stiff with salt. *Good heavens*, she probably also smelled of seaweed. No wonder he'd pulled away.

He shielded his eyes from the sun before returning his gaze to her. His frown deepened.

"I spent the entire day in the ocean. I probably reek of fish. You probably smell like fish too." But he didn't. He smelled like man, fresh air, and sea salt.

He blinked at her as if she were bacon-brained. "I need something that floats."

"Like what?"

He patted the length of his body and stuffed his hands into his pockets but found nothing. "A ribbon, a cork, a string, anything light."

Her pins and ribbon had fallen out long ago. She reached down and overturned the hem of her petticoat.

"That will do."

She yanked at the material, but it wouldn't rip.

"Here, let me." His eyes shifted in obvious discomfort as he tore a strip and dropped it into the water.

She folded her hem back and moved to her hands and knees to watch the ripple of fabric float in the current. "Why did you do that?"

He glanced back at the island and seemed to be calculating

figures in his head. "To assess current direction and speed." He pointed to the strip. "See how quickly it drifted?"

Already she was losing it among the distant waves.

"Our boat is being carried in that same direction just not as quickly." He massaged the back of his neck and met her gaze. "If we continue on this course, we'll never make it to the island."

CHAPTER 15

Deploy ships to gain dominion over the Mississippi River
and secure British control of the major trade routes for
the American South.

*~ Letter from Admiral Sims to British fleets stationed in
the gulf*

*P*riscilla shielded her eyes from the sun. "Perhaps
there's another island further down?"

"It's too risky." Tobias shook his head. "We're going to need
to abandon ship and swim for it."

It was Priscilla's turn to frown. The last thing she wanted
was to return to the water again. To think she used to swim
daily in the country for enjoyment.

"The longer we wait, the further we'll drift, and the longer
we'll have to swim."

Her shoulder's sagged, "By all that's holy…"

"Trust me. My aching bones aren't relishing the task either."
He tapped her under the chin with his index finger. "I'll go first."

It was an odd gesture, but Priscilla smiled. At least, on the
inside.

He stretched his muscles, pulling his arms over his head, giving Priscilla a view of his broad chest. He shook out his hands, and without a word, pushed off into the water.

It splashed onto her toes, and she curled them under the hem of her skirt.

His head bobbed up, and he wiped the water from his face. "Your turn."

A wave slapped the boat's side as though mocking her to hurry up.

Fine. If she must enter the water again, it was going to be on her terms. She rose to her feet. A wave had snatched her off the ship, and rough water had overturned the dinghy. This time she'd enter of her own will in her own style, the way her brother taught her.

She brought her arms above her head, and in one smooth movement, she pushed off and arched into a perfect dive. Priscilla reemerged and glanced back to find she'd gone a boat's length away with a nice head start on Tobias.

His white teeth flashed in the sun. "Nicely done."

He reached forward with long broad strokes, and Priscilla too began her swim to shore. Shortly after, her arms ached and protested. The water stirred around her. She raised her head to find him passing her. He paused and treaded water.

"I don't feel like I'm getting anywhere."

"See if you can tie up your skirts again or tuck them into something." He stilled and begun sinking before he turned to face the land. "I won't look."

Priscilla freed her legs from their cumbersome fetters. The now clear water didn't hide anything as it had yesterday, but it was life or death. Certainly, propriety should move to the end of the line. She twisted the fabric, wrapping it around her fist and pulling an end through as Tobias had done. "There." It should hold for the time being. "That should do it."

"Ready?"

"As much as I'll ever be."

They set off toward the land at an angle, not swimming directly into the current but still fighting it. Priscilla's shoulder blades ground like gears without any grease against each other. Her vision blurred as if she were swimming through a fog. Her legs kicked, but the shore appeared as far away as when they'd started. She needed to rest. Tobias kept swimming, his form at least two ship lengths away. He was going to make it. She mustered a cheer of encouragement, but only a gurgle emerged. At least one of them would.

She inhaled a deep breath and relaxed. Her body hovered underwater, slowly sinking. Something brushed her leg, and she opened her eyes to find a sea turtle pass. How did it carry its heavy body through the water with such ease? Saltwater burned her eyes. She kicked to the surface and sucked fresh air into her lungs.

"Priscilla!" Tobias paddled toward her.

"Keep going." She wanted to yell, but her voice couldn't find the strength. "You're going to make it. Leave me." She gulped in air.

He continued in her direction. "Don't be ridiculous. I'm not leaving you."

A ripple of a wave splashed her face. She closed her eyes and sputtered. When she opened them, his face bobbed in front of her. His hand raked through his hair, slicking it back.

His stormy gray eyes met hers like a thunderbolt. "We're going to make it together. Do you hear me?"

She nodded, but her arms failed her, and she sank below a wave.

He gripped her elbow and raised her. "Try swimming on your back for a while." He laid back in the water as though he were about to nap and kicked his legs.

She did the same. When her legs grew tired, she rolled over and scooped water with her arms. It worked. The shoreline grew closer each time she paused to look.

Tobias stayed by her side, dropping words of encouragement. "You're doing great. Keep it up. We're going to make it." Her favorite was, "Not much longer."

She was floating on her back, squinting at the bright sun when he touched her arm. "Priscilla."

She stopped and treaded water. Waves were breaking in the distance, and the land seemed closer than ever but still so far. She turned back to Tobias. Funny, he didn't appear to be treading water.

"Try to touch."

A wave pushed her into him. His gentle hands steadied her shoulders. He kept his eyes on her face, for which she was grateful. There was no hiding the amount of exposed leg. She put her feet down, and her toes touched sand. Never had anything felt so lovely. Her body relaxed.

Tobias's hand slid down her arm and clasped her fingers in his as he pulled her along the bank. "Watch where you step. Not only are we on a shoal where there might be sharp coral or shells, but you also have to watch for stingrays."

She coiled her legs close to her body.

He chuckled. "Don't worry. I'll drag my feet and stir them out of sand. You should be fine to walk."

She bobbed along behind him, admiring the colorful fish darting through the coral. "Is the water here always this clear?"

"Truthfully, this is murky for the Caribbean. Usually, it's so clear we can spy a shark a league away."

She stopped. *Sharks?*

"I shouldn't have brought that up. Forget I said it."

"There are sharks?"

He shook his head. "Not usually in shallow water." He nodded in the direction they'd been. "Back there, yes."

A nervous chuckle escaped. "I'm glad you waited until now to tell me." She spied something and pointed. "Look at that long yellow fish. Do you know what it's called?"

"A trumpet fish."

"Very fitting." She peered at the beautiful underwater landscape with its bright colors and odd shapes. He pointed out more brightly colored fish and coral by name—brain coral, stingray, fan coral, queen angelfish, bluehead wrasse, and yellowtail parrotfish.

Waves crashed against their backs, pushing them along. The knot fell out of her skirts, and so she held them up with one hand and allowed Tobias to pull her with the other. The sand bar sloped into deeper waters. The pale blue water darkened into a vibrant turquoise, but the island was within reach.

The last hundred yards dragged like a thousand. Tobias held her as they stumbled through the rough surf. Several large waves drove them to their knees. She would never have survived without his encouragement. He'd stayed strong throughout their swim and had shown no signs of exhaustion until they reached dry land. Tobias collapsed upon the sand, and without his support, she fell beside him. Tobias rolled to his back, his chest rising and falling with his heavy breathing. Fine grains of white sand stuck to the side of his face and his wet clothes.

They were alive. Somehow by God's grace, they were alive.

Priscilla would have danced with joy if she could move. Her muscles had turned to porridge and her bones to mush. The tip of a broken wave washed over her feet, carrying the hem of her skirt with it. Her arms and legs refused to budge, not even for propriety's sake, but when the wave receded, it drew the material back with it. Movement in her periphery drew her gaze. At least her eyeballs could move even though they still burned. A small crab, so light in its pale-yellow color, it was almost see-through, crawled elbow first out of a hole in the sand. Its claw was nearly as big as the crab itself. It stopped, spying her with black eyes suspended above its body before darting back into its burrow.

The crash of an impressive wave thundered. A few seconds later, it lifted her feet, swirled water about her knees, and left foam markings as a reminder of where its territory ended. Sunlight poked through clouds, warming her skin. They lay without saying a word for a good while, for the same crab now skittered in open sand, waving its massive claw at another crab. The sun drifted closer to the horizon, and the tide no longer reached them. It had moved back several yards by the time Priscilla summoned the strength to roll onto her side. With great protest from every inch of her body, she sat up.

Tobias still lay on his back with an arm draped over his eyes. His breathing had evened as if he'd drifted off to sleep.

She drew her legs to her chest and wrenched down on her wet skirts. She rested her chin on her knees and stared at the perilous beauty of the ocean. They'd survived those deadly turquoise waters, but it had only been by God's grace. An urge to thank the Lord for rescuing them flooded her being, but she didn't know the proper way to go about praying.

God, I may not be speaking properly to You. Please forgive my ineptness. I merely... I need to thank You for saving me. She glanced at Tobias. *For saving us. Um, I want to thank You for helping us endure the storm and carrying us to land. I know our survival was Your doing because it certainly was a miracle.*

Tobias stirred next to her. He removed his arm and squinted at the sun.

Thank you that I'm not alone. Um, well, that's all for now. Amen.

Tobias grunted as he pushed himself into a seated position. He rested his arms on his legs. His wet breaches molded to his thighs, and his white shirt and vest clung to his broad frame. His shoulders hunched forward, so unlike the stiff, upright captain she'd become accustomed to. Staring out at the vast ocean, he picked up a scalloped shell and shifted it in a circle between his fingers.

She sighed and pushed her wet mop of hair off her face. "Well, we're alive."

He continued to scan the horizon, likely searching for ships.

More than ever, Priscilla desired her friend Lottie. Not just to discover the truth about her brother, but because she needed a friend with a reasonable mind to help her untangle this knotted net of emotions. Why had Tobias risked his life to save her? Was he just doing his duty as a captain? Why did she feel a connection to him, but at the same time, always feel at odds? "Will any ships pass this way?"

He remained quiet.

"Do you think we could signal them?"

His jaw tightened, and he glanced at her. "I don't even know where we are." Raw, naked fear flashed in his eyes for a split second before he turned away.

Priscilla stared down at the sand. Her eyes burned as if expecting to draw moisture, but there was none. She bit her bottom lip as her stomach twisted into a knot. Of course, he couldn't have the answers. They had been lost at sea and could have drifted anywhere. For all she knew, they'd floated to Central America. Well, that might have been a bit far-fetched, but couldn't he allow her a bit of hope?

"Yes."

Her gaze flew to his profile.

The captain had returned, for he'd schooled his face to mask his emotions. "There is a possibility we could hail a passing ship."

She straightened, her newfound optimism masking the ache in her muscles with a surge of energy. No one would come looking for her, but Tobias was the ship's captain and a respected commander. Surely, His Majesty's Royal Navy would search for their captain. "If we could somehow light a fire." She scanned their surroundings. "It could hail a ship's attention. I still believe the *Trade Wind* might come for us."

His nostrils flared. "They'd be defying my direct order, but there is a slim chance they'll keep watch as they pass with the rest of the fleet on its way to the Gulf."

"Then, we must find a way to hail them or signal another vessel in the meantime." She crossed her arms on top of her knees and frowned, refusing to give up so easily. They'd reached the Caribbean. She wasn't far from St. Kitts and Lottie, yet without a ship, there was no means to get there. How long could they survive on an island without a ship's rescue?

His lower jaw extended, and he pounded a fist into the sand. "Hold your demands until we discover what's on the island." He paused, rubbing a hand down his face, and his voice calmed. "We must be cautious. This isn't a London ballroom. Not everyone in the Caribbean is civilized." An echo of pain flashed in his eyes, but in a blink, it vanished. "It's best to identify friend versus foe before we begin signaling anyone of our presence."

Priscilla forced herself to nod because words wouldn't come. Seeing his brief moment of vulnerability had shaken her. Aboard the ship, she'd tried to get the captain to drop his defenses, but now she needed them for courage.

He glanced away, exhaling, and dusted sand out of his hair before meeting her gaze once more. "There are dishonorable men out there, smugglers, bandits, privateers sailing for countries at war with England. We must not do anything hasty."

A long moment passed before she gathered the strength to ask the question needling her mind. "What is the plan?"

"Rest here for the night." He tossed the shell back into the sand. "Tomorrow, we'll search for freshwater and signs of settlers."

Until he said the words, Priscilla hadn't realized how thirsty she was. Suddenly, her tongue stuck to her mouth, parched from all the salt water she'd accidentally swallowed.

Could they still die of thirst? Of course they could. Not all these islands had freshwater. Hadn't she read such in one of her father's logs? "Shouldn't we look for settlers now? Perhaps they'd shelter us for the night?"

"The sun is about to drop below the horizon, and it will be dark." Tobias pointed to a grassy dune. "We need to move further up the beach, or the tide will reach us." He stood with a grunt.

"But, don't you think—?"

"We can barely move, much less scour an island for inhabitants."

Priscilla slowly raised to her feet like an old woman. Perhaps he was right.

They turned and stared at the small land mound—their refuge. It didn't seem like much. A long stretch of white beach encircled a rocky outcropping that rose into scraggly green shrubbery with an occasional palm tree waving its fronds in the brisk breeze. It looked scenic, as if she'd walked into one of the oil paintings hung in her father's study, but even more vivid in color. At the same time, it appeared rustic, secluded —deadly.

Her legs wobbled like a newborn colt's as they half walked, half crawled to the softer, dry sand closer inland.

Tobias dropped to his knees and picked shells and other sharp objects from where they'd lie. "It's not much, but sand will hold some of the day's heat to keep us warm most of the night. Tomorrow, we'll make a better plan."

Priscilla curled onto her side with her back facing Tobias, and he did the same. The breeze pelted her with sand, making her feel exposed and vulnerable. Despite her physical exhaustion, her mind worked overtime. "What sort of wild animals roam an island?"

"Nothing to fret about." He didn't shift to face her, merely let the wind carry his voice. "I'll be right here beside you."

Her muscles relaxed. *I'll be right here.* The sweetest words ever said.

Tobias yawned. "Get some rest, Priscilla. Lord knows we'll need it."

Her eyes widened. "Why? What are you expecting tomorrow?"

He didn't respond.

Whatever they did tomorrow couldn't be more challenging than what they'd endured over the last twenty-four hours, could it?

The sky morphed from blue to purple, and then black with stars in abundance. In between the crashing of waves, strange sounds of bugs and frogs littered the air. She held her breath and rolled to face Tobias's back. The sight of his form pushed away the rising waters of her fear, keeping it at bay.

She wasn't alone. Tobias had kept them alive. He would do so tomorrow, too, and once they haled a ship and arrived at St. Kitts, they'd have some grand tales to share. She had to hold onto hope, or else she would drown in despair.

Of course, anyone hearing those tales would know she'd been alone with a man for several days. There would be questions about her reputation. His life would go on, but hers would never be the same.

Unless he offered for her.

Marry into the Middleton family? Not unless her father held Tobias at gunpoint. How would she feel about a forced marriage to Tobias? He'd most certainly be a reluctant groom. She pictured him standing as captain of the *Trade Wind*, his face contorted in anger. *The Middleton name is a blight upon society.*

Then she remembered his face lined with concern after she forced her way above deck during the storm. Had his heart changed regarding her? Had he been concerned for her or feared for his men, believing she'd be in the way, putting them in danger? *I will not set the needs of a woman above my crew.* Yet, he'd saved her.

Her heart twisted between hope and despair.

Dear Lord, get me out of this mess.

CHAPTER 16

It pains me to relay the news, but a missive arrived from
Lieutenant Dalton of *The Trade Wind*. Your daughter and
Captain Prescott were washed overboard. I fear they are
lost to us. Please accept my deepest condolences.
~ *Letter from Captain Fuller to Admiral Middleton*

*T*obias awoke to sun warming his skin. The familiar
sound of ocean waves soothed him, but something
wasn't right. Memories rushed in, clouding his mind, invading
his peace like bolts of lightning veining through the sky. He
groaned. He'd lost his ship, he'd endangered his mission, and
every bone in his body ached from battling one of the worst sea
squalls he'd ever witnessed from a rowboat. One disaster after
another, and they all could be traced back to a single alluring yet
troubling individual.

Yesterday and the day before, he'd been acting on survival
instincts. He hadn't had time to breathe, much less consider
what had happened and the consequences of his actions. How
had he allowed a lone woman to ruin everything? The moment
he'd laid eyes on her, he'd known she would bring misfortune.

She was a Middleton. Trouble followed them like a plague. It was her fault he'd lost his ship, and therefore his mission. And if Britain lost its battle in Louisiana, he'd blame that on her too.

Tobias swatted at a pesky sand flea. His legs were dotted with red bumps where the fleas had made a meal of him. He rolled over to find Priscilla, the object of his problems, already awake. He was an early riser. Shouldn't she still be sleeping? Henry said most ladies attended balls until early hours and then slept until noon.

Of course, Priscilla would be contrary to his expectations. She sat in the sand, her knees drawn to her chest and her arms wrapped around her legs, staring at the sea. Wind whipped her golden strands of hair, flying them high like banners. If he weren't so riled, she would have made a fetching picture.

His stomach flipped, but he attributed it to hunger or to taking in too much seawater the day before. He'd hoped to get his bearings and start finding a source of water and food before she woke.

He stood and dusted sand from his hands, but it was a futile effort. Fine, sticky grains covered him. Sunlight glistened off the ocean waves. Thanks to the strong sun, by midday, all rainwater will have evaporated. He pushed to stand next to Priscilla.

She squinted at him but didn't rise. "It's beautiful in a wild, untamed sort of way, is it not?"

The ocean's aquamarine waters rose until they grew crystal clear with white caps dancing on top. They tumbled over one another in their haste to get to shore. Tobias recognized the mast of a sunken ship jutting near the reef's edge in the distance. Had there been any survivors? If there were, did they make it off the island, or would he run across their sun-bleached bones?

A large pelican landed upon the waterlogged crow's nest and stretched its wings before nestling down.

He grunted. There wasn't time to enjoy the view. His stomach rumbled, and when he tried to swallow, his parched throat scratched as if he'd drunk sand. There would be plenty of time to enjoy the scenery once their basic needs were met—if this small island even had the resources to meet them. "I'm going to find water."

"*W*ait for me." Priscilla jumped to her feet. "I'm coming with you."

He trolled the beach, searching for a way to maneuver through the island's scraggly underbrush. He heard Priscilla's footsteps squeaking in the sand. He turned around to tell her to stay put on the shore, but her expression silenced him. She marveled at the landscape with an expression of awe. He'd most likely held a similar look the first time he'd set eyes on the Caribbean's blue waters and its white-sand beaches. Over time from his travels, he'd grown accustomed to the splendor, but she had only heard about them.

"I've never seen the like." Her voice rose above the crashing waves.

He wasn't certain if she addressed him or merely spoke her thoughts out loud.

She tilted her head up. "I'm used to cloudy gray skies, but here it's so blue and the sun..."

Dark smudges underlined her eyes, and an all too familiar pang twisted his gut. He reminded himself that Anthony Middleton also had his good points and times when he'd been a decent chap, enough for Tobias to stick his neck out for him to help the man be promoted, but that was before Middleton revealed his true character.

Priscilla's expressive face and innocent wonder poked holes of doubt in his righteous anger. Had she merely been at the wrong place at the wrong time when the *Trade Wind* raised anchor—then again, hadn't Anthony lied, claiming something similar?

She shouldn't have come above deck, but she'd been terrified. No one could have faked such fear. And if he were truthful with himself, he'd broken his most fundamental rule, one he drilled into his men's minds from the first day they walked upon his decks—one hand for the ship, one hand for the crew. What had possessed him to take his hand off the rail? Why had he tended to Priscilla himself and not sent one of his shipmates?

He could try to blame her all he wanted, but reality bubbled to the surface, pushing him deeper into guilt until he drowned in the thick of it. He'd gotten himself into this mess.

He should have known better.

Now, he could only hope his crew would go on with the mission without him. Pray they succeeded where he could not. He wouldn't have the opportunity to help his country or prove himself in battle. One split-second decision had changed the course of his life. He'd lost his chance to become a hero like his father before him—to prove he deserved the support of those who'd provided for him as a boy.

His hand raked through his hair, which was stiff with salt. He must concentrate on keeping himself and Priscilla alive. *God is the God of second chances.* He'd provide another way for Tobias to live up to his father's legend.

Tobias had to believe it because, otherwise, he'd lose his purpose. He'd have failed his father and Lord Osterby, who'd paid for his commission, and that would devastate Tobias.

Focus on basic needs: water, food, shelter—in that order.

The storm would have dumped rainwater on the island. That would sustain them for the moment, but if they wanted to survive longer than a few days, they needed to find a way to store it.

"Is this a coconut?" Priscilla pointed to a hairy brown ball in the sand.

"Indeed."

"My brother brought one home once. He said you could eat the pulp inside."

Why must she keep reminding him of Anthony Middleton? "He's correct."

"Should I keep it then, for food?" She bent to pick it up.

"Not that one. It's been in the surf for a while and possibly even floated over from another island."

"Another island." The expression of wonderment returned. "I hadn't considered that."

"If we don't find another food source, we'll cut fresh ones down from the trees." He pointed to some ripe coconuts bunched in the center of palm branches.

"Do they taste like a nut or a fruit?"

He stopped. The shell would make a suitable container. Not only that, but coconut itself held water and food. Mayhap some sustenance would give them more energy. "How about we find out?"

"Truly?"

The only thing he didn't relish was expending energy climbing. He picked through scratchy grasses, vines, and palmetto leaves to the base of the nearest palm tree. He hugged the trunk with his arms and legs, alternating their support like an inchworm. Sweat broke out on his brow, but it became easier as he neared the top, for the tree curved at a forty-degree angle, and with his added weight, almost bent horizontally.

Priscilla blocked the sun with her hand, smiling as she squinted, and watched his climb. He stuffed down the impulse to impress her with his climbing skills and forced his gaze back to the coconuts. "Stay clear." He waved her away. "I don't want these to land on you."

She stepped back, and he removed a cutlass from his belt. More than ever, he wished he'd kept his sword. It would have come in handy. He sawed at the coconuts. One fell readily, the other he hacked until it plopped into the sand.

Priscilla collected them while he climbed down.

The coconut hull dulled his knife as he carved strips in each side and peeled off the fibrous cover, revealing a hard-shell underneath. He stabbed his blade into one of the three dark eyes of the protective cover and corkscrewed until it broke through to the pulp. He passed her the open shell and worked on his own.

Priscilla held the fruit between her palms, drew it to her nose, and sniffed.

"Go ahead and try a sip." He finished opening his, tipped it back, and drank. The sweet water, with its buttery aftertaste, soothed his parched throat and lips.

She sipped hers. "It tastes sort of like water, but sweet and woody." She drank more. "I didn't realize how thirsty I was."

"Saltwater will dry out a man." He cleared his throat. "Or woman."

She tapped the bottom to get every last drop.

He did the same, then found a rock to break a hole in the top of each so he could cut out a bit of pulp with his knife. "Greener coconuts contain more water, whereas the darker ones contain more oil."

"How do you know these things?"

He shrugged. "My men pick up tales in port or, in Raleigh's case, firsthand. He learned not to eat too many of the darker, more mature coconuts. He..." *Hit the head for two days.* Tobias cleared his throat. "Let's say he was indisposed." He held out a strip of white coconut for her.

She hesitated.

He chuckled. "Don't worry. This coconut was green."

She popped it into her mouth and chewed the fibrous insides. Her lips turned down. "It doesn't taste like the dried coconut Anthony brought home once."

"They add sugar to the dried stuff." He handed her more. "Eat up. It'll fill your stomach and revive your energy."

"I'd eat tree bark right now. I'm so famished." She stuffed another piece in her mouth.

Tobias understood her hunger. When was his last meal, the one where sneaky Pete interrupted their conversation? It seemed like forever ago. A companionable silence fell between them as they chewed their bites.

Priscilla peeked at him.

He offered her another slice of coconut on the end of his knife.

"Are we going to look for settlers?" She accepted the piece. Before he could answer, she launched into a diatribe. "I was thinking. If we started a big enough fire, the *Trade Wind* might still be within sight distance. They would see the smoke, and if we drew in the sand a big 'help,' the barrelman may spot it, and then they'd come for us."

"How do you plan to start this fire when everything is soaked by rain?" Why did he feel the need to cloud her optimism?

She licked her lips and stared at the coconut shell cupped in her palms. "I'm sorry."

"For what?" He winced at his harsh tone.

"You know." She bit her lower lip. "Putting us in this predicament."

"I thought we went over this already." He scratched his jaw with his thumb.

"But, you still seem angry."

Why did she have to ask so many questions to keep him talking? He exhaled a deep breath. "We don't need to get into this right now."

"But I need you to believe I truly am sorry. I never meant for any of this to happen." Her wide eyes reminded him of the turquoise water and pleaded with him for a sign of forgiveness. "If I could go back and change things, I would."

His hands tingled, longing to comfort her, but he didn't

know how. A curt nod of acknowledgment would have sufficed for his crew, but not Priscilla. Those wide blue eyes tugged at his heart as if ready to abscond with it entirely. "I know."

She perked up. "You do?" Her brow wrinkled. "But you're still angry at me."

The last part came out as a statement. "I'm frustrated is all." He held out his arms with the coconut in one hand, gesturing at the island. "All this is just a lot for one man to take."

Her chin lowered, and she nodded.

He pinched the bridge of his nose. How could he explain? This mission had been his chance to prove his worth. He'd hoped to show the same heroics as his father before him to win the battle for his country. He'd be hailed a war hero or die trying, and Lord Osterby's gamble to pay for Tobias's commission would have paid off. His lips parted several times to try to clarify his reasoning, but he abandoned each attempt.

Pricilla stroked the side of her coconut with her thumb. "When I was sinking and thought I couldn't swim anymore, one of the stories Miss Dodd read floated into my head. It helped me find the strength I didn't think I had."

"God does that." He cleared his throat. "I mean, He speaks to us through His word, bringing it to mind when we need it."

She lifted her head and peered at him with unblinking eyes. "You think God spoke to me?"

"Most likely."

They sat in silence. He allowed the conversation to die by devoting his full focus to making the most of his small meal until there were only a shell and a thin coat of pulp. Odd, but Priscilla didn't seem bothered by his ineptness at speaking, which set him a bit more at ease. It hadn't been the case with other ladies of his acquaintance. They stared at him as if he were the town idiot, which only increased the length in formulating what he wanted to say or caused him to stutter. To avoid feeling stupid, he kept conversations short and terse, not caring if he came across as rude or uninterested.

The sun had risen higher. If they wanted to collect water, then they needed to get going. Heat would soon be upon them. He rose and aided her to stand.

He wiped sweat already beading on his brow with the back of his hand. "Let's go inland to look for water."

"Do you know where you're going?" Her rosy skin accented her blue eyes, causing them to appear even brighter.

Obviously, he didn't know where he was going.

Priscilla followed on his heels. "I mean, do you know if it's safe? Are there poisonous creatures or plants? What about wild animals? I read about large lizard creatures from the African savannah who hold their bites like bulldogs."

"This isn't the savannah."

She followed him over the hot sand.

"I realize that, but I'm merely saying we may need to be cautious because we do not know what we might encounter." She paused and glanced down. "And we're barefoot."

He stopped where seagrass and scrub brush met the shore. "You can stay here if you're concerned." Would she be safe alone? "But it would be best if you stayed hidden until I bring water back." He pointed toward some rocks. "Rest behind that large rock and don't draw attention. I'll be back soon." He plunged into the undergrowth.

She chased after him. "I'll take my chances with you."

His jaw tightened at her lack of obedience, but perhaps it was best. She'd be safer where he could keep an eye on her. Spying a washed away section of brush, he picked his way up the natural path. The rocks dug into his feet, which had softened from soaking in the ocean's saltwater. He refused to acknowledge the pain.

"Do you see any signs of people?" He heard her soft footfalls crunching on dried leaves as she picked her way along the path.

"No." He glanced back to check on her.

"Could there be native islanders living here?" She winced and stepped off what must have been a sharp rock.

"Not likely." He wracked his brain for a way to protect her tender feet, but other than carrying her on his back, which would be highly improper, he had no solutions.

"You're not a man of many words, are you?"

He peered up at the blue sky and passing clouds. Tobias found it challenging to understand the female mind, and now he was stuck on an island with one. The good Lord had a sense of humor. He picked his way over some larger rocks and turned to offer her a hand. "No."

She placed her slender hand in his and held her skirts in the other. "I tend to ramble a bit when I'm nervous."

Without doubt.

Maybe he was paying penance for his failure to keep Annie alive. Was this a test? Could he redeem himself by keeping Priscilla alive? He spied an ample leafed frond holding water and tested it with his finger to make certain it was safe. "Would you care for the first drink?"

She leaned back. "You may do the honors."

He dipped and poured the water into his mouth. The collected liquid ran down his throat, refreshing him with its mineral taste and clearing residual coconut pulp. Nothing in his memory tasted better. He motioned her forward. "Tilt your head back and open your mouth."

"It's safe to drink?" Priscilla studied his face.

His lips twitched. "Safer than not drinking."

She flashed a dimple. "Well, when you put it that way..." She stepped forward and opened her mouth.

He had her bend her knees as he cupped the leaf for her. The water rushed down over her lips, filling her mouth. A drop traced the slender curve of her throat. She closed her eyes and moaned a sweet sound of pure ecstasy.

His gut tightened.

"That's the best water I've ever tasted."

He shook his head to clear it. *She's a Middleton.* "You're merely dehydrated." He focused on the task, holding his coconut shell out and funneling trapped water off the broad leaves into the container. She did the same with her coconut, all the while commenting on the plants, leaves, and flowers and asking questions, most of which he didn't know the answers to.

They hiked a path, collecting what water they could find in their coconut shells.

All seemed peaceful when she yelped and grabbed his sleeve. "What is that?"

He followed her gaze to a tiny green lizard blending into a leaf.

"It's a gecko. They're harmless, but you'll find them everywhere, so get used to them."

She nodded, and they continued until they stood upon a rocky clearing with a break in the canopy of scrub trees. From the height to which they'd climbed, the vast ocean spread out before them. In the distance rested another isle similar in size to this one. He'd hoped to see the smoke of a sugar cane boiling house or boats docked along the shore, but there was nothing, just lush green vegetation.

Priscilla gasped beside him, hushing to a reverent whisper, "I've never seen such a view."

He didn't reply. He'd appreciate the beauty around him more once they had food and shelter.

"Lottie wrote about the beauty of St. Kitts. Her descriptions were lovely, but I had no idea." A smile transformed her face as if radiating light like the sun.

The wholesomeness of her smile riveted Tobias, as did the delicate curve of her cheeks and slope of her nose—soft and dainty. So different compared to the rough, coarse men who'd always surrounded him.

Her smile faded as her eyes scanned the rest of the surroundings. "Shouldn't there be sugar cane fields or fisherman—some sort of settlement?"

He'd already drawn the same conclusion. So much for any help or an easy rescue. "It looks deserted." He scratched the stubble on his jaw, not yet used to being unshaven. "We won't know for certain until we've explored a bit more." However, he didn't hold out much hope. There weren't any paths or roads cutting through the underbrush. However, a chance to get a lay of the island before determining who was friend or foe could be a blessing.

She turned her head toward him. "How far do you think that island is?"

He quickly shifted his gaze and estimated twenty-five miles or so. "Far. Too far for us to swim." They'd swum not even a quarter of that distance yesterday, and the other island was also against the current. Unless they had a boat or grew gills, they wouldn't make it.

"Let's keep going and see what else the island has to offer?" They needed water and food if they were to survive on their own.

On the other side of the peak, the wind was considerable. Fewer trees grew, and the ones that did were wider than they were long and had contorted to the wind—their branches growing to one side. Tall grasses filled in between the trees, waving in unity with the direction of the gusts. They picked their way along a natural path cut from the heavy storm's running water. He scanned the terrain and listened for running water, but found nothing, not even a tiny creek or a small puddle. His shoulders slumped, but he hitched them back up and pressed on.

Dry sticks snapped underfoot, and loose fronds sliced their tender skin. Thorny vines woven amid the rocks compounded their injuries, but they had little choice but to limp on.

He should have forced her to stay on the beach, where she couldn't get injured, but he had no idea if there were any locals, natives, or fishermen who could drag her off, never to be seen again.

The ripping of fabric sliced the air. Priscilla stopped, and her breath hitched. He turned to see that her dress had caught on a spiny branch from a tangled bush.

"Let me." He set down their coconuts careful not to spill the precious water and pieced her skirt from the gnarly limb. The challenge of charting through rough and rustic terrain barefoot significantly slowed their progress. He shaded his eyes. The sun had already passed its highest point and started its slow descent.

"Thank you." She bobbed a small curtsy. "If I had known I was going to be exploring island terrain, I would have worn a sturdier gown." She held her hand to shield her eyes from the sun. "And boots."

He grunted with a nod before peering at his own bare feet. "Little good wearing my boots did for me."

Grass rustled, and a shadow shifted in his periphery. He grabbed Priscilla's hand and tugged her to a crouched position.

She clutched his arm. "What did you see?"

He put a finger to his lips and scanned the surrounding area, keeping his ears honed for any sound. Hair on the back of his neck rose, and his gut sensed they were being watched. He wasn't sure how long they squatted eye level with the tall grass, but the sound of Priscilla's soft breathing near his ear and the heat of her body so close to his became a distraction. He slowly stood, his knees groaning in protest.

Her eyes questioned him.

"I thought I saw something, but it was only my imagination."

Her lips quivered, and a smile formed.

He lifted an eyebrow.

She giggled and waved away his question. "I'm happy to know I'm not the only one hallucinating."

He shrugged, once again baffled by the female mind. His intuition had saved him and his men countless times. It wasn't something to laugh at.

The path widened, and she casually slid her hand around his arm. Tobias glanced at her slender fingers, curving around the inside of his bicep, and endeavored to ignore the strange sensation.

By the time they approached the summit, sweat dripped down the curve of his spine, and both of their feet were bleeding. He broke off a prolonged, straight limb from a nearby tree and clambered to the highest point. Wind blew in great gusts, pasting his shirt to his body. He bent down and hoisted Priscilla up the last steep incline. Her hair whipped in the stiff gale, stinging his exposed skin on his neck and face. She captured it with her hand, holding tight. Only a few loose tendrils escaped.

Tobias shaded his eyes with his arm and turned in a slow circle, searching the horizon for any sea vessels. Nothing. He'd hoped they'd be on the edge of a trade route or shipping channel, where ships would pass frequently, but the blue sky was separated only by a deeper ocean blue. There wasn't the white of a sail anywhere in sight. Unless the ships were hiding behind the other lone island, there was nothing to see, not even the previous storm's lingering clouds. Their rescue wouldn't be as easy as convincing a fisherman to charter them a trip. He rotated back the other way, examining the island's terrain for resources. They'd landed on the island on a curved stretch of beach sheltered by a reef. The isle's left side sloped sharply into the sea, and a rocky ledge curved back into a lagoon filled with flamingos. At least something was in their favor.

He yelled over the wind. "I found where we can get food other than coconuts."

Priscilla followed his line of vision to where he pointed. The wind curled the hem of her gown about his ankles.

"Those birds eat shrimp." He pointed to the pink dots below.

"We'll probably even find some clams." Turning on a forty-five-degree angle, he waved his hand over a flat outcrop of rock. "This is a good place to set up camp. The wind would protect us from mosquitoes"—he scratched a bite on his arm— "and there won't be any biting midges or sand flies. After we build a shelter, I can work on starting a fire where those rocks block some of the wind. There's one thing we can do now." He untucked his shirt from his trousers.

She stared at him, her thin eyebrows knitted together. "What are you doing?"

"I'm making a flag."

"To signal the *Trade Wind* or a fishing vessel?"

Or alert pirates or privateers to their location, but what other alternative did they have? "There is a chance that the fleet will pass, but I wouldn't get too hopeful." He tucked the stick under his arm to free both of his hands. "This flag is to claim the island for England if it hasn't been already." He gripped his shirttail.

"Wait." She bent down. "That won't be enough fabric." She grabbed the partial tear in her petticoat and pulled.

"You don't have to—" But it was too late. A section of her underskirt tore.

The hem wouldn't give as readily.

"Here, allow me." He slit the fabric with a searing rip and spread the not quite rectangular material on the rock. With his knife, he tore four strips and pinned them under his knee to keep them from blowing away. His fingers made quick work of tying the largest piece to the end of the stick. The opposite end, he plunged into a cracked spot between two boulders. "It may not be the Union Jack, but I claim this isle for England."

The stick didn't stand perfectly straight, but it was close enough. His chest swelled as they admired their creation.

She shifted her weight and winced.

He pointed to the ground. "Sit down."

"Whatever for?" Despite her protest, she sat anyway, folding her legs under her skirt.

Must she always question his commands? He grabbed a strip of cloth. "Let me see your foot."

"But..." Her toes peeked out from under the hem.

"I'm going to apply a bandage to those cuts."

She blushed and slid the rest of her foot out. He tied the strap around the ball of her slender foot, ignoring the intimacy of the moment. She was his responsibility. He couldn't let her wounds become infected. He knotted the bandage before proceeding with her other and his own feet.

The sun passed behind some low hanging clouds.

"We should head back before it gets dark. I'd prefer the sand over hard rock until the shelters are built." Tobias descended the rocky landing, grunting as one foot slipped on dusty pebbles. He regained his balance, but sharp rocks stung his feet, even bandaged. Ignoring the pain, he reached back to aid her descent.

She leaned on him to ease her step, and he breathed in the scent of saltwater mixed with sunshine.

He cleared his throat. "We can explore the cay for food tomorrow and build a shelter. Tonight, we once again dine on coconut." How long would the coconuts last them? A sunny blue sky was great weather for at sea, but how frequently did it rain here? There may be other food sources, but if it didn't often rain, coconuts could be their only source of water.

Priscilla placed a hand on her flat stomach and nodded.

Carefully they retraced their steps, briefly stopping to retrieve the coconut shells they used to store the water and for Tobias to harvest another coconut for each of them. They sat in the shade under a bed of palm tree fronds to eat the fibrous pulp.

A gecko zig-zagged its way through the underbrush and raised its head above a frond to peek at them.

Priscilla sipped water from her coconut. "Those tiny lizards are almost cute in a strange sort of way."

"A lizard can be caught in the hand, yet it is found in king's palaces." He chewed on a bite of pulp. "Proverbs."

"You know the Bible well. Do you read from it often?"

"Daily since September twenty-fifth, 1807, until yesterday."

She licked her rosy lips, and those intriguing dimples winked at him. "September twenty-fifth must have been a significant date for you to recall it."

He followed the gecko's movements as it slipped between the fronds. "It was the day I asked God to take the helm."

"Did He?" She leaned in and searched his face. "Take the helm?"

"Most definitely."

"How can you tell?"

What could he say to explain his transformation? Early in his commission, whenever he'd returned on leave to his stepfather's house, he'd endured his stepfather's ridicule. Tobias's mother had pleaded with him to make peace, never once defending her oldest son. Over time, his visits became fewer and farther between until he declined any leave and stayed aboard ship.

Learning God accepted him when his own family had forsaken him changed his despair to hope. How could he describe the thrill of having meaning, not merely doing one's duty, but working with purpose? His outward change might have appeared slight, but inwardly his life was restored. Words couldn't suffice. "I felt different."

"Like how? Is it a tingle? Or a clarity of mind?"

Of course, Priscilla would want details. He scratched his jaw with his thumb. "It's more of a heart change. There's hope, and life is no longer centered around our selfish motives. Priorities realign."

"Ow." She slapped at a mosquito on her shoulder.

He stood, grateful for the distraction so he didn't have to continue to formulate words. He aided her to stand. "We better keep moving and finish our supper later." He held back a branch so she could safely pass. "In the islands, mosquitos will carry you away if you're not careful. It's best to sleep near the shore where the breeze is stronger."

Sunset burnished the sky into bright reds, pinks, and oranges. He often caught her stopping and staring at the brilliant display. She'd surprised him that day. Instead of sitting on the beach fretting about their situation, she'd explored with him. Never once had she complained about the long hike or the rough ground that must have been painful to her delicate feet. And then she'd torn her petticoat to assemble a flag. Anthony claimed women cared more for their wardrobe than their husbands or siblings, but Priscilla didn't give him that impression. He found himself relaxing around her.

"When we get back," he said, "we'll need to soak our feet in the ocean. Water will clean the wounds, and salt will help them to heal faster." The little light left didn't afford him time to build them shelter. They'd have to make due sleeping in the open air on the beach.

As a cadet, he'd slept on a beach numerous times. When the ship grew too hot to slumber below deck, he'd take his bedding to the beach and hunker down under the stars. One evening, after the crew imbibed on too much rum and grew rowdy, Tobias and his closest mate, Adam, camped on shore. That night in the throes of a nightmare, Adam's sleep-uttered protests revealed that he wasn't who he'd claimed. Adam was actually Annie. Tobias had been so furious that she lied to him that he didn't speak to her the following morning as they boarded, nor a couple of hours later when the ship sailed. How could she have withheld her true identity after he'd told her everything about his awful stepfather, his mother tossing him aside for a new family, the pressure of needing to sacrifice himself for his country as his father had before him?

He rubbed his eyes to wipe away the pain of his memories. If only he'd asked her why she hadn't told him earlier or asked her forgiveness for ignoring her. If only he'd said something... said anything. His chest constricted. A week later, they'd fished her body out of the ocean—her pale face, dripping with water, staring at him with unseeing eyes.

If he couldn't keep Annie alive, how was he supposed to protect Priscilla?

CHAPTER 17

We'll catch their "Old Hickory" in a punishing crossfire
while our large contingent shall charge and crush the
American line.

~ Letter from Lieutenant General Pakenham to Admiral Sims

A strange cry stirred Tobias to consciousness.

Priscilla stumbled to her feet like a drunken sailor.
Moonlight reflected off her pale face and the wild glint in her
terrified eyes. "Help me," she whispered through cracked lips.

He leapt to his feet with his cutlass ready to fight off the
unknown attacker. His eyes scanned the beach, but all seemed
still except for the rolling tide. "What is it? What's the matter?"
He gripped her arm, but she yanked it away.

"No. I won't go with you." She slammed her heel on his foot
and turned to flee. She proceeded only a few steps, glancing one
direction and then the other. Her face crumpled. She gripped
the sides of her head and half screamed, half cried. "Where are
you. I can't find you." She sank to her knees and rocked back
and forth.

Tobias put away his knife and cautiously approached her from the side. She must have sleepwalked through a nightmare. Annie, too, had had similar dreams. "Priscilla," he softly called as he maneuvered to face her.

Her chest heaved with each breath. Her irises darted in nervous saccades, occasionally landing on him but not seeing.

He cupped her face between his hands. "Priscilla, look at me." He stared into her glazed eyes. "You're fine. I'm here."

She exhaled a whimper. "I can't find them. I don't know where they are." Her eyes glistened in the moonlight.

"Who?"

She blinked, and tears dropped over her cheeks, dripping onto his wrists. "Papa and Mama. I was following the balloon, and now they're gone."

He shook his head at her gibberish. "You're here with me—Tobias. You're safe."

A vertical crease formed as her eyebrows pushed up and together. She blinked again.

He stroked her cheek with his thumb. "Your parents are in England, and we're in the Caribbean. Remember? You boarded my ship, thinking it under your brother's command. We were washed overboard." He examined her eyes in the pale blue light for any signs of recognition and found none. "Now, you're stuck on an island with a grumpy captain you don't particularly care for."

She frowned, and her eyes cleared. "Tobias?"

He chuckled. Now she recognized him.

"Why are you awake? What's the matter?"

"You were having a nightmare."

Her curious expression left. "Was I...?" She tugged on her bottom lip with her teeth and lowered her chin. "What did I do?"

He released her and lowered to a seated position on the sand. He tugged on her wrist to encourage her to sit also.

She sank next to him. Her knee brushed his thigh, but she quickly repositioned.

"You were dreaming, searching for someone... your parents?"

"Oh." She plucked at the small tear in the hem of her gown.

"Would you like to tell me what happened?"

She wrapped her arms about her midsection as if chilled, and he wished he had his jacket to offer her, but it was left behind on the dinghy.

"I believe I was four or five, barely out of leading-strings." Her throat convulsed as she swallowed. "Everyone had gathered at Hyde Park for a hot air balloon launch. I can still remember the crowd—the women forming a wall of parasols clinging to men dressed in dark clothes like the trunks of trees. All eyes were fixated on the balloon as it inflated into a massive oval, blocking out the sun. At first, I was awestruck, but the preparations outlasted my attention." She laughed, but it rang hollow.

"It was all a mistake." A dimple flashed in one cheek. "I moved for a better view and got turned around. I tried to follow the balloon back to locate my parents. They had stood close to where it had first lifted." She heaved a sigh. "It could have been only a few minutes or several hours before I realized the balloon was drifting. Meanwhile, the crowd had thinned, and I'd somehow left the park." She rubbed her arms.

He placed a hand over hers and squeezed it. "I can imagine how frightened you must have been."

"I've never been so scared in all my life. A scraggly old man with a lazy eye and a mole on his cheek snatched my hand and asked me where my father was. I told him I didn't know. He yanked me down a back alley, covering my mouth with his hand to muffle my screams. I twisted and stomped on his foot to get away, but he cursed me with words I'd only heard slip from Anthony's mouth and tightened his grip."

Tobias resisted the urge to pull her into his arms and comfort her.

"He locked me in a cellar. I remember seeing dust fall in the dim light of a small window beyond my reach as his heavy footsteps above shook it loose."

He tensed, not liking the direction her tale was going.

"I sat there crying on the dirt floor amid a bunch of old dusty furniture and clutter. My whole body shook, scared of what he planned to do to me, when one of his footfalls rattled a pane of glass. The sill had come loose from the window and was falling into the cellar. I thought I might be able to wiggle through, but the footsteps above stopped, and moments later, the cellar doors flew open. The scraggly man tossed back the last of his drink and threw the empty bottle over his shoulder before coming in and locking the cellar door behind him."

She closed her eyes as if to gather the strength to continue.

Tobias shifted closer to her side.

"I squeezed between his food storage shelving and the stone wall. I scraped my cheek against the rough stone and screamed as his hand reached in after me. His body blocked all the light, and I waited for his fingers to grip my arm and haul me out. I can still feel the air of his flailing hand."

Her shiver vibrated through his being.

"Pulling back, he cursed me, my father, and my father's mother for bearing him. He shook the shelves and tried to pull them away but couldn't. After what felt like hours, he left for the upstairs, promising to return after retrieving a tool. As soon as he locked the cellar door, I scrambled out from behind the shelf, stacked up boxes under the window, and climbed. I had to tug with all my might on that cellar window. I remember heaving, thinking it would never budge. But then it did, smashing on the dirt floor and shattering the glass. I poked my head out as the heavy footsteps thundered across the upstairs floorboards.

Fortunately, the window exited the opposite side of the cellar door. I wriggled out before he could fit the key into the door lock. I ran back in the direction of the park, knowing I would be safer if I found people."

Her gaze lowered, and she inhaled a deep breath. "I've struggled with the fear of being alone ever since."

Guilt slapped him. "That's why you defied my order to stay away from my men. It's why I kept finding you with them in the crew room." He rubbed his chin. "It's why you came above deck during the storm."

She pinched her lips and blinked as if she might cry.

"I didn't understand." Tobias wrapped his arm around her in an awkward side embrace. "I'm sorry."

Priscilla didn't pull away. Instead, she leaned her head upon his shoulder.

His breathing shallowed, expecting her to jerk away. She was merely seeking comfort from her nightmare. Nothing more. When she didn't pull away, he relaxed and stroked her hair, enjoying the smooth, silky feeling under his calloused hands. "Did someone help you?"

Her head rubbed against his shoulder as she nodded. "I spied a gentleman helping a lady into a carriage. I could hear the scraggly man chasing after me. I screamed and pounded on the carriage door. When they opened it, the scraggly man turned and darted back the way he'd come. The young woman inside recognized me. She wiped my tears and the blood on my cheek with her handkerchief and offered to take me to my parents' townhouse."

"You were fortunate to happen upon them."

"I realize that now, but I can remember shaking the entire ride. The woman smiled and asked me questions, I think to calm me, but my teeth were chattering so badly, I could barely get a word out."

He understood more than she knew. His heart clenched for the slip of a girl.

"I ran up the front steps and through the door and into the parlor and fell into my mother's skirts. She had the maid clean me up and tell the story to Papa once he returned from searching for me. When I told Papa what happened, he grew eerily still, and his expression turned to stone. His words were terse and carefully controlled as he questioned me about the man's looks and location. I tried to recall as much as I could, but I kept crying. I could tell Papa was furious and frustrated with me. Something changed in him after that."

A long moment passed as they listened to the crashing waves, lost in their thoughts.

He heard the pain in her voice at her father's reaction and longed to console her but didn't know how. After the initial shock of Annie's death, he'd behaved similarly, battling his anger by withdrawing into himself. It was the only way he could keep from falling apart.

Priscilla broke the silence first. "Do you believe I'm crazed? Anthony told me not to tell a soul about my episodes, or I'd be admitted to Bedlam."

"You're not mad."

She relaxed against him as if grateful for his declaration. "I asked you about reading the Bible because Miss Dodd had started reading a chapter each night before bed. It helped me keep my fears at bay and fall asleep."

"Would it help if I recounted a story I know from the Bible?" Seeking God's word had helped him come to terms after Annie's death. Maybe it could help Priscilla.

"Yes, please." She nodded against his shoulder.

"There was once a boy named David, the youngest of seven brothers, who tended sheep for his father. One day, the prophet Samuel came to anoint the next king. All of the brothers lined up, but David wasn't even called in from the fields."

"Why wasn't he?" She stiffened, and he smiled at her reaction to injustice.

"He could have been forgotten, not believed to be worthy as the youngest son, or mayhap the sheep couldn't be left." He shrugged. "I truly don't know, but Samuel stood in front of each son and asked God if he was the anointed one, and God answered no over and over."

She snuggled until her cheek rested against the flat part of his chest.

He leaned back into the sand, and she nestled in the crook of his arm. The stars above shined bright in the night sky. "Samuel asked David's father, Jesse, if he had any more sons, and David was called in from the field. The Lord said, 'Rise and anoint him for he is the one.'" Tobias stroked her arm with his thumb. "It's a great example of how God often uses someone unexpected to accomplish His will, and that He doesn't forget his children."

He felt her cheeks round into a smile through the thin material of his sleeve.

Tobias relayed more of David's story. When he reached the part where he defeated the giant Goliath, Priscilla's breathing became even, her head heavy against his chest. He paused, thinking she'd fallen asleep, and closed his own eyes.

"Tobias?"

His heavy lids flicked open. "Hmm?"

"I gave you every reason to be grumpy."

He smiled. "That you did."

"I know we got off to a poor start, but you've shown me exceptional kindness." Wind blew her hair so that it tickled his chin. "And patience." She tucked loose strands behind her ear and folded her hands under her cheek. "What I'm trying to say is..." She sighed, and her voice softened to a whisper. "If I have to be stuck on an island, then I'm glad to be stuck with you."

Tobias swallowed. Could she feel his heart pounding under those delicate fingers? He fumbled for the right words to say. *I, too, hold you in high regard?* No, that wasn't right. Or should he discourage such thoughts? Even if they did survive the island, she was a woman afraid of being alone, and he was a captain at sea for years at a time, one whose next voyage could be his last. Surf rumbled in the distance, and frogs croaked and peeped behind them.

A long moment passed, she nestled against his shoulder. "You may continue the story."

He grunted at her command. He'd grown tired of explaining how, as captain, he should be the one issuing orders. "David moved into the palace to play the harp for King Saul, waiting for God's timing."

Her chest rose and fell like the motion of a calm sea, a sure sign she'd fallen asleep.

It could be their strange circumstance, but from his understanding of Henry's tales, women sought comfort from men they've started to fancy. Could that be the case? Did he want the possibility? He'd never considered courting. Traveling sea captains made for terrible husbands. He'd seen the effect on his mother.

Her fingers twitched—one hand sliding over his thudding heart.

He was beginning to care for her, also—a little too much.

◇

*P*riscilla woke at first light, horrified to find herself snuggled against Tobias's side. *Egad.* What must he think of her? Only wanton women curled up next to a man who was not their husband. She lifted her head. Would Tobias understand she'd been distraught? One would think exceptions would be permitted for such extenuating circumstances. A stirring tingled her stomach as she peeked at his profile, softened in sleep.

She shifted her weight, careful not to wake him as she stood and stepped downwind to avoid shaking sand on him. Warm sunlight caressed her face, and she rubbed her eyes with a big silent yawn. By noon, the rays would burn her fair skin. She squinted, and her cheeks ached. Already she'd seen too much sun. If only she had her straw bonnet, the one with silk flowers sewn with a wide ribbon. She scraped her hair back and held it with one hand so that the breeze wouldn't blow it in her face. What if the grass she'd seen yesterday could be woven into a hat of some sort? She had no idea how to go about such a task, but it couldn't hurt to try.

Bug bites on her legs screamed to be itched—blasted sand flies.

She needed to make herself useful. Tobias had done so much for her. She needed to start helping instead of hindering. She straightened and studied his sleeping form. He lay on his back, using his arm as a pillow. A shadow of a beard shaded the lower half of his rugged face, yet his features, relaxed in sleep, held a boyishness to them. He was a handsome man when he wasn't scowling. His nose was narrow, his jaw square. She hadn't noticed the scar on his chin, but it stood out in a stark white line against the dark new growth of his beard. The wind tussled his thick hair as his husky voice had soothed her ruffled nerves during the night.

Now he knew the silliness of her fears. Was he only being kind when he said he didn't think her mad? It seemed unlikely for a man who believed her bound for Bedlam to hold her and recite Bible stories until she fell asleep.

However, she'd been wrong about men before. An image of Mr. Goulart popped into her memory. What was to be trusted—words or actions? She shook her head to clear it, only to recall Anthony stealing a British ship to rendezvous with Lottie. She must discover the truth from Lottie, which meant she needed to survive and be rescued, and for that, she needed to be useful.

Perhaps she could find some shells that could be sharpened to cut reeds or more coconuts. Her stomach growled, thinking of food. Tobias had to be starving. A man of his size needed more than coconuts to survive. The coconut shells they'd eaten yesterday rested in the sand a few yards away. Perhaps, she could use one of those strings as a hair tie. Cool sand slid between her toes as she padded over.

A couple of unopened coconuts rested behind the ones they'd eaten. Had Tobias climbed up and retrieved more while she slept, or had she not noticed him tucking a few away? At least they had something to break their fast. She pulled a few brown strings from the husk, braided them into a tiny rope, and used it to tie back her hair.

Keeping Tobias's form in her periphery, she explored the beach. How could she be helpful? Sand crabs scuttled and darted into their holes. Later today, Tobias said they'd explore the lagoon for clams and fish. Perhaps she could help him find the creatures. She'd seen clam before, but only in a sauce. How did one spot one of those tiny, squishy blobs? Her stomach turned. There must be something else she could do to help.

In the Bible story Tobias had told last night, Samuel had prayed for God to show him the next king. Mayhap she just needed to pray? Yes, but Samuel was a prophet. Didn't they get special treatment? The husky timbre of Tobias's voice from the previous night echoed in her mind. *God often uses someone unexpected to accomplish His will.*

She paused in her walk, clasped her hands, and lifted her eyes to the horizon. "Um, heavenly Father"—Miss Dodd often kneeled to pray, so she quickly dropped to the sand—"I want to thank you again for rescuing us and for not leaving me all alone. If you could please continue to help us. I want to be useful, but I don't know how to find food or build a shelter. Could you show me or perhaps send someone to find us?" She squinted at the bright sun. "I guess that's all... Wait—if you could also help me learn the truth about why Anthony lost command of his ship, and if I said anything detrimental to hurt my country or my family the night of the masquerade." The knot in her stomach tightened. "I don't want to believe the worst." She started to rise but hesitated, adding, "And please don't let Tobias believe I have a few attics to let after last night's incident."

How embarrassing he'd witnessed her fear and listened to her childish story of being left in Hyde Park. Although he denied it, he must believe her to be nicked in the nob for still reliving that fear after all these years. Her shoulders sagged. A ninnyhammer was better than a traitor. She shook off the thought. The night of the Lemoore party seemed eons ago, and what she'd revealed so inconsequential compared to what she and Tobias had recently undergone.

"God, I'm a mess." She shifted from her knees to her bottom and wrapped her arms around her legs. "I try to pretend I'm fine, but I'm not." She dropped her forehead. "I'm scared. I hate being afraid, but it blinds me to the point I can't reason. If I ever get off this island, they'll surely lock me up in a ward." She peered at the horizon. "This time, I didn't merely endanger myself. I endangered Tobias. He could have died out there in the deep waters, and it would have been my fault. He still could. I don't know how to survive on an island. I'm lost, God. I need you. I've made a muck of things." Something tickled her toes, and she opened her eyes to find a sand flea crawling on her foot. She shook it off.

The sun rose above a thin strip of clouds, fanning its rays across the sky. Her heart pounded in her chest, not from fear but wonder. The vast ocean spread before her, deeper and wider than she could fathom. Compared to its immensity, she felt as small and insignificant as a grain of sand. No one would look for her, and even if they did, no one could find her.

A ray of sunlight glinted off a wave and lit upon her as if saying, *I know exactly where you are.*

Tears sprung to her eyes. She remembered the words Tobias whispered lying on the overturned dinghy.

Who hath gathered the wind in His fists? Who hath bound the waters in His garment? Who hath established all the ends of the earth? What is His name, and what is His son's name?

Priscilla whispered his name on a ragged breath. *Jesus.*

Peace settled in her, and her tears subsided. A gull glided over the waves soaring on wind, enjoying its freedom, and she couldn't keep from smiling. "Jesus." She said His name a little louder.

Was God trying to tell her something? Didn't Tobias say God spoke in various ways? Could that be how he communicated with her, through His Word and the wonder of nature?

She rose and inhaled a deep breath, absorbing the beauty before her. She missed London, the comforts of home, the thrill of attending crowded dances and balls, the delight of meeting people, but there was freedom in not having to pretend her fears didn't exist.

She chuckled. Here, she was the crowd.

Poor Miss Dodd, now a lone female on a ship. Was she worried sick about her charge or presuming they'd met their demise and mourning her lost soul? How was the crew faring without their leader? Would they truly continue their mission without stopping to locate their captain? Would anyone come to Tobias's rescue? She swallowed the turbulent swirl of her thoughts and forced her mind to concentrate on being grateful to be alive.

She gathered stones, spelling H-E-L-P on the shore. In the process, a lump on the beach caught her attention. She dusted her hands and strolled toward it, keeping an eye out for useful shells. Occasionally, she peered back to make certain Tobias was still there. Seagulls scurried, their jeering cries announcing their displeasure as she neared the object. A dead turtle had washed up on the beach. Its flesh eaten, only the sun-bleached shell and bones remained. Priscilla gasped and covered her nose and mouth with her hand. She turned her head and averted her eyes, hoping it wasn't the same graceful creature she'd seen glide by under the waves the day they'd swum to the island.

The carcass could have been hers washing ashore if Tobias hadn't dived under and saved her, or if God hadn't intervened and saved them both. Life was short. She couldn't count on tomorrow. More than ever, she understood the reality of it all.

Should she bury the creature in the sand?

She walked around the hard shell, admiring its unique composition. God designed everything in the islands with unique beauty. It seemed a waste to bury such a beautiful object. Could it be useful? The shell would make a nice bowl or a way to collect water when it rains. She peered heavenward, simultaneously asking for permission and forgiveness. It was already dead, and they weren't. Not yet.

She needed to be resourceful.

"Priscilla."

Tobias stood on the shore with his hands cupped around his lips.

She raised an arm and waved.

He rubbed his lower jaw, and she could just make out the shake of his head before he jogged to her.

She frowned at the turtle carcass. "Tobias most definitely thinks me half-crazed if not stark raving mad."

His white shirt billowed in the wind.

Her cheeks heated, remembering how she'd melted into the comfort of those strong arms and fallen asleep.

"Why didn't you wake me?" His stern gaze let her know his question was a command.

She hugged her middle and pushed a bit of sand into a pile with her toe. "The sun woke me early. You appeared so peaceful that I didn't have the heart to wake you. I had some things to mull over, and I had no idea you'd want to be woken." She dared to glance up only to be ensnared by his stormy gray eyes, demanding the truth. She sucked in a breath to gather her courage. "I was worried you'd think"—she turned to face the waves—"that you're stuck on a deserted island with a madwoman."

"Priscilla."

"You have every right to think that way."

He stepped closer.

His nearness charged the air like static, but she didn't turn. "You risked your life, your mission—" Her voice cracked.

"Priscilla—"

"I didn't deserve it. I'd been a handful, disobeying your orders and risking injury to your crew." She blinked away tears. "I promise I'll find a way to be helpful. I will make it up to you."

"Look at me." His words were gentle but rang with authority. He turned her to face him. "I've forgiven you."

She heard his words, but she couldn't believe them. Why would he forgive her after what she did? "When I return to London, I will speak to my Papa. He'll…"

He lifted his eyebrows, and his sharp glare silenced her. "You'll do no such thing. I will earn my honor by my deeds." His hands cupped her face. "I need you to listen carefully." His eyes darkened. "Indeed, you have been a handful, and you need a good lesson in trusting authority, but I was captain, and I was responsible for your safety. You are not solely to blame for our situation. I forgave you before we reached this island, but last night helped me better understand the situation. I witnessed firsthand the fear you've been hiding."

He leaned in until their foreheads almost touched. "You are not alone. I will not leave you."

"Why?" Words pressed through her lips before she could stop them. All her life, she'd heard, *not now, Priscilla, run along, I'm busy,* or *I have to go now. Maybe upon my return.*

A weak smile twisted the corners of Tobias's mouth. "Because God hasn't forsaken me."

Her breath caught. *Who hath established all the ends of the earth?* God had a plan. He brought her and Tobias together for a reason. She wasn't alone.

Tobias's smile grew, and his gaze flicked askance. "What have you found here?"

He stepped back, and her body, deprived of his closeness, craved more.

"It's a dead sea turtle." She crouched and reverently touched the grooved shell. "I thought it might make a good tray or bowl to carry things."

"Splendid idea." He rested on his haunches and examined the dead animal.

"Truly?" Her insides fluttered. Maybe she could serve a purpose.

He nodded and removed his cutlass from its sheath. He used it to cut and wedge the shell from the turtle's bones. He made short work of the task but needed Priscilla's help to pry it away. As the top gave way from the bottom with a loud crack, she reeled back, stumbling in the sand until she landed on her backside.

"Careful." He aided her up. "Look through the bones for anything else that might be useful as tools."

While he washed off the turtle shell and his knife in the waves, she broke off a few bones to serve as needles. He held out their new container, just a bit smaller than a bread basket, and she placed the small bones and other seashells that might come in handy inside the center.

Back at their camp, Tobias dropped the shell and peered at the tree line. "Let me find some coconuts to break our fast."

She pointed to the uncut coconuts she'd found this morning. "We already have some. Did you not cut extra yesterday?"

He peered down at the food. "Humph." He ran a hand over

his face. "I don't remember collecting more." He squatted and wiped off his knife. "Or maybe instead of sleepwalking, I sleep-climb."

She crossed her arms. "Lord, help us if we both wander the island at night."

He held one of the coconuts at arm's length and peered at it with a deep frown. "Very strange, indeed."

❧

*T*he sun was high in the sky as Tobias maneuvered the steep, rocky path to the lagoon. He talked Priscilla through the best footing and aided her when he could. She was heartier than her delicate appearance suggested and amazed him with her strength—first rowing, then swimming, and now descending a steep rock face, albeit with his help. This genteel woman raised to host parties for the upper-crust of Mayfair did it all without complaint. He'd seen greater men whine when their boots weren't polished to a shine. She rolled to her stomach on top of a smooth boulder, clinging with her finger-tips as she inched downward. He reached up, ready to grasp her. She let go, sliding until he caught her waist and placed her on solid ground.

Sweat dampened tendrils of hair and plastered them to her forehead. Without wind on this side, the humid air grew stifling, especially with their added exertion.

"Do you need a break?"

She exhaled a breath and wiped her forehead with the back of her hand. "We're getting close. Let's keep going."

He crouched and sat on his backside to slide down another incline. Sand covered the boulder, and he descended faster than he'd intended. He turned to warn Priscilla, but she had already inched herself after him. She yelped as she picked up speed.

Instead of moving straight, sand shifted her to the side near a sharp drop off.

He hurled himself on the rock and reached for her, fumbling to grasp her hand. She flung herself onto her side, clawing the ground, but momentum kept her slipping over the edge. Her fingers missed his.

She disappeared, plummeting over the side.

CHAPTER 18

Bonaparte and I have established a mutual trust. He is a polished and intriguing man, but his arrogance and candor know no bounds. He's convinced the sovereigns of Europe shall call upon him.

~ Letter from Colonel Neil Campbell to Lord Castlereagh

*P*riscilla landed a full body's length down on an outcropping of rock. Her calf and thighs burned, and dots of blood appeared where skin had been scrapped.

"Priscilla?" Tobias's voice pitched several octaves higher than usual.

The entire length of her side hurt. She eased up into a seated position, carefully moving her toes and arms to ensure nothing was broken. Besides a few scrapes, everything seemed to be in working order. "I'm all right." She crawled to the edge of the rockface and peeked over. It sloped a few feet before plunging into the ocean. Waves churned the seawater, crashing over dark crags and covering rock in a salty spray. Continuing down wasn't an option, and there was nothing to grab to climb back up to Tobias. She'd fallen too far to be reached.

Perchance if she skirted along the ledge of this boulder, they could meet.

"I'm coming," he said.

She could hear him grunt, and pebbles tumbled down upon her head. "Nothing's broken, but I'll sport some ugly bruises tomorrow." She twisted to see how badly her gown was ruined on her left side.

Something moved behind her.

Priscilla pivoted to see a gargoyle-looking creature the length of her arm eyeing her a step away.

She screamed and crab-crawled backward until her back bumped against a rock.

"Priscilla!" Tobias's guttural bellow spread the lizard creature's hackles further.

Rocks bounced off her head, but she didn't dare move. She and the awful monster were in the midst of a stare-down.

Thick, bent arms lead to claw-like fingers that spread wide and dug into the rock. Spikes jutted the ridge along its back, and a scaly flap under its chin fanned out underneath. It faced her, raising its head and opening its mouth, and moved as if barking a silent roar. The flaps under its neck waggled with each jerking motion like Nellie's father's jowls whenever he spoke in a rage against opposing political leaders.

Tobias's fingers curled over the edge. He grunted as he strained his neck to peek over.

Keeping her hand close to her body, she pointed at the beast. "What is that?"

He rested his chin on the cliff edge. "Heaven have mercy, Priscilla. I thought you were in danger."

"I'm not?"

The beast stopped its barking movements but continued to eye her warily.

"It's an iguana." He sighed. "They're relatively harmless."

"They don't look harmless."

"They sun themselves on rocks and can be found on all the islands, at least, all the ones I've seen."

She eased to a stand, and the thing restarted its jerking head lifts. "It's not going to bite me?"

"Not likely."

"That's not reassuring."

"They're not known to bite unless attacked. Just move away slowly." He stretched his neck. "See if you can maneuver along the side of this boulder, and I'll meet you at the bottom."

She skirted around the edge, keeping the creature in her periphery, only to run into a second one on the other side. "Ah, Tobias?"

She heard him scrambling down the side of the other rock.

"What now?"

"There's another iguana, and it's blocking my way."

"You'll have to go around it."

"I can't."

He murmured something, but all she caught was, "... should have stayed on the beach."

Priscilla stiffened, and her breathing shallowed. He couldn't leave her alone. She must be useful so he'd continue to bring her along. She gulped and raised her chin. The iguana also lifted its head.

"Shoo." She waved her fingers and inched forward.

The iguana opened its mouth and released a slight hiss.

She stopped moving. "It's hissing at me."

"Hold on. I'm coming to you."

They're harmless. Priscilla moved a step closer.

The lizard continued hissing.

You can't let Tobias think you're bird-witted.

She stepped forward. *God, if you're listening, please give me courage.*

The iguana's spikes seemed to lengthen.

She inched closer. "Move, big guy." She stepped forward until she was only a couple of feet from the creature.

One of its legs stepped back.

She scooted closer.

The iguana turned and scurried under a crevice. Its thin striped tail dragged behind.

"I did it." She did a little hop and continued around the rock. Another larger iguana rested at the corner.

She spied Tobias landing in the sand a few yards away, and the urge to run to him flooded her being. "Tobias."

His head snapped in her direction, and relief softened his expression.

She grabbed her skirt and scooted along the boulder, eyeing the stony lizard as she inched along.

It lifted its head and fanned out its headdress.

"Oh, yeah?" Priscilla gripped both sides of her skirt and held them up, spreading the fabric wide.

The iguana scurried away.

Tobias reared his head back and laughed. "You showed him."

Her smile erupted despite her embarrassment at being caught threatening something Tobias deemed harmless. She picked her way around the ridge. "Did you see that?" She glanced back the way she came, breathless, not from exertion but her incredible feat. "I scared them off." She patted her chest. "They were afraid of me."

Pebbles rolled down the rock above and behind her, ricocheting and bouncing in all directions.

Priscilla and Tobias froze and eyed each other.

She spoke first, whispering, "Was that an iguana?"

Tobias held a finger to his lips and shook his head. He pressed past her, disappearing down the path she'd climbed.

Prickly fingers of fear crawled up her back like the vines that grow along the shore. "Tobias?" she eked out between tight lips.

He slipped around the boulder, and a second later, strode in her direction. "No one was there."

She sagged against the side of the rock.

"You all right?"

She nodded.

He glanced back over his shoulder. "Quite strange."

She hooked her arm through his, drawing strength from his nearness. "Let's keep going."

They crossed the stretch of rocks toward the lagoon, but Tobias continued to glimpse back as though looking for someone. Now that their feet had begun to callous, he moved with fluid strides despite the uneven ground. A combination of sweat and humidity adhered his shirt to his muscular frame, and although they were on a deserted island, he was ever the captain in command. Even if she made for a pathetic crew, he didn't treat her as such nor complain about her slowing him down. On board the ship, he'd seemed rigid and daunting. She had taken an instant dislike to the captain's controlling behavior and had only seen him as a boorish man intent on making her life harder, except for those few instances when they dined together. But since their overboard mishap, she'd glimpsed the caring side of Tobias. Maybe she hadn't ever hated him, merely hadn't understood.

Priscilla stayed close to Tobias's side as they weaved their way down to the west side's sandy cove.

He jumped off the last rock into the sand and reached back to aid her. She gripped his sturdy shoulders, and he wrapped his strong hands about her waist. The simple touch sent her pulse leaping like dolphins racing in front of a ship's bow. His silver gaze checked hers as though gauging her fortitude while he lowered her to the ground. The intensity in his eyes heated her cheeks.

The connection broken, they continued walking. What was the matter with her? What was it about Tobias that stirred her emotions? Since their first encounter, she'd been flooded with outrage, fear, and now—she glanced at his chiseled profile—this strange stirring, like a longing mixed with need. She wanted to understand him, to be close to him, to mean something to him.

Why had he gone overboard to save her? She couldn't imagine her London socialite friends ever risking their lives for her. They couldn't be inconvenienced. Her parents probably wouldn't have noticed her disappearance. Anthony might have sent someone for her, but he'd box her ears for embarrassing him. Yet, Tobias, who had every right to curse the day she was born for turning his life into one big mess, hadn't blamed her nor complained. He'd forgiven her.

She remembered the panic in his voice as she slid over the cliff and the protective way he'd guided her. Why? Why would he risk everything for a woman who's been nothing but troublesome? Why would he even care whether she lived or died?

"How are you doing?" His Adam's apple bobbed. "Do you need to rest, or shall we keep going."

For much of her life, she'd been left to her own devices and lacked supervision. It felt lovely, yet strange, to have someone care for her. "I'm fine."

One side of his lips lifted in a half-smile. "Good because I'm starving."

They'd reached the beach, and the aches in Priscilla's feet eased due to the soft sand. An entire night of dancing didn't cause them to throb in such a manner. If Tobias's men came for him, she would never take a pair of shoes for granted ever again. They rounded the cove, and she halted at the flock of strange looking birds standing knee-deep in the water.

Tobias nodded at the lagoon. "Those are flamingoes."

"Flamingoes," she whispered. Their fluffed bodies, like pink feathery clouds, were propped on spindled legs with knobby knees. They peered into the water with graceful scrolling necks. Their pointed, black-tipped beaks appeared as if they'd been dipped in an inkwell. "I've heard of them but have never seen the like." She stepped forward, and three of the birds straightened their necks to peer at the newcomers. "A drawing in a book, perhaps, but never in real life, never up close."

"They eat shrimp and crustaceans. Which means, there's food." He removed the turtle's shell, which he'd strapped to his back between his suspenders, and handed it to her.

"You'll have to tell me what to do. I don't know what I'm looking for."

He waded into the shallow water near the mangrove trees and rolled his sleeves. The birds eyed them and pushed to one side. "You've never seen a scallop or mussel?"

"Only mixed with linguini after our chef visited Italy." She tied the bottom of her skirt to keep it from getting wet and stepped into the lagoon before Tobias could spy the indecent amount of ankle she revealed.

His head hung as he searched the water. "What about oysters? Those have become a delicacy."

The warm pool restored life to her tired feet. "Are those the slimy looking things in a half shell? The ones the Prince Regent likes to eat?"

"Indeed." He pulled out his knife and squatted, prying something off the reef.

"Anthony used to eat them daily," she said. "He told his friends they helped him court women or something along those lines."

Tobias jolted upright and almost dropped whatever he'd caught in the process. He juggled the slippery object until he clasped it tightly in his grip. He shook his head and muttered something under his breath about Middleton.

"Do you believe that's why the Prince Regent eats them?" She stepped on a hard piece of coral and quickly changed footing, careful to inspect where she tread. "If so, it doesn't appear to have had much effect on Princess Caroline."

He cleared his throat. "Let's pick a different topic of conversation, shall we?"

"I'm merely making an observation. I don't mean any offense to our prince." The muscles of Tobias's tanned forearms rippled as he pried another lump off the reef. "I know you can be sensitive regarding royal topics."

"I'm not sensitive." He frowned. "I merely don't tolerate any slander regarding our king or country." He waved her over.

She picked her way to him, grateful for the shade of the mangrove trees. "How do you know what is right and wrong if you don't discuss things?"

"How do you mean?" He continued his work.

"My father spends hours debating legislation brought before the House of Commons. Sometimes he'll pick a position he doesn't favor merely to argue the other side and draw out more questions." She stopped by his elbow. "He says it helps solidify what you believe if you consider the opposition."

"Fill the turtle shell with a bit of water."

She dipped the shell, and saltwater rushed over the edge into the center.

Tobias dropped four shells into the small pool. "When in battle, one doesn't have the luxury of questioning an order. To do so costs lives."

She inspected the black oval shells in her makeshift bowl. "What creatures are these?"

"Mussels." He slipped in a couple more.

"I hadn't considered how questioning an order could cost lives." She balanced the turtle shell between one hand and her hip and picked up a mussel to inspect. "I used to love to listen to Papa debate with various diplomats and delegates, especially on war topics. Did you know Napoleon was a second son and self-made man?"

He grunted his disapproval and plopped in a couple more mussels.

"The coup of people who put him into power hoped he'd chart a new course for France. They adored him because he was one of them." She placed the mussel back into the bowl. "If Napoleon ever escaped Elba, the people of France would rally around him once more, because even though the man is a tyrant, he offers hope to the common man."

Tobias stood and arched his back. "How do you know this?"

The tips of her ears burned. "You probably either believe me the bluest of bluestockings or a complete ninnyhammer, but I've never understood why men wouldn't value a woman with some sort of intelligence."

"Whoa." He held up both palms. "I don't believe you're either of those things, and women shouldn't have to hide the fact they have a mind, but where did you hear that about Napoleon?"

"I told you, my father debates—"

"I meant that particular conversation about escaping Elba." He waded around in the shallows a bit before crouching again and gathering a few more mussels.

She followed him and peeked over his shoulder to watch his work. "I have problems sleeping, as you know."

"Indeed. Most unfortunate." He shot her a sympathetic smile before wading over to a sharp-looking reef.

"I feared being alone in my room, so I used to sneak to the library. There was a bookshelf with a cabinet on the bottom. It contained a grate that looked into my papa's study. I'd curl up there most nights and memorize the maps on his wall while I listened to his voice. I never had a great view of my papa, but sometimes I could see the shadow of his legs pacing back and forth. I did have a good view of the men in his presence, though."

He dropped a couple of shells that looked like rocks into the bowl.

"What are those?"

"Oysters."

A strange pile of shells behind a tree caught her eye.

"Continue." He waved a hand.

She refocused. He was a bossy bit of goods. "I think that's how I became skilled at reading people. When I wasn't memorizing maps, I'd study the men's movements. As a young girl, I couldn't understand all the big words they'd use, but I could tell if they were angry, nervous, or excited by their gestures." She tracked a bright and colorful fish darting in and out of tree roots. "It became a game to guess their emotions before they exhibited them by laughing, crying, or storming out."

"Did your father know you were listening?" His head turned and twisted to look at something beneath the surface.

"I think not."

Tobias rose but continued to stare at the water.

"Most nights, I fell asleep in the cabinet. Sometimes I woke and walked back to my bed, but other mornings I'd wind up in my chamber without any recollection of how I got there. A servant most likely found me and carried me to my room." She followed his line of vision. "Is that shell moving?"

He stuck his hand into the water past his elbow and brought out a large shell with a pink inside the same color as the flamingos bathing nearby. "You could have sleepwalked like you did last night."

Priscilla heard his words but lost focus as the large snail-like creature stretched a tentacle out, feeling the air as if searching for ground. She wrinkled her nose. "What is that thing?"

He chuckled at her expression. "It's a conch, and it will make a nice dinner."

Her stomach twisted, no longer hungry. "It's the same kind of shell as the ones piled up behind this tree."

Tobias's eyebrows snapped together. "What tree."

She pointed behind the mangrove.

Tobias waded over and examined the pile. He grabbed a limb from the tree above and pulled himself onto shore. As if standing at the helm of the *Trade Wind*, he examined their surroundings, scrutinizing every yard.

A cold trickle ran down her spine, despite the heat. "What is it?"

"We're not alone."

CHAPTER 19

I suggest using a small force to cross the west bank of the Mississippi River and seize the dirty shirt's battery.
~ *Letter from Admiral Sims to Lieutenant General Pakenham*

The second day of eating mollusks didn't improve over the first. Priscilla's stomach heaved as the slimy oyster slid down her throat. She gagged and flung the half shell into a pile.

Tobias sat next to her under mangrove trees' shade as they rested from the hot sun and building shelters. He chuckled at what must have been her greenish tint. "They'll taste better when they're cooked, but first things first—eat, finish our shelters, then create a fire." He surveyed their rations. "We've done well with our find. We might be able to survive for a month off shellfish and coconut water."

"Only a month?"

"Maybe more if my inventory calculations are correct. I don't recall how long it takes for a palm tree to produce coconuts, but there are enough growing to sustain us for four or more weeks."

His eyes scanned up and down the shoreline once more. It was becoming a habit for him to search for whoever was lurking in the underbrush, watching.

"If someone else is on the island with us, why wouldn't they make themselves known?" She brushed some loose sand off of her arm even though sand had become almost a second layer of skin. The more she brushed off, the more it appeared to accumulate.

"I could be wrong, but either way, we should still be cautious. If someone is here, we want to make certain their intentions are good."

"Maybe someone survived the shipwreck and lived by eating conch, which would explain the stack of shells, and then they were rescued." She clasped her hands near her chest as if holding onto hope.

He shrugged. "There are lots of reasonable explanations. Pirates could have hidden in this cove and feasted until naval ships passed. Monkeys or some other dexterous creature could be eating them as food or merely collecting the shells for some reason, finding them valuable."

"We haven't seen any monkeys."

He shrugged, his focus moving to the food. He rubbed his palms together, and she could almost see him salivate over the treasure trove of shellfish they'd found. His obvious delight drew a smile to her lips.

"Whoever or whatever, they have sophisticated taste in seafood." He tilted his head back and let the oyster slide from the shell into his mouth, chewed, and swallowed. "Delicious."

A repulsed shiver wiggled from her shoulders and down her spine. "I think I'm going to stick to coconut."

"You need to keep up your strength. You can't sustain yourself on coconuts."

Intense hunger had clung to her for days, but she didn't dare embarrass herself by swallowing the mucous creatures and retching in front of Tobias. "I'll make due."

"Try a conch. They're meatier and less slimy." He held it out.

Priscilla struggled to keep her midday meal from making a reappearance.

"It has less of a fishy, ocean taste." He licked his lips. "The texture is nice and chewy with a salt flavoring. It's a delicacy, and around here, they appear to be plentiful. We have the luxury of eating them every day."

One of her eyelids fluttered shut at the thought of ingesting the slimy, chewy meat with residual grit crunching between her teeth. "If you continue to torture me with your jests, you will lose my favor."

"Ah, but I have a remedy for that problem, at least according to your brother." He held up another oyster he'd cracked open and slipped it into his mouth. "I merely have to wait until the oysters have their effect, and then you won't be able to resist me."

"You vile libertine." She swatted his arm.

He ducked a bit and burst out laughing.

She smiled and shook her head, leaning back on her palms. "What happened to the strict, uptight captain I first met. I don't even know this teasing, talkative person who appears whenever food is the topic."

His laughter died to a chuckle as he devoured another oyster.

Priscilla continued to grin at Tobias relaxing on the beach beside her. She didn't doubt his senses remained on high alert, but this teasing side of him and that disarming smile could grow on her. Might bearing responsibility for an entire ship have kept him rigid and ill-tempered?

"Talkative." He snorted and shook his head. "It's odd you say that. I've never been able to speak freely in front of a lady."

"Hmm. Talking, maybe. Yelling—well, that is a different matter."

He bumped her with his shoulder. "It's because you so easily raise my ire."

"That's what Anthony used to say." She sat up and dusted sand off her hands before resting her chin on her knees and peering at him. "Why do you think you can't talk to women? You're talking to me?"

He cast her a sideways glance. "You ask a lot of questions."

"It comes with being a younger sister. Along with a good dose of pestering if you try to avoid my interrogations."

"I can't believe I'm saying this but" —he glanced at the sky— "God bless Anthony."

She raised both eyebrows to say, *I'm waiting on my answer.*

"I've been aboard a Navy ship since age eleven, so I haven't happened upon many women."

"Certainly, you have leave? Don't you spend it with your mother and siblings?"

He rubbed his eyebrow with his index finger. "My mother remarried, and I have two twin brothers who were born a few months after my father's passing. The burden of three children was too much for my mother, so she pushed me to enlist. I agreed because it was my duty to be the man of the house. However, she remarried to a French baker four months after I left. I hadn't even finished my initial training." His jaw tightened. "I arrived home from my first leave to that surprise. I now have two additional half-sisters and a half-brother, but I've always been at odds with my stepfather. We had a falling out a while back. My mother pressed me to appease him by not discussing certain topics—especially my father or the crown. I was never well-received, and eventually, I stopped going home."

Priscilla raised her head. "But your poor mother and siblings. Surely they want to see you?"

He shrugged and stared at the flock of flamingos, pruning

their feathers in the midday sun. "They chose a family, and it didn't include me. My crew became my family."

A telltale muscle twitched in his jaw, so she backtracked to safer conversational ground. "What about when you're in port? Don't you go ashore with your men? Anthony always did."

"No. I couldn't. I..." His eyes darkened like clouds at a funeral.

She ached to comfort him. Whatever direction his thoughts had taken pained him. Instead, she bit her tongue and waited.

"When I first was commissioned, my bunkmates and I got along famously." He stacked empty shells as if unable to look at her. "One, in particular, I understood well. We both had fathers who'd passed, and we didn't like our new stepfathers. We became thick as thieves. I knew Adam had my back, and I had Adam's." The stack of shells toppled, and he let them fall.

"Adam slept in his uniform, said he always wanted to be ready."

Priscilla snorted a giggle. "I see why the two of you got along."

Tobias didn't even crack a smile. "When the other kids made fun of Adam, I defended him, but then one sweltering night, we slept on the beach to stay cooler. I woke to the sound of crying. He was in the throes of a nightmare, but what he murmured about his stepfather didn't make sense. Not for a boy." He exhaled a rush of breath. "I confronted him about it in the morning, and he confessed." Tobias paused as if reliving the moment in his mind. "Adam was a *she*."

"Oh my." Priscilla's lips parted. Did Tobias's friend suffer from nightmares similar to hers? Is that why he'd been patient with her, maybe even understood a little? "Why would she pretend to be a man?"

Tobias sucked in a deep breath. "Annie, which was Adam's real name, joined to escape her stepfather's abuse. We have lads on the *Trade Wind* who joined for the same reason. Benton is one of them. The Royal Navy is well known as a way for young boys to escape their living situation and develop a career where they're well paid, fed, and valued."

Her heart clenched for Benton and the other children. "What happened to Annie after you found out? Did you report her?"

"If only I had." His face shadowed, and his eyes closed tight. "If the up-and-ups had known, they probably would have sent her home but under safer watch. Maybe she'd still be alive."

Priscilla held her breath. Her hand moved as if of its own will and rested on top of his. He didn't pull away. Instead, his eyes opened, and her heart tore in two at the grief haunting his expression.

"I couldn't speak to her after I found out. I pretended like everything was normal and I could go back to the way it had been, but every time I opened my mouth, my tongue tripped on the words. I stuttered and babbled like an idiot." He shook his head as if disappointed in himself. "My reaction hurt Annie, and over the next few days, she grew angry. When we were alone swabbing the deck, she boxed my ears, calling me a clunch. 'Spit it out,' she said. 'Rail at me for lying or betraying you. Just don't act like a bumbling fool on my account. I'm still the same person you knew a week ago.'"

Cords along his neck grew taut, and he rubbed his wrist. "I tried. I honestly did, but I was so angry, so hurt that she'd hidden this from me, that the words wouldn't come. When I didn't respond, she told me she cared for me and then hauled back and planted a facer right into my chin." He pointed to the spot. "I still have the scar. Annie might have been a girl, but she packed a good wallop."

A sickening feeling soured Priscilla's stomach, and it wasn't from the oysters. She swallowed and braced herself for the truth. "What happened to Annie?"

"Some of the crew overheard her yelling. Word spreads quickly aboard a ship. I slept above deck, hoping to gather my wits. I remember the men had been extra rowdy that night, partaking of spirits until they were three sheets to the wind. When I couldn't sleep, I finally relented and went below deck." He rubbed his chin. "The rest of the story might be too much for a proper lady."

"I'd like to hear." She swallowed to steady herself for the rest of the tale. "It would help me understand."

He inhaled a deep breath. "Annie's bunk was still made as if she hadn't slept in it." His Adam's apple bobbed as he swallowed hard. "I can still feel the sense of dread in the pit of my stomach. I knew something was wrong. I scoured the ship looking for her, waking half the crew in the process, and then I heard the cry." He closed his eyes for a brief moment, and the cords on his neck strained. "Man overboard." His voice dropped to a whisper as if reliving the moment in his mind. "The midshipman fished her out, and men gathered around as her body was laid upon the deck. I pushed through the crowd. I had to see her. I didn't want to. I wanted to hide below, but I needed to know." He blew out a shaky breath. "I remember the captain, clasping a hand on my shoulder and telling me I shouldn't look, but I did." He blinked and gave his head a little shake as if to remove the image from his mind. "Annie didn't die from drowning. Someone on the ship had done terrible things to her and afterward tossed her body overboard."

Priscilla covered her mouth to hide her horror.

"Another cadet had to hold me up. I cast up my accounts right there on the deck." His voice trembled. "She was buried at sea, and the perpetrator was never identified."

"I'm sorry." Her heart broke for the man sitting beside her. At such a young age, he'd already dealt with much death.

He nodded as if to accept her sympathy. "I railed at God. How could He take her? Wasn't He supposed to be a father to the weak? It was that night as I lay in my hammock when I first heard God speak into my heart."

"What did He say?" She hoped the curiosity in her voice didn't make her appear flippant about such a traumatic death.

"He planted two scriptures in my soul. Isaiah forty-three, 'When thou pass through the waters I will be with thee,' and 'Whosoever shall offend one of these little ones which believe in Me, it were better for him that a millstone were hanged about his neck, and that he were drowned in the depth of the sea.' I had to trust God to avenge Annie's death. It was hard to move on, but I did, knowing God was with me even in deep waters." His gaze locked on her. "He still is, you know."

Her heart jolted. More and more, she understood.

"He has plans for you and for me." He held his palms up. "The fact that we survived proves He wants to give us a hope and a future." Tobias pushed himself to a stand and dusted sand off his backside. "Enough talk. It's time to get back to work. Those shelters aren't going to build themselves."

Priscilla stood and shook out her dress. Humidity and sweat caused it to stick to her legs. They'd spent yesterday searching for the right sticks to build the frame for two lean-tos and dragging them to their camp. Today they were collecting fronds for the walls.

As they climbed to the island's grassy side, Tobias grasped her hand to aid her over a steep incline. He paused midway. The silver-gray of his eyes shone bright as if he'd been granted a wish.

Her breath stilled. Oh, to be a genie with such an offering. Her fingers throbbed, longing to trail the line of his firm jaw and feel the pickle of his bearded stubble.

"I haven't spoken much to a woman since." One side of his mouth twitched into a half-smile. "Until now."

*T*obias contemplated what had come over him. Sweat poured off his face, dripping off his chin and drenching his shirt. The heat must be addling his wits enough to loosen his tongue. As he'd matured, he'd learned to converse with females, but only in a polite minimalist way, which was not how he'd just borne his heart to Priscilla.

He broke off another palm branch, tossed it into his pile, and glanced her way. Priscilla split palm fronds in half longways the way he'd shown her so the rain on their makeshift roof would run off in the same direction. She'd tied her blonde hair back to keep the wind from whipping her tresses and insisted upon helping him gather sticks, palm fronds, and bundles of grasses, even though he'd warned how tiring the work was. The plants' sharp blades scratched their legs and sliced tiny cuts into their hands.

She didn't shy from hard work, unlike her brother. The more Tobias came to know Priscilla, the more he believed her to be nothing like Anthony. Priscilla truly cared. Her soft heart shone in those expressive blue eyes. He could still feel the warmth of her fingers over his as she sought to comfort him. He should have pulled his hand away, but he hadn't realized how much he needed her touch until her warm hand covered his, and a sense of rightness filled him—except that it was wrong. His life belonged to his country as his father's had before him. It was not his to give to any woman.

The snap of a branch resounded through the air, but it didn't come from Tobias.

He and Priscilla stilled.

The grass rustled a few feet away.

Her eyes widened, and she mouthed the words, *what is it?*

Holding his knife, he parted the grass and cautiously stepped forward. The underbrush stirred, then stopped. He swept aside more tall grass but spied nothing. Instead of emerging, the creature retreated, swaying grass, headed in the opposite direction.

Priscilla wiped sweat from her brow with her arm and swatted a bug. "Whatever it was, it's leaving."

The hair on the back of his neck stood on end. He tracked the moving grass past the ridge to the lagoon. The creature was too large to be a monkey, but a human would be too big and wouldn't crawl on all fours through the grass. What kind of wild animal was tracking them? Was it friendly, or was it biding its time to attack?

"Look here." Priscilla plunged into the underbrush.

Tobias's breath caught. "Wait."

She re-emerged with two bottle-shaped gourds still attached to a vine. "We can use these to store more water when it rains." Tendrils of her hair danced with the breeze. Without using her hands, she blew them out of the way.

He grabbed the gourds from her. "Good thinking."

Her dimples flashed as she fought back a smile and tucked loose strands behind her ear.

His stomach flapped like a loose sail. "I acknowledge when my men do good work."

"Do you see me as one of your men?"

"No. I…" Blast. He fumbled for words.

"I was merely jesting with you." She laughed. The musical sound jingled like wind chimes.

He jostled the gourds, unsure how to respond.

Her smile faded. "I'm sorry. I didn't mean—I hadn't meant to reference Annie." She covered her mouth with her hand. "How thoughtless of me."

Was she expecting some sort of acknowledgment?

When the moment became awkward, she continued pulling apart fronds.

He sliced the gourd's tops off. An oyster shell he'd pocketed made for an excellent tool, but his fingers weren't protected from the mush as he extracted the seeds and pulp. Slimy orange pulp squished between his fingers. He shook his hand, plopping the innards onto the ground. His hand grew sticky as the sinew began to dry. He bent and picked out the seeds. "We might be able to plant these and grow more."

She stopped mid-rip of a frond. "You believe we'll be here for an entire growing season?"

He frowned and shook his head. "No. Not likely." *Possibly.* They'd more likely die of dehydration first. Priscilla kept referring to their being rescued, but he didn't have the heart to explain the low odds. His crew had probably already joined the navy ships anchored in St. Kitts and were charting a course for Louisiana. If by chance they retraced their route, sailing through the Lesser Antilles Islands, then he needed to build a fire near the white flag to signal the fleet. Perhaps they'd send a fisherman or passing trade ship for them or organize a search party after the battle was won. Without a fire, however, his crew would assume he'd drowned.

"Stay here while I bring these branches to camp." Tobias handed her his cutlass. "Take this for your protection."

She accepted the knife, but her brows drew together.

He bent down and hefted the gathered stick and palms.

He'd chosen the highest elevation where the wind blew away flying insects, but the brusque wind meant they'd grow chilled once the sun set—another reason for the fire.

"I'll join you." Priscilla tucked the knife handle into his belt and gathered her fronds.

Her touch, so near his sensitive stomach, sent a skittish sensation through his midsection. "It's too much for you to carry." He cleared his throat. "I'll come back shortly."

She laid palm leaves over the turtle shell and placed the gourds on top. "I can manage."

Tobias peered around his load. "Don't be ridiculous. You won't be able to see your footing."

"I'll be careful."

He didn't like it, but her fear wouldn't allow her to be left behind. He had no other choice. She stayed close as he verbally guided her through the terrain, and she made it to the top.

Tobias dumped his sticks on the cleared and level area of ground just below the peak where they'd planted their flag. He helped Priscilla unload the fronds.

She stared down at the sticky orange goo covering her gown's bodice, squeaked, and stepped back. Her foot slipped in a divot from a removed rock, and she toppled backward, landing on her backside. "Ow." She grasped her wrist and stared at her hand.

"Are you hurt?" He crouched to inspect her reddened palm covered in thin, tiny needles.

Sure enough, a small cactus plant grew out of a rock crevice near her fall.

He lifted her to her feet. "Time for us to go for a swim."

Her gaze flooded with worry. "It burns. Is it poisonous? Am I going to die?"

"It will sting something fierce, but soaking your hand in water will wash some of the needles out." He peered at his stained-orange fingers. "It's time to wash up anyway."

Their travels had already worn a wide path to the beach. Between searching for food, materials for building their shelter, and now firewood, they must have traversed the same path at least twenty-five times in the past couple of days. The midday sun set the sand ablaze, scorching their feet. He and Priscilla dashed as fast as possible into the tide. The clear water cooled their burning soles and swished around their calves.

Priscilla still held her palm in her other hand.

"Let's go past the breakers so you can soak your injury." He stared into the water. "Watch where you step. You don't want spines in your hands and feet."

"What about those red spiny urchin things we saw in the lagoon? Are they over here too?"

"The rough waves on this side keep the urchins away, but you will have to watch for stingrays." Tobias pushed through the breakers, relishing the feel of the water cooling his skin. Priscilla followed a couple of steps behind him. "You all right?"

She nodded.

He dove under the next wave and let the grime and sweat of the past few days melt away. He rose and wiped saltwater off his face. Funny how they could be surrounded by water but not have a drop to drink.

Priscilla surfaced next to him and dipped her head so her blond hair slicked back off her face. "Was it a few days ago I said I'd never swim again? I'd like to recant my previous statement. The water feels lovely." She floated on her back.

"Is it helping your hand?"

She peered at her palm through the clear sea. "It's cooled the burn quite a bit, but I feel the sting when the waves tug on them."

"It should start to work some of those needles out." He floated over a swell on his stomach. "The rest we can pick out, or your body will push them out over time."

"The body will do that?" She turned and treaded water.

"Aye. I once knew a chap who had a bit of shrapnel in his side. It became a dark lump as his body rejected it, and he was able to ease it out over time." He scratched his nose. "It was a sight to behold."

"Sounds awful."

A pang hit Tobias in the chest. "I beg your pardon. Such talk isn't meant for a lady's ears."

"Oh, tosh. I'm not squeamish." She floated over a swell. "Besides, I've heard far worse from my brother."

"Ah. The delightful Anthony Middleton."

"I know you hold a grudge against Anthony because you

believe he betrayed his country." She pinned him with her gaze, her eyes matching the turquoise water. "Your tone makes me believe it's more than that—something personal."

Tobias peered into the water, catching sight of a striped angelfish swimming nearby. He wanted to relax and savor this peaceful moment before resuming their work. Priscilla's glare told him she wasn't going to let this drop. "Anthony and I were stationed together once. We both quickly rose within the ranks, and we both had well-known fathers who'd made a name for themselves in His Majesty's Royal Navy. It created a rivalry between us."

"You and my brother competitive?" Her tone dripped with sarcasm. "Who would ever have thought?"

"Yes, well, after showing each other up, we eventually established a mutual friendship. I, however, was promoted to captain first, which flew Anthony into the boughs." Tobias clenched his teeth. "Behind my back, he spoke ill of me to my crew and my superiors to win their favor for himself."

"Could it have been a misunderstanding? Did you confront Anthony about it?"

"He denied it until he had too much to drink one evening and didn't realize I was in the room." Tobias treaded water over a wave. "Word spread about another captain's position opening up, and the admiral was going to defer to my recommendation. Anthony changed his tune then. Suddenly, I was his friend again. He begged me to nominate him. He even tried to buy me drinks to win me over and show me a good time with the ladies in port but pitching gammon and flummery has never been in my nature."

Tobias wiped a drop of water from his eyes. "Skillfully speaking, Anthony was the best person for the job, but his heart wasn't in the right condition. I ended up recommending him, but only after he gave me his word he would take the position seriously, give up spirits and foolhardiness. I put my career on the line for him, and he repaid me by using British naval property for personal gain."

Priscilla's brow furrowed as she absorbed his information.

He hated having to be the one to open her eyes to the ugly truth about her brother.

Priscilla treaded water over another swell. "I know it doesn't justify my brother's actions, but he's always been under tremendous pressure from our father to move up in rank. He's lived in my father's shadow."

His jaw clenched. "I know that feeling all too well."

Not wanting to put a dark cloud over such a lovely day, he stared at the wreckage of the ship, its mast sticking out of the water like a flagpole. "Want to explore the old ship? See if there's lost treasure aboard?"

Her face brightened. "A little treasure hunting sounds delightful."

"We'll need to keep an eye out. There is potential for sharks in deeper waters."

~

The tepid water became a balm for her hand and a refreshment for her soul. The longer she stayed in, the further she pushed back the disturbing black cloud of her brother's behavior and the more the current worked the needles out of her palm. The swim to the lone mast wasn't too far, but they moved slowly, keeping their eyes peeled for sharks. The ship had banked on a reef not far from shore where the shallows dropped into the deep on a sharp incline. She and Tobias grasped the slimy wood of the crow's nest at the main mast and held on, peering into the wreckage below.

Sand had piled high on one side, burying the ship, while on the other, the sand had eroded away. The wheel of the helm and the pointed bow grew seaweed. Colorful fish played among the rotting boards, making their homes in crevices or among the growing barnacles.

"I'm going to dive down and have a look." Tobias sucked in a deep breath and plunged underwater.

Her scalp tingled as she circled the crow's nest to locate him. Spotting him, she sagged against the mast. As long as he remained in sight, her fears stayed at bay. He inspected the helm, prying open a compartment she wouldn't have known existed, but didn't find anything salvageable.

A swell splashed Priscilla's face, and she reared her head, wiping water away with her hand. She peered back down, but Tobias was no longer swimming at the helm. She scanned the wreckage, searching for his figure but found nothing. Her blood ran cold.

Where did he go?

CHAPTER 20

Use the cover of the morning mist when possible for the element of surprise.
~ *Letter from Admiral Sims to Lieutenant General Pakenham.*

A splash sounded behind Priscilla, followed by a deep inhale of breath. She whirled around to find Tobias and lost hold of the wood of the crow's nest. She slipped under the water, but he caught her elbow and dragged her up.

"What's the matter?" He studied her expression.

"I lost you for a moment and panicked."

He remained quiet, catching his breath.

A gull screamed overhead and lowered toward the mast but spied them and flew away.

"There's a large crack in the hull." Tobias gasped for breath. "I can swim through, but you won't be able to keep an eye on me."

She shook her head, sending droplets of water in all directions. "I need to be able to see you."

A wave pushed him to her, and her leg bumped his. "Pardon."

He didn't move away. His hand grasped the crow's nest next

225

to hers, and he sucked in gulps of air until his breathing evened. "I'd hate for it to be a wasted trip. Do you feel up for diving?"

Diving sounded better than the alternative. She nodded.

"Take a deep breath." He inhaled and pushed off from the mast.

Priscilla did the same. Below the surface, barnacles covered the wooden structure, causing the ship to appear misshapen. She swam fast to keep up with Tobias, and pressure built against her eardrums. A school of yellow-and-blue striped fish parted her and Tobias before the fish zig-zagged away in perfect synchronicity. The eerie silence beneath the waves combined with the ship's skeletal remnants and forewarned they'd encroached on solemn ground.

Part of the rail had broken off and lay twisted in the sand. The ship's bow bent at an angle. The coral reef had shaved off the bottom half. As she reached the break in the hull, her untrained lungs cried for air. Tobias's white shirt billowed like a jellyfish as he inspected the ship's innards.

He beckoned her before disappearing within the hull's dark chasm.

She poked her head inside. Sunlight filtered through the holes and cracks, and little bits of plankton refracted light. Something moved on her right. Instead of finding Tobias, three large fish, almost her size, with oversized lips in a deep frown faced her. She back paddled and released a muffled scream, but only bubbles erupted from her mouth. The fish swam out of the hull and past her with a swish of their tails.

Her lungs screamed for air. Where was Tobias? She needed to breathe.

As if she'd summoned him with her mind, he emerged from the hole carrying a balled-up fishing net. He pointed up, and she nodded.

She broke the surface and grasped the crow's nest. A surprised pelican snapped its beak at her. When Tobias emerged inhaling a deep breath, the bird spread its broad wings and flew.

He wiped water from his face as they both sucked in deep breaths. "I think I found the galley, but I ran out of air." He gasped to catch his breath. "I'd like to try again and see if we can find any supplies."

He waited until their breathing evened. "Ready to dive again?"

Not quite, but he didn't give her much choice. Tobias filled his lungs and pushed off the crow's nest once more. Priscilla did the same. This time she didn't hesitate to enter the hull. Time was of the essence. She merely hoped those large frowny-mouthed fish didn't return. Tobias waved her down a dark corridor to the right, where a broken deck panel allowed in sunlight. A rusty iron woodstove, fallen on its side, lay covered in seaweed. Dishes rested strewn about in the sand. Tobias wrenched open a drawer, removed a ladle, and tossed it aside. Priscilla swam to another cabinet and opened it. Rows of jars covered in barnacles lined the shelves. She gurgled a sound in her nose to get Tobias's attention. He pulled a rusty knife out of the drawer before peering up at her. His eyes widened at her find, and he grabbed a rusty pot. They started shoving jars into it.

Priscilla's lungs burned. She couldn't stay any longer and pointed up, hoping Tobias would follow. She swam back down the corridor and into the room with the breach in the hull.

Tobias's hand gripped her shoulder and pushed her against the wall.

Her lungs screamed for air. She couldn't wait.

He pressed his index finger to his lips, his eyes wide and fixed on a shadow.

Priscilla followed his line of sight to a shark skimming the ocean floor inside the hull. Her body turned rigid. She wanted to scream but didn't dare attract attention.

Tobias's hand pressed her back into the side of the hull as if they could blend in with the surroundings, but the pale yellow material of her skirts floated around them like a beckoning hand waving the shark over. Her lungs and throat convulsed as Tobias inched them along the side and pushed her through the opening.

She kicked to the surface, following the wooden mast up to safety, not looking back. Emerging, she sucked in glorious air.

He burst through the surface with a large gulp of breath.

"T-there was a shark." Her teeth chattered, and she stared down into the depths for any movement.

"Let's"—he gasped for air—"give it a moment to swim away." Tobias put his face under the water to watch, coming up for breath several times.

Priscilla forced her breathing to steady as she clung to the side of the crow's nest and searched for any movement under the water.

He lifted his head and wiped away the water with his hand, treading water with only the use of his legs as he held the pot full of jars to his chest with the other. "It's gone. Let's swim back and see what we found."

She nodded, ready to be back on land.

Her knees quaked as she dropped the heavy fishing net on the beach and wrung her wet skirts. "That was close."

Tobias plopped into the sand and drained water from the pot.

"I know you told me there might be sharks, but it's different once you've seen them. If it had attacked us, we'd have been helpless."

"Indeed, it gives you a healthy respect for the water." He pulled out some jars and wiped at the barnacles with his shirt-tail. "It helps me better understand God. The ocean teems with life. It provides water and food, but it is also powerful and deserves our respect." He used one of the rusty knives to pry the cork out of the wide-mouth bottle. A popping sound split the air as the vacuumed seal broke. He sniffed the top and drew back. "It's pickled something."

He offered it for her to smell.

She peered at the sandy bottle that had a bunch of dark circles clustered inside before catching a whiff of the vinegar fragrance. "Pickled beets?"

He grimaced. "I hope not." His shoulder shrugged. "Then again, if we run out of coconut and crustaceans, anything pickled might taste good—even beets."

"You plan to eat one?" She handed the jar back to him. "You think they're still edible?"

He rose and stuffed the cork back into the bottle. "The seal hadn't been broken, and the ocean water would have kept it cool. Fifty-fifty odds say it's still good enough to eat." He offered her a hand to rise.

"I think I'll wait and see your outcome before I taste one."

"Suit yourself." He shrugged. "More for me." He returned the bottle to the rusted pot, plopped the fishing net on top, and hefted it onto his shoulder. "We still have a shelter to finish and a fire to build, and we're losing daylight."

Priscilla squinted at the sky. The sun appeared at its highest point, but she trusted Tobias's estimation. The man was a natural taskmaster with a plethora of knowledge when it came to survival skills. As much as she wanted to be useful, there was no doubt it had been his skills that'd kept them alive.

They picked their way up the steep incline. As they reached the level ground of their new camp, Tobias stopped short.

Priscilla skidded to a halt and listened. Her senses heightened. A yellow warbler stole a strand of grass from their pile before flying away. Leaves rustled in the breeze.

Tobias set the pot down and scanned the surroundings.

"What is it?" Priscilla whispered and stepped to his side.

He extended his arm back as if to shield her from harm and

crouched slightly, tiptoeing closer to where he'd set up the lean-to frame. Priscilla hovered so close she could feel humid steam emanating from his shirt. He studied the ground where a stack of coconuts rested.

Priscilla gasped. How did those coconuts get there? Tobias flashed her a be-quiet warning look, and she closed her mouth.

He examined nearby shrub trees and held up his palm. "Stay here."

She nodded.

He crept over to a natural parting in the undergrowth, fingered a broken branch, and studied the dirt around the area.

What did he see? Were they not alone? If not, why hadn't the person made himself known? All these questions welled up in her chest, threatening to burst past her lips to the point that she nearly gagged on them. She wrapped one arm around her midsection and pressed her other hand against her mouth to hold in her interrogation. It would only annoy Tobias, and she didn't want to ruin the friendly truce they'd maintained the past few days.

He stood with his hands resting on his narrow hips in a commanding captain-stance. He scanned the land in the direction of the lagoon. A warbler belted its song, and other birds chirped their reply. Tobias crossed his arms and furrowed his brow.

Would he never speak his mind? Hushed waiting curled her toes.

She couldn't take it any longer. "What is it? What did you find?"

After what seemed an eternity, he faced her. She wanted to grab the front of his damp white shirt and shake it out of him.

"I don't know what to make of it." He peered at her with clouded gray eyes. His glazed expression communicated his focus on putting the puzzle together.

Mayhap she could help? "Make of what?"

The furrow in his brow deepened. "The ground's too rocky to get a good imprint of tracks, but what I can make out appears small, almost human, and they lead toward the lagoon."

She sucked in a quick breath. "That time, the grass rustled, and we thought it was an animal. It also moved in the direction of the lagoon."

"It could be an animal, a large monkey or the like." He rubbed his chin. "I merely haven't seen any on the island."

"Why would a monkey bring us coconuts?"

He shook his head. "I haven't the foggiest. Perhaps we've settled where it stores its food?"

She swallowed. "Should we move to another area?"

"No. Either it will get used to us, or we'll get used to it." He picked up a frond and tied it to the lean-to frame with some stringy rope he'd collected earlier from the bark of what he called a mahoe tree. "Let's get back to work. We have a lot to do before dusk."

He reached down and handed Priscilla a frond and showed her how to tie it to the frame. Her fingers fumbled with the awkward makeshift supplies, but after a couple of hours, as gauged by the sun, she developed a knack for attaching the palm branches. Soon after, they had one lean-to finished, and they started on the other frame a few feet away. The primitive two-sided huts didn't allow much privacy, but they blocked the wind and would keep out moisture.

Priscilla's back ached from leaning forward, and her fingers hurt from pulling the ties tight. To make it worse, she could, on occasion, feel the tiny nettles of the cactus embedded in her palm. She refused to complain. They were alive and now had shelter. If they could manage a fire, which Tobias believed he could, they'd soon have cooked food and smoke to signal passing ships. She could spend Christmas with Lottie.

Her hands stilled, and the frond she'd been holding slipped

from her fingers. Tobias caught the leaf and handed it back to her. His silver eyes met hers, and her heart skipped.

Christmas with Lottie lost some of its appeal. Did she not want to be rescued? *Don't be ridiculous.* Of course, she wanted to be saved. She needed to discover the truth about Anthony and get back to her family to warn her father about those men.

She laid the palm frond on top of the others, tied it to the branch, and quickly picked up another. She had to admit she'd enjoyed working alongside Tobias. He might be quiet, but he listened when she spoke and patiently answered her questions. The story of Annie's death broke her heart, and the way he opened up endeared him to her at the same time.

Was she developing feelings for Tobias?

She knotted the rope. How could she entertain such a ridiculous thought? She merely enjoyed the personal attention. Nothing more. Besides, he had no one else to command, so as he said, he was only making the best of a bad situation.

Tobias's capable fingers tied the last frond. His hands exuded strength and surety. The muscles in his tanned forearms flexed as he pulled tight on a knot. What would it feel like to be cherished in those strong arms?

Merciful heavens. It must be the heat.

"You mentioned you have a friend in St. Kitts?"

She snatched her gaze from his biceps. Heat filled her cheeks at being caught staring. "Er—yes. My closest friend. Her name is Lottie Etheridge—ah, actually Lottie Winthrop. She recently married a Kittitian merchant. I plan to visit with her before returning to England."

"Ethridge." He grabbed another palm branch. "The name sounds familiar. I do believe Middleton had mentioned her."

"Anthony fancied her before she married. I'd hoped she'd become my sister as well as my friend, but Winthrop beat him to the altar."

"Wait." Tobias grunted as he tied the last knot. "I remember now. She's the one who dropped a candle and caught her skirts on fire. The poor bloke who extinguished the flames was forced to marry her."

She stiffened in defense of her friend, even if it was true. "They're a love match now."

"Bah, isn't she the one your brother committed treason to save?" He dusted off his hands, then his pants. His movements, a tad too hard, displayed his latent anger rising to the surface.

"I don't believe that story." She folded her arms. "I've known Lottie all my life. She wouldn't do such a thing."

His jaw set. "But your brother would. He could have persuaded her."

"Lottie is a highly moral woman." She shook her head. "And Anthony wouldn't do such a thing."

"Ha!" He burst out. "You don't think your brother would seduce a woman?"

Priscilla hesitated to answer. How well did she know Anthony? He'd been at sea for seven years. She only saw him when he was on leave for a couple of months every year. "No." She lifted her chin, not caring if it appeared defiant.

"I've witnessed the comings and goings of your brother's many conquests. Believe me. It is not above him."

"Why do you hate him?"

"I despise anyone who'd betray our country."

"What if he had a good reason?"

"He didn't."

"What if you haven't heard the full truth?"

He rounded on her. "What do you know?" He stepped close and pinned her with the wrath blazing in his eyes. "What lies has he told you?"

"Nothing." She squeezed her fingers into fists, tempted to rail him. "He hasn't told me anything, but I will find out the truth from Lottie. She'll explain the whole story and redeem my family." Tears clouded her vision. She turned before he could see her vulnerability amid the doubts that niggled in the back of her mind and mumbled, "She'll shed light on your vendetta against my family."

Silence fell once again between them.

Priscilla crouched and collected the extra fronds to set inside the lean-to. Behind her, Tobias sighed, but she refused to turn. She shoved the palm branches into the crook of her arm, not caring how they scratched her hands.

Her cheeks burned and ached when she squinted between the black mampoo trees with their scraggly limbs and the young saplings fighting for domain. Beyond them, palm trees popped above the undergrowth as if curious for a glimpse of the cays. Scraggly windblown limbs cast shadows longer than the height of the oak trees from home over the camp as the sun began its descent below the horizon. Already her skin had seen too much sun. It was time she did something about it. She settled into her lean-to and weaved dried palm strips like her fashionable straw bonnets.

Outside, Tobias worked. A strange rubbing sounded from his direction. She resisted her curiosity as long as possible, but she'd always been weak in that area. She poked her head out.

Tobias had crafted a bow the other night, similar to a violin bow, with a stick and his shirt's tie string. He looped a small branch in the string and rapidly thrust the bow back and forth so that the stem twisted upon a cluster of fibrous coconut husk. Now and then, he'd stop and blow on the mass. He'd tried the night prior without any luck.

"Blast." He scowled at the pile and started the motion again.

She settled outside her lean-to and went back to making her hat. It was best to let him be when angry.

A few minutes later, he blew upon the pile again. "Confound it."

She set aside her weaving. "Is there anything I can do to help?"

"No." He twirled the stick again by jerking the bow back and forth.

"Fine." She returned her project to her lap. The brim of a hat formed as her fingers bent and folded the reeds.

His grumbling continued as the sky turned from bright pink to purple.

Unable to see any longer, Priscilla set the makings of a very flat hat aside.

A little orange glow sparked within the coconut husk. Tobias knelt, blocked the wind with his body, and gently blew on the ember.

The scent of smoke wafted under her nose, and she held her breath.

He grabbed more husk material and added it to the small flame, which flickered to life.

"You did it."

He issued her a curt nod then followed the stern action with a boyish smile. "And a fire burnt among them."

Her traitorous stomach somersaulted.

He quickly piled leftover sticks, dry branches, and palm fronds and carefully lifted the burning husk pile onto the wood. "And God said, 'Let there be light.'"

She stared at the dancing flames spreading to the remaining wood. "I will never take a lit fire for granted again."

Flames spread, and so did his smile. "Neither will I."

They both stared at the source, emanating light and heat. Priscilla stretched out her fingers to warm them. The motion shifted the nettles in her palm. She winced and peered at her hand.

"Let me see." He didn't allow her time to refuse. Instead, he gently grasped her hand and pulled it closer to the firelight. He examined her palm, his breath grazing her skin. With his fingernails, he carefully picked out a few of the little needles.

"You don't have to do that." She pulled at her hand, but he wouldn't release her.

"I insist."

He continued to work on her palm as a surgeon would a patient, and she couldn't resist studying his profile. His tanned skin glowed in the firelight. The flickering shadows only enhanced the masculine quality of his firm jaw and straight nose. His shirt front lay open with the missing string, revealing tiny wisps of dark hair. She averted her eyes. Why did such a handsome man have to be so exasperating?

After a few minutes, he paused and glanced her way. The intensity of his gaze swallowed her. "I don't hold a personal vendetta against your family."

His voice crooned like soft velvet, and her rebellious heart tripled its beat.

"Yes, you do." She hoped he couldn't feel her hand tremble. "It's the barrier between us. The simmer easily rolls into a boil. I see it in the clench of your jaw, flare of your nostrils, and shadow in your eyes." She pushed the words past her lips. "I don't know the entirety of what my brother did, but when you look at me, you see him." If only she could pretend her feelings for Tobias didn't exist, attribute her remark to wanting his friendship or respect, but her heart protested otherwise, and those feelings grew stronger each day they remained on the island. She couldn't lose her heart to a sea captain. She wouldn't survive a day alone while he was away at sea, much less a full deployment of nine months or more.

The flicker of fire in his eyes warned her of danger but beckoned her closer.

"You're wrong."

～

*U*nder Tobias's thumb, the pulse in Priscilla's wrist throbbed. Its quickened pace coursed liquid fire through his veins. He blamed the heat on the campfire, but as his thumb brushed the sensitive skin, it only stoked the burning within him. He stared at Priscilla and saw a strong woman who'd worked tirelessly by his side, a courageous beauty who'd faced her problems and found solutions, and the gently-bred woman who'd sought the best of every situation no matter how desolate. What he couldn't bear to see in those admirably perceptive blue eyes was sorrow.

"You are...well...different." The right words failed him. Why couldn't he speak his mind? Why did his jaw lock tight whenever women were concerned? She was soft, kindhearted, open, vulnerable, strong, and beautiful. His lips parted to say those very words, but she spoke.

"I can't help who I am. I'm still a Middleton."

He swallowed and lifted her chin with his knuckle. "You are nothing like your brother." The words spoken from his lips led him to a new awareness of truth. The young woman who mistakenly boarded his ship was innocent of the crimes of which he'd condemned her. She didn't lie behind his back or abuse his authority. He'd learned Priscilla was brave enough to speak her mind even when he did his best to intimidate her. She wasn't lazy like her brother, using others for her gain. He remembered her tireless fight rowing the dinghy and building the lean-to. She wasn't a hardened sailor nor a war-torn officer, but she'd been through battle and had her world turned upside down, yet he'd not heard one complaint from her. Although she had been deceptive—merely to hide her fear of being alone—since then, she'd openly apologized for her actions and their consequences.

As captain, he was to know the state of his men at all times, as in Proverbs, *the shepherd should know the state of his flock.* In this case, he'd allowed his anger regarding Middleton to blind him to happenings on his ship. He should have been kinder and more understanding in his dealings with Priscilla, trusted his men's judgment of her character. Especially after how loyally they protected her. Raleigh and Cecil were ready to face being stretched over a barrel to keep him from discovering she'd been playing cards when she was supposed to be in her cabin. All she had wanted was to avoid being alone.

The warm glow of firelight and setting sun illuminated the soft curves of her face, and she watched him with such an innocent expression, the walls around his heart crumbled. She had a way of lowering his defenses, setting him at ease, drawing him out to speak his mind. Not since Annie had he told a soul the things he'd shared with Priscilla in the past few days, not even Henry, his second in command, who'd endured numerous battles by his side.

Tobias's fingertips traced the soft white skin of her forearm to the inner crook of her elbow and lazily traced a circle.

The hairs on her arm lifted. She couldn't be chilled this close to the fire. Was she responding to his touch? Did she long for him with the same desire that wrenched his heart? Her generous lips parted slightly, emphasizing their fullness.

He knew his silent contemplation only twisted her into knots. She would soon fill the silence with nervous babble, so he forced his thoughts into words. "You are an enigma I can't wrap my brain around. You are unpredictable and yet thoughtful. You are assertive yet gentle." His gaze plundered the depths of her eyes for understanding, and she seemed to soak up his attention like dew on dry wood. "You are infuriating yet lovable. You are challenging." He leaned closer. "Yet, I can't get enough of you."

CHAPTER 21

Everything is going according to plan. Our sources have obtained complete intelligence on the Elba Island's guards' names, their placement, and their shift rotation.
~ *Translated letter from alias Lord Fortin to French Rebels of the Bourgeoisie*

Tobias's hand brushed over the capped sleeve of Priscilla's gown, along the smooth line of her clavicle, and gently up the slender slope of her neck. He expected resistance but found nothing but a reflection of his own passion in the swirling pools of her eyes. All this—her nearness, his feelings, their connection—it was all new to him. He slowed so as not to appear like an overeager greenhorn. His fingers dipped into damp hair at the nape of her neck. Something inside him shifted like unstable air before a turbulent storm.

Right now, he couldn't be a hero for his country, but he could be her hero.

She closed the gap, pressing her lips to his.

Her swift advance caught him off-guard. He froze.

She pulled back as if shocked by her impulsiveness. Her teeth raked her bottom lip with sudden shyness. "I'm sorry."

The awkward moment should have rebuked him, but for reasons he couldn't fathom, her unexpected kiss emboldened him instead. The corners of his mouth twitched with a smile he couldn't suppress. He drew her back. "I'm not." He traced her cheek with his thumb as his gaze lowered to her velvety lips. A vehement surge of possessiveness stirred his blood.

He pushed aside the warning ringing in the back of his mind.

Her hands slid up his chest. His muscles reflexively contracted until her fingers curled over his shoulders.

Fire crackled beside him, but it was nothing compared to the inferno building inside him. His heightened senses warned of overload. He wanted to feel the sweetness of her lips pressed to his once more. How simple to covey his feelings with his kiss when his brain stumbled with words. He'd show her the burning passion she'd fanned into flames since invading his life, punish her for distracting his heart from its purpose, prove to her he believed she was nothing like her brother. His embrace tightened. His lips lowered.

His conscience nagged him to do the honorable thing, even if it took every ounce of his self-control. He hesitated.

She stiffened, and her quick intake of breath sucked the air from his lungs. His heart collapsed in upon itself at her pained expression. He read the doubt, rejection, and confusion etched in her eyes.

God, help him. He couldn't let her believe he'd rebuffed her.

He tempered himself from devouring her in a searing kiss meant to change them both inside and out, and instead brushed her lips in the lightest whisper kiss. She relaxed in his arms, leaning in until his mouth moved against hers. Heat, like a stoked fire, melded them together. She tasted of salt and coconut. Seeking the freedom he hailed on the open sea and the rush of taking command, he deepened the kiss. He demanded a response, and she willingly complied with a soft moan.

The brush behind them shifted, and the small hairs on the back of his neck lifted in alarm. They were being watched.

As if she sensed it too, Priscilla's eyes sprung open.

He broke the kiss.

The fire popped, and Priscilla jumped. He scanned the perimeter of their camp. Shadows danced from the flickering flames. All was still except for a single branch bobbing from the wind. Or did it a shake from a departing animal? Perhaps an unexpected visitor? He gave himself a mental shake. Had the deluge of emotion he felt for Priscilla set his imagination running wild?

Only the music of crickets and frogs serenaded.

"Is something out there?" Her breath tickled his neck, and she trembled.

He offered a reassuring squeeze of her arm, then allowed the cool night air to rush between them. He scoured the darkness, forcing his thundering heartbeat to slow. "It's nothing." He flashed what he hoped to be a reassuring smile. "Merely my conscience for taking advantage of a gently-bred woman."

Her eyes clouded. "Are you saying I should slap you for taking such liberties?"

"It was you who kissed me." He quirked an eyebrow, daring her to deny it.

Her jaw dropped. "Mine was a chaste kiss."

"Then let it be a lesson not to play with temptation." He brushed his thumb across her swollen lips.

Her throat convulsed as she swallowed, and her dimples flashed as she clamped her jaw tight.

His fervor renewed to pull her into his arms and soundly kiss her frown away, but he tamped it down and rose, dusting off his pants. "I think it's time to retire to our new"—and separate—"dwellings."

Priscilla hesitated, and the disappointment in her eyes was almost his undoing. A silent moment passed. She nodded and crawled into her lean-to.

He heaved some thicker branches onto the fire, enough to last them until morning. His stomach churned with guilt. *Lord, forgive my moment of weakness.* He should never have kissed her. Not when he couldn't provide her with a future. He was a sea captain, devoted to his country and crew.

Priscilla kept her back to him as she combed her fingers through her hair and plaited it into a braid with swift jerking movements.

It was better for them both if she remained angry with him. He meant what he said about playing with temptation. He should have known better. There was no denying the pull between them was growing stronger, but he was a captain, and sea captains made terrible husbands. He wouldn't resign Priscilla to that future.

He dusted off his hands and rolled onto his bed of palms. With a stretch and a long exhale, he closed his eyes to sleep.

"Tobias?"

His eyes sprung open.

Priscilla lay on her side with her head resting on her arm. Her blond braid curled around her neck and nestled in the cleft of her bosom. "Can you tell me another Bible story? It would help me sleep."

The sweetness of her ask punched his gut. How could she forgive his callous behavior so easily? What possessed him to kiss her, a gently-bred woman? He'd decided long ago he wouldn't allow his heart to be distracted from its purpose. He could not put a woman through the pain of loving a man who'd die serving his country. He'd seen the endless tears and soul-wrenching sorrow his mother had suffered, and he'd personally endured devastation at the loss of Annie.

He wouldn't subject anyone to that pain.

Forcing away his dark thoughts, he said, "Have you heard the story of Joseph?" He chose the story more for himself than for Priscilla's benefit. He needed a reminder of a man who pursued God even though he was rejected by his family—a man who'd defeated the temptation of Potiphar's wife.

The leaves rustled as she shifted positions. "It sounds vaguely familiar. Please do tell."

Tobias laced his fingers behind his head and concentrated on Joseph's firm resolve as he told the story. However, despite his efforts, his mind drifted to the contradictory woman only a body's length away who proved to be tenacious and valiant when facing storms but delicate and yielding in his arms.

He might survive the island, but could he survive his desire for Priscilla? He needed to change tactics, or he'd only hurt her further.

~

*P*riscilla didn't want to awake from her slumber. For the first time in a long time, she hadn't been plagued by nightmares. Instead, she'd dreamed of being held in Tobias's strong arms and relived the sweetness of their shared kiss.

Tobias's rich baritone voice sang a sea shanty from behind the cover of the thick underbrush. She'd set the rule that, if either were to leave camp without the other, the one who'd left must sing so the other would know they were faring well. He must consider her utterly mad, but he complied. She rose and stretched, glimpsing the back of his head several yards away gathering firewood. He carried the tune well, slipping between tenor and baritone octaves.

He must be horrified when it was her turn for privacy. Although she loved to sing, she couldn't hold a note.

The smell of burnt ashes hung in the air, different than the aroma of the hearth at home, possibly due to the native types of firewood or the fact that the soot mixed with the fresh tropical breeze. Last night in the campfire glow, he'd called her an enigma, but the more she got to know the rigid captain, the more layers she discovered under his tough exterior. The same harsh man who demanded perfection also pardoned her mistakes, from the unforgivable, like falling overboard and marooning them on a deserted island, to the minor, like slipping and landing on a prickly cactus. Her stomach flipped at the memory of his gentle fingers plucking each tiny needle. The intensity of his protective gaze, for a precious moment, had suggested she was the center of his world. She reveled in his words, *I can't get enough of you.* She had welcomed the sweet, possessiveness of his kiss like a wanton woman.

She lowered her head as heat swept into her cheeks. He certainly hadn't seemed shy around women last night. But then again, she'd expected him to continue their kiss—longed for him to linger, if she were being honest—but instead, he'd suggested they turn in for the night.

Of course, such a disciplined captain would consider her behavior atrocious.

She licked her lips for moisture, but her mouth was parched. In England, Priscilla wouldn't consider it a good morning without sipping a warm cup of chocolate in bed while the servants lit the fire and drew back the curtains. Now, a lovely day was one where no sand fleas bit her legs. For the first time since arriving on the island, she'd awoken in the lean-to without a single new bug bite. Perhaps her body, dotted with welts, a few she'd scratched until they bled, would now have a chance to heal.

Before stepping into the break in the trees, she stared over the vast expanse of ocean. It had become a habit to start her day talking to God, pouring out her thanksgiving and requests.

Lord, thank you for another day. Thank you for the beauty that surrounds us. Provide us enough food and water to make it through until we're rescued. Keep us safe in your care, and help them to come soon.

She remembered how Joseph had waited in the pit for his father to come for him, but he never came because his brothers had faked Joseph's death. Her heart wept at the disappointment and uncertainty he must have felt as he sat isolated from society in a dirty jail, amid varmints and other creatures, until Pharaoh needed his dream interpreted. All that time, God hadn't forgotten Joseph.

A small bird darted past her, landing on a nearby branch, and a chorus of cheeping followed. Three scrawny birds held their beaks open as the bright, yellow-bellied mother held a caterpillar out for them. God didn't forget about the birds. He provided for even them.

Tobias returned, dumping his load of sticks and wood for the fire. He combed his unruly hair with his fingers, and greeted her with a groggy smile, his chin darkened by a beard. The crisp white uniform he'd proudly donned had become dirtied and stained. It didn't detract from his appearance, only enhanced his rugged manliness and relaxed demeanor. On the deserted island, he sang, teased, and spoke openly to her, unlike the brooding commander of the *Trade Wind*.

"I do believe I like this side of you." She unplaited her braid and ran her fingers through her hair to remove any tangles.

"Hmm?" He glanced up from stoking the fire.

"Your casual side is less intimidating than the stiff captain in his high polished uniform."

His gaze honed on the sliding movement of her fingers through her hair. His Adam's apple bobbed before he returned his attention to the fire.

"I didn't understand all that was demanded of a captain. All those people who counted on you for their survival." At the hard angle of his jaw, a muscle twitched. "I now hold a better under-standing."

He remained silent.

Smoothing back her hair, she tied it with coconut string. She had grown accustomed to his contemplative moments, but something seemed off. "Are we going to try fishing today if the net is in decent shape? Otherwise, we'll have to swim further out to find more oysters."

His grunt sounded like approval.

Each stick he pitched into the fire erected a barrier between them and only made her more determined to re-establish their tentative truce. Had their kiss changed the dynamic? Perhaps he discovered something in their shared moment he didn't like? "I daresay, cooked fish sounds better than slimy oysters." She moved to his side and sat in front of the fire. "The question now becomes, can either of us cook?"

Tobias rose and fetched a coconut.

Yesterday, he would have at least chuckled at her question or teased her about being a hopeless case. He cracked the coconut to break their fast and their thirst.

She'd spoken too soon. The guarded captain had returned.

Her heart withered, but she forced a smile as he passed her a half of a shell and a knife. They sipped the water, relishing it, for it might be all they received for the day, and ate their meal in relative silence.

With each bite, doubts bombarded Priscilla. Had she imag-ined what transpired between them? Had she done something to deserve his silent treatment? Foolish, foolish, girl. Had he been disappointed in her impulsive behavior? She should never have pressed her lips to his or curled her fingers over his shoul-ders. Only a romp would be so forward. Or had she been too timid, breaking off their kiss in her nervousness? She stared into the coconut shell and sighed. She'd, once again, ruined everything.

Finished with his meal, he stood and grabbed the fishing net. "I'm going to the beach."

She stood as he marched down the path with the net draped over his shoulder. The belt sheathing his knife hung loose on his hips. He was going to leave her there. She bit her quivering lip, hating that she'd run after him like a frightened child. *For heaven's sake, get a backbone, Priscilla.*

He paused at the bend and turned. "Aren't you coming?"

Relief flooded through her body, but she acted as if nothing were amiss. "One moment." She scurried into her lean-to and grabbed the hat she'd been making and the pot. Holding the container in the air, she said, "For when we catch something."

"Good thinking." He waited for her.

She dared to meet his gaze as she reached his side, desperate to re-establish equilibrium between them. He nodded, and she accepted his comment and nod as a good sign.

They traipsed to the beach. Morning breeze shook palm leaves and lifted Tobias's hair. She helped him spread the net and retie a few damaged areas. They worked as a team for a good hour, and the tension of this morning's interactions melted away. Together they weighted the edges and picked the best spot to toss the net and capture their dinner. They chose a cove several feet deep where they could stand on rocks and see fish pass. Several fish escaped while they learned the art of net fishing.

She pointed to a stingray through the rippling clear water, burying itself in the sand. "My word. They disguise themselves and wait. You can only see their eyes."

Tobias rubbed his chin. "That gives me an idea." He added some braided line and returned, dropping the net into the water. "We'll set a trap in the sand, and when a fish swims by, we'll hoist the net, catching the fish inside."

Sun beat down as they waited and waited.

He wiped his brow and tilted his head toward the shade.

"Why don't you get out of the sun. I'll wait a bit longer before giving it a rest."

Her skin already felt burned from the sun's intense rays, so she didn't protest. She stretched out in the sand under a shady palm and folded more grass into a hat. It began to take shape, appearing more like an inverted cone, but it would provide the shade Tobias needed. She started on an eleventh row. After a while, her fingers ached, and she decided to check on how Tobias fared.

He still stood on the rocks, focused on the water, his white shirt pressed against his flat stomach and billowing in the breeze. One hand rested on his hip, the other at the ready to heave the net. He stood frozen as if fused with the rock beneath his feet, his proud frame daring the ocean to try and wash him away. It was the same stance he took with her. Somehow she'd become the surf beating against the wall of his heart, probing to get inside. To no avail.

Her friends in London would have swooned over such a display of virile maleness, but it wasn't merely physical attraction that drew Priscilla. She admired his masculinity but melted at the vulnerability in his eyes when he'd spoken of Annie, the determination as he'd remembered his father, and his deep, reverent tone when he'd relayed a Bible story to calm her. His soft heart had taken her prisoner. He was completely unaware of the power he held to lift her to joy or plunge her into sorrow.

"You're a fool ten times over, Priscilla Middleton," she muttered to herself. "Tobias Prescott is the epitome of practical, and you are the complete opposite." Her fingers fell into a rhythm, sliding the grass under, folding, turning. "He's stuck with you is all."

Tobias glanced her way.

Lord, help her. All she needed was for him to hear her talking to herself. He'd already seen her crazed behavior during her episodes. There was no need to draw more attention to her madness.

He hoisted the rope, and the net folded in on itself.

Priscilla sat straighter and set the hat aside. "Did you catch something?"

His face beamed a triumphant smile as he hauled in the net. A large fish flopped in its center. "We have our supper."

She jumped up and grabbed the pot. From the edge of the rock, she leaned over and filled it with water as Tobias set the net on the rock ledge. The fish stilled. Its gills expanded and contracted. Tobias carefully peeled back one side of the net and then another.

She set the pot down. "Strange how they appear so colorful under the water but dull outside of it."

He reached for the fish.

The fish flipped itself over.

Tobias grabbed for the slippery creature, but it flopped to the water's edge.

"Oh, dear!" She lunged for it as it flung itself back into the ocean.

Tobias's arm caught her around her midsection before she splashed face-first into the water.

The fish remained stunned as if catching its breath, then darted away.

"Blast." Tobias scowled at their departing meal.

Her stomach tingled where his hand lingered.

As if realizing he still touched her, he flung his arm back. "Er — you almost went for a swim."

"Indeed, if not for your quick reflexes."

He lowered his gaze to the drooping net and sighed. "I guess we try again." He plucked something off the rock and held it up for her to see. "Or else it's snails for dinner."

She grimaced but held his gaze, his jest restoring their pre-kiss balance. "Would you like me to have a go?" She leaned forward and pressed her thumb to his tanned forehead. "Give you a chance to get out of the sun?" The light pressure left a white mark on his skin, which filled with red before returning to its usual tan color.

He cleared his throat. "I'll keep going. I don't mind. You stay in the shade."

She rose and dusted off her skirt. "Hold on. I have something for you." She grabbed the cone-shaped hat and brought it over. "It isn't pretty, but it will shade your face."

He examined it, turning it over in his hands.

She twisted the fabric of her skirt. "It's a tad uneven, but the weave is tight and should hold."

His eyebrows lifted as he checked the quality. "It's impressive. How'd you learn to do this?"

She warmed at his compliment. "Mother used to shop for hours at the milliners. She brought me along to keep her company, but then she'd spend most of the time talking to the shopkeeper. I used to peek through the curtain into the backroom and watch the women weave. They made quick work of it, threading in and out like intricate dance steps. One woman could make four hats in an hour if she didn't take a break."

"That's forty hats a day." He grunted. "I imagine they received a pretty farthing for each."

She nodded. "And then some."

"I might have gone into the wrong line of work."

She burst out laughing.

He tilted his head. "What's so amusing?"

"It's merely that..." She stifled her mirth. "Our milliner was... well, to put it nicely, a fop. He'd wear his collar points so high he couldn't turn his head without poking himself in the eye."

Tobias snorted his chuckle.

"When I pictured you in his garb"—she fought her smile—"it struck me as ridiculous."

He tugged up his collar points. "You don't think it would be a good look for me?"

She giggled. "It seems a bit impractical for you."

He smiled in full, and a shout of *huzzah* welled up in Priscilla as if she'd singlehandedly won the Battle of Trafalgar.

~

*T*obias's stomach growled. As much as he wanted to enjoy the natural beauty of Priscilla's smile, those dimples were too tempting not to kiss. Focus on his duty—to keep Priscilla and him alive until he could return to battle. They needed full bellies tonight, because they had to travel further to find wood for the fire and food each day. If he could catch a fish, perhaps they could find a way to smoke it and store it for days when their hands came up empty. He stuffed the inverted cone hat on his head. "Time to get back to work if we want to eat something other than snails tonight."

She nodded and dusted the sand off her gown.

Sand had become part of him. It was always under his nails, in his hair, gritting in his teeth. He'd given up bothering to remove it. As much as he'd tried to prevent it, Priscilla had become like his sand, difficult to remove, ingrained in his heart, and pervading his life.

She was nothing like what he'd wanted for a wife. If, for some reason, he didn't die in battle serving his country, then he'd planned to retire at a ripe old age from His Majesty's Royal Navy, purchase a boat, and charter passengers across the channel or start a fishing business. He'd find himself a nice quiet wife to keep him company, one who didn't mind him being away on long sailing expeditions. Priscilla wasn't in the least bit silent, nor could she handle him being gone for even a moment. They were entirely unsuitable for each other.

He strode to the rock outcropping and dropped the weighted net into the water.

Why then had he kissed her? It wasn't like him to be moved by the moment, nor to not reason through actions and counter-actions. He knew better than to mislead a woman into thinking he'd be in pursuit of courting her.

Priscilla walked the beach, shielding her eyes from the sun while scanning the treetops. Wind swept the hem of her gown, giving him occasional glimpses of her womanly curves. She'd strolled farther than he'd anticipated she would, considering her fear. She stopped under a bent palm and glanced in his direction.

He quickly turned his head. Only a small sunfish drifted nearby, but he cast again and came up empty. A moment later, he scanned the coastline for Priscilla but saw no sign of her. His spine stiffened.

Leaves of a bent palm shook, and a coconut dropped into the sand.

A flash of pale yellow showed among the green. Priscilla sat in the tree. She had somehow shimmied up it and cut coconuts.

She could fall. He stepped in her direction until the rope tugged his hand. He'd have to hoist the net and start over. The palm leaves shook, and Priscilla walked backward along the bent trunk, hand over hand and foot over foot. She reached a point and jumped. Her skirt flared, revealing her calves, but she landed like a cat in the sand.

He averted his gaze. Her dangerous stunts provoked him. It had been her impulsive nature that got them into this mess. He wiped sweat from his brow with his sleeve.

By gum, this was entirely her fault. She'd opened Pandora's box by kissing him first, and he was left to restore everything to its proper place. She didn't understand the temptation she posed, but it would take a lot more than a shapely calf and alluring blue eyes admiring him as if he were her hero to sway him. God had made him of sterner stuff. He was created for battle, like his father before him. He must be more cautious, keep a strict distance, and not relinquish his guard. It was the only way they'd make it off this island unscathed, if they made it at all.

A bubble popping woke him from his deep thoughts. A large kingfish drifted on the tide, sunning itself in the middle of his net. He jerked the rope, catching the fish unaware. Water sprayed as the fish flailed.

"You caught another one." Priscilla dumped the coconuts and palm fronds into a pile and ran over with the pot. Her face lit with excitement. "Huzzah! You did it."

In the radiance of her admiring smile, his chest swelled like it had his first time at the helm. He moved the net onto the beach this time before opening it and held the fish for her to inspect.

"It's a beauty. You are an excellent fisherman."

Its tail flicked, splashing a mix of water and sand in their faces.

With the back of her hand, she wiped her cheek and stared with an awed expression at the creature. "He's a feisty thing."

Not as feisty as you.

"You held so much patience standing out there. I had to keep checking to see if you'd become a statue. You are a man of utmost determination."

Indeed. Extreme determination. His pulse quickened by her nearness. *And extreme self-control.*

He moved back to the solid rock surface, bringing the fish with him.

Priscilla followed.

He pulled out his knife and filleted the fish.

Her lips parted. Her expression varied between fascination and disgust.

He tossed the head and bones into the pot and chuckled at

her expression. "Had I known fileting a fish would render you silent, I would have tried fishing earlier."

She frowned at him. "How do you know what to do?"

"From doing what you're doing now." He slid his knife between the meat and the skin. "As a young lad, we all had our turn at kitchen duty. I'd be stuck peeling potatoes while the cook prepared the meal. When I showed my curiosity, he was happy to talk me through the steps." He grunted. "I never figured it would come in handy until now."

The waves crashed in the distance, and the breeze picked up, whipping her hair about her face. In the past few days, her skin had obtained a healthy glow and a smattering of freckles across her nose and cheeks. A strand caught in her mouth, and he ignored the urge to pull it free by stroking a finger down her pink cheek.

"It certainly looks big enough to make a good meal." Her dimples flashed.

He captured his thoughts and pushed them aside before his control broke and he did something he'd regret. He rose, hauling the empty wet net onto his shoulder. "We best head back to camp. We'll need to add another log to the fire so it doesn't burn out." He lifted the pot with the kingfish, and she gathered the coconuts and her makings of another hat.

"Do you know how to cook it?"

He heard her footsteps in the sand following his. The ground grew hot beneath their feet, so he hurried to the shaded entrance to the path before answering. "I suggest over a fire."

"No, silly." She nudged him with her elbow. "I mean, do we roast it? Boil it? How does one cook a fish?"

Her family had servants who tended to the kitchen duties, so he decided to tease her. "I was hoping you'd know."

She chuckled. "This could be interesting."

"What would you suggest?"

Her lips pursed and pushed to the side, revealing a dimple. Why did he hold such a fascination with those indentations?

"I think boiling might be easiest since it's already in the pot."

Her logic seemed agreeable. Thankfully, the ship's cook had also taught a curious young lad how to poach a fish. "Boiled fish it is."

He stopped at their camp entrance. Dirt had been thrown on the fire, smothering it. Only a thin strand of smoke trickled towards the heavens. "The fire's out."

CHAPTER 22

A treaty has been signed in Ghant between Britain and the Americans. Send word for our troops to return. I fear our commands shall not reach General Pakenham before he wages battle.

~ Letter from Admiral Sims to the British Fleet in the Gulf

*P*riscilla's shoulders drooped. "Ugh. Do you think you can light another?"

Tobias crouched and examined the remnants of charred wood. Handfuls of dirt had been tossed over the embers, smothering the flames. The muscles in his tanned forearms tensed as his fingers curled into fists.

"Someone extinguished it on purpose."

She glanced about, half expecting someone to spring from the bushes. "Do you think they have ill intent? Do you think it's savage natives?"

"The fingerprints are tiny." He pointed to a four-finger indent near the ashes before dusting off his hands. "It could be a mischievous monkey. They have plenty of those in the Leeward Isles."

She planted her fists on her waist. "It would have to be a smart monkey to know to throw dirt on a fire."

"Quite right." He stood and raked a hand through his hair. "It's time to take extra precautions." He strode from the camp.

She set down the turtle shell. "Tobias, wait." She ran to catch up and instead slammed into his hard chest as he returned with a handful of dry mahogany leaves. "Ooof."

"I'm not going far." He dropped the leaves and turned to get more.

She dogged his steps. "Are you angry?"

He expelled a deep breath and faced her. "That I have to start another fire? Yes."

"But not with me?"

His stiff shoulders dropped, and he tucked a loose strand of her hair behind her ear. "I guess we both find it hard to understand each other." He issued her a weak smile. "I'm not angry, merely frustrated at the circumstance."

Priscilla helped him, gathering armloads and spreading them around the edge of the camp. "How will leaves keep the monkey, pigmy, or whatever it is out?"

"They won't." He filled in the circle with more leaves.

"Why are we doing this then?"

"So we hear the scamp coming."

"Oh." She dumped another armload and scratched where leaves had itched her skin. "Why don't you let me finish while you work on lighting another fire?"

His lips tightened, but he consented with a nod.

Priscilla strayed farther from camp, searching for more leaves, but felt safe as long as she could hear Tobias's grunts and rapid rubbing of the stick. Once she'd covered the entire circumference, she wiped sweat from her brow and plopped in front of her lean-to. She reeked of dirt and leaves. What she wouldn't give for a hot bath and a bar of lavender soap. She picked up the makings of her hat and worked on it while Tobias continued stoking a fire. Her stomach announced its hunger with a loud gurgling.

Tobias glanced her way.

She pressed a hand to her tummy to quiet it.

"Hungry?"

She shrugged. "A little."

"Why don't you grab one of the jars we pulled from the shipwreck." He pointed to their food stockpile. "It should be preserved. Smell it first to make sure it's not rancid before you eat."

She leaned over and seized a jar. They'd taken six, but there were only five remaining, including the one in her hand. "I think one was stolen."

He frowned. "I hope it took the jar of pickled beets. It's welcome to those."

She picked off the dried barnacles with her fingernail revealing a yellow color inside. "I think this might be apricots or peaches." She wiggled the cork, but it wouldn't budge. She stuck the jar under her arm and yanked on the stopper.

"Let me assist you." He held out his hand.

"I've got it." She grunted and tugged with all her might. The cork popped off, and Priscilla toppled, almost spilling the contents.

"You sure?" A smug half-smile twisted his lips.

She ignored the look and sniffed the jar. Her stomach leapt at the sweet aroma. "It is peaches—sweet, delicious, fruit—that's not coconut."

"If I get this fire going, we'll dine like kings and queens tonight."

She dipped her fingers into the warm liquid and pulled out a peach slice. The juice dripped down her hand, and she nibbled, testing a piece. The nectar tasted like the peach jam served with scones at home. She plopped the rest into her mouth and savored the sweet tang. It had a bit of a zing, but never had food tasted so good. "Mmm. You must try some. They're heavenly."

He leaned over and blew on the coconut husk. Smoke billowed from the small pile, then snuffed out.

She pulled another peach slice from the jar and closed her eyes to relish the flavor. The rubbing of sticks resumed. She opened her eyes and snuck another peach. "I could eat this entire jar."

Tobias set down the stick and once again blew on the husk. His shirt stretched over his back, outlining his muscular frame. She should look away, but her mind drifted to the kiss they'd shared. A warmth filled her stomach and spread to her extremities.

"You are a man of many talents."

He remained focused on his task, which was fine with her because she stole another peach slice.

"Your captain bravado can be intimidating, but now I know you also have a sweet side." She plopped another peach into her mouth and licked the tip of her finger. "Just like these peaches."

An orange glow devoured the husk. Tobias coughed on smoke and rolled back onto his heels before adding sticks to the fire.

"You know how to find food." She held up the jar in salute and bit into another peach slice. "You know how to make shelter and start a fire."

Maneuvering a stick inside the fire, he pushed stones closer together. Then he rested the pot on top.

"I would never have survived without you." Priscilla sat back. A tingling sensation spread through her extremities. "I owe you my life."

He pried open a ripe coconut and poured its crème into the pot with the fish fillets. "You'd have found a way. You're made of sterner stuff than you realize."

She giggled. "I don't know your definition of stern, but mine doesn't include a fear of being alone. That's another thing you're good at—putting up with me." She ate another peach slice. "Anthony hated me dogging his every step." She held out the container to him. "You really should try one of these before I eat the entire jar. They're delicious."

He furrowed his brow and accepted the jar.

She propped her head with her elbow. "You're my hero."

His fingers dug into the glass bottle and pulled out a peach slice. He frowned and sniffed it before popping it into his mouth.

"Truly. You're my rugged rescuer, my island champion." She pointed at him and shook away the fuzzy thoughts clouding her brain. "Another thing you're good at—surprisingly good at—is kissing."

He stopped chewing. "These peaches have fermented."

She peered heavenward and sighed. "You're not listening to what I'm saying."

"You're foxed."

She burst out laughing. "We don't have any spirits. We don't even have a bottle of Madeira. You're funning me." She shook her head. Why must he be so confusing? It hurt her brain. "Funny, that's something you're not very good at—jesting. Teasing, yes, jesting, no."

"You need to eat something."

The setting sun cast his face in shadows, outlining the hard angle of his chiseled jaw. "I'm not foxed. I would know if I was. I can assure you."

He handed her a slice of coconut and checked the pot. "Would you now?"

"I don't appreciate the sarcasm in your tone." She chewed on the coconut. It tasted plain compared to the peaches. "Here I am trying to compliment you, and you keep trying to distract—" The delicious scent of crème de coco fish sauté wafted under her nose. It reminded her of a dish Anthony convinced their

French chef to prepare when he was home on leave. The flavorful scent enticed her family to the dining room early, and they spent a half-hour talking before dinner was even served. "That smells lovely."

Even though his face was shadowed, the white of his smile shone as he shook his head at her.

"Don't tell me I must add chef to your list of talents."

He wiped the turtle shell with his shirttail, then slid the fish out of the pot into the makeshift dish. "It's hot, but try to eat some."

She reached out. "Ow." She quickly withdrew her hand.

"I warned you it would be hot." He shifted next to her as if to protect her from harming herself again.

She leaned over and blew on the plate. His face rested only a few inches from hers, along with his firmly molded lips, raising memories of his kiss and renewing the storm inside her.

"Priscilla." He said in his captain-tone. "You need to eat something."

She sighed. Now wasn't the time to focus on the velvety feel of his lips—much like the soft skin of a peach. She shook her head. "My parents would be horrified at my lack of table manners." And the direction of her thoughts. Priscilla blew on the white fish before pinching off a bite. The creamy hint of coconut filled her mouth, and she released a low moan. "You're not a good cook. You're a splendid chef." She ate another bite. "I should have known."

Her fingers bumped his hand as they both reached for a bite of fish. "Should have known what?"

"That you'd be a good cook. The meal is delicious, a thousand times better than cold mollusks."

He chuckled. "Tomorrow, I'll see if we can dig up a few clams and steam them. See if you feel differently. You cannot form a strong opinion until you've tried them dipped in butter, however."

"How did you become so good at everything?"

"Good and having a basic understanding are different things. I know how to survive and do a lot of things out of necessity. The weight of being responsible for myself and my men has fallen on my shoulders since a young age."

"There is the difference between you and me. While you shouldered the responsibility and learned from your challenges, I squandered the opportunity."

"How so?" He draped one arm over his knee and, with the other hand, placed another bite of fish into his mouth.

"My father hasn't passed, so I can't compare my situation with yours, but my parents weren't...well, they weren't attentive. I was more of an afterthought." She disliked how negative she sounded, but she spoke the words more to hear the truth herself than to garner Tobias's sympathy. To outsiders, their family seemed ideal— her father a respected admiral, her brother following in his footsteps, her benevolent mother involved in numerous charities.

The flames' light deepened the shadow of his frown.

She waved. "I've had nannies, governesses, and you've met my duenna, Miss Dodd. I haven't lacked, but I've always been left to my own devices. Whereas in your case, you chose to learn and develop. I chose poorly, usually out of desperation for attention. I put on a good face, but inside I pitied myself, instead of bettering myself." She released a sigh, dispelling her regret. "I realize now I'm good for nothing, and I have no one to blame but myself."

Tobias's brow furrowed. A hunk of white fish in his fingers stopped before it reached his mouth. "Why would you say you're good for nothing?"

She scooped more fish into her mouth, chewed, and removed a small bone. The fog surrounding her brain began to clear. Why had she been so loose with her tongue? No one wanted to hear a woman of privilege spin a tale of woe, especially not Tobias. Only Lottie knew Priscilla's whole story. It was past time she changed the subject. "This is a thousand times better than cold oysters."

"You didn't answer my question."

"Isn't it obvious?" Her gaze refused to lift to meet his eyes. "I've tried my best to be helpful, but as you've discovered, I'm hopeless. I can't find food, nor make a shelter, nor build a fire. I serve no purpose. Even at home, I wanted to help my mother by addressing invitations, but I addressed the envelopes with the back-flap upside down. I tried to help plan meals with the housekeeper, but I didn't know what foods paired well together. My father didn't want me underfoot in his office, so he sent me away. Anthony considered me a pest because I wouldn't leave him alone." A lump formed in her throat, and she swallowed around it. She wasn't about to embarrass herself by bursting into tears. "The harder I tried to be useful, the more of a hindrance I became until they shooed me away."

"I don't find you a hindrance."

She ate another bite of fish, and her stomach proclaimed its fullness. "Truly?" She arched an eyebrow, doubting his sincerity.

"You are a quick learner and notice things others would not."

Her ears strained, and her heart thumped against her rib cage, eager to hear more—needing to hear more.

"You may disagree with an order, initially, but when my reasoning is explained, you capitulate." He pointed at the turtle shell. "You anticipate needs, like using the shell and making the straw hat." One side of his mouth lifted. "I can make a fire, but I could not weave a hat. And don't forget the coconuts. I saw you climb that tree and chop down several this afternoon. How did you learn to scale a palm tree?"

She shrugged. "I guess from watching you."

"See, now that's an example of you being a quick study and anticipating us running low on water."

Priscilla straightened. "Speaking of water, now that we have a fire, do you think it would be possible to boil seawater to collect freshwater?"

"You mean condensation?"

"Exactly, we could hold the turtle shell above and collect the drips when the steam cools. There hasn't been a single cloud since the storm passed, and we're going farther out to find coconuts. I'm afraid we shall run out eventually if we're not rescued soon."

He rubbed his chin. "Another brilliant idea."

Her chest warmed, and she fought a smile. Fire crackled between them, and they both stared at the dancing light.

A strange scent drifted on the breeze. How odd. She sniffed. "Do you smell olives?"

He tilted his head up and inhaled. After a moment, he shrugged. "You don't give yourself enough credit. I know grown men who would have drowned during that storm, but you fought courageously. You've proved yourself as well as most men."

Part of Priscilla basked in the praise, and another ruffled at his second comparison of her to males. Funny how with Anthony's friends or with the crew playing cards on the ship, she'd wanted to be considered one of the men. However, now with Tobias's Corinthian physique resting so casually next to her and his appealing virile scent wreaking havoc with her senses, she longed to be seen as feminine and fetching. She curled her dirty feet under her ripped gown. So much for appearing desirable.

A breeze wafted the scent of olives through the air again and rustled nearby leaves. Tobias excused himself and strode from camp.

Priscilla assumed he'd left to relieve himself, so she pushed the remaining bites of fish into a pile and pitched any small bones into the fire. When he returned, they would need to trek back to the beach and scrub the pot with sand and ocean water so it didn't attract animals.

The air around her seemed to still. Darkness crouched in around her, and she gulped down a breath.

"Tobias?"

No response.

She turned in a slow circle, searching the darkness for him. "Don't forget, you're supposed to sing."

Silence.

"Tobias?" The ocean breeze swayed the leaves in the palm trees.

Movement flashed in her periphery, and her gaze snapped to the second hat she'd almost finished. The woven husks seemed to move slowly of their own accord as if ants underneath carried them.

Wait. Priscilla's breath caught. Dirty fingers touched the brim and were pulling it out of the clearing into the shadows.

Priscilla froze.

The small hand retracted, and a dirtied face tipped its ear up. A child jumped to its feet. It was nearly as tall as Priscilla's waist. The dim firelight revealed layers of dirt, matted hair, and a pair of wide green eyes. The child turned to run.

"Wait." Priscilla lunged forward. "Come back. I didn't mean to scare—"

Strong arms clasped around the child.

A shrill, high pitched squeal burst from the little red mouth lined with tiny white teeth. The two in the top-middle were missing.

Tobias's face emerged from the shadows with the kicking and screaming youngster in his arms. "I think I found the source of our mystery olive scent and the missing jar. It wasn't a monkey."

The little moppet bared its teeth and growled, struggling like a wild animal. A ratty dress three sizes too small clung to the girl's thin body, holding onto her shoulder by one frayed strap.

"Sweet mother of Job." Priscilla inched forward, careful to

avoid the girl's flailing legs. "What happened to her? Where are her parents?"

"Confound it." Tobias flinched with a grunt.

Priscilla reared back at the sound of water trickling on rock.

The child had urinated on Tobias's leg. Remarkably, he didn't toss her or tighten his grip. Instead, he slowly lowered her to the ground with a shushing sound.

Sinking with them, Priscilla ached for the poor thing. She reached out to push a tangled strand of hair out of the girl's eyes, but the child's jaw snapped shut, almost biting Priscilla's finger.

"Careful," Tobias warned. "See if she'll accept some fish as a peace offering."

Priscilla scooped the leftover fish and offered it to the child.

Tobias released her thin arm so she could take the food, but he kept a grip on her other.

The child sniffed the cooked meat and eyed Priscilla with suspicion.

"It's food." She held it to the girl's mouth.

The girl snarled.

"We're not going to hurt you," She spoke the words in a gentle, soothing tone. "What is your name?"

The child ignored Priscilla but once again sniffed the food. A timid pink tongue poked out of her mouth and licked the fish. Green eyes fixated on Priscilla as the girl's small fingers snatched the fish and stuffed it into her mouth. Instead of chewing, she opened her mouth and let the meat fall to the sand in disgust. She clawed the rest off her tongue with her dirt-encrusted nails.

Priscilla glanced at Tobias. "Perhaps I was a little premature in declaring you a good cook."

Tobias snorted. "I'm not sure she's accustomed to cooked fish."

Priscilla's heart melted for the poor thing. "My name is

Priscilla." She touched her chest. "Priscilla." She glanced at Tobias. "And his name is Tobias. We're not going to harm you. What is your name?"

The girl eyed the barnacle-covered containers near the campfire.

Tobias nodded to the supply from the shipwreck. "Open one of the jars and see if she'll eat those."

Priscilla slowly stretched, careful not to startle the girl, and reached for a container. As she worked to open it, the child's gaze dashed back and forth between Priscilla and the jar.

Priscilla grunted and put all of her strength into uncorking it. It popped with a loud bang, and all three of them jumped. She giggled, easing some nervous tension. She sniffed the jar before offering it for Tobias to smell. "I think it's pickled peppers, which should be good, but then again, I thought the peaches were fine."

He stuck two fingers into the jar, pulled out a long yellow pepper, and bit into it. The child shifted around and watched him chew.

"You want one?" He pointed at the jar Priscilla held. "You may have one."

Priscilla pulled out a red pepper and offered it. The girl snatched the pickled vegetable and shoved the entire thing into her mouth. Spittle and bits of pepper trickled from her lips as she chewed.

"I think she likes those." Tobias shifted his weight after resting on his haunches for so long.

She handed the child another, and the girl devoured it. Eventually, she offered the child the entire jar, and they all sat on the ground. Priscilla and Tobias watched her eat.

"Look at the poor thing. She's covered in dirt, and there are scratches, insect bites, and scars all over her arms." Priscilla tugged on her bottom lip with her teeth. "I can't imagine what she's been through."

Tobias lessened his hold on the child, but she stayed put, focused on eating. "I wonder if she survived the shipwreck. The boat was mostly intact. If I happened a guess, I'd say the ship ran aground two or three years ago."

Priscilla gasped. "You think she's been living on her own for three years?"

"I'd say it's likely." He scratched his now bearded chin. "Look at her. She's feral. She can't even communicate."

"What do we do with her?"

Tobias shrugged. "This is all new to me. I haven't a clue."

"How old do you think she is?"

"She looks the same age as my youngest stepsister the last time I saw her. She was six. I remember because we were celebrating her birthday, and she showed me where she kept the top teeth she'd lost."

Priscilla regarded the little girl. Six years old, which meant she'd probably been alone since she was three or four? "She's so thin. How did she survive all this time?"

The girl finished the peppers and belched. The scent of vinegar wafted under Priscilla's nose. She and Tobias waited to see what the child would do next. A breeze rattled palm leaves and shook underbrush. The girl stiffened as though listening. She smelled the air. After a moment, she relaxed, and her gaze strayed to the straw hat.

Priscilla handed it to her.

The child studied it, turning it over in her hands before plopping it on her head. She eyed Priscilla and Tobias as if waiting to see what they would do.

"It looks good on you." Priscilla smiled. "You may keep it. I'll make another."

The girl leapt to her feet in one bound and dashed into the underbrush.

"Wait! Come back." Priscilla rose and lifted onto her tiptoes, searching the locustberry shrubs.

Tobias also stood, but he didn't look for the girl.

"We must find her." Priscilla clasped her hands to her chest and implored Tobias with her eyes. "She's by herself in the dark."

"She's been by herself for some time now."

"But what if she gets hurt? What if she falls or gets attacked by a wild animal?"

"She's survived this long without us. Besides, I don't think it's the last we've seen of her." He shook his wet pant leg. "I need to wash."

Her hand flew to her lips to hide her smile. "I'd forgotten in all the excitement."

He strode to the pathway leading to the beach and paused. "Coming?"

"Most definitely." Priscilla grabbed the pot in need of cleaning but continued scanning the underbrush for any sign of the little girl.

Lord, I know you love children. Watch over that little girl. Her heart clenched. *She's even more lost than I am.*

CHAPTER 23

Bonaparte has settled into his role as the Emperor of
Elba. His mood has stabilized now that his mother and
sister have joined him on the island. He works to
improve the land by ordering the building of hospitals
and providing more drinking water.
~ *Letter from Colonel Neil Campbell to Lord Castlereagh*

*T*he following morning, Priscilla prayed again for
God's protection over the poor child—that He'd
bring them back together so they could help her. While she and
Tobias resumed their daily routine of searching for food and
water via coconuts, she scrutinized the island for any signs of
movement but spotted nothing unusual.

Lord, help us to find Your lost sheep as You helped me.

Tobias heaped a few of the larger sticks onto the fire before
they returned to the shoreline. Priscilla perched on a log to
work on her weaving, while he wore his wide cone hat and used
the fish head from their previous night's dinner to attract other
fish. Before the sun reached its zenith, he raised the net, which
was heaping full of a catch, but he hadn't captured fish. Instead,

a mass of crabs writhed in the net, their pinchers poking through the holes.

His white smile contrasted against his dark beard and tanned skin. "We feast again tonight."

Priscilla laughed. "Is food all you think about?"

"When trapped on a deserted island, it is." He strode to her and watched her fingers as she folded under the last reed. She put the hat on. "What do you think?" She squinted at him.

The sun's rays illuminated him in white light. "Lovely." He dropped the net in the sand. The crabs poked their pincher through the holes but couldn't escape. Tobias plopped beside her, wafting the scent of sweat and salt.

Her cheeks heated at his compliment.

He stared at the distant crashing waves, and she longed to rest her head upon his shoulder. How fickle her heart had become. Two weeks before, she'd blamed this man for all her woes. He'd taken over her brother's command. He'd refused to turn the ship around. With his overbearing ways, she'd believed him intent on making her life a misery.

Now, she respected Tobias's discipline and hard work. She enjoyed his presence more than anyone's she could remember, even Lottie. They could rest side by side without talking, and she didn't feel compelled to fill the silence... at least not always.

She stared at the churning ocean. The swirling water had signified death, but now it sustained them. Accidentally sailing with the *Trade Wind* had seemed like a tragic mistake, same with being washed overboard, but she was learning that God could turn all things around for His good.

Their talk last night had changed her. When Tobias praised her for being a quick learner, noticing things, and anticipating needs, her heart had shifted. Her parents, her brother, and even Miss Dodd to some extent had never recognized what she did right. They focused on what she'd done wrong. But Tobias noticed her positive qualities, and it drew her to him like a feral child to pickled peppers. Hearing his accolades shone a light into her darkness. He'd strengthened the hollow shell of her soul. And deep down, she knew she could also help support him. She'd seen it in how he'd opened up to her, how he relaxed and spoke his mind. Perhaps she could be a safe harbor for him, especially after all they'd been through together.

He may not love her, but she held the capacity to be loved. If Tobias noticed her good traits, there was hope someone else might also, if her reputation wasn't ruined beyond repair.

Tobias and rugged island life had revealed the courage she'd possessed all along. Like the jars they'd found, her value had been covered in barnacles. Slowly her insecurities had been covering her significance, eating at her worth, but her value was within. Her time free from the expectations of society—being stripped down to bare essentials—had revealed that her life held merit. If God knew when a single sparrow fell, and the Great Shephard would leave the ninety-nine to go after one lost sheep, if He would send a protector in Tobias to keep her from certain death, then surely, He must believe her worth loving.

"Do you smell that?" Tobias continued to watch the ocean.

Priscilla sniffed the air. "Smell what?"

"Vinegar."

"Vinegar?"

"As in pickled pepper's vinegar." He slowly turned his head and peered over Priscilla's shoulder.

She inhaled a deep breath with a hint of the acidic, sour odor.

"She's nearby. Watching us."

Priscilla straightened and glanced back over her shoulder.

"Don't move." Tobias stilled her with a hand. "You might scare her."

"Where is she?"

"On your ten o'clock."

Sure enough, crouched in gnarled underbrush, the child

observed them. Her dirty knees and feet poked from under the straw hat Priscilla made yesterday. Priscilla sucked in a breath. "What should we do?"

Tobias slowly stood and peered down the coastline. She could almost see his mind working on a solution to their problem. His confident gaze snapped back to Priscilla, and he aided her to rise. "Let's walk to the lagoon and see if she'll follow."

Her heart ached to help the poor child. She wanted to pull her into her arms and let her know they would protect her, that she didn't have to be alone anymore. Priscilla would clean her face, untangle the knots from her hair, and make her feel safe. She gripped his arm. "What if she doesn't follow?"

"I have an inkling she will." He scooped up the net, careful of the protruding pinchers.

The surety in his eyes relaxed her. He didn't want the child to leave any more than she did. She could read his care in the gray depths of his eyes, and she'd witnessed it last night in his patience. He hadn't flung the poor thing after she'd relieved herself on him. His hold was gentle yet firm, and he'd spoken in a soothing tone. Her heart fluttered then glided like one of those stingrays through clear water. She'd witnessed the makings of a great father. She slipped her arm through his as they skirted along the beach.

How romantic this moment might have been if they'd been strolling the beaches of Somerset, her hand on the arm of her suitor, her parasol spread wide behind her. She wasn't in England, nor was she being courted by the dashing Captain Prescott, yet her future still held promise. Would she want to be the wife of a sea captain? Her father had spent her infancy at sea, but his voyages grew few and far between as he was promoted to work for the War Department. It might not be the same for Tobias. He could be gone for months or years at a time or parish at sea.

An ache seized her chest, and her steps slowed.

Tobias's tanned face focused on her. "Something wrong?"

"I'm fine. Merely thinking." The thought of having an absent husband welled up a new sense of fear. Over the past week, Tobias had become a part of her—a comforting presence. He'd filled a hole within her. If he left, the hole would return along with the pain of loneliness. Was she strong enough to bear the emptiness again? Could she overcome her fears?

The answer clasped upon her like an iron shackle.

At the bend of the island, they rounded stacked boulders the size of London townhouses.

Wind died as they approached the lagoon. Several flamingos raised their heads briefly before returning to search for shrimp as if thinking, *those strange-looking creatures didn't bother us last visit.*

If anyone had told her two weeks ago she'd be stuck on a deserted island with a handsome captain and striving to befriend a feral child while surrounded by pink birds, she'd have thought they were the ones who'd taken leave of their senses.

"I'm going to swim out and search for another conch." Tobias dropped the netted crabs back on the beach and pointed to a small pile of conch shells resting under the mangrove trees. "I think she may like those better than cooked fish."

"You think she ate those?" Her tone pitched high.

A crooked smile twisted his mouth. "I've had my suspicions."

"How do you think she learned to survive? Surely someone had to teach her. I would have been so frightened. We have to help her."

"We will try. She's testing us to make certain we're safe. She's a smart little girl." He waded into the glassy water. "Why don't you wait here and listen for her. If it helps to appear busy, you could dig for clams or search for more oysters deep in the mangrove roots."

Priscilla swallowed back her fear. If a little girl could live alone on an island, Priscilla could make it a few minutes. Icy prickles tingled her spine. She clamped her jaw tight to keep the words in place, but they burst through her lips. "You're not going far?"

He glanced back over his shoulder. She expected to hear a heavy sigh and see an annoyed expression similar to what she'd often spied on Anthony's face, but Tobias didn't smirk.

His eyes remained warm, his tone gentle. "The water's clear. You should be able to see me even if I dive under."

"Very good." She waved as it had been an offhand question which had nothing to do with her fear.

"Come tap me if the sun moves a hands-length above the horizon. By then, the fire will need another log." He didn't wait for her nod of agreement to resume wading out.

She shielded her eyes from the sun reflecting off the water. His shoulders swayed as the water deepened, and bright sun illuminated the rolling of his muscles through the thin, wet material of his shirt. His head turned the slightest amount as his eyes scanned the sandy bottom for a creature dragging its weighty shell. As he drew near the flamingos, their heads popped up. As if of the same mind, they all flapped their wings. Black-tipped feathers flashed between the pink, and their long legs appeared to walk on water before they soared to the far edge of the lagoon and resettled.

Priscilla scanned for any sign of… she couldn't keep calling her girl or child.

A large black bird, similar to a Magpie back home, picked up a shiny shell in its beak. It dropped it into a pile at its nest and puffed out bright red plumage under its chin, which to Priscilla looked like the shape of a heart.

That was it. The child was like a little magpie. She appeared to be as shrewd as the notoriously smart bird, and she was attracted to new or curious objects. Maggie. She'd call the crafty little girl Maggie in her mind.

Grass near the island peak moved like a green wave, but

there was no sign of Maggie. Had Tobias left knowing Priscilla would be more approachable alone? Perhaps if she pretended to work, Maggie would feel more at ease.

Priscilla found one of the halves of an oyster shell Tobias had discarded when they'd last been at the lagoon. She trolled the area where the water lapped. The clams dug deep, leaving dime-sized indents in the sand and a small bubbling hole. Scooping the oyster shell, she flicked away the sand but found no sign of a clam. She moved from spot to spot, digging every tiny bubbling air hole until the beach became littered with dots.

Determined not to let Tobias find her empty-handed, she focused on the task at hand, almost forgetting her original goal. She swallowed a startled scream as a pair of dirty feet moved into her line of vision. Broken, uneven toenails wiggled, and the breeze flapped the hem of her thin and filthy gown. Her tangled mass of hair jutted in all directions. Maggie peered at her with fisted hands on her waist and a frown pursing her lips.

She stomped.

"You don't think I'm doing this correctly?"

Maggie squatted next to Priscilla and waited for the bubbles to return. She dug with her fingers, flinging sand in five or six fast scoops. She plunged her hand into the hole halfway up her elbow and pulled out a closed shell.

"You did it!" Priscilla smiled and clapped her hands.

Maggie picked up the oyster shell Priscilla had been using to dig and pried open the clam. Before Priscilla could react, the girl ripped the clam out with her teeth and discarded the empty shell over her shoulder. She started the process over, except this time, after prying open the clam, she offered it to Priscilla. Uncertain how to decline without hurting her new friend's feelings, she ate the shellfish, also removing it from the shell with her teeth. The live creature moved in her mouth, and Priscilla gagged. She forced it down, swallowing it whole. For the next few minutes, she was certain it squirmed in her belly. Her stomach threatened to cast up its accounts.

Maggie kept digging and ate a couple more. She offered more to Priscilla, but Priscilla held up a hand. "I'm going to save mine for later."

The girl seemed to understand, for she didn't continue to offer. Instead, she placed them in the hat Priscilla had given her. Priscilla talked to her as they worked. "You are the bravest little girl I've ever met. I'm scared of being by myself, and here you are alone on an island. I do believe you're alone? Aren't you?"

Maggie dropped another clam on top of the two she'd already collected. Her green eyes, rimmed with blue, peered at Priscilla. A low groan erupted in her throat, and her lips moved as if testing out the sound. Her mouth opened a bit too wide, but Priscilla distinctly heard, "Ma...Ma."

Not only did she understand, the girl was attempting to speak. Priscilla leaned forward. "Your mother is here." She pointed to the ground. "On the island?"

Maggie stared at her.

"Your mama is here?"

She nodded and pointed in the direction of sand-colored boulders, at least a story high, with one outcropping leaning against the other. The tops and surroundings were covered in moss and vines.

Priscilla followed the girl's gaze. "She's over there? In the cave?"

Maggie nodded. She jabbed her finger several more times.

"Can you take me to your mama?"

She bounced up and darted to the boulders.

Priscilla pushed to her feet. She waved her arms to signal Tobias in the distance, but his head dove underwater once more. She couldn't lose the child. Tobias would have to find them. She rushed after Maggie, catching glimpses of her matted hair or a dangling leg as she scaled the crags.

The climb was steep. Maggie crawled over the large rocks leading up to the outcropping, which explained the scratches and callouses on her knees. The child slowed and glanced back.

Priscilla clamored over boulders until she reached two rectangular stones leaning on each other. Maggie slipped between them, entering the darkness.

Priscilla called after her. "Wait."

Maggie's face reappeared inside the cave. Priscilla glanced over her shoulder for Tobias but only viewed the tops of the mangrove trees and the still turquoise lagoon beyond. *God, I hope he finds us.* She swallowed the tightness in her chest, shook her tingling fingers, and followed Maggie into the recesses. A warning cry sounded in the back of Priscilla's mind, but she ignored it. If Maggie could be brave, so could she. As her eyes adjusted to the dim light, she made out what essentially was two rooms of a cave, one in which they stood and another section that sloped down. A gap in the rocks high up in the other area allowed in some light and cast a water pattern on the ceiling. There had to be water below. Flashes of the reflected light illuminated a few sleeping bats dangling upside down with folded wings. Priscilla shivered. Maybe she should have waited for Tobias.

Priscilla cautiously walked the perimeter, exploring the colorful markings drawn on the wall—made by Maggie or her mother? "Is this where you live?"

Maggie frowned and tilted her head.

"Is this your home?"

She nodded.

No one was here. Was her mother out looking for food?

The upper enclosure sloped to a lower canyon room with a high ceiling and a narrow corridor that likely led to the ocean. Its floor consisted of sand and a couple of inches of rippling clear water. More light spilled in from a crack in the ceiling where a boulder had eroded, and a bit more came from the narrow back entrance to the cave, which was probably inaccessible during high tide.

A dripping sound echoed, and Priscilla followed it to the source—a small pool that trickled over the ledge running into the seawater below. Maggie knelt, scooped up a handful, and drank.

Priscilla gasped. The child couldn't be drinking seawater. She lowered and dipped her hand in the pool, glancing at Maggie for permission.

She nodded her head, and her matted hair flopped back and forth.

Priscilla drank, and fresh spring water quenched her parched throat. She gulped down several more handfuls. *Wait until Tobias hears of this.* She couldn't resist washing her face, too.

Maggie tilted her head, observing her.

Refreshed, Priscilla turned her focus back to the upper room where she spied a small pallet made of palm leaves. She turned to Maggie. "Is this where you sleep?"

Maggie blankly stared.

Priscilla folded her hands and rested her face against them, which Maggie seemed to understand. She nodded.

"Where is your mother?"

The little girl pointed to a dark alcove on the opposite side of the cave. A withered pile of palm leaves rested in the dark recess. The alarm in Priscilla's head roared once again as the hollow eyes of Maggie's mother peered back at Priscilla.

CHAPTER 24

Our great leader has fooled the guards into complacency.
They believe Bonaparte's claims that his time of greatness has passed. Start preparing the small fleet. Paint the
brigs to resemble a British vessel.
~ Translated letter from alias Mr. Goulart to French rebels

*P*riscilla's scream bounced off the rocks and startled
the flamingos in the lagoon into flight.

Tobias's foot slipped, scraping his ankle against a rock, but
he barely acknowledged it. A sense of urgency drove him as he
followed muddy footprints over the boulders. He'd caught a
flash of Priscilla's gown before it disappeared into the crags, and
he'd left the lagoon in pursuit. He should never have left her
alone. Pirates or wild natives could easily have moored,
witnessed a beautiful lone woman on the beach, and taken her
by force.

The conch shell he carried clattered on the rock as he used
his hands to climb. In his haste, he'd forgotten about the creature. The opening between the two boulders lay ahead, where

he'd caught a quick glimpse of Priscilla's blond hair before she disappeared. *God let them be safe.*

He launched himself into the unknown darkness. "Priscilla?"

He spotted the child's outline in the cave's center, her hands capped over her ears. Thank heaven, she was all right. Nearby, Priscilla's hands covered her mouth as she stared into an alcove.

In two swift strides, he was by her side. She spun and bumped into his chest, and he wrapped her in his arms, shielding her from whatever had frightened her.

"It's her," she murmured into his shirt. "It's Maggie's mother."

A shudder ran through her body, and he cupped the back of Priscilla's head, drawing her closer into his embrace. His need to protect her nearly brought him to his knees. He vowed to hold her and never let her out of his sight again.

Behind her, a yellowed, intact human skeleton lay upon withered palm leaves. The hollow, dark eyes of a long-decomposed skull stared at them.

His gaze flicked to the young girl. Her big eyes also seemed hollow, but for a different reason. "It's all right. We're safe." He spoke the words not only for Priscilla's and the child's benefit but because he also needed to hear them.

A moment passed, and Priscilla sagged against him. This was where she belonged, in the protection of his arms. The way she turned to him for comfort, touched him with ease, and leaned against his shoulder when they sat together on the beach stirred him the same way the helm of a ship invigorated him. He would guard her with his life.

She pulled back.

"Maggie's here. She found us." Priscilla held out her hand, and the girl cautiously stepped closer and clasped her fingers but hid behind Priscilla.

His eyebrows raised. "Maggie? She spoke her name?"

"Well, not exactly." Priscilla's gaze lowered, and she stepped aside so he could see Maggie, but the child shifted with Priscilla, peeking from around the full skirts. "That's the name I started to call her in my head, but she can speak. She's already said, 'Mama.'"

Tobias slowly dropped to one knee in front of her and offered the conch shell.

Maggie butted Priscilla's legs, causing Priscilla to readjust her footing to remain upright. Tobias patiently waited for her to grow accustomed to him. After a long moment, her little hand reached out and accepted the conch. She slowly backed away, eyeing him until there was a row boat's length between them. Then she turned and ran for the exit.

Priscilla gasped and grabbed her skirts to chase her, but Tobias clasped Priscilla's hand to stall her. "Let's see what she does."

Maggie stopped at an outcropping of rocks near the entrance and raised the conch high, slamming it pointy-end first against the boulder. She sat on the hard ground and easily pried open the conch door with her fingers and ripped out the mollusk. It squirmed as she bit into the meat like a wild beast, tearing off pieces using her back teeth.

Priscilla's hand moved to cover her mouth, and Tobias heard her gag.

Maggie devoured the conch as if she hadn't eaten in days, even though she'd recently eaten a whole jar of peppers and another full of olives. He couldn't blame her. When one didn't know when or where the next meal would come, one didn't waste food.

Priscilla's fingers splayed across her stomach, and she peered at him with wide, concerned eyes. She must be horrified to see a young girl eat in such a manner.

He shrugged it off. "It's all she knows."

Maggie finished the mollusk. Her tiny belly appeared

slightly rounded, pressing against the material of her much too small gown, especially compared to the rest of her, which was all bones and skin.

Priscilla rounded on him. "There's freshwater. Listen."

A drip splattered into a puddle.

"Over there." She pointed. "It must be a spring or pooled rainwater."

He followed the sound. Sure enough, water ran off a stalactite into a pool. He dipped his hand and drank, closing his eyes in sweet relief. More and more, he believed in their chances of survival.

When he rose and backed away, Priscilla held out her palm, which the little girl timidly accepted, and they strolled to the water in the lower section of the cave. Priscilla encouraged the child to wash, and Maggie reluctantly allowed her to remove the dirt. She dipped the hem of her gown in the water and used it to wipe the grime from Maggie's face and in between her tiny fingers.

His heart broke at the way Maggie studied Priscilla. Her tiny face shone with awe at Priscilla's mothering, as if the movements felt familiar, yet strange. Sloshing water echoed off the solid walls. Her loving fingers gently mothered the child. Tobias's heartbeat picked up its tempo. Priscilla's gentle nature with Maggie stirred something alive inside his chest. For a moment, a future with Priscilla caring for their children became a possibility. He pushed the image aside, facing facts. He was a sea captain, one destined to give his life for his king and country, and she was a Middleton with a fear of being alone.

The girls stood and started back toward him.

Maggie paused to scratch what must have been a bug bite on her leg. They continued, then paused again at the palm branch pile across from the alcove where Maggie must have slept. Priscilla's gaze passed from Maggie to Maggie's dead mother to

Tobias. "How long do you think she's been"—her throat convulsed— "dead?"

"By the looks of it, at least six months, probably longer." Tobias scratched his sideburn, still startled to find whiskers.

Her voice lowered to a whisper as she glanced back at Maggie, who pulled some palm leaves out of her bed. "What do you think happened?"

Tobias stole a glance at the bed of bones. The tibia was broken in several spots. "It looks like she might have fallen. Her leg was broken, but somehow, she was able to crawl here. Could have been the loss of blood, or perhaps infection set in. A whole host of things could have done it." He grimaced. Wounds were painful, but infection was a horrible way to die. He'd witnessed men under his command burn with fever one minute and shake with cold the next. Their skin would turn red and slough off in sheets, and their minds would deteriorate as they wavered between their half-awake, half-asleep nightmare.

"I haven't seen any signs of another human." Priscilla drew against his side and slid her hand around his arm. "Do you think they were the only survivors?"

"It appears so."

Maggie babbled with only a few distinguishable words like *no, mama,* and *ohm,* which he believed sounded like home.

His chest tightened. How did he go from avoiding women entirely to being responsible for the care of not one but two?

Priscilla looked past him to where Maggie played with what looked like dolls made from palm leaves. The tiny knots and braided arms indicated Maggie's mother must have made them for her.

Priscilla squeezed his arm then crouched next to Maggie. "Are those your dolls?"

As she spoke to the child, Priscilla's blond hair fell loose from its makeshift tie and cascaded over her tanned shoulders.

He never wanted to feel the panic of loosing her again. He'd grown accustomed to her quirks, chattiness, and gentle touch. He wanted to protect what was his.

A jolt slammed through Tobias, and he staggered back a step. He loved her.

∽

"*A*re these dolls you and your mama?" Priscilla re-tied her hair back.

Maggie's big eyes seemed to encompass her entire face. Her gaze dropped to the dolls before looking back at Priscilla. She gave the barest of nods.

Priscilla's heart broke for the poor child who'd watched her mother die. Had she continued to curl up next to her mother's dead body after her spirit left? Did she understand what happened, or had she thought her mother slept until the stench of death became so pungent, Maggie had to move her bed and sleep alone? *Oh, God.* Priscilla's throat tightened, and she swallowed back tears. Unable to speak, she opened her arms wide.

Maggie launched herself at Priscilla. Her thin legs wrapped around Priscilla's waist, and her tiny body curled under Priscilla's arm as a hermit crab clings to its shell.

Tears streamed over Priscilla's cheeks as she rocked Maggie with calming words and stroked her matted hair. "We're here now. You're safe, and you're not alone. We'll make sure you're never alone again."

Tobias's fingers slid around her waist in a possessive hold. His firm jaw was set and his stance wide. The relaxed castaway had been replaced, once again, with a resolute-captain, but she now recognized the gentle tenderness in his eyes that she'd overlooked onboard the *Trade Wind*. She leaned into his strength, her head tucked nicely under his chin, and her cheek rested on his firm chest. His arms wrapped around them both, cocooning Maggie within their offer of protection.

A pang twisted Priscilla's heart. She'd been selfish with her wishes to stay on the island. She loved being the center of Tobias's attention and feeling useful building and doing things, but she'd put her desires above the man who'd sacrificed so much of his life for her. It was now important not only for Tobias to return to his crew but also for Maggie to be returned to society so she could be reunited with her relatives. A new determination struck, infusing Priscilla's spine with fortitude. From now on, she'd pray with renewed fervor for their rescue.

Tobias cleared his throat and lowered his arms. "We need to head back before the fire burns out."

As she stepped away, she caught Tobias blinking a couple of times before he turned. Was he as touched by their little unit as she was? A mosquito buzzed around her ear, and she swatted it. More appeared, as if smelling a feast. She slapped one on her arm and chased another off Tobias.

"The insects will only get worse as it grows dark." Tobias waved his hand about his head. "It's amazing the mosquitoes didn't carry Maggie and her mother away. See if there is anything Maggie needs from here. We'll have her come back to camp with us."

Priscilla nodded and searched for anything a child might find valuable. A stack of conch shells sat in a corner, and there was the bed of dried palm branches. She crouched to speak with Maggie. "You're going to stay with us. Is there anything you want to bring?"

Maggie clutched her dolls. Her hollow eyes wandered around the cave and lingered over her mother's bones. Maggie shook her head before burying it again in Priscilla's shoulder.

"I think we're ready." Priscilla nodded at Tobias and rose.

Priscilla held Maggie as Tobias climbed down to retrieve the crabs and the net. Birds had picked a few legs off the crabs, but they would still provide a good meal. Maggie went willingly into Tobias's arms when he offered to carry her up the incline toward their camp. The route over the crest of the island would be shorter than skirting along the beach and back up. Whereas Priscilla had huffed and puffed under the additional weight, Tobias carried the girl as if she weighed a feather. They conversed on the way back about his stepsister, and he even took a moment to commend Maggie on how clever she was to figure out how to open a conch and get coconuts.

They settled into camp. Maggie played with her dolls, Priscilla boiled the crabs, and Tobias held the turtle shell over the pot, collecting the condensation into an empty coconut.

Maggie refused to eat the cooked crab, but Priscilla figured she must be full from the conch.

After filling their tummies, Tobias relayed the Bible story about Jonah and the whale.

Maggie sat in Priscilla's lap and listened as he acted out the story with his hands. Priscilla's heart swelled at the wonderful father Tobias would make someday. Each time Maggie shifted, Priscilla worried Maggie might run back to her cave the way she'd done the night before, but as the story concluded, Maggie's breathing had deepened, and her body grew limp against Priscilla.

Tobias's voice trailed off to a whisper, and he smiled at Priscilla. "She's asleep."

He moved to sit next to her, and they both stared at the fire while Maggie dozed.

Priscilla leaned against his shoulder and inhaled his scent, feeling needed for the first time—even wanted. She released a contented sigh, but as she exhaled, traces of guilt seeped back in. "I have a confession."

Tobias didn't speak, but his head tilted toward her.

"I know it's my fault you're here, and I regret all I've cost you." Seeing the remnants of Maggie's mom made the possibility of never being rescued feel all the more real. "But I don't regret being here." A sad chuckle burst from her lips. "I know it sounds ridiculous, but being here is the best thing that's happened to me in a long time."

"Why do you say that?" His tone rang with surprise.

Because of you. She bit her tongue, unwilling to confess such thoughts. Or how being here bided more time from having to explain what happened the night of the party and witness her parent's disappointment. After all she'd endured, how could a slip of the tongue be considered treason? It was likely she'd overblown the whole incident. The real reason she longed to remain on the island sat beside her, and now another rested curled in her arms. "I serve a purpose here." She swallowed. "In London, life was little more than one party after another. My parents threw hundreds of them so the world would believe our family was happy, but we aren't. My dad buries himself in his work while my mother pours herself into her charity groups so they can ignore how miserable they are. My life held little meaning except to keep up their farce and eventually marry into what I assumed would be another sham of a marriage."

The fire popped. Tobias tensed, likely because of the noise. He poked a log with a long stick. "Why do you think marriage is a farce?"

"My parents barely speak to one another. It's another reason why I babble so. I hated quiet. The tension screamed at me until I hushed the blaring silence with my ceaseless prattle." A new clarity settled over her. "You've helped me become comfortable with silence. With you, the quiet is comfortable. It doesn't blaze with unspoken judgment or criticism."

He laced his fingers through hers and pulled her hand onto his lap. The simple gesture displayed more love than anything she'd witness from her parents in years. "Then we're even. You've helped me to talk to females." He chuckled. "Two females to be precise, one woman and one little girl." He gently squeezed her hand. "It's not uncommon for marriages among the *ton* to be based on bloodlines and finances. Love matches are atypical."

"I know. I thought I could be happy in such an arrangement, but now..." Her throat tightened, choking her words. What could she say? That he'd changed her heart, made it his for the taking?

Tobias's breath rushed in and out between his parted lips. It synched with the rise and fall of her chest as if they were the same being.

She steered the conversation back to safer ground before she professed her love and begged him to make a life here with her on the island, as ridiculous as it sounded. "I hope you'll get to meet my friend, Lottie. You'll like her. She's very respectful and obedient."

"And the two of you were friends?"

She shook her head at his mocking tone. "Indeed. Even though we were exact opposites. Her mother, Lady Etheridge, held tight rein over Lottie, whereas my parents..." How many times had they opened their mouths but didn't know what to say to her? How often had she driven them away with her ceaseless chatter? "They didn't know what to do with me. Being abducted set a rift between us. Instead of dealing with the awkwardness, they ignored it and allowed me to do as I pleased."

He grimaced. "I understand how not dealing with an issue can harm a person."

The bitter tone insinuated he was thinking of Annie. Not wanting this special moment of sharing to turn gloomy, she once again attempted to lighten the mood. "It turns out I'm not great with freedom. It chokes me."

"Truly? I thought you preferred your freedom. You certainly dislike direct commands."

How could she explain? "I saw my parents' lack of boundaries as an absence of caring. When they railed at me, at least I knew they cared."

"Earning their respect might have gotten you farther." Tobias's gaze lowered to the sleeping form curled in her lap.

She swallowed. By telling him the truth, she might condemn herself in his eyes. Tobias was the epitome of loyalty and respect, and after her reckless actions caused them to go overboard, she deserved neither. "I knew something wasn't right with me. Other kids could play by themselves, read books in a corner, or sleep alone. I wasn't one of them. I worked so hard to appear normal when I knew I wasn't. Lottie was the only person I trusted with the secret of my nightmares. After she married and left for the islands, my episodes seemed to grow worse— more frequent and uncontrollable. I became desperate for companionship. I befriended people who only led me into more trouble." She stared into the fire. "The passage in Proverbs was right. Miss Dodd often recited it to me. 'He that walketh with wise men shall be wise, but a companion of fools shall be destroyed.' It's why I went to see my brother the night the *Trade Wind* sailed. I'd overstepped. My friend convinced me to attend a soiree I knew wouldn't be above reproach, but I hadn't expected it to be so political. Merely being seen could have ruined my father's reputation with the Whigs."

The horrid events of that evening flooded back. "My friend disappeared with a man who wasn't a gentleman who convinced her to drug her chaperone. My dance partner left instead of helping me find her." And then her father was there. Her chest heaved with each breath.

He drew her head onto his shoulder and trailed his fingers along her jawline. "Psalm 107 says, 'They that go down to the sea in ships...will see His wonders in the deep.' Those who are willing to change, to step out of what is comfortable, will see God's wonders. Sometimes we have to witness disaster before God can bring us into our safe haven."

Maggie snuggled deeper into her lap.

"That's just it." She turned her head to face him.

Tobias sat so close his nose practically touched hers.

His eyes darkened to deep blue.

Her voice strained above a whisper. "I feel safe here with you."

CHAPTER 25

It is complete Bedlam. The Americans arranged a motley crew of soldiers consisting of everything from bare-footed frontiersman, to negro slaves, to Indians, and even to blasted pirates.

~ *Log of Lieutenant General Pakenham*

A surge of protectiveness shot through Tobias's body. His arms reflectively tightened around Priscilla's shoulders, aching to embrace the spirited, maddening woman who'd taught him how to be vulnerable by humbling herself and baring her wounds to him. He'd blamed her for all he'd lost, but he'd sacrifice everything—his ship, his career, his future—all over again for this moment.

Beyond the reflection of smoldering firelight, her luminous eyes brimmed with tenderness and passion, sparking a desire to create a new future. He'd assumed his purpose in life was to become a martyr for his country as his father had, but could a life with Priscilla be as meaningful? Could saving one lamb be as great a sacrifice as saving the ninety-nine?

The sweetness of her breath lured him like the tropical

breeze, and her full lips, inches from his, tempted him with their softness. His discipline slipped. She'd affected him, wearing down his rigid fortifications and showing him the thrill of spontaneity. He claimed her mouth in a soul-reaching kiss. His lips absorbed her gasp, and he relished the curve of her smile. He shifted his body, his hands curving around the nape of her neck. He held nothing back, drinking in the glory of her ardor as she responded and matched it with her own.

A muffled whimper sounded between them.

Priscilla broke their kiss, and an emptiness swept over him. He forced his eyes open. Murmurs turned to cries, and Priscilla soothed Maggie. Her slender fingers gently stroked the damp hair on Maggie's forehead.

How could he have forgotten about Maggie?

The child's eyes squeezed tight, and her dark brows furrowed. She curled deeper into Priscilla's midsection as the cries softened back to whimpers before ceasing.

Glistening tears brimmed Priscilla's eyes, but she blinked them away. "Do you think she suffers from nightmares like I do?"

He studied the child's fragile frame. "It's likely."

"I'm glad we found her."

"Me too."

"I think I can help her."

Tobias's breath hitched. Was it God's plan for him to save Priscilla so she could save Maggie? For a long moment, he sat holding Priscilla as she cradled the child. Was altruism like a wave expanding out to affect others? They might have fallen overboard, but more and more, he suspected none of this had been an accident.

Priscilla's blinks slowed, and her head lolled until she jolted back awake.

Tobias grinned at her efforts. "I think it's time to turn in."

He scooted away from Priscilla and scooped up Maggie. The

child barely weighed a stone and hung limp in his arms. He aided a drowsy Priscilla to her feet and walked her the mere two yards to her lean-to. After she braided her hair and settled into the bed of palm branches, he laid Maggie next to her. The child rolled against Priscilla's side and released a contented sigh.

Tobias strode to his lean-to and lay down. Typically, he was a back sleeper letting the stars navigate him into sleep, but tonight he lay on his side, observing the delicate curves of Priscilla's outline. The rest of Psalm 107 ran through his heart. *They were glad that the waters were quiet, and He brought them to their desired haven. Let them thank the Lord for His steadfast love, for His wondrous works to the children of man!* As his eyelids drew to a close, his heart praised God for His wonders and safe haven.

~

A frantic moan tore Tobias from his needed sleep. The full moon illuminated their camp in a bluish light. Priscilla tossed her head in the throe of a nightmare. It was her wail that had woken him. A smaller whimper echoed. *Maggie.* He pushed to a stand, shaking off cobwebs of sleep. Palm leaves rustled as Maggie stirred. "Priscilla." He tiptoed to them. "It's just a dream."

She flopped onto her back with a groan. Her blond hair glowed pale blue in the moonlight. She twisted from side to side, wagging her braid like the line of an untrimmed sail.

Maggie's small, sleeping form shivered, likely from the lack of warmth since Priscilla had rolled away.

Tobias crouched beside them. "Priscilla, you need to wake from this nightmare."

Her head rolled to face him, and shiny tracks of tears shone upon her cheeks. Her lips parted in a squeak of a whimper.

He held her shoulder to wake her, but instead, she rested her face on his fingers. The soft dampness of her cheek twisted his stomach. She cried in her sleep.

God, rescue them from this torture.

Maggie wiggled close as if searching for warmth.

He shifted to sit beside her just outside the small lean-to and, with his free hand, stroked Maggie's hairline as Priscilla had. The child's body relaxed, and her breathing deepened. His father may have been distant, and his mother may have chosen his stepfather over him, but these two fragile women needed him even more than his men. His crew required a leader for direction, but Priscilla needed him to support her emotionally, mentally, and physically. He'd failed Annie by not being there for her. Maybe being there for Priscilla was his chance for redemption.

Priscilla rolled onto her side, nestling Maggie between them and freeing his hand.

He stretched out on his side next to Maggie, content to watch them sleep.

Two people were now in need of his protection. More than ever, he needed to get them off the island, but would leaving the island change what was growing between them?

～

*P*riscilla woke to giggling. Maggie sat near the campfire, eating strips of coconut while Tobias sang from the private area of the bushes. He sang a sea ditty, and every time the chorus belted a long "Ohhhhhh," Maggie erupted into another fit of giggles.

Priscilla sat up and unbraided her hair, running her fingers through it before re-braiding.

Tobias returned to camp. A genuine smile broke over his face to find them awake, greeting him.

Maggie jumped up and grabbed Tobias's finger. She led him

through the underbrush. Several minutes later, they returned with an armload of large greenish-yellow orbs. Maggie bit one, spitting out the peel, revealing a juicy bright orange fruit center. She handed it to Tobias.

"I think Maggie is rewarding you for your singing." Priscilla chuckled.

He examined the fruit and smelled it. "I believe it's a mango. I haven't had enough of them to be certain."

Maggie yanked it from his hands and bit into it once more before handing it back as if to show it was safe to eat.

He accepted the fruit, tasted it, and nodded his head while he chewed.

Maggie clapped her hands.

"It's quite good. I think Maggie just showed us another food source."

She touched her lips and gestured, fluttering her fingers as if they were musical notes floating into the air.

"You like my singing?"

Maggie mimicked his "Ohhhhhh" of the chorus and then burst into another bout of childish laughter. Priscilla covered her mouth to keep from giggling.

"Do you know this one?" Tobias erupted into England's national anthem, *God Save the King*. She didn't show any sign of having heard it, so Tobias taught her, which served as the perfect distraction for Priscilla to detangle Maggie's hair. Maggie appeared to enjoy the attention. Only once, when Priscilla pulled too hard, did Maggie snarl and act as if she might bite, but Tobias stopped her with a firm "no."

Maggie lowered her head, appearing contrite. Several hours must have passed before Priscilla had most of the knots out. By then, Maggie could sing the tune of *God Save the King*, even if she babbled most of the words.

Later that day, while Tobias caught a fish for their supper, Priscilla and Maggie crouched in the sand, digging for clams.

Their holes turned into a moat, which needed a castle, and soon Tobias joined them, declaring the fortress needed a tall tower and a front gate. They found seaweed and seashells to decorate the exterior, and Tobias created an elaborate story of a knight rescuing a princess who lived in the tower. Priscilla was as enraptured by the tale as Maggie and noted Tobias no longer fumbled for words, not even the slightest bit.

Several days later, as Maggie began to emulate their actions and act less like a wild beast and more like a young girl, Priscilla decided all young ladies must learn to dance a proper minuet.

On the beach, Priscilla hummed a tune and taught Maggie the steps, and Tobias patiently partnered them both. Maggie stood on Tobias's toes as he moved her through the dance. As Priscilla watched, the empty aches of her heart, the ones that had always cried to be fed, filled to overflowing. She'd heard the words of Jesus read to her from the book of Matthew, *I have come so that they may have life, and have it to the full,* but this was the first time she believed those words could apply to her.

The next weeks passed. They worked together in the cool morning and, in the evenings, gathering wood to keep the fire ablaze, making repairs to clothing, the fishing net, and the lean-tos, all the while scrounging for food and water. However, each midday was spent in satisfying bliss for Priscilla, for they rested out of the scorching heat in the shade of a palm tree and enjoyed one another's company.

This morning, she manned the net ready to heave if a fish passed into their trap, but her attention drifted. Tobias, who'd made several grueling trips to the spring and back, stood on the beach and taught Maggie how to play a game similar to cricket. He used a broken paddle they'd found washed ashore to whack a coconut toward a stick in the sand. It was Maggie's turn at-bat. Her dark hair hung in two braids that Priscilla had fastened.

Lord have mercy, had the child squirmed when Priscilla had fixed her hair. Removing tangles had grown easier once Tobias whittled a comb from another turtle shell. He'd presented the comb as a present on the day likely to have been Christmas. Truth be told, their sense of time had diminished. Days blended into one another, but they celebrated anyway with a coconut-and-conch feast, which remained Maggie's favorite food. She even ate some of the shellfish cooked, though her preference for raw meat persisted.

Priscilla had presented Maggie with a new long dress, which she'd fashioned from the gown Maggie's mother had worn. The stitching was crude due to the coconut string thread and fish-bone needles, and so was the shape, since Priscilla had only learned to embroider not sew, but it served Maggie better than her too-short, threadbare gown. She'd given Tobias a woven mat to cushion his bed and a telescope she'd found on one of their dives into the shipwreck.

Her fingers moved to the necklace Tobias had made for her. He'd carefully drilled a hole through a piece of teardrop-shaped sea glass. She'd witnessed him sanding and polishing something for weeks, but he'd refused to show it to her. Now the precious gift dangled from her neck fastened by washed-up fishing line. She treasured the necklace more than the expensive gifts purchased by servants on her parents' behalf.

Tobias had hidden it behind his back while they each exchanged gifts. He hesitated as if uncertain before holding out a coconut shell to her. She'd laughed, thanking him for the coconut, but he urged her to open it. Her fingers shook as she lifted the lid. Blue-green sea glass sparkled against the white of the coconut, and she held it up to the light, exclaiming over its exquisite color and shape. He brushed back her hair and gently tied it around her neck. When she turned to him and asked how it looked, his eyes held hers for a long moment. "Its color reminded me so much of your eyes. I knew I had to give it to you." The muscles worked in his throat. "But, its clarity reminds me of your goodness and your purity."

Her lips parted, and she couldn't find words. A yearning she'd never experienced throbbed inside her entire being. It was the loveliest thing anyone had ever said to her.

Thankfully, Maggie broke the silence with her insistent, "Me see. Me see."

Priscilla blinked back to the present. A sunfish lazily swam over to the net, but it was too small to bother capturing.

"Keep your hands in the middle of the handle." Tobias modified Maggie's grip. Her saucer-like eyes stared up at him as he demonstrated. When she nodded, he walked a few paces and bowled the coconut to her. She missed it the first time, but Tobias was patient. Several more rolls, and Maggie swung the paddle with her entire body. The coconut skittered past him. Tobias whooped and rushed over to congratulate her. The breeze swept their words away, but it ended in Tobias tickling Maggie's side. The little girl's peal of laughter rose above the wind.

"Did you see little Miss Mag-pie's hit?" Tobias proudly smiled at Priscilla, and her heart swelled until bursting. How long could she hide her feelings for him?

"You see, Cill-ah?" Maggie's expression widened with excitement. "You see?"

Priscilla laughed and nodded. "You swung hard. I saw you."

Tobias lifted Maggie onto his shoulders. She giggled and wrapped her tiny arms around his head as they ambled to where Priscilla stood.

Maggie stiffened, and the smile disappeared from her face. "No, Toe-be. Down." She fell to the right with full confidence Tobias would catch her. He set her on the sand, and she darted up the path that led to camp.

"Where is she off to?" Priscilla cupped her hands around her mouth without releasing the net. "Maggie. Come back." When the girl didn't listen, Priscilla turned back to Tobias. "Do you think we should go after…"

Tobias's face paled, and he stood stiff on the shore with his fingers clenched by his sides.

Her stomach dipped, and she whirled around to follow his stare. Off in the distance, she could see the dark lines of masts backdropped by white sails. She shielded her face from the sun and could make out not just one ship but an entire fleet. Even in the heat, a chill penetrated her core. Would the sailors see them? Would they be rescued? Was the life they'd established here at an end?

Behind her, she heard Tobias move. By the time she turned, he'd sprinted the coastline, waving the broken paddle above his head. "Here! We're over here," he shouted above the crashing waves.

Priscilla remained frozen to the spot. Her gaze traveled from the rocks she'd set out to spell H-E-L-P on the beach to the wisp of smoke emanating from their fire. The truth slapped her in the face. She no longer wanted to be rescued. She wished to stay here with Tobias and Maggie permanently. They were her family now. This island was her home. Things were simpler here. Her life in England reminded her of peering through shattered glass, distorting and confusing her purpose, but here things were clearer, like the ocean in front of her and the sea glass dangling around her neck.

Tobias tossed the paddle next to her, huffing from his exertion. "I don't think they saw me. We need to stoke the fire and hope the smoke attracts the eye of a barrelman in the crow's nests."

She followed Tobias as he dashed up the same path Maggie had ascended. His feet pushed off the rocks with smooth agility, and she scrambled to keep up. At the top, he skidded to a halt, and a tortured groan erupted from deep within his gut. He gripped his head with both hands as if holding it in place.

The fire was out. Someone had smothered it—like before.

Maggie.

Tobias burst into action. He dropped to his knees and pulled out burnt logs from the fire with his bare hands. "We have to find an ember to start the fire again." He winced and shook his hand after touching hot coals.

She passed him the turtle shell to use as a tool and scanned the area for Maggie. Why would she extinguish the fire? Was she frightened of the ships?

Tobias continued to pick through the remnants blowing on ashes.

A hiccupped breath drew Priscilla's attention. Crouched in the shadowed corner of the lean-to sat Maggie. Her knees drawn to her chest, she rocked back and forth, hugging her legs. Priscilla crawled into the lean-to, sat next to Maggie, and opened her arms. Maggie clung to Priscilla and wailed. Priscilla shushed her, cupping her back and reassuring her everything was all right.

Tobias paused and rubbed the lower half of his jaw, staring off into the distance, a muscle twitching in his temple. "Confound it." Tobias hurled the shell onto the ground, rose, and stomped off.

Priscilla hugged Maggie closer and squeezed her eyes shut. She should also be angry. Those ships were the closest they'd been to rescue since they had arrived on this island. Didn't she want to see Lottie, her parents, her brother, her other friends?

Her heart answered with clarity. *Not if it means losing Tobias and Maggie.*

Maggie's sobs turned to sniffles and then to heavy breathing. Priscilla laid the child down for a nap on fresh palm branches and stood. She observed Maggie's sweet sleep for several minutes before dusting off her hands and seeking Tobias.

She found him at the overlook, where she often spoke to God in the mornings.

He stood in his captain-stance, his legs wide, his head high, and his hands folded behind his back. His telescope was clutched in one. He stared over the ocean, watching the ships pass. She moved to stand by his side. A thousand questions piled in her mind, but she remained quiet, merely offering her presence as solace, which he seemed to prefer.

When he finally spoke, his voice sounded hoarse, as if he hadn't any water in days. "I calculated the dates. They're two weeks late, but I suspected they'd pass. It's the *Trade Wind*, right there in the front." He pointed to the furthest ship. "I can tell by the flag hung above the spanker. She's leading the others." He passed her his telescope.

She accepted it but didn't look.

The emotion drained from his voice. "Maggie was the one who'd extinguished the fire before, but I figured it was because she was afraid it would spread. This time she deliberately put it out so as not to attract the ships. Why would she do such a thing?"

Priscilla let silence fall between them as she inhaled a steadying breath. "I don't think she wants us to be rescued. She may believe we won't take her with us."

The muscle at his jaw twitched. "This was my opportunity to rejoin my men, to lead them into battle." He raked his fingers through his hair. "It was my chance to be a hero like my father." His voice dropped to a whisper. "I was supposed to do whatever it took to win the battle for our country—to die for my king."

Priscilla blinked. "Die? I know you wanted to be a hero like your father, but why would that include dying?"

"I swore an oath to defend my king and country at all costs. My blood must spill so others might live."

"Don't be ridiculous." He must be confused. He couldn't mean that. "The crown doesn't expect you to die. If that were true, there'd be no naval forces left to fight the next battle."

"You don't get it." He rounded on her, eyes blazing. "It was asked of my father, and now it is expected of me."

"Who? Who expects this of you?"

He pinched the bridge of his nose and inhaled a deep breath. "The man who gave his last coin to pay for my commission, every commander who trained me and invested in me, every sailor who has served under me and looked up to me—they all expect greatness. They expect something profound, something grandiose. Lord Nelson was able to live to fight at Trafalgar because my father threw himself in front of a cannonball to save Nelson's life."

Her heart squeezed, wanting to weep for the small boy whose father never returned home—the little man who grew up desiring to be like his father before him. "I'm sorry."

"Don't be." He shifted his gaze to the passing ships. "It was my father's greatest glory to give his life for his country. 'Greater love hath no man than this, that a man lay down his life for his friends. John fifteen-thirteen.'"

He shook a fist at the ships growing tiny on the horizon. "This mission was my chance to prove I could live up to his legacy."

Surely, Tobias didn't hope to die to live up to his father's legacy? She shook her head with the barest of shakes. He was too practical to do something so ridiculous.

An odd glint of determination lit his eyes. "I will not fail in this."

"What about those you can only help by being alive? What about Maggie? What about me?" She choked back a sob. "If you die, then you fail us and the others you could have helped in the future."

"You." He raked his fingers down his face. The cords of his neck strained. "You were not part of my plan."

"Your plan? What about God's plan?" She wrapped her arms around her midsection, feeling like she might come apart. Did he want to die? How could Tobias hold such little regard for her after all they'd endured? Didn't he know how much she needed him? "Do you really think God is done with you? Do you truly believe you've finished the race—you've served your purpose? Didn't you say God has plans for me—to give me a hope and a future? Doesn't that also apply to you? Have you even consulted Him? Have you prayed about this?"

"Yes!" he shouted, but then he lowered his gaze. "I have." This time his voice didn't sound as confident.

"Didn't you tell me, 'The heart of a man plans his way, but the Lord establishes his steps?' Well, might God perchance be changing your course?" She watched the sails fading into the distance. "It certainly seems as if He may have other plans for you because, if you were supposed to die saving your crew and country, why would you have risked your life to save mine?"

Vicelike hands gripped her arms and spun her to face him. A vein protruded from his forehead, and his face reddened. "I don't know."

Did he mean he didn't know God's plan or that he'd felt he'd made a mistake in saving her? The direct hit of his words penetrated her heart. A nagging voice from her past spoke once again. *He's right. You're a menace, always in the way. Your life isn't worth saving. No one cares for you.* Her life wasn't worth those of his crew or the heroism he'd receive for saving his country. A chill swept through her as blood drained from her body and gushed from her wounded heart.

Tobias squeezed his eyes closed. Anguish creased his face, and he released her as if his hands had been burned.

Tears streamed down her cheeks, and a sob tore from her throat. Her knees, no longer willing to hold her, sank to the ground. She'd been a fool. All this time, she'd thought he'd come to care for her, that he understood the grip of fear that bound her, but she'd lied to herself. The truth was there in his eyes. He blamed her.

His hand clenched into fists. He pivoted on his heel and stormed from the clearing.

The shattering of her heart pierced her ears.

CHAPTER 26

We have suffered massive casualties, including the noble
Lieutenant General Sir Edward Pakenham, who
succumbed to lethal wounds sustained from grapeshot
fire.
~ *Letter from a wounded Colonel Peters to Admiral Sims*

"*B*last!" Tobias hauled up an empty net. The fish
escaped through a hole Tobias had unintentionally
created. It had caught on coral, but instead of saving the net and
letting the fish escape, he yanked harder. He didn't even need
the fish. The three he'd caught over the past few hours was
more than they could eat in a day, but he wanted to stay occupied so he didn't have to acknowledge the turbulence warring
within him. He held up the torn section of net to assess the
damage. He'd already swum out to the wreck and returned with
another jar of olives. He'd lit another fire and found a taller
branch to hoist the white flag. However, when Priscilla sparked
conversation, he kept his responses to brief one-word answers.

It wasn't Priscilla's fault, and sweet little Maggie was too
innocent to understand the disaster of her actions. Even with a

fire burning, there was a good chance the ships wouldn't have spied it or broken protocol for a rescue. *Thunder n' turf*, he wouldn't have stopped the mission. He'd have sworn to come back around after the Americans and their General Andrew Jackson were defeated. Years of training beat into him the emphasis of the greater good—king and country over the individual. Who was he to second-guess?

Other frustrations also mounted, tainting his mood. He'd seen how Priscilla's enthusiasm to be rescued had wavered over time. Now that Maggie was part of their misfit family, it seemed as if Priscilla was content to stay here forever. She'd lost sight of the main objective, and now only he was left to fight for the mission.

Might God be changing your course?

Her poignant words latched onto his thoughts. Was God redirecting his steps? Had the mission changed? He couldn't deny his overwhelming desire to protect Priscilla and now Maggie. The longer he stayed on this island, the more he lost his objectivity, the more he imagined a life with Priscilla by his side, and the more his traitorous heart moved into her hands.

He smacked the net against the rocks.

Stay the course, and remember your mission. No matter what the cost.

Tobias squeezed his eyes shut. He wasn't angry at Priscilla or Maggie. He was upset with himself because, truth be told, he wanted to stay.

If his crew caught wind of his feelings, or if his father or his father before him looked down from heaven and saw his selfishness, they'd hang their heads in shame.

He'd failed them, and in his heart, he'd betrayed his country.

∾

*T*he knot in Priscilla's stomach left little room for food, but she swallowed her supper anyway to keep up appearances. Maggie's guilt for putting out the fire seemed to weigh on her small shoulders. She even ate cooked fish instead of holding out for the uncooked portions she preferred. All the while, she peeked up at Tobias to see if he noticed.

"Good girl." Tobias acknowledged her efforts, but he didn't smile or tease her like he'd done the night before. Instead, his gaze drifted back to the distant horizon, ruminating in his thoughts.

Priscilla double-praised Maggie's efforts to compensate for Tobias's inattentiveness and babbled like a henwit to fill the uncomfortable sullenness quieting their camp.

Maggie's shoulders slumped lower as their meal progressed, and when Tobias wasn't looking, she snatched a grasshopper off a rock and popped it into her mouth.

Priscilla gagged on the fish she'd eaten as the rest in her stomach threatened to make a reappearance.

Maggie's big eyes questioned Priscilla as she swallowed. Her lower lip trembled.

Priscilla patted the girl's hand. They would have a discussion later about how little girls don't eat bugs and how it's proper for food to be cooked, but Priscilla didn't have the heart to broach it with Maggie right now. The poor child's expression already held a hollow, dejected-look while she helped Priscilla clean up the remnants of dinner.

Tobias brooded in silence as he mended the fishing net and collected more firewood. Their pile of wood grew substantial, and yet he left to retrieve more. Priscilla wanted to scream at his retreating form and pound his back with her fists. When they retired for the night, instead of crawling next to Maggie like a rearguard while she slept, Tobias lay in his lean-to. Priscilla glanced in his direction more than once, but he rested on his back with his eyes closed.

How long would he torture himself and them in the process? Maggie had already suffered through so much. Over the past month, Maggie had come to love Tobias as a surrogate father, and Priscilla had come to... Her eyes burned with unshed tears. Lord help her, she'd come to love him, for all his odd traits. She loved him still, and she didn't know how much longer she could endure the torment of his moody silence. Tobias might feel lost and left behind, but he wasn't alone. They were in this together. God hadn't forgotten them. He would pull them through. She must help him believe.

That night Priscilla's dream returned. She raced down dim streets, searching unfamiliar faces. This time she wasn't her six-year-old self, but a full-grown woman barefoot in a tattered gown stiff with saltwater, running through Hyde Park and weaving along London streets begging strangers to help her find Tobias, but they shook their heads. A wail sounded, and she pivoted around to find Maggie crouched in an alley next to a broken barrel. She lifted the girl onto her hip, shushed her, and scrambled after a passerby. A pair of well-dressed men strolled ahead of her, and she tugged one of the men's jackets. He turned. She opened her mouth to inquire if he'd seen Captain Prescott, but she recognized this man—Mr. Goulart, her former dance partner, and beside him, turned his friend Lord Fortin.

Mr. Goulart rubbed the side of his nose with his thumb knuckle and grinned a wicked smile. "We've been looking for you."

Lord Fortin reached for her, his hand turning to the shadowy tentacles of the darkness. She clutched Maggie to her chest and ran.

Priscilla awoke, choking on her scream. Maggie's face had curled into Priscilla's chest, and her wet tears soaked her skin. Had Maggie, too, had a nightmare, or had her moans frightened the child? Priscilla rubbed her back. "You're fine. It was just a dream. We're all right." She glanced over at Tobias, who slept on his side, his back facing them.

Her heart clenched as she swallowed her sobs.

~

*P*riscilla couldn't shake the residual fragments of her dream. The face of Mr. Goulart prickled a sense of eerie foreboding at the back of her neck.

Tobias greeted her with his usual, "Good morning."

Had things returned to normal? Priscilla stretched, plaited her hair, and shook the wrinkles from her gown. "I had my dream again last night, but this time it was different."

Tobias whittled the tip of a stick into a spear instead of responding.

"I ran frantic through London, stopping people to ask them if they'd seen you." The vividness of her dream returned in full. She hugged her midsection and watched a gecko climb a nearby tree. "Maggie was there, and so was Mr. Goulart, a former dance partner of mine." She glanced over at Tobias.

He paused his whittling but didn't look in her direction. Soon the rhythmic scraping continued.

"He was with Lord Fortin, the same men from the party I had left to find Anthony on the *Trade Wind*."

He grunted his acknowledgment.

Would he continue to withdraw from them? He needed time to process, but how long? She turned to Maggie, still sleeping in the lean-to, so he wouldn't see the disappointment on her face. Poor Maggie had tossed and turned most of the night. She needed her rest.

Muttering something about formulating a new plan, Tobias set his knife and stick aside and excused himself before striding down the privacy-path. He didn't sing.

She watched him until he disappeared behind a cluster of trees. Needing to pray, Priscilla strode to the opposite end of camp, where the short path to the clearing began. If she stood partway, she could see Maggie's sleeping form but also peer out over the rocks to the vast ocean and speak to God.

The sun glinted off the water, and a stiff breeze whipped the tendrils of hair not pulled back in her topknot. She brushed them away from her face and frowned at the dark clouds moving in on the horizon.

"Lord, how do I navigate these stormy waters? I'm afraid Tobias is cutting me off because he feels betrayed. Like he did to his mother and like he did to Anthony. I'm afraid I'm losing him. God, I think I'm in love with him. No man has angered me the way Tobias does, nor made me as happy and carefree with a single glance. I love the way he plays with Maggie, and I love his heart for You and his country."

She glanced back to check on Maggie, still sleeping. "I'm afraid if we are rescued, Tobias will return to his life as a captain, and I'll be forgotten. Even worse, he'll do something half-crazed like get himself killed. If I were to lose him, I'd might as well have drowned in the ocean, for my life would be nothing." The emptiness of facing a future alone stirred the darkness back to life. Its tendrils fingered her neck, tightening the roots of her hair.

The wind picked up, pressing her skirt tight against her legs.

My love is enough. The wind seemed to speak to her, and a calm warmth flooded her heart. *Your name is carved on the palm of My hand. That is how precious you are to Me. So much so, My Son gave up His life for you.*

Hadn't these past months demonstrated how far God would go to recover His lost lamb?

The tentacles of fear retreated.

"You're right." Sucking in a ragged breath, she asked God to forgive her. "I've tried to fill my void with the love of others when Your love can fill me to overflowing. All I needed was to accept it." She raised her chin and closed her eyes, feeling the warmth of the sun shining upon her and God starting to mend her broken heart.

Those who go down to the sea in ships... will see the works of the Lord and His wonders in the deep.

A scream ripped through camp.

Maggie.

Priscilla hitched up her skirt and dashed to the lean-to.

Maggie stood, her arms held stiff by her sides. "No leave. No leave."

Falling to her knees, Priscilla gripped Maggie's shoulders and pulled her close.

Maggie clung tight, sobbing.

"Shh. It's all right. I'm here. I won't leave you." She rocked Maggie in her arms as Tobias bounded over a small hedge of locustberry bushes. Fresh rips in his shirt and pants revealed the urgency with which he returned to camp.

He, too, dropped to his knees, his face a mask of worry. "What's wrong? Why was she screaming?"

"I was behind the lean-to. I believe she woke, couldn't locate us, and panicked. She kept saying, 'no leave.'"

"I thought..." Tobias's hands scraped back his overly long hair. "I feared..."

"She's fine." Priscilla flashed a weak smile. "We're all fine."

Tobias's shoulders crumpled, and he wrapped his arms around them both, hugging them tightly. They remained that way for a long moment until Maggie squirmed. Tobias released them and pushed back on his haunches.

Maggie pressed her tiny hands against both of his cheeks, staring him in the eye. "No leave, Toe-bee."

Tobias once again wrapped her in his arms.

Priscilla caught a flash of affection in his eyes before he squeezed them shut. Rising, she wiped tears from her cheeks and moved to make them food to break their fast. Tobias settled on the ground and kept Maggie on his lap, teasing her about the hole he'd ripped in his sleeve on her behalf.

"Cil-ah fix," Maggie said with all confidence. She accepted the half coconut shell of water Priscilla passed her.

Tobias accepted his cup also, but his fingers grazed hers, and their gazes held. His clouded eyes searched hers for understanding. She could only offer him a glimpse of the peace God had provided her.

She cut slices of coconut and the fruit with the yellowish-orange inside and a large flat seed. Mandarin? No, mango. After they ate, Tobias suggested they walk along the beach.

Waves rolled onto the white sand, leaving traces of foam in an outline indicating how far the water stretched. Maggie ran ahead, chasing away seagulls or running back to show them a hermit crab she'd discovered, a piece of coral, or a sand dollar. She held up a pale-purple shell still connected to its other half like a pair of butterfly wings.

Tobias examined it and handed it back to her. "That's a splendid find you've got there, Little Miss Magpie."

Maggie's face broke into an infectious smile, and she ran around with the shell held high, pretending it was a butterfly flitting from flower to flower.

He clasped his hands behind his back in his captain-fashion and followed Maggie with his gaze. "I apologize for my behavior. It was wretched of me to take out my frustration on you and Maggie."

She caught her breath, startled by his admission. His chiseled profile contained hard lines and sharp angles, and he held his chest high and proud, but she knew a soft heart dwelled within. "You are forgiven." A smile tugged at the corners of her lips as Maggie began to skip and hum the song Tobias taught her, *God save the King.* "And I do believe Maggie has put the whole thing behind her."

"I just…" He stopped walking and shook his head.

Priscilla drew to a halt.

"I thought you wanted to be rescued?" He stared at her. "It seems you no longer care."

She fingered her braid. "At first, I was afraid no one would come for us, but then I became afraid of being rescued and our lives never crossing paths again. I'm frightened of the emptiness I'd feel if something happened to you in battle. I'm terrified you'll go back to your crew, and I'll be forgotten. I'm trying to be strong, and I'm trying to hear from God—to know His plan and trust His will to do what is best for Maggie and us, but I don't want to do it alone."

Her words hung in the air like a challenge.

She exposed her vulnerable heart even further. "Don't you understand what you've come to mean to Maggie? To me?"

Tobias closed his eyes and pinched the bridge of his nose. "I'm trying, Priscilla." He stared out over the ocean. "I understand how to run a ship. I can plan battles and strategize for war. I can navigate the seas and keep us alive on an island, but I cannot pretend to understand the female mind. Henry said I was too harsh. He told me to treat you like a delicate flower. Taylor said to be honest and regard you as one of the men. I took all of their recommendations, but none of them worked. None. I do not, for the life of me, understand what a woman wants, and I'm beginning to believe I never will."

Her stomach knotted at the pain etched into the lines on his face. She waited for what seemed like an endless moment for him to look at her. He finally peered her way, and her breath was stolen by the deep agony evident in his eyes.

"To be loved," she whispered. "We want to be loved." She lifted a hand to his bearded cheek and swallowed. "I want to be loved."

His eyes closed, and his shoulders slumped. "It's too late for that."

She'd ruined her chance. She'd let her fears destroy her opportunity to be with the man she'd grown to love. Her fingers traced his jaw another moment, reluctant to relinquish the touch. Her hand fell to her side. "I see." She failed to keep the hurt from her voice. "I don't blame you. My follies have left scars. Who would want, much less love, a grown woman who cannot control her fears? Who sets herself and others in danger due to her irresponsibility?"

His eyes opened but remained clouded like a London sky. "You misunderstand." His hand cupped the back of her neck, and he held her gaze with the electric intensity of a tropical storm. "It's too late because I've already fallen in love with you."

Priscilla's bottom lip trembled. Her heart pounded against her chest like a horse waiting for a gate to open so it may run. She wanted to believe it, but it didn't seem real. She couldn't trust her ears, not after all those years of fear telling her she was nothing, worthless, and unlovable.

"I fell for you the moment you defiantly told me my commands were unreasonable. I realized I loved you when you held out your skirts and showed the iguana who was in charge. I knew I'd lost my heart when you sat for hours combing knots out of Maggie's hair, and I knew I couldn't live without you when you made us sing songs and dance in the sand."

Little arms wrapped around their legs. Maggie's green eyes peeked up at them.

Tobias brushed his knuckles down the side of Maggie's cheek.

A sweet little smile emerged before she buried her face against his thigh.

"I love you, Priscilla Middleton." His eyes darkened, and he rested his forehead against hers. "And if we never get rescued, then I pledge before you and before God, I will do everything in my power to love, honor, cherish, and protect you for as long as I live."

Her heart savored his words engraving them into her being so she could remember them always. She tilted her head up to meet his gaze, hoping he could feel the joy pulsating through her. "And I you."

A love she never witnessed before shone in his eyes. It flooded around her, soft and fluid. It permeated her skin and should have filled the deep holes within her. She'd craved for love all her life, but the crevices in her heart were already full. God had filled them with His love, and now instead of only taking it in, she could return His love. She could let it flow outward to others who needed it, too She smiled even though tears streamed helplessly from her eyes.

He wiped the tracks with his thumb. "You see how confusing you are? You cry and smile at the same time. What am I to make of that?"

A chuckle snorted through her nose. "I'm merely overwhelmed with joy." She blinked away tears. "Because I love you too, Tobias Prescott."

∼

*T*obias lost himself in the affection shining in her eyes and her alluring dimpled smile. He sealed his promise with a reverent kiss—gentle but compelling. He needed her to feel the depth of his feelings, for words didn't seem adequate. He hadn't anticipated the softness of her lips, how she'd taste of coconut, nor how her heat would scorch his skin, branding her into his heart. Her hands slid up his chest and curled around the nape of his neck, trapping a guttural groan in his throat and igniting a blaze within him. It stirred images of a future filled with love, passion, and devotion.

A giggle erupted, and they broke apart to discover Maggie clinging to Priscilla's skirts.

He cleared his throat, but his voice remained hoarse. "Magpie, I need to talk with Miss Cil-ah. Can you build me a sand-castle like we showed you?"

Maggie nodded and sat closer to the water. Her brows furrowed with purpose as she dug.

He turned his attention back to Priscilla. Her lips were swollen from his kiss, and her eyes dazed-over with passion. He cupped her cheeks in both his hands. "Where were we?"

"I believe you were proving how confusing a woman can be, and I was confessing my love for—"

"Priscilla?" He grinned at her nervous babble.

It took a second for her to tear her gaze from his mouth. "Yes?"

"Do stop talking." He reveled in the slow widening of her eyes as he reeled her back into his safe harbor for another thorough kiss, deciding their fate. She conformed to his arms like a sail adapted to the wind and filled him with an intense desire to weave himself into her life. He wanted to be introduced to her parents, befriend her friends, and affiliate himself with her acquaintances. Dash it all. He'd even forgive her brother and spend his Christmas around the table with the disloyal bloke. His hand roved over Priscilla's back and into her hair, but it wasn't enough. He wanted all of her.

Tobias broke their kiss, afraid of his ardor. His chest rose with each ragged breath, and his pulse thundered erratically, but he couldn't let her go. Not yet. He pressed a kiss to her forehead before gripping her to his chest and resting his cheek on the crown of her head. She clung to him, her fingers curled into the material of his shirt.

She stiffened.

He pulled back and searched her face. Had he offended her with his fervor? Her heart raced much like his, and her rapid breathing meant she'd been as affected as he. Her blue eyes stared past him over his shoulder, and she gripped his arm, her fingernails digging into his skin. A shadow fell over them.

Maggie glanced their way and jumped to her feet. He released Priscilla and turned to see what was the matter.

Maggie's tiny fingers slid into his.

The sails of a merchant's frigate emerged from between the two islands heading straight for them.

No one dared move. The mast waved a British flag, but that didn't always mean the ship was friendly. Dumbstruck by the importance of this moment but also by the implications, they waited together to see what fate awaited them.

The ship's sails partially blocked the sun as it dropped anchor. The captain waved his hat in a friendly gesture from the rail.

Tobias's heart ceased beating, and his blood drained from his face, pooling in his feet.

They were rescued.

CHAPTER 27

I fear Bonaparte is restless. I shall return to discuss the
situation in person.

~ Letter from Colonel Neil Campbell to Lord Castlereagh

*P*riscilla scooped Maggie into her arms. A tremble
ran through the small child's frame. She squeezed
her eyes shut and buried her face into Priscilla's shoulder.

She rubbed Maggie's back and leaned against Tobias's side
for strength. He stood stiff and tall with a wide stance, shoulders back, and head high, his steady gaze assessing.

"Is it one of ours?" She winced at the squeak in her voice.
"Are they friendly?"

"We'll soon find out." His fingers wrapped around the hilt of
his knife sheathed in his belt. "It appears to be a merchant ship. I
don't know why it would put in at a deserted island, but it's
flying British colors."

A dinghy lowered, and several men rowed it into shore. A
large bald man jumped into the breakers and dragged it onto
the sand.

"Ahoy there," Tobias yelled over the waves to the approaching crew.

A dark-haired man stood and, with leopard-like grace, hurtled the bow of the rowboat, splashing into the few inches of receding surf. Priscilla squinted against the sun peeking through the flapping sails of the massive ship in the distance. Something about the man looked familiar. She'd seen him before. A merchant...at a ball...dancing with Lottie. She stepped forward. "Mr. Winthrop?"

A smile spread across the man's face. "Praise God." He peered over his shoulder back at his men. "It's them." He turned to face her and bowed. "Miss Middleton, splendid to see you alive and well. You've given my wife and many others a good fright."

Her heavy sigh of relief melted to her bare toes. "How did you find us? Is Lottie well? Is she aboard?" The drive to see her friend returned. "May I see her?"

Nathaniel Winthrop's smile widened. "I see why the two of you are friends. Lottie is...er...ill and was unable to make the voyage."

She gasped. "Ill? Oh no, her fevers have returned?"

His smile faded as he rubbed the back of his neck. "It's more of a condition."

"A condition? You don't mean..."

He peered at the sand, but a proud smile lifted the corner of his lips. "My wife is with child."

Priscilla grabbed Tobias's arm and squeezed. "Did you hear that? Lottie's having a baby." Tobias nodded but remained stiff.

Mr. Winthrop's gaze raised to her hand on Tobias's arm.

She immediately released her hold. "My heavens, in my excitement, I forgot my manners. Captain Prescott, let me introduce you to Mr. Nathanial Winthrop from the Leeward Island of St. Kitts. His wife, Lottie Winthrop, is my dearest friend." She peered at Mr. Winthrop. "Mr. Winthrop, it is my honor to introduce you to Captain Prescott, Captain of the *Trade Wind* in His Majesty's Royal Navy. He risked his life to save mine."

Tobias stepped forward and bowed and Priscilla ached to once more be in his embrace, yielding to the demands of his kiss. She cleared her throat and forced her pulse to return to normal.

Mr. Winthrop bowed. "A pleasure to make your acquaintance, and my sincerest gratitude for saving Miss Middleton's life. The bond between my wife and Miss Middleton extends beyond an ocean. She has been beside herself ever since Miss Dodd appeared on our doorstep."

Her eyelids fluttered. "Miss Dodd, God bless her."

He pointed his thumb at the ship. "She's aboard the *Katherine*, anxiously awaiting news."

Maggie slipped between Priscilla and Tobias. She shyly assessed Mr. Winthrop.

His tone turned playful. "And who have we here?"

Priscilla hefted Maggie up. "This is Maggie. At least, that's what we've been calling her. She doesn't speak much."

Tobias held out his arms, and Maggie leaned into them. She sat on his hip and eyed their visitors. Her tiny sleeve drooped off her shoulder, so Priscilla reached over and tugged it back up. "We discovered her alone on the island and think she and her mother might have been shipwrecked."

Mr. Winthrop followed their gazes to the mast protruding from the ocean. "And her mother?"

Tobias nodded. "Her remains lie in a cave. She passed some time ago."

Mr. Winthrop's brows raised. "She survived here on her own?"

"It seems so." She touched Maggie's bare toes. "She's a brave little girl."

"I'd say so." Winthrop nodded, disbelief in his expression.

Maggie's shoulders shook, and a giggle escaped her lips. Priscilla followed the direction of her gaze to the large bald man, making a silly face as he winked at Maggie. As if feeling all eyes were upon him, the bald man straightened and resumed a deadpan expression, which only made Maggie giggle once more.

Mr. Winthrop gestured to the man. "This here is my midshipman, Baby. He has a couple of little ones of his own at home." He gestured behind him. "And manning the dinghy is Salt."

The men bowed, and both Priscilla and Tobias nodded.

"I don't mean to rush you, but I'm itching to get back to Lottie, and I know Miss Dodd is pacing the deck anxious to see for herself you're alive." He wiped sweat from his forehead with the back of his hand. "Is there anything you need to gather?"

Priscilla glanced back at the path leading to their camp. All the precious treasures, straw hats, bottles of pickled vegetables, the pot, the net—everything that had kept them alive—wouldn't be necessary anymore. She strode to where Maggie had last played on the beach and picked up the palm dolls her mother had made for her. She handed them to Maggie, who squeezed them tight under her arm. Priscilla glanced at Tobias. "I do believe that's it."

Mr. Winthrop assisted Priscilla into the rowboat. Tobias climbed in after her with Maggie. Baby and Mr. Winthrop pushed the dinghy back into the waves before embarking half wet. Salt strained against the oars.

Tobias and Mr. Winthrop conversed on sailing the Caribbean waters. Mr. Winthrop explained how the smoke from the fire signaled their presence, and Tobias explained the sudden storm that washed them overboard. Mr. Winthrop knew the exact one and said it set his other ship, the *Emory,* off course by forty leagues.

Priscilla stared at the island, their refuge and home for three months. Palm trees waved farewell in the breeze, and turquoise waves pushed them back to shore. She should be relieved and excited. *Huzzah*, they were rescued. Nevertheless, the foreboding fizzled the joy she should be feeling. Would Tobias's attitude change toward her once they returned to polite society? Did he plan to catch up with the *Trade Wind*? Did he still hold the fantasy of becoming a martyr for his country? Of course his duty would return him to sea, but how quickly? How much time did they have? He'd undoubtedly become engrossed once again in the demands of a captain, the trainings, the needs of his crew.

Her throat constricted.

God, please don't let him forget us.

~

*P*riscilla felt as though she were reliving the past. As if they were back aboard the *Trade Wind*, Miss Dodd, Tobias, and she dined in the captain's quarters. Except in Lieutenant Dalton's stead sat Mr. Winthrop. Exhausted from all the excitement, Maggie had eaten a meager portion of dinner and lay curled asleep on Mr. Winthrop's bunk.

Earlier that day, Priscilla had filled in Miss Dodd on what transpired after she'd retired the night of the storm, including a humble explanation of her fear of being alone, which led to her being swept overboard and Tobias's rescue. Miss Dodd blustered, upset that Priscilla hid her fear from her, and wavered between berating herself for not noticing and sympathy for Priscilla's plight. After she calmed, Priscilla detailed their means of survival, careful to mention their building separate lean-to's.

However, when the retelling was finished, Miss Dodd arched a thin eyebrow. "Yours and Captain Prescott's adherence to propriety will be irrelevant. All society will hear is that you spent several months in the company of a bachelor without a chaperone. I hope you have prepared Captain Prescott for the fact that your father will expect him to do right by you."

She poked around at the bread pudding set before her and mulled over her earlier conversation. Tobias marrying her out of obligation held little comfort. Lottie had been fortunate she and Nathaniel Winthrop had fallen in love after their marriage of inconvenience. However, Priscilla couldn't stand a marriage to Tobias being one-sided. She loved him and needed to know he loved her in return. This morning, she was sure he loved her, but since their rescue, he'd been respectful but distant.

Tobias and Mr. Winthrop swapped seafaring tales. Their laughter drew her thoughts back to the people present at the table. Tobias and Mr. Winthrop had hit it off brilliantly, having much in common to discuss.

Tobias snorted. "Captain Anthony Middleton is a thorn in a man's side."

Including their mutual dislike of Anthony.

"What did Middleton do to you?" Mr. Winthrop sipped his drink.

"Besides belittling me behind my back?"

"Not surprising."

"He also stole a British frigate for his personal use and claimed it was to rendezvous with your wife."

Mr. Winthrop choked on his watered ale.

Tobias waved a hand. "Do not fear. He didn't gull anyone. He lost his command for his traitorous actions."

"Middleton spoke the truth." Mr. Winthrop coughed.

Priscilla leaned forward over her bowl. "Anthony wasn't pitching gammon?"

"Lottie had been abducted by a man who planned to sell her to a band of pirates."

"Pirates!" Priscilla's mouth fell open in an undoubtedly unladylike display. She snapped it shut.

"Indeed. My ship had been damaged during a storm and

wasn't seaworthy. It was Lady Etheridge"—he glanced at Tobias —"my mother-in-law's idea to commandeer the British warship under Middleton's command. We boarded the ship stationed in the bay at Brimstone Hill and convinced Middleton to sail to Barataria."

"He risked his command to aid you." Priscilla's shoulders lowered. Anthony had good reason for his unpatriotic actions. He'd been helping Lottie.

Mr. Winthrop smirked. "Let's just say our convincing left him little choice."

"Whatever do you mean?" Priscilla frowned.

"Pardon my insensitivity, for I know Middleton is your brother, but Lottie was in danger. I would have risked everything to save her and more. Either Middleton sailed with us, or we sailed without Middleton."

The burst of hope for Anthony faded. Lottie was her closest friend, and he hadn't held the courage to save her.

Tobias shifted in his chair, and a muscle in his cheek twitched. "You stole British Naval property?" His stiff pose and tight expression conveyed Tobias's disdain of such a disloyal act, at least to her. She guessed his deep patriotism warred against the moral obligation to save a woman in distress.

"I had to reach her." Winthrop's eyes reflected a haunted look. "I couldn't lose her." His gaze flicked to Tobias. "Much like you abandoning your post to rescue Miss Middleton, but imagine your love for her was beyond reason."

Tobias met Priscilla's gaze and held it. His gray eyes deepened to the color of the sea during a storm—and held as much tumult. For a moment, she forgot to breathe.

"Technically"—Winthrop shrugged—"since Middleton was aboard the entire time and the ship was intact, it was more of an unsanctioned expedition."

An awkward silence fell over the room.

Miss Dodd inhaled a slow breath and raised her glass. "Well,

I for one am most grateful to Captain Prescott for keeping my charge alive and to Mr. Winthrop for the use of his ship and time for their search and rescue."

Priscilla lifted her cup. "Hear, hear."

They saluted with their glasses. Tobias raised his also.

In her heart, Priscilla added another praise—to God that Anthony was not the liar she'd been convinced he was. *God, forgive me.*

~

*P*riscilla leaned against the rail, enjoying the commotion of men shouting from the crow's nest and climbing the rigging to adjust the sails. Wind ruffled the skirt of her muslin walking dress. Her fresh gown, one which wasn't filthy and torn, swirled about her ankles. Miss Dodd, the blessed woman, had brought along Priscilla's change of clothes, the same ones she'd packed the night she'd boarded the *Trade Wind*.

Maggie giggled at Baby sticking a coil of rope on his head and batting his eyelashes like a girl. Miss Dodd sat nearby, watching the exchange. Priscilla bit her lip to keep from smiling. In a short time, Maggie had set up residence within Priscilla's heart. If she hadn't boarded the ship, she would never have found Maggie.

Nor met Tobias.

He stood near the helm in his dress uniform—also packed by Miss Dodd at Lieutenant Dalton's insistence. He stood in a wide stance observing as Mr. Winthrop explained their merchant routes. As if he sensed her, Tobias's gaze flicked in her direction.

Her stomach flipped. She missed being the center of his regard, washed in the depths of those gray eyes, rattled by the husky timbre of his voice. She held his stare until her heart pressed against her ribcage and threatened to break off a rib and poke its way out. She stepped to him, drawn like a passing ship.

Mr. Winthrop pointed to the map and said something that caused Tobias to break their trance and nod.

Perhaps God was showing her she was only one piece of a puzzle. She'd been trying to fit into one place, but it turns out she belonged in another. Mayhap God rearranged the pieces to create a new picture—a family picture. She clung to that hope.

Maggie laughed even harder when Baby used Maggie's braid as a mustache. How Maggie's lesson on tying a sailor's knot turned into such a display, Priscilla had no idea, but it seemed to amuse both Maggie and Miss Dodd, who smiled from her barrel seat. Priscilla had asked Miss Dodd how she knew they'd still be alive, and she'd replied, that she'd prayed, and God had given her the faith to believe it in her heart.

Thank you, Lord. Priscilla hadn't stopped thanking God for their rescue, but she'd also been praying that Tobias would not forget his pledge to her on the beach. He'd proclaimed, *And if we never get rescued, then I pledge before you and before God, I will do everything in my power to love, honor, cherish, and protect you for as long as I live.* If only she could erase the words "if we never get rescued."

Now that they were rescued, had his sentiments changed?

"Maggie appears to be adjusting nicely." Tobias's baritone voice lifted her hopes like a flock of flamingos raising their heads. He joined her in his captain's garb, his hat tucked under his arm. The white of his shirt front and clean trousers gleamed in the sun almost as bright as the gold buttons. His free hand flipped back his jacket and casually hooked his thumb into his pocket.

"The crew has helped draw our little hermit crab out of her shell. The first two days, if she wasn't hiding in my skirts, she was endeavoring to crawl into my skin."

He smiled. They both watched as Maggie followed Baby's

instructions on how to tie a knot. Her face scrunched in concentration, and after pulling the ends tight, she looked to Priscilla and Tobias for approval.

"Well done," Tobias said as Priscilla clapped.

Baby pulled apart the knot and began another instruction.

"I'm sorry I misjudged your brother." Tobias stood erect and stared straight ahead. "I will be certain to convey the actual accounts to our superiors."

"Thank you. I know he would appreciate the gesture to clear his name." She studied the firm line of Tobias's jaw. "Anthony, too, longs for our parent's approval. His pride probably took a blow." She inhaled a deep sigh.

Tobias's gaze slid to her. "It was quite a turn of events. Stealing a ship. Lottie in the hands of pirates." Tobias grunted almost inaudibly. He didn't fool her with his controlled expression. Over three months with him had cued her into his little nuances. His nostrils flared, and muscles in his forearms bulged.

She turned and placed her hands on the rail, leaning out to feel the rush of wind on her face. "You've taken issue with Winthrop and his crew?"

He leaned next to her, propping his boot on the bottom rung of the rail. His arm brushed against hers. The single touch washed her in memories of their last kiss.

"What Winthrop did was treason."

She frowned. "What if it were the only way to save Lottie?"

A wave splashed up against the ship's hull, spraying them with a fine mist. A long moment passed as he stared over the ocean. "There had to have been another solution."

"Even if time was of the essence?"

He remained silent.

She placed a hand on his sleeve. "Winthrop and Lottie might have been forced to marry, but they have become a love match. Lottie confessed as much in one of her letters. You must have seen the way Winthrop's eyes lit when he spoke of her."

His shoulders slumped, and his voice grew solemn. "A true Englishmen puts his king and country above all else."

The firmness of his tone unsettled her. "What about God? What about family?" She straightened back to a standing position.

"A true countryman finds a way to protect all three." Tension exuded from his taut muscles as if an internal winch had been cranked. He scratched his jaw with his thumb. "Speaking of family and marriage. I wanted you to know I will do my duty."

Her eyebrows rose. "Duty?"

His lips parted and then closed into a firm line. His Adam's apple bobbed as he swallowed.

Priscilla searched his face for hints of whether he was struggling for words or distraught by the idea of marrying her. A vice tightened on her chest, not allowing her to breathe. After all they'd been through, could she have misunderstood his feelings? Had he kissed her simply because he'd resigned himself to having no other options? Her heart cracked like a coconut and leaked out her hopes and desires.

"I will do the honorable thing." His gaze locked on hers. His lips tightened as if forcing the words. "Because we were alone on an island unchaperoned."

"The honorable thing?" She pushed off the rail and straightened. "I will not be considered a duty. I'm already a pest to my brother and problem for my parents. I'm not about to strap myself to a husband who sees marriage to me as an obligation. I survived on an island. I will no longer stand being a burden to anyone. I can take care of myself."

"Priscilla, that's not…" Tobias sighed and squeezed her hand. "Why is it we're compatible on an island but at odds on board a ship?"

Priscilla swallowed, but her throat constricted and wouldn't allow any words to pass. She refused to succumb to her emotions. He wouldn't see her tears. She turned her head.

"Look at me," he said in a gentle tone. His fingers touched her chin, turning her to peer at him. "You are not a burden. Not to me. Winthrop's loyalty to the crown might be in question, but I can understand his reasoning. If it had been you who'd been captured, I would have sailed the world to find you."

"You would?"

"I may not express myself as I should, but the depths of my feelings for you have taken the place of reason. I've become attached to your unpredictable, spontaneous nature. When you speak your mind, I want you to speak it to me. When you lift someone's spirits, I want them to be mine. When you disagree and argue, even then, I want it to be with me. I want us to raise Maggie and be a family. When I see a future, I see you."

When? His words raised a warning flag, but with her heart bursting and her mind focused on the love in his eyes, she was too overjoyed to consider it further. "Really?"

"The thought of your absence is unsettling… no, unbearable. I'm not offering to do my duty. I'm afraid I'm more selfish than that. I want you because I've grown accustomed to you."

He must have witnessed the confusion on her face, for he quickly rephrased. "I need you. You've changed me into a better person." He gripped her hand. "I haven't worked out every detail, but I'm certain I don't want to let you go." His husky voice lowered to a whisper, and his eyes shown clear with steadfast assurance, "Priscilla, marry me?"

Before he could think twice, she stretched and pressed a kiss to his lips, not caring who saw. "Yes! I will marry you."

CHAPTER 28

In my absence, Bonaparte has escaped Elba!
~ *Letter from Colonel Neil Campbell to Lord Castlereagh*

"*P*riscilla!" Lottie waved from the shoreline. Her red hair shone like a beacon in the sun. In place of the timid, pale, sickly woman from her memories stood a confident, tanned, healthy woman beaming a smile.

Priscilla waved back.

The dinghy couldn't beach fast enough. Tobias held her hand to aid her out of the rowboat, and Priscilla leapt over the side, running to embrace her friend. Lottie squeezed her tightly, and they rocked back and forth for a long moment before leaning back to get a good look at each other.

"Look at you! You're glowing." Priscilla glanced at Lottie's enlarged waistline. "I heard the news. Congratulations, I'm so happy for you both."

Lottie's hand moved to her stomach, and a motherly smile touched her lips. "We couldn't be more pleased. I knew Nathan wouldn't be able to hold in our secret." Her gaze slid to her husband, and she held out her hand.

Nathan's arm wrapped around her shoulder in a side hug, and he planted a kiss on her forehead. "It's good to be back. I missed you."

Lottie gazed at her husband with such love in her eyes Priscilla wanted to swoon. "I missed you too."

Priscilla glanced over her shoulder. Miss Dodd held Maggie as they exited the dinghy. Tobias moved to stand by Priscilla's side, with Miss Dodd and Maggie following. Did she and Tobias look at each other that way? She rather thought so. His eyes flashed as he peeked at her, and his warm hand possessively settled in the small of her back. "Lottie, let me introduce you to Captain Tobias Winthrop of the *Trade Wind*. Captain, this is Lady Charlotte Winthrop, whom we affectionately refer to as Lottie."

Tobias removed his hat and bowed. "Pleasure to meet you."

Lottie fell into a graceful curtsy. "The pleasure is all mine, especially for saving my dearest friend from drowning. Miss Dodd told us how a storm washed you overboard, but I'm dying to know the entire story."

When Tobias said nothing, Priscilla jumped in. "You wouldn't believe all we've endured. Battling the waves was—"

Maggie's little arms wrapped around Priscilla's skirt.

"Please forgive me." Priscilla cupped a hand around Maggie's cheek. "This is Maggie." She peered back at Miss Dodd. "And you've met my chaperone, Miss Dodd."

"Indeed." Lottie nodded at Miss Dodd. "How fortunate she came to us as soon as the *Trade Wind* anchored. I had Nathan setting sail to search for you within the hour. I was beside myself with worry." She bent down to smile at Maggie. "How old are you, Miss Maggie?"

Maggie pressed farther into Priscilla's skirt, but Lottie patiently waited.

Priscilla opened her mouth to explain but caught the slightest shake of Tobias's head, before he focused on Maggie.

Maggie bit her lower lip until it completely disappeared into her mouth. Her small hand rose, and she folded back all but three fingers. Her brow furrowed, and she released the other two fingers one at a time and frowned at them. Her hand dropped back to her side, and she shrugged.

"We're not certain of her age." Priscilla tucked Maggie's braid back over her shoulder. "I can explain."

Lottie kept her focus on Maggie. "Age doesn't matter when you're loved for who you are, now, does it?"

Maggie's chin dipped to her chest, but a shy smile spread across her face.

"I have so much to tell you." Priscilla sighed.

Lottie stood. "Why doesn't everyone come and sup at Calico Manor. Our cook, Adana, has been preparing a feast ever since the *Katherine* was spotted on the horizon."

"That sounds lovely." Priscilla clasped her hands in front of her chest. "I can't wait to see where you live."

"I must report to Naval headquarters." Tobias placed his hat on his head. "They will have to await my reassignment orders from England." His gaze locked on Priscilla's as if he hated to be separated. "I shouldn't be long." His voice lowered so only Priscilla would hear. "Depending on how hard it is to locate a reverend."

Heat rushed to her cheeks, and she nodded, resisting the urge to kiss him good-bye and tell him to hurry.

Tobias asked Winthrop for directions and bid everyone farewell until later. His purposeful stride ate up ground, and she found herself admiring his strong posture and the natural sway of his arms and shoulders.

Lottie moved to her side and led Priscilla toward the wagon. She leaned in and whispered, "You're in love with him, aren't you?"

Priscilla sucked in a breath. "How did you know? You've just met him."

"I can see it in your face. It's the same way I look at Nathan."

~

*T*he entire ride to Calico Manor, Priscilla shared what had transpired since boarding the *Trade Wind*. Lottie interrupted with multiple questions.

Mr. Winthrop pulled to a stop and announced, "Welcome to Calico Manor."

A charming two-story, white-washed house with blue shutters and a wraparound porch stood beside a large Saman tree with branches that hung to the ground.

Surrounding the property, a lake of green sugar cane rippled in the breeze. It flowed to the beach and also a good way up the mountain.

Priscilla couldn't help contrasting the island of St. Kitts with the deserted island that had been their home for three months. The island they'd been stranded upon had tropical palms and lush undergrowth. It also had jumbles of rocks and arid sections. St. Kitts was carpeted in a lush green that rose into a tropical forest near the cloud-covered summit. As the crunching of the wagon wheels slowed to a stop, she heard distant voices lifted in song. "Where is the singing coming from?"

Lottie smiled. "It's the men and women working in the field."

The music unlocked a memory of sitting in their family box in West Minister Abby, staring up at the delicately carved fan-vaulted ceiling and listening to the chorus of voices. The musical offering rose as if floating to heaven. The song from the field was the same. "Are they singing *Rock of Ages*?"

"Lovely, isn't it."

"Splendid."

Lottie gave them a tour of the house before the men and women returned from the fields to dine. She hadn't been exaggerating about their cook preparing a feast. Plates were filled with beans, rice, and mango chicken.

Priscilla and Lottie dined on the porch with Mr. Winthrop, the plantation overseer, Mr. Tallant, and his wife Adana, who held a bundled baby close to her chest. As they ate, Lottie relayed the extraordinary tale of being abducted by Nathan's back-stabbing friend and being taken to a pirate's lair on Grand Terre.

"Privateer." Her husband corrected her.

They exchanged a knowing smile before she continued to boast about how Mr. Winthrop came to her rescue with none other than her mother.

Priscilla blinked. "Your mother? Lady Etheridge."

"Indeed, we reached a sort of understanding and have set healthy boundaries—for the children's sake." She patted Nathan's hand. "Don't forget she'll be arriving on the next ship from England."

"Don't remind me." Mr. Winthrop sighed. "The understanding is more of a truce."

Both Priscilla and Lottie giggled. Priscilla's mother's long-term friendship with Lady Ethridge had thoroughly acquainted Priscilla with Lady Etheridge's acerbic nature.

"Come now. She has mellowed."

Mr. Winthrop eyed his wife with a smirk.

Priscilla smiled. She imagined she and Tobias sitting here as a married couple visiting with the Winthrops. They'd secretly hold hands beneath the table and tease each other the way Lottie and her husband had.

Mr. Winthrop and Mr. Tallant excused themselves to inspect the fields. Mr. Winthrop had left in the middle of planting season to search for Priscilla and itched to know how things had progressed in his absence. Miss Dodd ushered Maggie away for a nap before her heavy eyelids closed.

Adana cleared the table, but her eyebrows rose at Maggie's hardly touched dish. "She didn't like da food?"

"She's still growing accustomed to her food being cooked." Priscilla scratched the base of her throat.

Both Adana and Lottie's eyes widened.

"The meal was delicious." Priscilla suggested a change in subject. "It's the best I've had in some time."

Adana nodded and set off to scrub the dishes, leaving the pair of old friends to chat.

Lottie's brow furrowed. "What did you eat on the island?"

"Coconuts mostly, but we also caught conch, kingfish, clams, and"—Priscilla concentrated on saying the word without gagging—"oysters." However, a shiver of disgust wiggled her shoulders.

"Oh, but I've heard oysters are the Prince Regent's favorite food," Lottie chided. "Not liking them is almost disrespectful to our king."

"Hardly." Priscilla giggled.

"Surviving on a deserted island. I've always been envious of your independence, but that takes it to an extreme." Lottie tilted her head. "You are still my fun-loving, carefree friend, but there is something different about you. You seem at peace."

Priscilla reached across the table and squeezed Lottie's hand. "You might have been jealous of my independence, but I wasn't free. Fear controlled me. I was in chains but didn't realize it. I spent all my energy putting on a show to hide my fright. On the island, it was as if I could feel God's greatness—his beauty. Compared to Him, I was small, insignificant, and unworthy, but He loves me anyway. He values me. I know it because He saved us."

The memory of being under the water surrounded by inky darkness... her lungs burning and her limbs weary. Sinking. "I believed my life over. I was too tired to swim. I should have drowned, but He pulled me out of the deep. Tobias didn't see me, didn't know I'd gone under, but God did. He searched for me like a shepherd hunts for a lost sheep. He pulled me from a watery grave."

Lottie's eyes misted.

"Delighting in Him has shown me what real freedom is."

"You don't know how happy that makes me." Lottie blinked back tears, and she squeezed Priscilla's hand back. "God is good." She wiped the corner of her eye and leaned in. "So tell me about Captain Prescott. You love him, and from the way he looks at you, I can tell he returns the sentiment. You were on the island alone for a long time. Will nuptials be announced?"

Heat flooded Priscilla's cheeks. Lottie knew her past and how she'd allowed a suitor to steal a chaste kiss, but it had been a cry for attention. The kiss she'd shared with Tobias had nothing to do with defying her parents or being the first to tell her friends of the experience. It had been only the two of them expressing feelings that could no longer remain unsaid. God's love had unlocked a new chamber of her heart. Because God loved her, her heart became free to love Tobias. Their kiss left her changed forever.

"Please don't tell me Nathan must call him out?" Lottie asked, her expression slipping to anger.

"Nothing of the sort." Priscilla shook away her reminiscence and issued Lottie what she hoped was a jaunty smile. "You're beginning to sound like your mother."

Lottie burst out laughing. "Island life has taught me a new respect for her." Her eyebrows lifted. "But don't think you can get away with changing the topic. What about Captain Prescott?"

"After reporting to the Naval Base, he's off to locate a reverend who will marry us." Priscilla sat back in her chair and crossed her arms. "I'll have you know, he was a complete gentleman."

Lottie drummed her fingers on the table, waiting. She had always had a talent for drawing out the full story.

The weight of silence pressed upon Priscilla, and she lowered her gaze. "We shared three kisses, but that was all."

"And?"

She melted into the back of her chair. "It was lovely."

Lottie burst out laughing. "You are in deep."

She sighed. "I'm afraid so, but it wasn't always that way. At first, we could barely tolerate each other. He saw all Middletons as a plague upon society, but—"

"But being stranded with you changed his mind." Lottie rested her hand on top of her belly.

Horse hooves pounded the ground behind Priscilla. She rose. "That must be him now." She shielded her eyes from the sun. Sure enough, Tobias rode up the lane ahead of several other men dressed in military garb. One drove a wagon.

She tensed at the tight expression on Tobias's face, and her fingers gripped the chair. Something was wrong. Would they be shipping off soon? Why were these men with him? Was it to see them married before they promptly escorted Tobias to a ship leaving for battle in America? Her stomach tightened into a sailor's knot.

The horses neighed and drew to an abrupt halt. Dirt clouded around their hooves. The musty smell of earth and horse sweat drifted.

Tobias leapt from his horse and stormed in her direction while a red-faced superior, as announced by his shiny gold buttons and the collage of ribbons pinned to his red coat, barked to Tobias to get back in rank. The other men remained stiff in their saddles.

Unease slithered down her spine.

Tobias scaled the few porch stairs in one leap. "Tell them it's a mistake. You didn't give the French any intelligence."

Priscilla's blood froze in her veins.

"I told them you'd never do such an atrocity."

"I..."

He skidded to a halt. His gaze searched hers for answers, his face awash in confusion when she didn't immediately deny the claim.

The red-faced military official launched off his horse, bounded the porch steps, and tackled Tobias.

Priscilla screamed.

Three men rushed over and restrained Tobias. He ripped free from their grip. "She's innocent. Give her a chance to explain—"

"Tobias!"

Priscilla's warning came too late. A large, burly man struck Tobias in the temple. Tobias's eyes rolled back, and he collapsed to the ground, his head lolling to the side. She dropped to the ground beside him. "Tobias?" Her hands cupped his face as tears streamed down her cheeks.

Lottie turned to the servant, Adana, who stood frozen in the outdoor kitchen, a half-peeled onion in her hands. "Go find Nathan quickly!" The woman sped off in the direction of the fields. Lottie rounded on the official. "What is the meaning of this?"

He ignored her and addressed his men. "Bind him and toss him on his horse. He'll spend a night in the brig for such insolence."

Priscilla shielded him with her body. "I won't let you. He's hurt. You could have killed him."

The official gripped her arm and yanked her to her feet. "Are you Miss Priscilla Middleton?"

Two men pulled Tobias upright and dragged him, unconscious, to his horse, where a third helped drape him over the saddle.

The official shook her. "Are you Miss Priscilla Middleton?"

When she still didn't answer, he turned to Lottie and jabbed a finger in Priscilla's chest. "Is she Miss Priscilla Middleton?"

"Who is asking?" Lottie raised her chin.

The officer leaned as if to threaten Lottie.

Priscilla tore her gaze from Tobias's form to the man addressing her and straightened. "I am, Priscilla Middleton, daughter of Admiral Middleton, and once he hears of this, you'll be the one sleeping in the brig, or Newgate for that matter."

He didn't acknowledge her claim, merely turned and nodded. Two other men dismounted and charged at Priscilla, grabbing her arms.

"Unhand me." She glanced past the naval coats.

Malice shown in the red-faced officer's hard eyes. "You are to be held in lock-up and transported back to England to stand trial in the House of Lords."

"On what grounds?" Priscilla struggled against the man's grip, praying her worst fears weren't coming true.

His voice projected with disdain. "For high treason against the crown."

CHAPTER 29

We have a new development. Shall I assume you are
handling things on your end?
~ *Letter from Agent White to Admiral Middleton*

A sob caught in Priscilla's throat.

"Treason!" Lottie scooted around the table. "There
must be some mistake. Miss Middleton would never do
anything of the sort."

Rope scratched the soft skin of her wrists as the red-faced
officer bound her hands.

A scream turned everyone's attention.

Maggie stood in the doorway in front of Miss Dodd, her
small face etched with fright. She reached for Priscilla, but Miss
Dodd scooped her up and held her close.

The soldiers ignored the wailing child and ushered Priscilla
down the steps.

Priscilla twisted, struggling against her bindings. She
couldn't see around the men's navy coats, but she yelled to
Lottie or Miss Dodd, whoever was listening. "Watch over
Maggie. Tell her not to be scared."

They wrenched Priscilla's arms behind her, propelling her toward the wagon, but she kept her head high.

"Are you claiming you've had no contact with a French spy by the name of Goulart?"

She stiffened, the name and memory coming back to life to haunt her from her past.

"He's been known to go by the alias Lord Dawson, but I believe you met him as Mr. Goulart from the Lemoore party."

Her meal threatened a resurrection. This couldn't be happening. Maggie's muffled cries sounded nearby. A man escorted Miss Dodd and Maggie to a horse. "You'll need to accompany us for questioning," said a younger soldier.

He thrust Priscilla into the back of the wagon. Her shoulder hit dry, splintered wood, leaving scratches. She scrambled to push herself into an upright position as another cantankerous soldier smelling of body odor and rum climbed in with her.

"Dirty traitor." He spit on her before sitting with his hands on his musket. She wiped what she could off, but she had little movement with her arms pinned behind her back.

"Be courageous, Priscilla." Lottie stood beside the wagon. "Nathan will get to the bottom of this mix-up."

"Ya!" The solider snapped the reins, and the wagon lurched, tipping Priscilla over.

"God is with you. Be strong. I will…"

Horses hooves and wagon wheels drowned Lottie's voice.

Priscilla's panic threatened to swallow her whole as her friend's image shrank into the distance. Her throat tightened as if a noose had already been placed around her neck, but all she could see was the ache of betrayal that had slashed in Tobias's gaze before he was knocked unconscious.

The image tormented her more than the rough handling of her captors as she was dragged aboard a ship, taunted, mocked, and finally untied just before she was thrown into the lockup deep in the ship's belly. Splinters dug into her palms as she slid across the deck boards. Her hair blocked her view, escaping its coiffure and dangling in her face, not that there was much to see in the dim light of the retreating oil lamp. The sound of the door slamming and locking behind the British naval men permeated her anguish. She scrambled to her feet, blindly chasing the men. "Don't leave. I can't be alone." Her fists pounded on the thick oak. "Please. I'll die."

Hollow laughter rang from the other side, followed by a snide, "No one cares."

She pounded harder until her hands were bruised, swollen, and bleeding. Tears coursed down her cheeks as choking, gasping sobs ransacked her body. She slid down the side of the door and hugged her knees to her chest. The darkness surrounded her—salivating, taunting her.

There's nowhere you can run. Nowhere to hide.

She covered her ears to block out the voice, but it made little difference.

No one will hear your screams, and if they do, no one will care.

Her body quaked, and her teeth chattered. She tried to hold herself together, but it was as if her entire being had shattered into a thousand small pieces, too tiny ever to put back together. Her heartbeat erratically pounded, thumping so loudly in her ears that she could barely formulate a coherent thought. But from the recesses of her mind, a still small whisper silenced the noise.

Who hath gathered the wind in His fists? Who hath bound the waters in His garment? Who hath established all the ends of the earth?

She forced the answer past the convulsive rattling of her teeth. "Jesus."

The darkness gasped and recoiled back a step.

She sucked in a breath and said it louder, "Jesus."

The darkness raged, whipping up a frenzy around her, but it didn't touch her. She squeezed her eyes closed, and a candle lit in her mind's eye. It's warmth and glow drew her deeper.

Peace I leave with you; my peace I give to you. Do not let your heart be troubled, and do not be afraid.

Priscilla turned her head and rested her cheek on her knees. "Jesus, I know You are with me." She inhaled a shuddered breath. "Thank You for not leaving me and for making Your presence known. Thank You for coming after your lost lamb." Her shoulders relaxed even though she could still feel the darkness prowling around her. Its hot breath spilled over her neck, swinging her loose tendrils of hair, but fear no longer bound her. She wasn't alone. "God, I am not afraid because I know you are with me."

Hours ticked by, and as the darkness remained at bay, Pricilla poured out her heart in prayer. "God, be with Tobias and Maggie. Let them, too, feel the strength of Your presence. I pray they will know how much I love them, but even more importantly, how deeper, wider, higher, and longer Your love is for them. I know You will provide for them, no matter what happens to me."

Sometime in the middle of the night, Priscilla drifted to sleep and woke to the ship's creaks and groans. A beam of sunlight filtered through the cracks in the overhead floorboards, landing upon her face. A couple of things hit her at once:

The ship had sailed.

And she'd survived the night alone.

God hadn't forgotten her. He'd stayed with her even in the dark belly of the ship. His angels stood guard around her, keeping fear and its tentacles at bay. It was like how God had closed the lions' mouths when Daniel lay in their den.

The dust particles sparkled in the sunlight and shifted in such a way that she could almost glimpse an outline of her sentinel angel. Or maybe it was Jesus. His calming presence guarded her. Just like how Jesus walked about in the fire with

Shadrach, Meshach, and Abednego, she could sense Him protecting her from the dark.

At her lowest, weakest, most humbling moment, she didn't feel alone.

～

*T*obias's jaw throbbed. The ache stirred him awake only to be met with stiff pains in his back from the wooden floor. The planks beneath him rocked. He was on a ship. His ship? He squeezed his eyes tight as the haze of events slid back into place in his memory. He'd visited the general's office at Brimstone Hill. The general had stripped him of his command until his involvement in the accusations against Priscilla were proven false.

Priscilla.

He jolted into a seated position. The ship groaned. Above him, the crew echoed back the muffled commands of the captain. Barrels and crates surrounded him. He was locked in the ship's hold. Where was Priscilla?

"Priscilla?" He called to her with the hope she might be locked up nearby. "Priscilla?" He tried again louder.

"Here." A faint reply sounded from the far corner.

Tobias scrambled in that direction, pushing a crate out of the way with his shoulder to hear her better. He bent on all fours near a crack in the floorboards. "Priscilla? Are you all right?"

She grunted, and although he couldn't see her, he could hear her climbing up something, most likely a barrel, to get closer. "I'm here. I'm well… or at least still sane."

"I'm going to get you out of there. Somehow I'll speak to the captain, tell him his intelligence is wrong. At Brimstone Hill, I tried to convince General Seaton he was mistaken, but he wouldn't listen. They were intent on arresting you on the spot. I tried to warn you first, but I couldn't get to you in time. I wasn't familiar with the island to gain a head start." He rubbed his jaw at the memory. "For heaven's sake, your father works for the War Department. You'd never be involved with a French spy. I tried to explain, but the General was all out of sorts because of word that Napoleon Bonaparte has escaped Elba Island."

She gasped.

Tobias ran a hand through his hair. "I told him he was mad if he believed you had anything to do with Bonaparte's disappearance."

"Tobias, I swear I didn't know." Her voice cracked. "I never meant for anything like this to happen. Please don't think ill of me."

He jerked away, scooting back until the edge of a crate dug into his back. "What...?" His throat had gone dry. He cleared it. "What didn't you know?"

"If I'd have known who he was..." She sucked in a ragged breath. "I never meant to tell him anything."

He leaned closer to the crack. "What did he do? Did he threaten you? Try to hurt you? Did he use blackmail?"

She let out a sob. "No."

"What's going on in here?" The door to the hold slammed against the jam, and a burly crewman held his cutlass toward Tobias. "Move away from there."

Tobias raised his palms and slowly rose.

"The captain wants to speak to you." He twirled a finger. "Turn around and put yer hands behind yer back."

Tobias obeyed, and the crewman bound his hands.

He jerked him toward the door. "You can be certain he'll be hearin' 'bout this."

The crewman shoved Tobias into the passage so hard his shoulder could have cracked the wooden paneling, but Tobias didn't feel any pain.

Only numbness.

~

"She's been alone with me on an island for months. How could she have been part of an international spy ring?" Tobias stood in the captain's quarters, risking being flogged for defiance, but he didn't care. He needed the truth.

The captain rounded on him, sending the gold tassels on his shoulders swinging. "I will overlook your insubordination, but take this as a warning." He leaned over his desk, which was stacked with rolled maps. "The only reason I'm offering you a chance to defend yourself is out of respect for your father."

"She boarded my ship unintentionally. I hadn't a clue she and Miss Dodd were asleep in the captain's cabin when we set sail. I only learned of their presence once I decided to retire." Tobias shook his head. "I've come to know Miss Middleton well over the past four months, and I'm telling you, she doesn't have the capacity to be a spy."

The captain sighed. "You are not the first man to fall for a woman who isn't what she seems." Pity shown in the captain's eyes. "Because I know firsthand of your loyalty to the throne, I'll recount what the general told me." He counted on his thumb. "Miss Middleton listened to top-secret information meant only for her father's ears."

I used to curl up in the cabinet that shared a wall with my father's office. An old grate allowed me to see and hear the men's faces, and I learned to read their gestures. Tobias shoved the errant thought to the side.

The general lifted his index finger. "Miss Middleton passed the information to a French spy going by the alias, Goulart— Mr. David Goulart, or should I say, monsieur."

I had my dream again last night, but this time it was different. Maggie was there, and so was Mr. Goulart, a former dance partner of mine. A cold sweat formed on Tobias's brow.

He held out a third finger. "Her friend, Miss Nellie Archard, thought the man looked suspicious and asked to leave. Miss Middleton must have realized she was compromised, so she sent Miss Archard home in their conveyance and boarded the *Trade Wind* with her companion, Miss Dodd."

Tobias leaned against the wall, afraid he might wretch.

"Have a seat." The captain pulled out a chair and aided Tobias into it since his hands were still tied behind his back. "She would have had the perfect alibi if only you hadn't tossed Middleton out on his ear for previous miss-actions regarding the command of his ship." He clasped Tobias's shoulder. "In my personal opinion, you are a hero for taking down an espionage operative."

Tobias's chest compressed to the point he couldn't draw breath. How had he not seen it? He'd failed his crew, his family, and his country. The acid of betrayal burned his insides. He'd fallen in love with a spy for France.

~

*T*obias hadn't slept other than a few spotty hours here and there in three weeks. Captain Fuller, who'd taken pity on him, allowed him his freedom and put him to work, stating all hands were needed on deck. Tobias threw himself into hard labor, working himself into oblivion to block out all thoughts of *her*, but despite his exhaustion, he couldn't sleep. The creaking wooden beams were answered by the crew's snores—not his crew—they were serving their king and country in battle, which was where he should have been. Unable to doze, Tobias worked to build a rampart around his brain strong enough to block the bombarding images of Priscilla.

He'd almost made her his wife.

Her dimpled smile remained vivid in his mind, torturing him with what could have been, but Priscilla had used him. She played him for a fool, as had her brother. White heat raged through him until his insides charred. Why hadn't he stuck with his gut? He knew Middletons couldn't be trusted. How did he let the sneaky liar lower his defenses? On his ship, Priscilla had been insubordinate and defiant, but on the island, he'd witnessed her vulnerable side. He'd believed her rebellious behavior aboard the *Trade Wind* had been a coverup to hide her irrational fears. She'd been open and honest with him, bearing all her insecurities, only to pry him for information.

The sharp ache in Tobias's gut hadn't lessened over time. She left him as hollow as the shell of the shipwreck. Like the tall mast, he might still be present, but underneath the surface, his insides were rotting. Logic told him that if Priscilla was so good at deceiving people, she must have misled him. Why then the constant ache? Why was his spirit not settled?

Tobias shifted in his hammock. His endeavor to force sleep hadn't availed much. Pressing his palms to his eyes, he rubbed, hoping to blot out her image. He had loved her. He would have given up his purpose for a future with her.

He dropped his hands back to his sides and opened his eyes. Inches away, a face stared back at him. Tobias jolted but quickly recognized Maggie. "Mag-pie. You're supposed to be sleeping."

Reaching over the edge of the hammock, careful to keep his balance centered and not topple onto the deck, he pulled Maggie onto his chest. "Where's Miss Dodd?"

Maggie yawned and closed her eyes.

"She's sleeping?"

Maggie nodded.

Miss Dodd had purchased herself and Maggie passage upon the ship, but this wasn't the first night Maggie snuck out of her cabin and found him. The small child inhaled a shuddered breath and tucked her head under his chin. She lay on his chest, one little hand on top of his heart, and starred at the wall.

At least he hadn't been the only one. Maggie had trusted Priscilla also. Priscilla had sewn a dress for Maggie and spent hours combing the knots from Maggie's hair. How could someone so kind be so devious? Logic and his patriotic upbringing clashed with his heart, pushing sleep farther into the recesses. He stroked the back of Maggie's head, and her eyes drifted closed.

In the morning, he'd explain how unsafe it was for her to wander the ship at night. This brave little girl had been through so much and would endure more, but Maggie was a survivor. She wasn't afraid of the dark. She'd traversed the island in the cool of the night. Maggie wasn't scared of being alone. She'd survived alone on the island for some time.

The heavy rise and fall of Maggie's chest indicated the deeper breaths of sleep. His hand stilled. At least he could comfort her.

Faint singing floated through the cracks in the floorboards. Priscilla's off-key voice sung a hymn as he used to do on the island so she'd know he was near and not to be afraid.

A sick feeling spread through Tobias. He closed his eyes, hoping it would pass.

Priscilla was petrified of both the dark and being alone.

He could console Maggie, but who would comfort Priscilla? He mentally cursed himself. Why should he care? After all the lies she'd told him, why would he still worry about her? Why did he still feel the need to claw his way through the deck boards to get to her? How could he rid himself of the restless need to protect her that surged through him?

God, what would you have me do? She's betrayed me, but even worse, she's betrayed her country.

The ship's creaks and men's snores faded, but Tobias's heart echoed a phrase he hadn't been able to drive from his mind for the past fortnight.

Go after my lamb.

~

*P*riscilla awoke to a scuffling sound. A chill ran through her. The musty, damp floor seemed to have seeped into her bones. Her side had cooled, which meant Maggie had already risen to go back to Miss Dodd's room. As much as it thrilled her to see Maggie when she snuck in and squeezed through the bars to snuggle in Priscilla's arms, she feared it wasn't safe for Maggie to roam the ship, especially at night. She could accidentally slip and fall overboard or step in a coiled rope and be hoisted into the rigging, among many other things. Hadn't Tobias issued Priscilla a similar warning once? He'd been right. If only she could tell him.

But he wanted nothing to do with a traitor.

Over the past few weeks at sea, she played out different scenarios she hoped would redeem herself in his eyes. Each resolved with her pleading with Tobias to forgive her. She fantasized about him telling her it didn't matter because he loved her, but the lines she'd scratched in the cold, damp floorboards to mark the time were a stark reminder that, if her fantasy were true, he would have come for her by now. His devotion to his country was admirable—one of the many things she'd come to love about him. He might have forgiven her for other things, but not this—not treason.

Priscilla would be exiled from his life, thrust from his mind. He'd cut her off as he had Anthony and his own mother. She knew all too well how easily she could be forgotten.

Her mother would be horrified by the shame this accusation would bring upon her charity work. Her papa would lose his status and seniority at the War Department. Anthony would lose his distinguished naval career. Everything she'd done to rectify her silly mistake of attending the Lemoore party had been for naught. How easy it would be to blame Nellie, but Mr. Goulart's question rang in her ears:

"Have you seen Officer Neil Campbell lately—the man you said

sees you as an interloper?"

"Last week—perhaps. He paid father a brief visit."

"I thought he'd been supervising Bonaparte?"

How easily she'd been gulled into revealing information. She didn't realize such a small tidbit could lead to Napoleon Bonaparte escaping from Elba. Had she thought for the tiniest moment her dancing at a party would lead to a prolonged war with France, resulting in more deaths, she never would have left the house.

All she could do was tell the House of Lords the truth and plead for mercy. Her life was in God's hands now. She released a deep exhale, thinking of falling overboard, nearly drowning, and surviving on a deserted island. *I guess it always has been.* For the three weeks they'd incarcerated her on this sailing vessel, she'd cried out to God for strength every day, and He had been faithful.

She shifted a bit to ease the ache in her back. The hard deck boards provided little comfort, and she woke often. Funny, she never thought she'd yearn for her palm-leaf bed in the lean-to. She rolled to her side to allow her blood to flow into the sore muscles. A scratching sounded closer.

Rats? Her eyes sprung open, and she scanned for an assault from the pack of loathsome creatures, seeking any droppings of crumbs from the hardtack and mealy worm-infested bread she'd eaten as her supper. Where was Sneaky Pete, the weasel, when she needed him?

The memory of Tobias's laughing face flashed before her, his teasing smile mocking her for thinking he'd been playing footsy with her under the table. The pain in her heart surpassed that of her back and side. She missed Tobias so severely she could almost smell his masculine scent. She squeezed her eyes tight, refusing to shed more tears. The British Navy would never condone one of their captains marrying a traitor, but that didn't matter. She was dead to a patriotic man such as Tobias. She swallowed back the lump forming in her throat. If only she'd had a chance to explain further, but he'd either been relocated to a different deck, or he'd condemned her in his heart. No matter how long she sat on top of the barrels and called to him through the crack, he no longer responded.

How many years had she sought the peace and security of feeling loved? She'd thought she could find it in her parents, but they'd had other priorities. She'd thought she'd find fulfillment in being loved by Tobias, but his love, although precious, couldn't drive out her fear. Only God could send darkness fleeing.

A board creaked, and fabric rustled, shooting her eyes open. She rolled over and sat up. Her heart slammed into her throat.

Tobias leaned against a barrel beyond the cell bars. His face appeared haggard in the dim shadows of the early morning light seeping through the cracks. His knuckles turned white as he gripped the top of the cask beneath him.

"Why?" His raspy voice reverberated with pain, the single word filled with condemnation.

She rose and gripped the bars. "I didn't know." Everything in her pleaded for him to believe her.

"Thunder n' turf." He pushed off the barrel and pounded his fist into his open palm. "Don't play innocent with me. You were with Goulart that very night. You told me so yourself. You planned to sneak onto the ship and use your brother as your cover, but your plot went awry." He ran a hand down his face and neck. "I can't do it." His fingers curled into fists. "I loved you, but you've done the unthinkable. I can't save you from this."

"I know." Her heart threatened to shatter. She refused to allow his harsh words to phase her. Instead, she looked upon him with all the love she held in her heart. It flowed from God, through her, onto him. It was his choice to accept it or not.

Tobias dropped his gaze and ran a hand over his head,

appearing tormented as he paced the small room. "Even if I could, it would betray my father, his memory, and everything he died for if I helped a traitor. My career, my reputation, the respect of my men are all on the line."

"One hand for you, one hand for the ship. You see the bigger picture. It's one of the things I love about you."

"Don't." His harsh command ripped through her.

Quiet permeated the air. Even the ship seemed to still as if eavesdropping on their conversation.

Priscilla's voice softened. "I know you must take care of yourself because your men depend on you."

"Confound it, Priscilla. You depend on me."

"I did depend on you." She nodded her head. "But now, I depend on God. He will pull me through."

"And what if He doesn't? Lying, if you've forgotten, is a sin."

"I've asked for His forgiveness for whatever part I played in this. If I'm found guilty, then I will die and live in heaven with God. My only sorrow will be knowing I hurt you...and not being there for Maggie. It was never my intention."

"Never your intention? Napoleon escaped. Men will die in battle." He pounded his fist against a beam, and dust fell from the rafters. His lips curled, and he ground out from between clenched teeth, "I would have believed you if you hadn't slipped and revealed the name of the spy you'd been with at the party." Anguish, like an unfillable pit, darkened the depths of his eyes. "What else did you give him besides secrets? Why did you do it? I need to know. Was it for recognition? Money? Did you love him?"

The suffering etched in his countenance sliced through her heart. "I had never laid eyes on Mr. Goulart before that night. I would never have danced with him if it hadn't been for Nellie's persistence. She was bent on distracting me so she could run off and be alone with Lord Fortin." Memories of that night flooded back.

"My worry over Nellie kept me from paying close attention, but I remember he flirted with me. I believed it to be an act by the way he'd rub his thumb against his nose each time he lied and in the sneaky way he'd ask me questions. He wanted to know if any of the men visiting my father took an interest in me. I said they were all old except for Neil Campbell. He was insistent upon knowing why Campbell visited with Papa, but I never told him anything. I didn't know myself."

"Don't play me for a fool. Your friend claims she overheard you passing secrets of the guards' patrols."

"Nellie?" Her mouth dropped open. "Nellie said *I* passed along secrets?" She pulled back from the bars and crossed her arms. "That's what Lord Fortin meant when he said 'I have what I came for.' I thought he meant he'd tupped with her. I didn't think... I didn't realize..."

Nellie didn't have the brains nor the courage to create a story. That night, she'd spilt everything when confronted about drugging her duenna. She'd easily played into Lord Fortin's hands, proving how gullible she was to manipulation.

Nellie's father held political power, and he was known for doing everything in his control to protect it. How easy Priscilla had made it for Nellie by boarding a ship and then disappearing as if guilty. Nellie had fabricated a lie to appear innocent, and Pricilla as the culprit involved with a French spy. Her legs turned to water, and she sank into a pool of skirts. "Oh, Nellie, what have you done?"

Tobias closed his eyes and pressed his fingers against his brows.

Dropping his hand, he tilted his face toward the ceiling as if beseeching God. "I don't know what to do." His shoulders sagged, and he held a defeated tone. "I can suggest leniency to my superiors." He strode from the room. His countenance strained with deep sorrow. "It might give you a chance not to hang."

CHAPTER 30

I know your desire to reunite with your daughter, but I recommend her to remain imprisoned for her safety.
~ *Letter from Agent White to Admiral Middleton*

S *ave my lamb.*

Visiting Priscilla didn't settle the disquiet in Tobias's spirit, but the image of her collapsed on the cell floor branded his mind. Her dazed look with her skirts puddling around her as if she'd melted into despair haunted him day and night. He prayed for her soul and begged God to have mercy on her, but each time his heart screamed, *Save my lamb.*

He paused in clewing the mainsail and shouted heavenward, "What would you have me do?"

The sailors about him didn't pause in their work, for they were busy preparing to dock, but their gazes slid in his direction.

Tobias quickly finished his task and knotted the line. Usually, his pride swelled at the sight of English shorelines, but this time his heart was too heavy-laden. The winds favored the ship as the starboard rudder applied for them to browse into the quay. When the wharf appeared ready to catch their lines, Tobias had to hold in the commands for mooring. This wasn't his ship, and the captain wouldn't appreciate his usurping. Eventually, the order was given. They dropped anchor, and the boat settled into port.

"Prescott." The senior captain hailed him over with a wave of his hand. Tobias strode to the helm and saluted the man.

Captain Fuller held up a folded piece of paper. "You are to be escorted immediately to the War Department along with…" He frowned and unfolded the missive, scanning it. "Along with Miss Dodd. Gather your belongings. You are dismissed."

He thanked the captain and saluted before going below deck. His personal items were already bagged and ready.

The sailors he passed appeared giddy to be home, eager to see their families. He'd never had a family welcome his arrival. His stepfather made it clear he didn't belong and wasn't wanted. For a moment, Tobias wished to remain disillusioned and return to life on the island—to Priscilla. She would have been the wife who anxiously awaited his arrival. He would have walked back to their hut after a day of fishing. Spying him, she would have run to him, and he would have taken her into his arms and kissed her breathless. Little Maggie would wrap her arms around both of their legs and giggle.

Dreams were for fools.

He hoisted his bag over his shoulder and set out to find Miss Dodd and Maggie.

What would become of Maggie now? He couldn't take her with him on his next mission. His mother already had too many mouths to feed. He hoped Miss Dodd would be the answer. He could pay her wages to take care of Maggie.

As he rounded a bend, two guards roughly hauled Priscilla up the ladder to the middle deck. She stumbled with her hands tied, and Tobias reached out to steady her, but one of the guards beat him to it. He jerked her upright, and she winced at the pain of the man's tight grip, leaving white marks that filled into red when he released her.

A foolish surge of protectiveness coursed through Tobias's veins. His fist clenched to draw the guard's cork before he remembered Priscilla was a traitor. He flexed his fingers as she tilted her face up to shake back the blonde tresses that covered her eyes. She caught sight of him, and their gazes locked.

Priscilla didn't look away. She didn't act as a traitor would when about to be brought before the House of Lords. Her gaze held his without shame or fear. In those clear blue depths, he saw only love.

It blazed through him like a powder keg exploding, knocking him back against the passage wall. The first guard squeezed past him in the tight corridor. Priscilla mouthed, "I love you." How he'd ached for her to say those words on the island, but now it hurt too much.

The hem of her gown curled about his ankles as if wrapping him in a hug as she passed. Her sad dimpled smile winked at him before the guards pushed her up another flight to the upper deck to be placed in a paddy-wagon and taken to the gaol until she stood trial.

Save my lamb.

～

*W*omen were masters of deception.

Tobias was seeing another side of Miss Dodd. The woman who'd stayed quiet in Priscilla's shadow while aboard the *Trade Wind* was not only an operative of the War Department but also held a sharp tongue that could peel the skin off any man. Currently, she was in the process of flaying Lieutenant Sparks alive.

Tobias stood in a corner office of the drafty War Department. The smell of old paper, drying ink, and musk swirled about the room with each gust of the March wind that seeped through the cracks in the walls and rattled the glass window panes. Miss Dodd slammed her fist on Lieutenant Spark's desk with such force that her tightly pinned hair bun jiggled.

Maggie startled in his arms and snuggled her face deeper into his chest. A second later, her curious eyes peeked over the wool blanket he'd secured to keep the child from freezing. The cold English air had to be a shock after all her time on a tropical island.

Miss Dodd leveled her gaze on the lieutenant. "This is a classified matter. You know, if even the slightest hint of this slips out, gossip columnists will be salivating outside your door."

The change in the prim Miss Dodd's demeanor left Tobias speechless. His holding Maggie was the only thing keeping his boiling rage in check. Was any woman true to how they seemed?

He no longer should be surprised by the deceitful actions of a woman. Every woman in his life had deceived him. His mother claimed to have loved his father but married another with the dirt still fresh on Father's grave. Annie had pretended to be a man. Priscilla lied to him and betrayed her country, and now Miss Dodd. Or should he refer to her as Agent White?

"I will not allow the client I swore to protect come to ruin." Her face hovered over the man's desk like an eagle perched to swoop in on its prey.

The man fumbled in his pocket for a handkerchief before releasing a rattling cough that hurt Tobias's lungs merely from the sound. He beat on his chest with his fist. "I will do my best to keep her arrest discreet, but we are at war once again. Men are dying because of leaked information that allowed for Napoleon's escape. The blame doesn't fall at my feet for this mess. She was under your care."

Miss Dodd straightened. Her lips pinched so tight it left a white ring. "I was pulled from my assignment for the night to infiltrate the office of one Mr. Goulart, and I found enough information to incriminate the wretched brigand." She pointed a finger straight at Lieutenant Spark's nose. "It was you who allowed the brigand to get away, to change his name and appearance once again."

"This doesn't fall just on me. While you were searching his office, the man extracted vital information from your charge." The lieutenant rubbed his temple. "Admiral and Captain Middleton will be here at any moment." He glanced at Tobias. "Inform us again of what Miss Middleton said to you?"

Tobias re-explained everything pertinent to the investigation from the moment Priscilla boarded the *Trade Wind* until their last encounter in her cell. The whole time he spoke, he had to contend with the persistent interruption of Maggie asking, "Where Cil-la?"

He quietly shushed Maggie with his finger and finished. "The last thing Priscilla said before dropping to the ground was, 'Oh Nellie, what have you done?'"

Maggie, who'd apparently had enough of him ignoring her question, grabbed his face in her tiny hands and pressed his cheeks together. "No. Nell-E. Cill-la!"

Something in Maggie's tone set off an alarm in Tobias's head. He heard the echo of Priscilla's voice in his mind's eye, but this time instead of hearing her say, *Oh Nellie, what have you done,* as if her friend had given her up, he heard it as, *Oh Nellie, how could you have done this to me?*

Save my lamb.

He straightened. Was God trying to tell him something? Who was this Nellie person? Could those around Priscilla have manipulated her? Those she trusted?

He saw Priscilla on the island, opening her heart to him. He saw her holding out a hat she'd made for him. She might have hidden her fears, but when confronted, she never hid the truth from him. *I'm not a traitor.* Her voice rang in his memory, her clear blue eyes filled with love, begging him to believe her.

The room grew silent.

Miss Dodd studied his expression.

Nellie insisted I dance with Mr. Goulart. As if a floodgate opened, more recollections of their conversation surfaced. *That's what Lord Fortin meant when he said I have what I came for. I thought he meant he'd tupped with her. I didn't think... I didn't realize...*

They arrested the wrong woman. The fog cluttering his brain the entire voyage to England cleared, and something deep within him saw the truth. Priscilla was innocent.

Maggie wiggled out of his arms and ran over to Miss Dodd, grabbing her hand and pulling. "See Cil-la."

Miss Dodd picked her up. "Not now, little one. Soon."

Tobias raked a hand through his hair. How could he prove Priscilla's innocence?

The door burst open, and in marched Admiral Middleton. "Sparks, I want my daughter released this instant."

Anthony Middleton followed his father. Upon spying Tobias, he released a menacing growl and dove at him. Tobias raised an arm to block Middleton's blows. Using the momentum of a dodged swing, Tobias pinned Middleton with a restraining grip.

Lieutenant Sparks shot to his feet. "Now, see here."

"You may have ruined my life, but devil take it if I allow you to ruin my sister's." He struggled against Tobias's hold. "Name your second. I'll see you in a field at dawn."

"There'll be no talk of illegal dueling within my office." Sparks flew into another coughing fit.

Tobias pressed Middleton's face into the faded wallpaper. "Neither of us can help Priscilla if we're battling each other. She needs us." He released Middleton and stepped back.

"You blackguard." Middleton adjusted his collar. "You should be the one hanging."

"Anthony."

Middleton's gaze bounced to his father, who was standing beside Miss Dodd with his arms crossed. "As much as I'd like to see this man at the point of my gun, I think we should hear him out."

The scowl never left Anthony's face, but he reluctantly relented.

"I owe you an apology." Tobias had to unravel the chain of misdeeds from his wrong assumptions. "Nathan Winthrop explained to me the truth of what transpired in Grand Terre. I shall do my best to restore you to your former position, but first, we must sort out the truth to save Priscilla."

Anthony Middleton's nostrils flared. "How dare you use her given name, you blackguard. You had the chance to defend my sister and didn't. Why would you want to help her now?"

All eyes in the room honed in on Tobias.

He boldly met both Admiral Middleton's and Anthony Middleton's gaze.

"Priscilla and I are betrothed."

~

*P*riscilla drew the rough blanket tighter about her shoulders to keep out the draft. Despite her neighboring cellmate's wracking coughs, the accommodations at Newgate were far better than those on the ship, but after three months of living outdoors on an island, she'd grown accustomed to sun and fresh air. After a month in the dark, dank belly of a boat and now a prison cell, she craved the open sky.

She did have a window and could sit in the sun for the hour it shined upon the floor, but to see outside, she had to climb the cracks in the stone wall and cling to the window bars. She could get a few fresh breaths of air before her fingers hurt from the exertion and the cold.

Although her situation seemed dire, she thought of Joseph in his jail cell, David standing before Goliath, and Daniel in the lion's den. They maintained their faith, and so would she.

~

*P*riscilla spent the next few days praying, only stopping to eat the meager slice of moldy bread provided and pray for Maggie, Tobias, and her family. She attempted to forge a conversation with the woman in the cell next door, but the woman huddled in the corner muttering incoherently or cackled with vicious laughter that sent chills up Priscilla's spine. Guards removed the woman for questioning only to return frustrated and toss the disheveled woman back into her cell. On the third day, keys jingled, and an old married couple shuffled into her corridor. The man's back was bent, and he hung on his wife's arm. As they drew closer and stopped in front of her cell, she recognized a familiar face.

"Papa." She clutched the bars and rose onto her toes. "You came."

He straightened to full height and gripped her hand. "How are you, angel?"

"Oh, Papa. I'm sorry. I should never have gone to the Lemoore party. I thought I could protect Nellie by accompanying her, but instead, I pulled myself and our family into a horrific mess. The more I tried to fix it, the worse it became."

"I'm the one who's sorry. I knew if word leaked out about my actual duties for the War Department, you'd become a target. It's why I hired Miss Dodd to watch over you and keep you out of trouble. I'd never have pulled her from her mission to identify the spies if I'd had known they would come after you."

Priscilla's brow furrowed. "Miss Dodd?"

"Yes, dear." The elderly woman peeked around her father and waved a gloved hand. Except the elderly woman wasn't elderly. It was Miss Dodd in a powdered wig. "I can tell from your expression you've never suspected me of being an agent."

"An agent?" She blinked as images of Miss Dodd flipping back the covers fully dressed passed through her mind. Strange, but so many things were starting to make sense. "I-I was a target?" She eyed her father. "Is Mama also an agent?"

"Heavens, no." He frowned. "She's much too delicate of a woman. I do hope you will keep all this quiet. She'd take to her bed for a month if she knew the whole of it. I tried to explain once and had to revive her with hartshorn. Your mother has never brought up the subject again. It's why your mother and I don't converse much. I believe she wants to remain in denial."

"You were undercover. That's why you were at the Lemoore party?"

He shook his head. "I came looking for you. We'd received intelligence a French spy was using his wiles to manipulate the daughters of officials to offer information or pilfer it from their father's desks."

"I never meant to give him any information." She reached through the bars, placing a hand on her father's sleeve. "You must believe me."

"I do, angel." He took her hand. "But I need you to tell us everything you remember from that night."

She relayed the events in as much detail as she could. Every time she mentioned Nellie, her papa and Miss Dodd exchanged a look.

"I hadn't meant to tell him Officer Campbell had visited recently. If it in any way led to Bonaparte's escape, then I will accept my punishment."

The woman in the cell next to Priscilla cackled a wicked laugh.

Miss Dodd stared at the woman until she quieted. With a sigh, Miss Dodd returned her focus to Priscilla.

Papa flashed a gentle smile and drew closer, lowering his voice. "We are doing what we can on our end, but you are the only one who can identify the spies."

Priscilla pressed her face to the bars. "I know I can if you get me out." If she could prove she wasn't a traitor, would Tobias speak to her? Would he allow her back into his life?

"No. You are safer here." He frowned. "I don't like you in this place, but your life will be in danger if they discover you're alive. They came to the house after the masquerade. I believe they intended to do you harm."

She gasped. The male voices. Miss Dodd sleeping in her clothes. It all made sense now.

"These men are masters of disguise and good at their job. We need to know any nuances, any gestures that would give them away."

She smiled. "Which one would you like to start with?"

 ❧

Tobias reviewed the plan, mentally walking through each scenario until what needed to be said and done was committed to memory. He lifted his chin while Anthony Middleton's valet tied his cravat into the perfect knot.

Anthony inspected the work. "If you didn't need to open your mouth, you could pull this off." Anthony rubbed his chin, his eyes trailing over Tobias's borrowed suit. "You've always coveted my position, my ship, and now you fill my shoes."

"In order to save your sister." He frowned. Anthony thought him jealous?

"You'll get the credit for that too." Anthony's gaze lowered, and he murmured, "As you did in Bermuda."

"You left us to fend for ourselves alone. You were supposed to fight beside us as a united force."

"We took a hit in the belly." He raised his head. "The ship was taking on water. If we had stayed, the ship would have sunk, and my men would have been captured. We'd have been no help to you."

Was Anthony lying? Tobias straightened and searched Anthony's face for answers. Anthony met him with a fierce glare.

Tobias's gut said he spoke the truth, at least for what he knew. Had he sorely misjudged Anthony? "I was never informed of such."

Now it was Anthony's turn to look surprised. "They never briefed you?"

He shook his head. "They must not have figured it necessary. I was also not told the entire story of what happened in St. Kitts until I spoke to Nathaniel Winthrop. I owe you an apology."

Anthony blinked.

"I will speak to the higher-ups. You should be reinstated as captain. I don't know whether they'll pay me any heed since now I've been stripped of my command, but I will try."

"You'd do that?"

Tobias nodded.

The valet tightened the knot. He wanted to bat the man's hands away. He could dress himself, but both Anthony and Miss Dodd insisted. *It's for Priscilla.* The all too familiar pain slicing through his heart returned at the thought of Priscilla alone and cold in a London cell. Admiral Middleton assured him she was in the best, safest place possible. *But she's terrified of being alone.* He sent up another prayer for her protection. He itched to get tonight underway. The sooner the truth was discovered, the sooner Priscilla could be free.

"Let's go over the plan once more."

~

*T*obias strode toward the steps of the Barringford party, swinging the ridiculous cane Anthony handed him, saying, "It's an extra touch. Most gentlemen of the aristocracy carry one."

The outrageous object threw off his gait and made him feel conspicuous. *Thunder n' turf.* He could walk unaided. When no one was looking, he cast the cane into the hedge. Anthony could find it tomorrow. Tonight, Tobias must focus on extracting information from Miss Archard.

Anthony's voice resumed in his mind. "Now remember, Nellie's bird-witted. She'll fall for any bit of flattery, but her father keeps a tight rein upon her as of late. She's infatuated with rogues and libertines, so you'll need to act"—Anthony's lips pursed—"as unlike yourself as possible."

Tobias raised his top hat and ran a hand through his hair to vent the nervous heat emanating from his body despite the night's chill. He strode up the steps and handed the butler his card. *Here it goes.*

Anthony would have been the better man for the task, but being Priscilla's brother would raise suspicions. The murmur of the guests' chatter grew louder as a livered footman ushered him down the marbled hall to the grand ballroom.

His alias was announced to the revelers, and he descended the staircase. Anthony stood in position at the bottom in a cluster of acquaintances. Spying Tobias, he raised his glass above the head of Miss Archard to identify the target. "Ah, here comes someone I haven't seen in a while. I figured mundane social gatherings were beyond your black reputation."

Miss Archard's gaze shot to Tobias.

Let it begin.

As Tobias joined the group, Anthony clapped him on the shoulder. "Heard you won the Manton estate in a hand of cards, you lucky chap. How does it feel to own land in three territories?" He held up a finger. "I forgot your plantations in the West Indies. Make that four."

Miss Archard peeked over her shoulder toward two men standing aside her father. Mr. Archard's shoulder shook as if sharing a jest with the men, but his gaze shot briefly to his daughter. Miss Archard's expression turned somber, yet she inched her way over to Anthony Middleton's elbow.

Tobias thanked God for the material of his gloves, absorbing the sweat from his palms. He could do this. He would do this—for Priscilla's sake.

"Ah, Miss Archard." Anthony stepped back and pushed Miss Archard forward. "Have you met Lord Seaton?" He didn't wait for her to answer. "Lord Seaton, may I introduce you to Miss Nellie Archard."

Tobias issued them a curt nod. His mouth refused to utter a single word.

Miss Archard fell into a regal curtsy and peeked at her father once more. "Your reputation proceeds you."

"I..." His lips twitched an awkward smile. How would a libertine respond? "The..." He cleared his throat to cover his stumble. He must do this for Priscilla. *Think. What would Middleton do?*

"The pleasure is mine." He lifted Miss Archard's hand and raised it to his lips. He forced his gaze to rove down over her curves. "I daresay, were you the lovely Greek goddess who attended the Lemoore masquerade?"

She eyed him in a coquettish manner from behind her fan. "Indeed."

"I'd hoped to sign my name on your dance card, but another held your attention."

Her gaze flicked to the man with the long nose and high hairline standing near her father.

He sighed like a forlorn lover. "I can see you are distracted.

Perhaps you'd like to take a turn about the room so we may draw some attention?"

Miss Archard's eyes sparkled, and she half hid her smile behind her fan. "A splendid idea."

He held out his arm. "To be seen with one so lovely would make me the envy of all the gentlemen in the room." The words began to flow from his mouth. For the moment, he was no longer Tobias Prescott, the responsible captain, but an English spy on a mission.

Miss Archard giggled and slipped her hand into the crook of his arm. She stole a glance once more at the men surrounding her father.

"He must be blind or an imbecile to allow you on another man's arm." He placed his other hand overtop hers. "Perhaps a little jealousy will bring him to heel?"

She studied Tobias with new interest and a bit of a spring in her step. "Quite right."

Tobias snuck a glimpse of her father and the two men. The one with hair unnaturally dark for someone so pale rubbed the side of his nose with his thumb. Tobias's breath caught. What had Priscilla said? *I could tell it was all an act by the way he'd rub his thumb against his nose each time he lied.*

Was that Goulart?

Lord, give us wisdom. He shot Anthony a pay-attention look and glanced in Nellie's father's direction. Anthony's gaze flicked toward the group of men before returning to Tobias with questions in his eyes.

Tobias rubbed the side of his nose with his thumb and raised his eyebrows at Anthony in a silent message.

Anthony lifted his chin, excused himself from the crowd, and beelined in the direction of the men. He pretended to bump into the man with dark hair, begged his pardon, and struck up a conversation with Miss Archard's father.

"He's looking this way," Tobias said under his breath.

Miss Archard turned to see, but he tightened his grip on her arm.

"Don't look." He stopped her inside the frame of the doorway to the terrace. "Why don't you laugh at something funny I've just said, and then we'll take a romantic stroll in the garden?"

Miss Archard giggled and slapped his arm with her fan in a flirtatious gesture. "Lord Seaton. You are every bit the rogue as your reputation claims." She lowered her lashes. "I'm beginning to see I've been betting on the wrong horse. Mayhap it merely took the right thoroughbred to come along to turn my tastes." Her lashes swept up, and her gaze held an open invitation.

Tobias swallowed. Blast, the woman was forward.

Her grip on his arm grew possessive. "I know a little corner where we can become more acquainted."

Feeling like the predator who suddenly became the prey, Tobias allowed her to lead him to the darkest regions of the garden. "Won't your father become alarmed?"

She stopped and ran her hands up his lapels. "Not while his assistant is with him."

"The man you desire is your father's assistant?"

She stepped closer and tipped her face up. "I no longer care for his attention."

Was Goulart working for Archard—Archard, who was privy to the topmost officials within the government and Whig party?

She pressed her body to the length of him, and her hand slid around his neck, pulling his head toward her upturned lips.

He recoiled. "Is that why you lied? To safeguard the man you fancied?"

Her eyes sprung open.

"Are you going to stand by and let Priscilla hang so you can continue to protect your love interest?"

"What?" She shrank from him with a dazed expression. "No. Priscilla sailed to the islands."

"Does your father know his daughter is involved with a French spy?" He loomed over her. It was past time she understood the consequences of her actions, because Priscilla certainly did.

She stepped back. "H-he'd disown me."

"But you knew Fortin was a spy." He inched forward. "You've been asked to do things, overhear things, pass along information." He pressed her so she'd crack. "And let your friend take the fall. What did they promise? Power? Riches? A title?"

She backed, wringing her gloved hands. "The season is expensive. Appearances must be kept. Papa says a government salary isn't enough."

"So, like Judas, you sold your friend's life for a few coins." His gaze traveled the length of her. "Or in your case, a new gown."

"He never said Priscilla would get hurt."

"Fortin?"

Her bottom lip quivered. "He said he'd see to it Priscilla wouldn't return."

A cannonball ripped through Tobias's chest, stealing his breath. She'd confirmed not only her guilt but also the danger Priscilla faced.

"There you are." Anthony skidded to a stop, his breath coming in gasps. "They've risen to the bait. We must go."

CHAPTER 31

Our plan is underway to flush out the French spies. Upon their apprehension, I shall provide a full report.
~ *Letter from Agent White to the British War Office*

a wooden plate with a crust of bread and a tin cup of water slid through the bars of her cell.

Priscilla pressed the Bible her papa obtained for her against her chest, the verse she'd just read from Isaiah implanted deep within her heart. *When you pass through the waters, I will be with you; and when you pass through the rivers, they will not sweep over you.*

She dropped to her knees and whispered her heartfelt prayer. "God, bless this food. Thank you that I no longer live on bread alone. I used to believe I needed my parents or others to fill my needs. On the island, I thought I depended upon Tobias, and then for a while, I assumed I could fend for myself, but it's You I need. You have gone to tremendous lengths to find your lost lamb, and you continue to tear down my walls and cast out my fears. I love you. Amen."

She fingered the bread slice. It was still soft and the first she'd received without a thin green mold coating. Her stomach growled, and mouth salivated to devour the scrumptious smelling piece, but something didn't feel right. She broke off a tiny section and carefully bit into it.

It's yeasty smell and light and fluffy texture melted in her mouth like the rolls Cook used to bake for her to break her fast. Swallowing, she tore off another piece but hesitated as the bread touched her lips. A warning rose within her.

"Ah, chérie, you were a special treasure. Yet, sadly, here we are."

Priscilla recognized the voice from the Lemoore party. She set the bread aside and turned to face her former dance partner, posing as the prison guard delivering food. He stood outside her cell, observing her against the far wall. His beard had been shaved, and his light brown hair was now pitch black. "Mr. Goulart, are you here to confess to your crimes? Can you no longer bear the guilt of knowing innocent people die because of your actions?"

He chuckled. "I'd forgotten about your charming sense of humor. It's a pity such beauty and intellect must meet an end. Ah, but don't let me disturb your meal."

"You're here to kill me, then?"

"See, it's such perceptiveness that requires your demise. Miss Archard saw only the costume, but you saw every nuance. You easily saw through the disguise and past my persona. I admit, very few people make me nervous, but that night, those clear blue eyes—so observant, so discerning—kept me on edge."

"There is no evidence to keep me from hanging. Why add another black mark on your soul?"

"France cannot risk it." He shrugged. "I cannot risk it. You have connections, and from what I've learned, somewhat of a genius at identifying people through gestures. I'm curious to know what it was that gave me away. I pride myself on being a master of disguise."

Her stomach clenched. "I knew Lord Fortin preyed upon helpless females, but you had a heart."

His eyes grew distant. "My heart died at the guillotine during the revolution." His nostrils flared. "Now, I do what I must for a new France under Bonaparte's rule. You were never supposed to be involved, chérie. Miss Archard willingly passed on the information from her father's desk regarding Napoleon's location and guard schedule in the name of young love."

He crossed his arms and leaned against the wall. "You weren't so easily charmed, but you would have been used for blackmail if Miss Achard didn't work out." His lips twitched. "So tell me, what gave me away? How did you know I was lying to you?"

"How could you use me for blackmail?"

A metal hinge creaked, and Fortin's gaze snapped in that direction.

The woman in the cell next door flipped her wooden meal tray with a cackle and muttered something about time to wash the dishes.

"We are wasting time. How did you know I was lying?"

She refused to let him change the subject. "I had no information. I knew nothing." Sweat beaded on her forehead.

He snorted. "It wouldn't have mattered. One only needs suspicion and doubt to blackmail. Your father would have complied on suspicion alone."

"That's where you're wrong." She shook her head. "He wouldn't have exchanged information for me."

"I would have and more." Her father stepped around the corner. "It's why I was at the party. I'd hoped to find you before they did, but they beat me to it."

Goulart jerked upright. His shifty gaze darted to the nearest exit.

"Papa." She extended a hand through the bars.

"I love you, darling. I know I didn't show it. I didn't want to make you more of a target than you already were, but I used to whisper it to you each night when you were asleep as I carried you to bed."

Papa, not one of the servants, had carried her to her bedchamber?

Goulart dashed for the hall, but the adjoining cell door flung open, and Goulart smashed into it, ricocheting and landing in a heap on the ground.

"Good work, Miss Dodd." Her father saluted the woman in the cell next door.

"Miss Dodd?" Priscilla's mouth hung open.

Miss Dodd winked at her before turning to Papa. "Our plan worked. I heard enough of a confession to hang the bloke."

How did she? When did she? Priscilla remembered the guard removing the woman for further questioning. Miss Dodd must have taken her place, donning a wig and similar clothes.

"Bind him and bring him to the cell with Fortin and Archard on the third floor." Her papa tugged a ring of keys from his pocket.

Would Nellie hang for treason?

"Priscilla!" Tobias yelled from the hall before he bounded into the walkway and gripped her arms through the bars. "Are you all right?"

"Tobias." She pressed her face to the cold bars. "You're here?"

He ran a hand into her hair. "Yes, darling, if you'll forgive me for doubting you, I promise never to leave you again."

Priscilla inhaled a gasp and trailed her fingers down the side of his face, searching his warm gaze for confirmation.

His gaze pulsed with love, and his calloused hands cupped her cheeks with a reverent touch. "I promise to love, honor, cherish, and protect you as long as I live."

Her papa, Miss Dodd, and the dingy prison melted away until she and Tobias stood alone on the beach. Oh, how she'd longed to hear those words once more from his lips. She gripped his lapel, pulling him closer to feel his lips upon hers and prove with a kiss not only that she'd forgiven him, but that their love survived the deep and grew stronger, richer, and sweeter for it.

Her stomach clenched in a sudden revolt. She pushed from him and stood in the center of her cell. Sweat dripped down the sides of her face, and pain ripped through her insides.

"Get that cell open!" Tobias roared as her father fumbled to insert the key into the lock.

Miss Dodd's eyes widened. "The bread. Goulart could have poisoned the bread."

Priscilla fell to her knees and cast up the minimal contents of her stomach as waves of pain coursed through her. The wooden plate of freshly baked bread with one bite missing rested near her face. The smell of yeast tormented her. *Lord, help me.*

"Priscilla!" The agony in Tobias's voice stirred her. Placing a hand on the damp stone wall, she used it to support herself as she stood. She wanted to look at him one last time, to tell him she loved him.

Key's jingled. Hinges creaked.

Nausea overtook her, and the room spun. She stumbled back to the floor.

"Call for a physician."

The bellow sounded muffled as if she were once again underwater. Her eyes opened, but her vision grew dark. She was falling, suspended, once again, in the deep waters without the strength to swim back to the surface.

A strong pair of arms caught her.

～

*P*riscilla awoke, feeling shaky and muddled. She peeled her eyelids open to find Tobias's face next to her, holding her hand. Anthony's shape came into focus by his side, along with her papa and mama, Miss Dodd, and the family physician. All had gathered in her bedchamber.

She was home.

"Praise God. You're awake." Tobias placed his other hand overtop hers and pressed it to his cheek. "If I'd lost you..." His voice died as he struggled to regain control. "I wanted to protect you. You should never have been left alone. I should have been there, but your father warned it would alert the spies to your location."

"God protected me." She swallowed to remove the raspy tone from her voice. "I was never alone. God was with me the whole time, so I wasn't afraid. And now God has sent me you and Maggie." She trailed her knuckles down his cheek. "You and Maggie are my family. Whatever happens, I pray you'll never forget that."

"Never." The vehement declaration resounded from the core of his being. "How could I, darling? You've had my heart from the moment you confronted me on deck, looked me in the eye, and told me my order was unreasonable."

"You told him that?" Anthony peered at her with new respect. "Captain Prescott is feared among the best of men."

She smiled at Anthony, but it quickly turned to Tobias. "I love you too."

Her mother and father exchanged a look. Papa must have updated Mama on some things.

Papa leaned forward. "You gave us quite a scare, angel."

"How are you feeling?" Mama still held a bewildered look as if all that had transpired was too much for her delicate sensibilities.

"I'm not dead. I'm no longer in jail, and I'm surrounded by the people I love. I'd say I'm doing quite well."

"Despite her optimistic spirit," the family physician interrupted, "my patient needs her rest, so I'm going to have to ask you all to leave."

"I'm not leaving." Tobias squeezed her hand as if to impart the promise of his words.

Her mother stiffened. "It's improper."

"Come, Lydia." Papa grasped her shoulders. "There are some things I must explain further."

"I'll stay." Anthony offered.

"It's my duty." Miss Dodd arched an eyebrow.

A chuckle rumbled in Priscilla's chest, but her lids were growing heavy. "I shall be fine, I assure you."

The physician shooed everyone toward the hall. Only Tobias hesitated. He eyed her with an are-you-certain look. "I can sing in the hall if that helps."

"Truly. I will be fine." She need not be afraid. God was with her. He always had been and always would be. Tobias kissed the back of her hand, and her heart turned over, bursting with love. "But don't wander too far."

"Never." The fervent intent of his words struck a chord. "I'll give up sailing. I'll become a landlubber so I can stay by your side always."

"I cannot hold you to that promise. You love serving the crown, and I love that about you. I will hold you to your promise to honor and cherish me all the days of our lives."

Tobias cupped her face in his hands. "I'm ready to fulfill it the moment you're well enough to stand at the altar."

~

*G*uests mingled, expressing their sentiments about the lovely wedding ceremony and offering well-wishes to the newlyweds. Her mama flung herself into wedding preparations as she absorbed the full truth of all that transpired. Hosting a large gathering of guests in their country home in Essex helped to take her mind off the shock. As Mama flittered about the flower-adorned veranda welcoming everyone, Priscilla recognized the loving glances her papa cast toward his wife. His divulging all his secrets brought a new spark to their marriage. For a few days, her mother had stayed in denial until Papa wrapped her in his arms and held her until she wept. Her proud father humbled himself and asked for his wife's forgiveness. He'd wanted to protect her but not at the cost of her feeling unloved, which led to what must have been the first meaningful conversation they'd held in ages.

Priscilla smiled at the distinguished man beside her. As if sensing her heart, Tobias slid a hand around her waist and possessively drew her closer to his side. He, too, had humbled himself in many ways. Instead of donning his captain's naval uniform, Tobias wore formal gentry dress as the groom, for he'd given his notice to the higher-ups. It had been entirely his decision to forgo his distinguished naval career to stay closer to home and start a family. Over the years, he'd saved enough earnings to purchase some land. Perhaps he'd become a gentleman farmer, or mayhap his new father-in-law knew of a quiet desk job within the department.

Tears had cascaded down her cheeks when Anthony explained how Tobias had played the part of a libertine and swayed Nellie into divulging information regarding the French spies. No one understood as she did, what courage he must have summoned for such a task. He, too, had faced his fears—not only learning how to speak to women but how to trust them. She leaned her head against his side—at least one woman in particular. God had brought him through the deep and blessed him for it.

A man Priscilla didn't recognize approached them. He paused to cough into his handkerchief before stuffing it back into his pocket.

Tobias turned at the noise and greeted him. "Lieutenant Sparks, glad to see they let you out of the department for special occasions. May I introduce you to my wife, Mrs. Priscilla Prescott."

Hearing her new name sent a thrill through her being.

"It is good to finally meet the woman who has been a frequent topic of discussion at the War Office." He bowed. "Congratulations on your nuptials."

She glanced at Tobias for answers, but he merely grinned at the lieutenant.

Sparks fiddled with the button on his jacket. "You may not know, but I've worked with your father and Miss Dodd for years. I wanted to thank you personally for catching the French infiltrators. Without your help, Lord knows how long those spies would have hidden within our political ranks. You will soon be invited in front of the House of Lords for a special recognition ceremony."

"That is very kind"—she dipped a small curtsy—"but unnecessary. I appreciate you clearing my name, and I'm humbled to assist my country in any way I can."

Tobias's thumb rubbed her side, the intimate touch sending tingles to her toes.

Priscilla lifted her hand. "May I ask what happened to Miss Archard?"

"Since England no longer allows penal transportation, the Archard family has willingly offered to relocate to Australia instead of facing charges. I believe it was the wisest choice."

Sparks scratched his temple and then wagged a finger in their direction. "In fact, after hearing about your gift of observation and Captain Prescott's pretense, we would like to gauge yours and the Captain's interest in positions at the War Department. Your combined skills would be an asset to your king. However, if you choose this opportunity, you would need to remain anonymous and not accept the display of gratitude from the House of Lords." He eyed Tobias. "It would be best for you and your wife to become forgettable."

Tobias reared back his head and laughed.

Priscilla joined him, drawing the attention of most of the guests.

Tobias clapped Lieutenant Sparks on the shoulder. "I'm not certain that's possible." His eyes twinkled at Priscilla, "But we shall consider it."

A familiar band of men approached from the stairs. Priscilla touched her husband's arm, and Tobias's gaze swung to the door, a broad grin spanning his lips. "It's about time the best man arrived."

Lieutenant Henry Dalton strode forward, followed by Cecil St. Ledger, Jacob Raleigh, and Speck. Their clothes were pressed, and they were clean-shaven.

Henry shook Tobias's hand. "We docked this morn. Imagine my surprise to learn not only you lived, but you survived each other and are getting married. The last thing I remember, you were about to wring her neck for being a card sharp."

Tobias draped an arm around Priscilla's shoulders. "A lot has changed in a short time."

"We cleaned ourselves up right quick because we had to see with our own eyes." Raleigh tugged his lapels. "Congratulations, Captain." He bowed to Priscila. "Mrs. Captain," he added with a saucy smile.

Tobias grew serious. "Returning word about the battle of New Orleans didn't sound good. I feared for my crew."

Henry paused and lowered his gaze in a moment of silence. "The battle was a massacre. British troops were slaughtered for naught. Nary but a few ships returned. A treaty had been drawn between England and the Americans the day before Christmas. Word, however, didn't reach Pakenham's fleets in time."

"But the *Trade Wind* lasted through the battle?"

Henry's gaze caught sight of Miss Dodd as she helped Maggie to a glass of lemonade, and his face softened.

Tobias had to clear his throat to regain the man's attention.

"We only survived because we'd been delayed. I know it would have been against your wishes, but we scoured half the British Isles in search of you and Miss Middleton."

Priscilla issued him a sideways I-told-you-so glance.

"There had to be at least forty small islands. We surveyed as many as we dared before Miss Dodd suggested we enlist the help of a merchant friend."

Maggie, dressed in a proper gown, pulled Miss Dodd over to their group. She released Miss Dodd beside the lieutenant before pressing into the folds of Pricilla's gown. They'd commissioned the War Department to discover any leads on the ship that sank off the British Isles in hopes to locate Maggie's relatives, but nothing yet had surfaced. Priscilla rubbed Maggie's arm. Tobias had agreed that there was no point in waiting. They'd officially adopt Maggie as their own child.

"Lieutenant Dalton." Miss Dodd curtsied, her face glowing like a young schoolgirl in the presence of the lieutenant. "I thought it was in poor form to gossip about a person when they aren't present, and I distinctly heard my name."

Henry's face flushed. "It was to sing your praises, madame. I assure you."

Priscilla saw another wedding in the near future.

The lieutenant returned his attention back to Tobias, and his face sobered. "We all know you wanted to be there to give your life for your country, but it turned out when you saved one"—all eyes shifted to gaze at Priscilla—"you saved many. I believe it was the Lord's will."

Tobias drew Priscilla against his chest and cupped Maggie's cheek as her green eyes peered up at him. God held his lambs close to his heart. That truth had never felt so real. A cloud shifted and sunlight spilt upon the small gathering like God's face shining upon them. His love overflowed from her to Tobias and Maggie, and it cascaded over every friend and family member celebrating.

"I know it was God's will." Tobias tipped Pricilla's head back with a gentle touch of his finger, and she absorbed the love radiating from his expression. "Because my heart is full, and my cup runneth over."

Did you enjoy this book? We hope so!
**Would you take a quick minute to leave a review where you
purchased the book?**
It doesn't have to be long. Just a sentence or two telling what
you liked about the story!

Receive a FREE ebook and get updates when new Wild Heart
books release: https://wildheartbooks.org/newsletter

GET ALL THE BOOKS IN THE LEEWARD ISLANDS SERIES

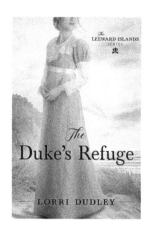

Book 1: The Duke's Refuge

Book 2: The Merchant's Yield

Book 3: The Sugar Baron's Ring

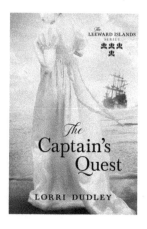

Book 4: The Captain's Quest

ABOUT THE AUTHOR

Lorri Dudley has been a finalist in numerous writing contests and has a master's degree in Psychology. She lives in Ashland, Massachusetts with her husband and three teenage sons, where writing romance allows her an escape from her testosterone filled household.

Connect with Lorri at http://LorriDudley.com

ACKNOWLEDGMENTS

God is good.

I'm so thankful for the opportunity to write about His awe-inspiring love through fiction.

Thank you to Misty Beller and the entire Wild Heart Books team. You are a pleasure to work with and have made this series such a joyful journey. I continue to be amazed at all the hard work and effort it takes to develop a story into a published work. Erin Taylor-Young, I don't know what I would do without your input into the heroine's struggle and the encouraging way you help me to see things from another perspective. Robin Patchen, not only have you blessed me with your eye for detail and questioning things I hadn't considered, but you've been my writing mother-bird, encouraging me to fly from the nest. I can't say enough about the Wild Heart Book's design and marketing team. Somehow, they're able to take what's in my head and make it into a beautiful cover and then spread the word through various campaigns.

Special thanks to Robyn Hook for steering me in the right direction with the storyline and forcing me to go deeper into the character's point-of-view. You are incredible and such dear friend to help me. Also, big hugs and kisses to my beta readers, Kristen, Lizzy, Shannon, and Louise. Additional thanks to Kristen, at Sugar Peonies, for making the awesome promo gifts for my launch team.

Speaking of my launch team, thank you for promoting my books with your friends and family, your kind remarks on Facebook, and posting reviews. I've loved hearing from all of you. A special shout out goes to the Louisville Rebecca's Circle group. You wonderful ladies are dear to my heart. Also, much love for my church family and small group. Thank you for being my cheering section.

I'm blessed to have a supportive husband who will always be my dashing hero. Thank you, babes. I'm grateful for my boys who listen to me ramble about island survival techniques and who ate raw coconut so that mom could hear them describe their first taste. To my parents, who are my constant source of encouragement and my biggest promoters, I love you. God has blessed me with an incredible family.

And I cannot forget all my wonderful readers. May God bless you all abundantly.

If you love historical romance, check out the other Wild Heart books!

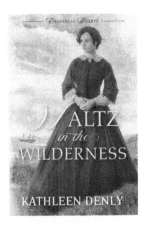

Waltz in the Wilderness by Kathleen Denly

She's desperate to find her missing father. His conscience demands he risk all to help.

Eliza Brooks is haunted by her role in her mother's death, so she'll do anything to find her missing pa—even if it means sneaking aboard a southbound ship. When those meant to protect her abandon and betray her instead, a family friend's unexpected assistance is a blessing she can't refuse.

Daniel Clarke came to California to make his fortune, and a stable job as a San Francisco carpenter has earned him more than most have scraped from the local goldfields. But it's been four years since he left Massachusetts and his fiancé is impatient for his return. Bound for home at last, Daniel Clarke finds his heart and plans challenged by a tenacious young woman with haunted eyes. Though every word he utters seems to offend her, he is determined to see her safely returned to her father. Even if that means risking his fragile engagement.

When disaster befalls them in the remote wilderness of the Southern California mountains, true feelings are revealed, and both must face heart-rending decisions. But how to decide when every choice before them leads to someone getting hurt?

~

Marisol ~ Spanish Rose by Elva Cobb Martin

Escaping to the New World is her only option...Rescuing her will wrap the chains of the Inquisition around his neck.

Marisol Valentin flees Spain after murdering the nobleman who molested her. She ends up for sale on the indentured servants' block at Charles Town harbor—dirty, angry, and with child. Her hopes are shattered, but she must find a refuge for herself and the child she carries. Can this new land offer her the grace, love, and security she craves? Or must she escape again to her only living relative in Cartagena?

Captain Ethan Becket, once a Charles Town minister, now sails the seas as a privateer, grieving his deceased wife. But when he takes captive a ship full of indentured servants, he's intrigued by the woman whose manners seem much more refined than the average Spanish serving girl. Perfect to become governess for his young son. But when he sets out on a quest to find his captured sister, said to be in Cartagena, little does he expect his new Spanish governess to stow away on his ship with her six-month-old son. Yet her offer of help to free his sister is too tempting to pass up. And her beauty, both inside and out, is too attractive for his heart to protect itself against—until he learns she is a wanted murderess.

As their paths intertwine on a journey filled with danger, intrigue, and romance, only love and the grace of God can overcome the past and ignite a new beginning for Marisol and Ethan.

∾

Lone Star Ranger by Renae Brumbaugh Green

Elizabeth Covington will get her man.

And she has just a week to prove her brother isn't the murderer Texas Ranger Rett Smith accuses him of being. She'll show the good-looking lawman he's wrong, even if it means setting out on a risky race across Texas to catch the real killer.

Rett doesn't want to convict an innocent man. But he can't let the Boston beauty sway his senses to set a guilty man free. When Elizabeth follows him on a dangerous trek, the Ranger vows to keep her safe. But who will protect him from the woman whose conviction and courage leave him doubting everything—even his heart?